Praise for Highland Press Books!

BLUE MOON MAGIC is an enchanting collection of short stories. Each author wrote with the same theme in mind but each story has its own uniqueness. You should have no problem finding a tale to suit your mood. *BLUE MOON MAGIC* offers historicals, contemporaries, time travel, paranormal, and futuristic narratives to tempt your heart.

Legend says that if you wish with all your heart upon the rare blue moon, your wishes were sure to come true. Each of the heroines discovers this magical fact. True love is out there if you just believe in it. In some of the stories, love happens in the most unusual ways. Angels may help, ancient spells may be broken, anything can happen. Even vampires will find their perfect mate with the power of the blue moon. Not every heroine believes they are wishing for love, some are just looking for answers to their problems or nagging questions. Fate seems to think the solution is finding the one who makes their heart sing.

BLUE MOON MAGIC is a perfect read for late at night or even during your commute to work. The short yet sweet stories are a wonderful way to spend a few minutes. If you do not have the time to finish a full-length novel, but hate stopping in the middle of a loving tale, I highly recommend grabbing this book.

Kim Swiderski
Writers Unlimited Reviewer

~ ~ ~

Legend has it that a blue moon is enchanted. What happens when fifteen talented authors utilize this theme to create enthralling stories of love?

BLUE MOON ENCHANTMENT is a wonderful, themed anthology filled with phenomenal stories by fifteen extraordinarily talented authors. Readers will find a wide variety of time periods and styles showcased in this superb anthology. *BLUE MOON ENCHANTMENT* is sure to offer a little bit of something for everyone!

Reviewed by Debbie
CK²S Kwips and Kritiques

~ ~ ~

NO LAW AGAINST LOVE - If you have ever found yourself rolling your eyes at some of the more stupid laws, then you are going to adore this novel. Over twenty-five stories fill up this anthology, each one dealing with at least one stupid or outdated law. Let me give you an example: In Florida, USA, there is a law that states "If an elephant is left tied to a parking meter, the parking fee has to be paid just as it would for a vehicle." In Great Britain, "A license is required to keep a lunatic." Yes, you read those correctly. No matter how many times you go back and reread them, the words will remain the same. Those two laws are still legal. Most of the crazy laws in these wonderful stories are still legal. The tales vary in time and place. Some take place in the present, in the past, in the USA, in England, may contain magic... in other words, there is something for everyone! You simply cannot go wrong. Best yet, all profits from the sales of this novel go to breast cancer prevention.

A stellar anthology that had me laughing, sighing in

pleasure, believing in magic, and left me begging for more! Will there be a second anthology someday? I sure hope so! This is one novel that will go directly to my 'Keeper' shelf, to be read over and over again. Very highly recommended!

~ ~ ~

HIGHLAND WISHES - This reviewer found that this book was a wonderful story set in a time when tension was high between England and Scotland. Burroughs writes a well-crafted story, with multidimensional characters and exquisite backdrops of Scotland. The storyline is a fast-paced tale with much detail to specific areas of history. The reader can feel this author's love for Scotland and its many wonderful heroes.

The characters connect immediately and don't stop until the end. At the end of the book, the reader wonders what happens next. The interplay between characters was smoothly done and helped the story along. It was a very smoothly told story. This reviewer was easily captivated by the story and was enthralled by it until the end. The reader will laugh and cry as you read this wonderful story. The reader feels all the pain, torment and disillusionment felt by both main characters, but also the joy and love they felt. Ms. Burroughs has crafted a well-researched story that gives a glimpse into Scotland during a time when there was upheaval and war for independence. This reviewer is anxiously awaiting her next novel in this series and commends her for a wonderful job done.

Christmas Wishes

Highland Press

High Springs, Florida 32655

Christmas Wishes

ISBN: 0-9746249-1-8

PUBLISHED BY HIGHLAND PRESS

A Wee Dram Book

To those of us who love the magic and beauty of Christmas. And to everyone who believes in and loves Christmas and all that special day stands for.

ACKNOWLEDGEMENTS

Grateful thanks are due to the many staff editors who helped with this book:

Kristi Ahlers
Cheryl Alldredge
Victoria Bromley
Patty Howell
Deborah MacGillivray
Marilyn Rondeau
Diane Davis White
Polly Williamson

And a very special thanks to
Monika Wolmarans

~ LLB

Table of Contents

Christmas at Home............... Leanne Burroughs......... 13

The Christmas Store............. Ann Marie Bradley......... 43

Love's Eternal Hope.............. Amber Dawn Bell........... 63

Operation Family.................. Billie Warren Chai........ 81

The Gift of You..................... Kimberly Ivey................. 101

The Patient Gift..................... Patty Howell................. 127

In Time for Christmas........... Cheryl Alldredge........... 149

Once Upon a Snowflake......... Shelli Stevens............... 171

Joy's Christmas Wishes......... Gerri Bowen................. 191

Miracles and Mistletoe........... Kimberly Grant............. 211

The Christmas Wish.............. Rebecca Andrews......... 231

All I Want for Christmas is   DeborahAnne
A Hula Hoop...and a Mother..   MacGillivray................ 253

Christmas at Home

by Leanne Burroughs

"Mommy, stop. Please stop!"

Allison stopped walking as her five-year-old daughter, Becca, tugged on her coat sleeve.

"What is it, sweetheart? We have to hurry or the store will close before we get there." They didn't have many ration coupons left, but this was a special occasion.

"But, Mommy, look at the music box in that window. It looks just like the RCA Victor Victrola you said my daddy bought you. And look at that dolly, Mommy. Oh, please, please can I have her?"

She peered into the window. Yes, the music box was a miniature version of the one Albert had bought her for a wedding present. He'd known how very much she loved music. Pain gripped Allison's heart seeing the doll resembled Becca—cornflower blue eyes and blonde hair that refused to stay neatly combed. More each day, her daughter reminded her of Albert.

How could she explain—again—that she had no money for things like dollies and toys? Since Albert had joined the RAF, and not the home troops, she received no widow's pension from good old Uncle Sam. Sometimes they barely had enough for food. Sadly, Becca was too young to understand.

"Not today, sweetheart. I've saved our ration coupons to get sugar for your birthday cake." Gently putting her arm around her daughter's tiny shoulders, she urged her away from the tempting window. Bracing

13

against the cold wind, they hurried down the street and through the door to the general store.

Inside the general store, radiant heat from the cast iron stove enveloped those who entered. "It's warm in here, Mommy. Not like our apartment."

Her daughter's innocent observation weighed on Allison's heart. Heating was another thing they had to ration.

Becca carelessly pulled off her mittens and Allison quickly gathered them. There'd be no money to replace them if they were lost.

Stepping briskly through the grocery aisles, so as not to be tempted to buy something she couldn't afford, she placed only necessary items in her hand basket.

Before heading back to the half of the building that housed the general store, Allison decided to check the butcher's counter. She always enjoyed talking with the mild mannered man. "Good morning, Mr. Garner. Have you any breakfast bacon today?"

He smiled, but shook his head. "'Fraid not, Mrs. Monroe. Bacon's still too hard to come by. We sold out of what little I had within an hour of opening the store."

"I was afraid of that. I didn't see any sugar on the shelves either. It's the main thing I came in for today." With a smile and a wave, Allison turned and hurried up the aisle, stopping in front of the Coca-Cola display. Allison knew she shouldn't, but...she had promised Becca.

"Can we buy one today, Mommy? Please? You promised you'd get one on my birthday."

Allison looked down at the hopeful look in her daughter's eyes. For once she wasn't going to say no. "I'm sure it's all right to celebrate—just this once."

A wide grin crossed her daughter's face.

Flinging her arms around Allison's legs, Becca beamed up at her. "You're the best mommy in the world!"

A fist closed around Allison's heart. Allison was doing the best she could, but it never felt as if it were enough. She'd do anything to protect Becca from the realities forced on them by the war.

Letting Becca hold the ice cold Coca-Cola, Allison hurried up the aisle while digging in her purse for her returnable bottle. Distracted by Becca's happy chattering, she placed her meager items on the counter.

"This is all for today, Mr. Burgess. Becca and I are going to share a Coke for her birthday." Allison started to place the deposit bottle on the counter, but drew it back. "Oh, I'm sorry. I wasn't paying attention. I thought you were Mr. Burgess. He always tallies my order."

The man smiled, stared at her like she'd surprised him.

She set the empty bottle on the counter. "I made sure to bring this in. I can't afford to pay another huge deposit on a Coca-Cola bottle. This war is taking a nickel treat and turning it into a luxury."

The man glanced at the bottle, then to her. His eyes met hers and her world shifted. What eyes! Azure blue like Lake Michigan on a summer day, they mesmerized her. Held her in sway. Only Becca tugging at her coat sleeve drew her back to the present.

"Mommy, can I have a candy?" Her eyes pleaded with Allison.

"I'm afraid not, sweetheart. We agreed we'd get the CocaCola. Maybe some other—"

"But Mommy, it's my birthday!"

"Just your lucky day, little girl," the man behind the counter said. "When we opened the shop today my father told me we were running a birthday special. He said I was supposed to give a penny candy to the prettiest little birthday girl who came in the shop."

His eyes swept from Becca's to Allison's, daring her to belie his words.

"Oooooo, Mommy! Did you hear? The man said I could have one. Can I, Mommy? Can I please?"

15

The blue eyes that met hers when she looked back held a hint of humor.

"Of course, sweetheart. Tell the nice man which one you'd like."

Shyly Becca asked, "May I have a Tootsie Roll?"

"You may have whichever one you want."

"I want a Tootsie Roll." She pursed her lips and said conspiratorially, "They're chocolate, you know."

The clerk laughed. "Yes, I knew that. Servicemen often carry Tootsie Rolls in their pockets since they won't melt."

"Mommy, did you hear? Soldiers like them, too. Did my daddy like them?"

Before Allison could answer, he handed Becca the prized candy. "Oh, Mommy, look! There's two here."

"Of course there is, little lady. The other one's for the second prettiest lady to enter our store today." His eyes never left Becca's face. "Can you do me a favor and hold that one for your mommy until she gets home?"

Puffing up with importance, Becca put the candy carefully in her pocket. Removing the paper from her candy, she bit off one end and smiled.

Finally, the clerk's eyes rose to meet Allison's. "Now, let's get the rest of these groceries ready for you, Mrs..."

"Monroe. Allison Monroe."

"Nice to meet you, Mrs. Monroe. I'm Ryan Burgess. My parents own this store."

Allison frowned. "I'd heard their son was overseas." She watched as he bent awkwardly to pick up the pencil he'd dropped. A cane rested by the counter.

"Been gone for several years. First, away at college, then I joined the war effort." A short, bitter laugh escaped and his eyes darkened. "Thought sure the war would be over in a shot once I joined up. Didn't quite happen that way." He lifted the cane. "Came home with this instead."

"I'm sorry you were injured, Mr. Burgess. I—"

"Ryan. My father's Mr. Burgess."

Allison moistened her lips with the tip of her tongue. "I hate to bother you, but I didn't see any sugar on the shelves. I know it's difficult to get nowadays, but I've saved my ration coupon just for today. I'd hoped to bake Becca a small cake for her birthday."

Ryan Burgess stared at her for the longest time, saying nothing. Then, slipping off the stool, he grabbed his cane and walked unsteadily to the family's personal quarters, When he returned, he carried a small ball—a fist full of sugar—covered with wax paper, a bright pink bow tied at the top making it appear like a present.

His eyes met hers, but he said nothing. Merely placed the sugar with her groceries and completed her transaction.

Tears clogged her throat and she struggled to keep them back. "But...I can't let you—"

Reaching for his cane he lifted her basket of groceries, slipped in two Tootsie Pops, and interrupted, "Can I carry these to your car for you?"

"I don't have a car."

His look said he understood—she couldn't afford one. "Too many people are making sacrifices for the war effort these days. If it's any consolation, men fighting overseas appreciate everything everyone is doing." He hesitated, then blurted, "As I'm sure your husband's already told you."

Allison's hand shot to her chest. Grief washed over her like the tide swept over the shore. Would this never get easier? Would the pain stab her heart every time she thought of Albert? Even after all this time? She turned to see Becca had wandered over to the toy counter and was absorbed in watching the small train going round and round.

"My h-husband is dead. He wrote me last November and told me he'd be home for Christmas. His Bomb Group flew over the Channel toward Germany on one of his final missions—and he never came home." *His plans—our life—came to a crashing end.*

17

Her hand clasped to her mouth to stop her sob, Allison snatched the basket from Ryan, grasped Becca's hand and rushed out of the store.

Two weeks later, Ryan stood at the tall racks in the nearby record store, flipping through the 78s, in hopes of finding a few songs. He particularly wanted either *Swinging on a Star* or *I'll Be Seeing You* by Bing Crosby. He'd always loved music. Turning to look through the selection on the other side of the aisle, he lost his balance as a whirlwind of motion bumped into him.

"Oh, Mr. Ryan. Sorry, I didn't mean to hit you. I was looking for Mommy." A smile lit little Becca's face at the sight of him.

Ryan grasped the counter to steady his balance. Kept his voice level to not let her see his pain. "Hello, little lady. It's good to see you. Are you coming to our store later today? I'm on my lunch break now, but I'll be back there shortly."

Becca furrowed her brows. "You're in the wrong store for lunch, Mr. Ryan. You can't eat here. They only sell records." She pointed toward the front door. "You should go to the *deli-tessen* across the street. They have food there."

Ryan chuckled. "Right you are. I'm glad we ran into each other so you could make sure I went to the correct store."

"Are you okay, Mr. Bur—Ryan? You look like you need to sit down."

He glanced up and saw Allison watching him, her eyes on his tense, white knuckles.

"I almost knocked Mr. Ryan down, Mommy," Becca said looking up at her mother. "Said I'm sorry. He isn't mad at me."

Allison frowned as she glanced from Ryan to her daughter. "Becca, how could you? I've told you not to run in stores. I—"

"I'm fine, Allison. Don't fuss at the child. It was an accident."

Allison inhaled sharply and looked at Ryan. "Did she hurt you?"

"No. Nothing happened, and she apologized. If we hadn't run into each other I'd still be trying to find lunch in the record store." He looked down at her daughter, then laughed at Allison's confusion. "I told her I was on my lunch break and she politely informed me I wouldn't find lunch here. That I had to go across the street to the deli."

"If you're sure you're fine..."

Wanting to spend time with her, Ryan jumped at the opening she'd given him. "I think I do need to sit a spell. I planned to head over to the deli across the street. Would you...walk with me?"

After a moment's hesitation, she nodded. He held out his arm to escort her—more to support himself than he cared to admit—and they crossed the street to the deli.

Though her touch was light on his arm, he thought he could feel her warmth through his overcoat. He didn't want that feeling to end. Before he could change his mind, he asked, "Have you and Becca had lunch?"

"No, but we—"

"Good, then you'll both join me. My treat," he added quickly.

After what had turned into a delightful lunch, they'd walked back to his family's store. His eyes following her every move, Ryan watched Allison gather her few meager groceries. He'd enjoyed the brief time together. Wished he could see more of her, but accepted that wasn't possible. Why would she want to be with him when other men—whole men—were around to court her? The thought of another man winning her affections made his stomach clench. He was selfish. He didn't want her with another man. He wanted her with...him.

In the background, *It's Love, Love, Love* by Guy Lombardo taunted him with what could never be.

Becca stood beside him nibbling her Tootsie Roll. He gave her candy whenever they'd come into the store—always on the pretext of some lame promotion. If only he had something he could give Alli to cheer her. *Alli?* When had he started thinking of her that way?

Then again, when wasn't he thinking about her? She was one of the prettiest women he'd ever seen, though he doubted she realized it.

He wanted nothing more than to ask her out on a real date. Lunch today had been fine, but only made him hunger for more. Made him want what he couldn't have.

Her husband had been a waist gunner. She'd told him the bittersweet story of how he'd enlisted in the Bomb Squad stationed in Nuthampstead, England, been a part of England's RAF.

Ryan hadn't told her yet that he was a pilot—or had been. He'd flown with America's 8th Army Air Force. Now he was nothing, had nothing to offer anyone. Certainly not anyone as beautiful as Allison Monroe. *She deserves someone whole.*

But oh, how he wanted her.

People said these were the nation's darkest days, but Ryan doubted they could be any darker than his thoughts. After all, what did he have to live for? He'd asked himself that question a million times since coming home.

He'd talked to numerous men while in and out of hospitals. All told him to put the past behind him. He'd tried. How could he with his leg as a daily reminder? When he wasn't even man enough to walk without a stupid cane? When he barely kept his balance after a small child bumped into him?

He hated it! He wanted to take Allison for a long walk through the park. Watch the remainder of the autumn leaves fall to the ground. Or go to a nearby club. Wanted to put his arms around her and hold her close. Sway with her to the music.

He loved music. Hell! He couldn't dance. Couldn't even drive anywhere. Couldn't do anything except help people in his father's store. He didn't need a hale, hearty body to take people's money and ration coupons. It was all he was good for anymore.

Only, as he looked at Allison, he wanted more! The pain in his heart more than he could bear, he turned away.

Later that week, Ryan sat in a booth in the nearby soda shop. He needed a break. His body screamed like the dickens from standing in the store so long. The tinkling of the bell above the door drew his attention.

His heart soared—then plummeted. Allison and Rebecca Monroe entered the store.

Before her mother could stop her, Becca skipped over to him. "Guess what, Mr. Ryan? Mommy brought me for ice cream! She said I did reeeeeeeally good in school this week so I deserved a treat. I'm going to have chocolate. It's my favorite. Mommy's, too—isn't it Mommy? What's your favorite ice cream, Mr. Ryan?"

He smiled at Becca. Lord, how he'd have loved a child like her one day. Unfortunately, that day would never come. Not anymore.

Riffling her hair, he leaned forward and whispered, "I like chocolate, too, but my very favorite is butter pecan. But with the price farmers are getting for nuts these days, most stores can't afford to order it."

He smiled up at Allison as she moved forward to take Becca's hand. "Hello, Alli."

He'd startled her by his greeting. It showed in her eyes, but she quickly recovered.

"Hello, Ryan. It's good to see you taking a break. You work too hard."

He laughed. "This is coming from a second grade teacher? You're telling me you don't?"

A flush crept up her cheeks. "Well, I...no...it's just that..."

Ryan pointed to the seat opposite him. "Join me. Please."

"We shouldn't impose."

The words had scarcely left her mouth when Becca clambered up on the bench next to him. "Come on, Mommy. Mr. Ryan said we can join him." She climbed on her knees to inspect his food. "Oooooooo, Mommy. Mr. Ryan has apple pie! Can I have some, Mommy? Can I?"

Allison closed her eyes and sighed, then slid into the booth opposite them.

"No, Becca. We said we were sharing one scoop of chocolate ice cream. Your exact words were, 'I want that more than aaaaaaanything.'"

"Well, it was before I saw the pie. We haven't had any since I was little."

Ryan hid a smile.

"Why don't you share the ice cream with your mom like you planned, and while you wait, you can help me with my pie? The waitress brought a piece big enough for both of us."

Becca's eyes widened and her head bobbed up and down, her blonde curls bouncing.

"Ryan, I can't allow you to..."

He shot her a glance that told her he wanted to do this. Moistening her lips, she nodded acquiescence. Lust shot straight to his groin. He wanted to taste those lips. Wanted to taste all of her. Wanted to...

Stop it! Strains of *It Can't Be Wrong* by Dick Haymes taunted him from the shop's Wurlitzer. He had to cease torturing himself with thoughts of what could never be.

"Mommy, I have to go to the baff-room."

"Of course, sweetie, it's right over there." She started to slide from the booth.

"I'm a big girl. I can go by myself."

Allison hesitated, but finally smiled. "Of course you can, sweetheart. If you need me, just poke your head out the door and I'll come help."

"Okay." Climbing down from the booth, she skipped to the nearby door.

Allison watched her daughter, concern etched in her eyes. Ryan reached across the table and placed his hand over hers. "She'll be fine."

She turned to face him. "I know. It's just..."

"You're trying to protect her. I understand. War does that to people. Makes us more protective of those around us."

Allison nodded. "You're right, it does. Ryan, it's rude of me to ask, but you've never mentioned what happened overseas—to your leg."

His throat constricted. His mouth felt like cotton. He'd talked of it to no one but his parents, hospital staff and Mr. Garner, the butcher.

He forced himself to look her in the eyes. Warm, brown eyes that offered comfort. Eyes that held a promise of—what? Things that could never be, that's what.

"We were on a mission. We'd lost two planes from the squadron the day before, but that day things had gone well. We were just returning to base when we came under fire. Everything went wrong after that." He tried to keep the images from flooding his mind. "I was the pilot. My men's lives were in my hands. I had to get them back. Couldn't have lived with myself if we'd gone down and been captured. I desperately tried to get my plane under control. I left our formation and somehow made my way back to England."

His fork clattered to the table. He hadn't realized his hand shook until Allison placed hers over his to steady it. He closed his eyes.

"The crew jettisoned everything they could to lighten our load. Although I landed her, I crashed into a barrier."

Still holding his hand, Allison squeezed it. His eyes rose to meet hers. "They kept me in the infirmary...forever. They feared they'd have to amputate, but in time it healed." He laughed mirthlessly and held out his stiff leg. "If you can call this mangled leg healed."

"You're alive, Ryan." He saw tears well in her eyes.

Damn! Why had he been so selfish, heartless? She'd lost her husband. To her he was probably the luckiest man in the world.

Becca came back to the booth, a smile lighting her entire face. "I did it, Mommy. I told you I'm a big girl now."

Ryan leaned over and helped her back onto the seat beside him. "We made it back, but my plane suffered extensive damage."

Becca looked up from the ice cream she'd immediately started eating. Licked some from the corner of her mouth. "You flew an airplane, Mr. Ryan?"

He nodded.

Becca's eyes shifted from Allison to Ryan and back. "Mommy, is Mr. Ryan going to be my new daddy?"

Allison and Ryan both jumped. Allison released his hand as though it had scalded her. "Becca, why would you ask such an embarrassing question? Of course, Mr. Burgess isn't going to be your father."

Her head shaking so hard her blonde curls bounced, Becca insisted, "Didn't you hear him, Mommy? He flew planes just like you said Daddy did." She turned to Ryan. "Mommy said Daddy was watching over us from Heaven. Did my daddy send you here to take care of me and Mommy? I bet he did, didn't he? I bet—"

"I'm so sorry, Ryan. Please forgive Becca. She doesn't understand. She was too young when Albert left to remember him. She..."

Exiting the booth quickly, Allison drew Becca away. Her eyes held more anguish than Ryan ever wanted to see in them. Tears streaming down her face, she turned and dashed out the door.

Rising slowly, Ryan braced himself with his cane and went to the counter to pay for their food. He planned to do something about her running away from him all the time. Stepping out into the snowy afternoon, he carefully walked back to the store.

This week was Thanksgiving. Since waking up in the infirmary, he'd thought he didn't have anything to be thankful for. Maybe he'd been wrong. He'd stopped believing in magic and wishes as a child. Yet maybe...maybe this tiny girl today had shown him he had something to live for after all.

He stopped before entering the store, let the cool breeze swirl around him. He stared up at the sky and prayed. "Lord, I haven't talked to You in a long time. Not since the day of my accident. I don't know if You grant *wishes* or not—don't even know if You answer prayers any more—but You kept me alive for a reason. I believe that now. Show me what that reason is. If I do get to make a wish, could I ask for a wife and family? Yeah, I know that's pretty presumptuous—especially since I have the wife already picked out—but I think You spoke to me today. Through the mouth of a child. Just like in the Bible. If I misunderstood, I'll understand, but..." He closed his eyes and whispered, "I'm sorry I ignored You for so long. Thank you for keeping me alive."

Taking a deep breath, he turned and opened the door to the store. Took the first steps toward his future.

When the bell over the door tinkled, Ryan looked up. Just like he had every time it had opened since he'd seen Allison in The Soda Shoppe. When she entered, his heart stopped.

"Well, Burgess, there's no time like the present," he muttered and steeled his resolve.

Moving around the store, Allison gathered her items quickly. Head down, she walked to the counter and handed her basket to him.

"Good afternoon, Allison. It's good to see you."

Her teeth worried her lower lip as she looked up. "I-I didn't know if you'd ever want to see me again. I'm so embarrassed, Ryan. Not only did Becca say something inappropriate the other day, I ran out and forgot to pay for our ice cream. I—"

He reached out and placed his hand over hers on the counter. A bolt of warmth shot through him. Yes, this was right. "Of course I want to see you again. As a matter of fact, if you hadn't come in today, I was going to come to your house to invite you both to our Thanksgiving dinner. Mother always fixes enough to feed the entire neighborhood. War on or not, I doubt this year will be different. She's already invited everyone from the block."

Becca tugged her hand free from Allison's, then walked around the counter to join Ryan. He smiled at her, pleased she felt comfortable with him. If only Alli did. He pulled the tall stool up to sit on, lifted Becca onto his lap and handed her a penny candy. "I believe this is your favorite?"

Becca beamed, unwrapped the candy and put the Tootsie Roll straight into her mouth.

"Ryan, we couldn't possibly—"

"You couldn't possibly come to dinner. I know. Knew that would be your answer before I asked—so that's why I'm not asking you." He turned to the child on his knee. "Becca, my mother's going to cook a really big dinner the day after next. My dad and I can't eat that much food. Remember when you helped me with my apple pie?"

Busy chewing her candy, Becca nodded.

"Well, would you like to come to my house and help me eat Thanksgiving dinner? I already know what Mom's going to make. She's going to have turkey, English peas, snap beans, dressing, mashed potatoes, yams, rice and gravy, and hot rolls." Becca's eyes grew bigger with each item he listed. "And for dessert, she's going to have pear salad and cup cakes." He bent his head to whisper in her ear. "And chocolate ice cream."

Bouncing on his knee, Becca shouted, "Yes, yes, yes. Mommy, we're going to eat with Mr. Ryan!"

Ryan tried to stifle the groan that tore from his lips at her bouncing.

Rushing around the counter, Allison grabbed her daughter and took her back to the other side. "Ryan, I already told you we couldn't—"

His eyes met hers. "I know what you said, but I didn't ask you. I asked Becca, and she's delighted. Surely you wouldn't deprive her of a day filled with my family and friends. And after the meal we could go to the Fall Carnival. I think Becca would like that. Unless you're planning on spending the day with your family, of course."

A tear slipped down Allison's cheek. "No, Becca and I will be alone. The only family I have left is my cousin, Samantha. I invited her, but she said she can't take time off from work. She's trying to save enough money to put a down payment on her own apartment, so she just took a second job at a shopping mall for the holidays."

"Then you have no reason not to join us. Let Becca spend the day with us. My sisters and their families will be there—and I mean it when I say most of the neighborhood will be there as well. Isn't that what Thanksgiving is about?"

Allison chewed her bottom lip—something he noticed she did whenever she was nervous.

"Or do you just not want to spend the day with me?"

Her eyes shot up, met his. Pain filled their depths. "You know that isn't true."

"Do I?"

Finally she nodded. "All right, we'll join you." She met his gaze, and though she clearly tried to fight it, her lips curved in a smile. "But I must tell you, Ryan, it's quite unfair to use a child to get what you want."

He smiled and quirked a brow. "I haven't begun to get what I want, Allison. Not yet. But I will."

With the house overflowing with people, the noise level was just a few decibels shy of the fair he planned to take Allison and Becca to. Finally everyone was seated at the long table. The noon day prayer was lengthy. As patriarch of the family, his father offered a prayer for those still serving in Europe. Offered a prayer for families keeping the home fires burning while waiting to hear about their loved ones.

Soon arms reached in front of each other to grab plates piled high with food.

His mother rolled her eyes. "Could we do this in a more civilized fashion? We have guests."

He and his sisters looked at each other, then reached for more food. "Nah."

Allison placed small portions on her and Becca's plates.

Sitting beside Becca, Ryan reached around the child and placed heaping portions on both plates. "Eat up, girls. There's plenty of food today. Mother's been saving it just for this meal."

While others ate, his father proclaimed, "I'm thankful our men are pushing those Germans back."

"I'm thankful our son is home safe and sound," his mother chimed in. At his raised brow, she added, "Yes, Ryan. You're sound. You may have an injury you'll have to live with the rest of your life, but other than slowing you down when you walk, you can do anything you want." She looked meaningfully at Allison. "The only limitations you have are those you place on yourself."

Leave it to his mother to cut to the heart of the matter!

"I'm thankful most of my men survived the mission. And I am thankful for coming home. I missed you all. We don't realize how much home means. You should've seen the faces of GIs in their foxholes last Christmas as they opened their packages from home. Every one of them grinned from ear to ear." He sobered, because the next day some of them were dead.

Soon everyone around the table said something with the exception of Becca and Allison. Her mouth full of mashed potatoes, Becca chirped, "I'm thankful, too."

Everyone turned to look at her. "I'm thankful Mr. Ryan gives me penny candy!"

At everyone's laughter, Allison gave her daughter a hug. Tears filled her eyes as she looked up. "I didn't think I had much to be thankful for this year, but I was wrong. I have the most precious daughter in the world—and I have wonderful friends who are gracious enough to open their home to us on a day meant for families." Her eyes met Ryan's, an unspoken message seeming to be locked behind their depths.

Ryan had spent every spare minute with Alli and Becca. He needed them as much as he needed air to breathe. When she'd agreed to spend the day with him and then attend the Fall Carnival, his heart had leapt.

So here he was, holding cotton candy with one hand and his cane with the other. It was difficult walking on the uneven ground, but Allison walked slowly. He knew she measured her steps to match his.

At the Ferris wheel, he threw the empty cotton candy cone into the trash. He reached for her hand, then laughed—hers was as sticky as his. He pulled her forward, wrapped his arm around her waist and lowered his voice so only she could hear him ask, "Come ride with me?"

A thought flashed through his mind. Allison lying naked in his bed. Her long, auburn hair spread across the pillow. It wasn't the Ferris wheel he thought of riding! Wasn't the cotton candy on her hand he thought of licking! A bolt of lust shot through him, all blood heading south.

Shifting uncomfortably, he stepped forward. Drew Allison with him. Becca had already run forward and sat on the seat. Right in the middle. So much for a romantic moment at the top of the ride.

Still, he laid his arm across the back of the seat, toyed with Allison's hair at the nape of her neck. He wanted to touch her. Wanted to be with her. *Forever.* Did he have the courage? He'd always had daring in combat. Only the thought of Allison saying no to him almost cut him off at the knees.

He wasn't ready yet to risk all.

Running ahead of them as they got off the ride, Becca's eyes widened with each booth they came to. When they came to one with rifles and targets, Becca jumped up and down. "Mommy, Mommy, look! Please, pleeeeeeeese can I have that teddy bear?"

She pointed to the largest bear. The one people never won. Everyone knew the games were rigged. Still, Ryan thought he might finally have a chance to win something for her—even if it was the smallest bear.

"I can't guarantee anything, Becca, but I'll give it a try."

She tugged her mother's arm. "Mr. Ryan's going to win me that teddy bear, Mommy."

Ryan's heart sank. How could he let this small child down? She went without so much already. Stepping toward the counter, he laid his money down and picked up a rifle. Three shots. Only three shots to win a prize.

Bam! Down went one clay duck. *Bam!* Down went another. Ryan braced himself against the counter and aimed. *Bam!* A third duck flipped backward.

"We got a winner here, folks," the man behind the counter yelled as he reached for the smallest bear. An ugly bear no child would want. "Who wants to be the next person to win a bear?"

Ryan plunked more money on the counter. "I'll keep trying if it's okay with you."

The man smiled, revealing a mouth with two missing teeth, the rest of them yellowed. "Fine with me." He handed Ryan a different rifle.

"If it's all the same to you, I'll keep using the one I already have. Just need more pellets."

The man's eyes narrowed, but with a small crowd looking on, he handed them to Ryan.

Bam! Once again a moving duck flipped over backwards. *Bam!* Again. *Bam!* Ryan smiled as the third duck toppled over.

As Becca squealed with delight, Ryan reached down to rub his thigh. He couldn't put his weight on the cane while he was shooting and pain spread from his foot to his hip. One look at Becca's face when the man selected only a slightly larger bear and handed it to her and Ryan knew he couldn't quit now. "Keep it," he said.

"Ryan, please, you don't have to do this," Allison pleaded.

He brushed her protest aside. For the next twenty minutes, he laid down money and kept reloading his rifle. Intense throbbing burned through his leg, Ryan could barely speak as the man kept reaching for larger bears. Determination egged him on. Only one goal would suffice—he had to win that bear. The one with the bright blue bow that matched Becca's eyes.

Only one more round to go. The crowd continuing to gather behind him grew quiet as he took aim. Closing his eyes, he grabbed the counter and swayed. Breathing deeply, he willed himself to stave away the dizziness.

You will not pass out, Burgess. She's a child. You can do this for her...for yourself.

Bracing himself, Ryan took aim. He had to prove he could do something. Prove he could stand up to the pain—and win. If he quit now, he'd be quitting the rest of his life.

Bam! Down went a duck. *Bam!* Down went another. *Bam!*

"Here you go, little missy," the man ruefully said as he handed over the prized bear. "Your daddy must love you an awful lot."

Becca's look of joy was all the thanks Ryan needed. *He'd done it.* He'd won the bear. He wasn't a failure.

Allison rushed to his side, picked up his cane, and braced his arm across her shoulders. "Let's sit awhile."

When Ryan looked into those beautiful brown eyes he didn't see the pity he expected.

He saw love.

Surely he imagined it.

"All right, I want you alone for a little while, Alli. I need you close tonight. Let's go sit by the carousel so Becca can ride it."

Allison rolled her eyes. "Is everyone in your family as bossy as you?"

Ryan laughed, a deep guttural sound. He hadn't done that in ages. Not since his plane had crashed into the barrier and the world as he'd known it had changed. It felt good. So did being with this woman.

"As a matter of fact they are. It's one of the things I love about them. They know what they want and go after it."

He pulled her closer. "When I was overseas, I watched men open parcels from home. Some got bars of soap, powder, maybe a sweater or a muffler. Simple things, but they meant the world to them. Meant home. I came home to a fancy house while many of those men died. I didn't appreciate it, thought my life was over. Merely because my leg hurts and I limp. I feared no one would ever want me. Figured I'd never want anything—anyone—ever again enough to take the risk." Sounds of the carnival carried on the cold night air.

"Until I met you." He turned her toward him. "But instead of making me feel good, for a while I felt worse. Sure, I knew there was plenty in this world to live for—but I thought I'd never have it."

"That's silly, Ryan. You have everything to live for. What could you have possibly wanted that you thought you couldn't—"

"You." At her gasp, he placed a finger over her lips. "I want you, Alli. Want to hold you in my arms. Want to feel your sweet lips against mine, to make love to you all night. I knew you'd never want me because I'm no longer whole. I'm damaged goods."

"But Ryan—"

"Then I changed my mind. Remembered I'm a Burgess. We go after what we want. Claim it. Take it. I'm going after you, Alli Morgan. Prepare yourself for that. I'm claiming you as my own. Some day very soon

I'm going to take you. For now I'll woo you. Win your heart. I'm going to start by kissing you." He eased his hand around the back of her neck and moved his mouth within an inch of hers, a smile tilting up his lips. "What's this? No argument? You're not going to tell me you can't?"

Her eyes met his. Never wavered. "No."

With only a few days until Christmas—armloads of gifts in hand—Ryan thought he couldn't walk another step. *White Christmas* played as he followed Allison out the door of the toy store. *That Crosby fellow must be raking in piles of money with all the records he has out right now.*

"Why don't we go get a cup of hot chocolate? I could use a break," he suggested. Allison's eyes immediately went to his leg, but he assured her, "I'm fine, Alli. I just need to rest."

She bit her lip. "Why didn't you stop sooner? I told you we didn't need to—"

"Shhh, love. I'm fine. Let's just go sit and rest a spell." He leaned forward and brushed his lips over hers. He edged closer to Allison on the padded bench, his leg now touching hers.

Have Yourself a Merry Little Christmas played on the jukebox in the corner. Yeah, right. As if that would happen. Oh, he wanted it—but did he really have the guts to go after it? Ryan's emotions were on a teeter-totter—up one minute, down the next.

The heat from her seemed to scorch his skin through the sleeve of his shirt. He wondered what it would feel like to have her warm touch on his naked body. He wanted her to run her fingers down his arms, across his chest, down to his... *Stop it!*

He didn't know if that would ever happen. He must have been a fool to buy her a ring. He placed his hand in his pocket, fingering the small box he'd picked up right before meeting her that morning. Could he make Alli happy? Did he have the right to hope?

Could she see herself in a life with him? Forever?

That's what he wanted. A life with her forever. Waking up with her every morning, making love to her every night. Having a child with her. *His child.*

He wanted...too much.

Nearly frozen by fear, he removed his hand from the pocket.

Since his family traditionally opened their presents on Christmas Eve, everyone sat in the crowded living room. His nephews and Becca laughed as they placed ornaments on the tall tree. Ryan held Becca up to place the star on the top of the tree.

Soon his nephews ran around the room, 'riding' their new stick ponies. Becca proudly held her prized doll, the one Allison told him she'd wanted on her birthday.

Shyly, Allison reached beside her and held out a package. "It's not much. I hope you'll like it."

He hadn't expected a gift from her. Knew she had little money to spare. Lifting the cover on the box, he pulled out a brown sweater. His eyes went to Allison's.

"I knitted it myself. I told you it wasn't much. I—"

"It's perfect. It will suit me just fine in the store. Thank you, Alli." He reached in his jacket pocket and pulled out a slender box.

She shook her head. "You don't need to give me anything, Ryan. What you've done for Becca is more than enough."

"It's not much, Alli. Please open it."

Her fingers shook as she unwrapped the gold bracelet he'd bought for her. As tears slid down her cheeks, he leaned forward, took it from her trembling fingers and fastened it around her wrist.

"Are you going to be my daddy now, Mr. Ryan? 'Cause my daddy's an angel now. Did he send you to watch over us?" Becca sat near the tree, watching them. Silence filled the room at the hopeful smile on her face. "Can I have a baby sister now, too?"

"Becca!" Allison gasped.

"Well, it's what I asked Santa for when I saw him at Gimbel's last week. I told him I wanted a new daddy and a baby sister."

Ryan smiled. *I wouldn't mind doing something about that last request.* Mindful that his family was watching, he touched his lips lightly across Allison's cheek, then brushed his knuckles against it. "It gets easier, Alli. Time will lessen your loss."

He wanted to be the one to take away her pain. Wanted to take her in his arms and hold her forever.

Behind them, his mother turned on the record player. Bing Crosby crooned, *Silent night, holy night. All is calm, all is bright.*

Was his future really bright? He'd know tomorrow— if he didn't chicken out.

His mother walked over and placed her arm around his waist. "It's not so very late. Why don't the two of you head over to the USO? I heard they're having a farewell early Christmas Eve party for some of the men ready to be deployed. They have a band tonight."

When Allison shook her head, Mrs. Burgess persisted. "You both deserve a night out. Becca can stay here and play with my grandsons. She can spend the night in one of the girls' old rooms upstairs."

"What a wonderful idea," Allison heard Ryan say. "We won't stay out late. Just long enough to listen to some music and relax a bit."

"No, I couldn't possibly do that. I should take Becca home now. We've imposed on you too much as it is."

"We've loved having the two of you visit and hope you'll come back often. But go, have fun. You're only young once," his mother insisted.

Returning with her coat and Ryan's overcoat, Mr. Burgess handed them both to Ryan. "Make sure you bundle this sweet girl up now. It's mighty cold out there. Mother, I don't see a neck scarf for the young lady. Do you have one she can borrow?"

While Ryan helped with her coat, his mother quickly returned with a long cashmere neck scarf. Ryan took it and wrapped it gently around Allison's neck. "There, that's better."

Allison just stood there, her mouth open. She'd never felt anything so luxurious. "But I can't—"

"Certainly you can, dear." She glanced over at her husband and received the briefest of nods. "In fact, I rarely ever wear that one. It looks lovely on you, so why don't you keep it?"

"I can't—"

As Ryan ushered her out the door into the blast of cold air, he laughed. "There sure are a lot of things you seem to think you can't do. Time to start thinking of what you can."

His mother had played Christmas music throughout the entire day. Bing Crosby had crooned, *I'll Be Home for Christmas*. Yes he was. Home. This was right. He had his family around him, Alli by his side, and Becca inside playing with his nephews. What more could he ask for?

He could ask for Alli to be his wife.

Out at the curb, he stopped beside the family's two year old Packard. "I wish I could drive us to the USO,"— he patted his leg with his gloved hand—"but the clutch and this old leg don't get along anymore. It's too cold to walk, but if you don't mind, I think it would be fun if we took the trolley."

At her agreement, they headed to the nearest trolley tracks. Placing his cane over his arm, he helped Allison up and then pulled himself onto the first step. As they sat in the rear seat and rode toward the center of town, he eased his arm along the back of the seat. "Why don't you move closer? It's cold in here and I don't want you to catch a chill."

He edged her closer, then his lips met hers. Gently. Sweetly. His tongue brushed her closed lips, urging them to open. When they did, he thrust his tongue inside, claiming what he'd wanted for over a month. What he planned to have for the rest of his life.

When the trolley stopped near the club, he helped Allison down the steps. Strains of Duke Ellington filtered out into the cold night air.

The trolley rolled on, but Ryan didn't move. Instead, he wrapped his arms around Allison and drew her closer.

Allison moaned as his hand brushed over her hair, eased a tendril behind her ear. He hugged her close. Moved his hand up and down the column of her back. Lust shot straight to his groin. He'd worried his injury might have messed up more than his leg. Allison's body pressed to his proved that wasn't so. He could make love to her—and some day he would. Of that he no longer had any doubt. He moved his hand inside her coat and brushed it over her plain, cotton blouse. The tip of her breast hardened instantly under his fingertips. Just as he'd hardened holding her.

He groaned. If he didn't stop now, he might not be able to. He wouldn't behave like a rutting stag. Gathering what little control he had left, he pulled back. Looked at Allison's very kissable mouth and had to close his eyes and count to ten. Mercy, but he wanted her.

Helping her straighten her coat, Ryan held his arm out for her and headed for the club. They waited their turn to enter. Bing Crosby's *Moonlight Becomes You* lilted through the door each time it opened. The song was right. She was beautiful, and the moonlight glinting off the snow on her silky, auburn hair had him wanting to run his hands through it. Wanting to run his hands over every inch of her body.

Inside, he helped her off with her coat, then handed it to a hatcheck girl and led Allison to an empty table.

This is where I'll discover if I truly have a chance with her or if she'll only be happy with another man— one who can spend the evening dancing with her. He watched the happy couples on the dance floor and saw her keeping time with her fingers on the table. So she liked to dance. Somehow he'd known she would.

Seeing one of his neighbors, a young man who'd been 4-F and couldn't go to war because of poor eyesight, he motioned him over. "James, this is Allison. Why don't you two dance while I get us something to drink?"

Allison started to protest, but James quickly pulled her out onto the dance floor. Ryan's heart slammed against his ribs as he watched her dance. Her smile was beautiful. He'd seen it so rarely. She always looked worried and sad—or had she been lonely?

Just like him.

He wended his way through the crowd to the bar to get their drinks. Uncertain how to carry them back to the table while he leaned on his cane, he cradled them both between his arm and his body. Then walked slowly around the outside of the room so no one would bump into him. Placing the cane across the table, he set the filled mugs on it, then lowered himself to a chair. He watched Allison and James do the jive, then collapse into giggles as the dance ended.

He'd never heard her giggle before. She sounded musical, like an angel.

She came back to the table, laughing. "Oh, that was wonderful. I haven't danced since...since..." She stopped. "Since the night my husband left."

"Did you dance together often?" Ryan asked as he pulled her chair out and seated her beside him, then shot a look of thanks at James and the man left them alone.

A sad smile crossed her face. "Yes, we did. Albert loved to dance. And all the girls loved to watch him. He was blond and blue-eyed, just like Becca. He gathered a crowd wherever he went."

"You're very good as well."

"We entered several dance contests. Won some, too," she added shyly.

A soldier approached their table. "I hope you don't mind, but I have to leave soon. My plane will be taking off shortly. I saw you dancing a minute ago and would love it if I could have just one dance with you. Do you know how to do the Lindy?"

Allison nodded. "I do, but I'm here with my date. I..."

She'd called him her date! He wanted to grab her and pull her to him. Keep her safe within his arms, never let anything or anyone ever hurt her again. She'd been hurt too much by the war. Instead he said, "It's fine, Alli. I don't mind if you have one more dance."

Oh, but he did.

He didn't want her dancing with anyone else. Didn't want anyone else touching her. Didn't want...despair shot through him. Hell. It didn't matter what he wanted. He'd been right all along. He'd never have her. He saw how the men looked at her. She was beautiful. And gentle. And kind.

And his!

By the time she came back to the table, Ryan had worked himself into a state. He wanted her far away from these men.

She started to sit beside him, but he stood. "We need to leave, Allison. It's time to go home." His voice was brusque, clipped.

Allison frowned and looked at him questioningly. He turned away and headed toward the cloakroom, handing the checker the ticket for their coats. When Allison reached him, he gave her the coat instead of helping her on with it. He felt like a heel.

Grabbing her elbow, he guided her to the door without saying a word. Out on the street, people still waited to get in. *You'll Never Know* by Dick Haymes played as they walked away. Truer words were never spoken. He wouldn't know. He'd only been fooling himself. What made him think he stood a chance with her?

He was a fool.

Almost to the trolley stop, Allison stopped. "Ryan, you're upset. Are you angry I danced with that young man?"

He didn't say anything. Kept walking.

"Don't you walk away from me, Ryan Burgess. You told me to dance with both those men. Now you're angry with me? How dare you—?"

She broke off when he stormed back to her, dragging his weak leg awkwardly behind him. Pulling her into his arms, he crushed his mouth to hers, kissed her with all the pain inside him. Kissed her with all his fragile hopes, his love. Finally pulling away, he ran his hand through his hair.

"I'm sorry, Alli. I didn't mean to do that. I mean, I did, but not like that. I went crazy seeing you dancing with other men. I can't do that. Can't take you in my arms and dance with you. You deserve better than that. Deserve better than me."

Allison watched him. Watched the myriad emotions flicker in his eyes. He looked so lost. So forlorn. In that instant Allison knew she'd lost her heart to him.

She hadn't meant to. Had fought it from the moment he'd slipped the Tootsie Pop in her basket.

She wrapped her arms around his waist and he leaned against her. Rubbed his hand along his thigh.

"Did you hurt your leg when you stormed back to me?"

"I didn't storm. I—"

"Acted like a cave man."

He leaned his head against the top of her head. "I'm sorry, Alli. Really. I wanted this evening to be special."

"It was special, Ryan. It *is* special—because I'm with you."

"Alli, don't. I don't need your sympathy."

Again she watched him. Watched the emotions in his eyes—pain, hurt. Hope.

"Put your arms around me."

He stepped back. "What?"

"I said put your arms around me." She moved closer, wrapped hers about him again. He finally did as she asked and pulled her close. She wrapped her arms around the back of his neck and began to hum. Then swayed slowly from side to side.

Ryan closed his eyes. Let her lead him.

"You're dancing, Ryan."

His eyes flew open. "What?"

"You're dancing. *We're* dancing. Right here, right now. Under this street lamp with the stars in the sky and a light dusting of snow around us. I don't have to dance the Lindy or the Jive to be dancing. I'm dancing with you."

Ryan looked around to see if anyone watched them. His steps were unsteady. "In the middle of the street?"

"Yes, in the middle of the street. Where I'm dancing doesn't matter. Who I'm dancing with does."

He inhaled deeply and rested his head against hers.

"I love you, Ryan." Standing on her toes, she brushed her lips gently over his.

Ryan reached into the inside pocket of his coat and pulled out the box. So small, yet it held something very big—the answer to his prayers.

If only...

Drawing a breath, Ryan thrust it at Allison before he changed his mind. "Merry Christmas, Alli."

She held it, but didn't open it. Her eyes met and locked with his, a myriad of questions in them.

His voice caught. "Aren't...aren't you going to open it?"

Tears slowly trickled down her cheeks as she nodded and gently undid the wrapping paper. Her breath caught as she flipped open the lid. A sparkling diamond twinkled up at her. "Ryan...I..."

"Allison Monroe, if you tell me you can't marry me, I'll—"

"Yes!" she interrupted and flung her arms around his neck.

Dumbfounded, Ryan just stood there. Stared into her eyes. Finally he regained his senses. "Yes? As in yes, you'll marry me?"

"Yes. I'll marry you!"

"You're not going to argue and tell me all the reasons why you can't?"

"No."

"You're not going to run away from me?" A smile tipped up the corner of his lips.

"No."

"You're going to marry me, let me adopt Becca, and live with me in the house we're going to buy next week?"

"Are we now?"

"Yes, we are."

"Then, yes, I guess I'm going to marry you."

"I love you, Allison Monroe."

"And I love you, Ryan Burgess."

He brushed his lips over her eyes, her nose, lightly across her mouth.

"Remember when I told you I was coming after you? That I was going to have you some day?"

Allison nodded.

"And I started it all with a kiss?" He put his hand behind her neck just like he had that long ago night—and claimed another kiss.

One that sealed the present. Sealed the promise of their future.

Down the street, the doors to the nightclub opened and the strains of *You'd Be So Nice to Come Home To* filled the snowy night.

"Dance with me, Allison."

Visit Leanne's website at:
http://www.leanneburroughs.com

The Christmas Store

by Ann Marie Bradley

New-fallen snow glistened like millions of diamonds across the sidewalk and crunched beneath Aine's boots. Miniature white lights criss-crossed bare tree branches and lined rooftops, twinkling on and off. Elvis crooned, *I'll have a blue Christmas without you* through overhead speakers.

"He's got that right," Aine mumbled. She sucked in a deep breath and hurried to catch up with her best friend, Holly.

"Aw, come on, Scrooge. Just look at this window display and tell me it doesn't put you in the Christmas spirit." An easy smile played at the corners of Holly's mouth.

Aine studied the exhibit. *The Christmas Store* was emblazoned across the top half of the window in large red letters. Underneath, spread on a layer of snow-white cotton, lay a tiny village, complete with Victorian houses, stores, and a small church with a steeple – straight from Currier and Ives. In the center of the small town, a happy couple skated hand in hand on a mirror pond. *Everyone has a partner except me.*

"Come on, Aine, let's go in." Holly pulled her by the arm and almost dragged her inside the quaint shop. A bell jingled as the door opened, and Santa Claus peeked around a large Christmas tree in the middle of the store.

"Ho, ho, ho! Welcome to The Christmas Store, ladies." He finished straightening a shiny gold star on the fresh cedar tree, then motioned toward a round

43

table in the corner. "Help yourself to a cup of hot cocoa and some of Mama's fresh-from-the-oven sugar cookies."

"He's good," Aine whispered, leaning closer to Holly.

"I told you you'd love this store." Holly flashed her friend a wide grin. "Bet they don't have anything like this in Florida."

Santa joined them at the lace-covered table and popped a snowman-shaped cookie into his mouth. "Mmm, mmm, nobody bakes like Mama."

Aine stirred miniature marshmallows into her hot chocolate with a cinnamon stick and glanced about. A real contrast to the fancy department stores and specialty boutiques she normally frequented. Every inch had been stuffed with handcrafted toys and gifts. Candy canes and sparkly gold garland hung from the edges of shelves, and the rich, spicy scent wafting from the window display told her the village houses were real gingerbread.

"Now, Papa, save some of these for our guests."

Aine smiled as a seventyish woman, dressed in a long, red velvet skirt and green silk peasant blouse scolded Santa. The old woman playfully tapped his hand away from the large Christmas-tree-shaped tray of cookies.

"Have to keep up my appearance for the children, Mama." Santa rubbed his round belly and chuckled, amusement flickering in his eyes.

Aine couldn't control her burst of laughter at the gentle teasing between the happy couple. The cold, empty feeling inside her vanished, replaced with something warm and enchanting. She hadn't felt this good in months. Since before she'd walked into her apartment and found her fiancé in bed with another woman.

Mrs. Claus set the tray on the table and reached inside a deep pocket of her apron. "Have you girls hung your Christmas wishes on the tree?" She handed them each a candy cane pen and sheet of sparkly gold paper.

"I'm afraid I haven't believed in Santa Claus for a long time." Aine laid her pen and paper on the table.

"Oh, come on, party pooper," Holly whined. "Don't spoil the fun." She wrote out her wish and hung it on the tree with a snippet of red ribbon supplied by Mrs. Claus.

Santa adjusted his wire-framed glasses a bit higher on his nose. "Tsk tsk. You don't believe in Santa Claus? Mama, did you hear this child?"

His wife shoved a wisp of snow-white hair from her forehead and sighed. "I heard, Papa. But I'm sure you can change her mind."

Aine rolled her eyes. "Twenty-nine is a little old to be making Christmas wishes to Santa." Her pulse pounded in her head.

"Old? You're never too old to make Christmas wishes." He picked up the pen and paper, and his chubby hand reached out to her. "Just write your heart's true desire."

Aine threw up her hands and sighed. "Okay. I'm outnumbered." She reached for the pen and paper. Her hands shook visibly as she composed her Christmas wish. She bit down hard on her lower lip and wrote:

Dear Santa,
Please bring me a husband and family for
Christmas.

Love,
Aine Ross

A band tightened around her heart. She took a deep breath, folded the note, attached the gold string Mrs. Claus offered and tied it to the highest branch she could reach.

"There. Satisfied?" In spite of her reserve, a tinge of frustration came into her voice. *Santa is going to accomplish in two weeks what I haven't been able to in almost thirty years? Sure. And eight tiny reindeer pull this man around in a sleigh on Christmas Eve. Damn you, Peter Browning. Damn you for cheating on me.*

"That's much better, young lady." Santa's jolly voice pulled her out of her reverie. "Wishes come true at The Christmas Store. You'll see."

"What'd you wish for, Aine?" Holly stretched on tiptoe, trying to read the message.

"None of your business." Aine closed the door on her painful memories and gave Holly a friendly jab on the arm. "You didn't tell me what you wished for."

"You can't guess?" Holly laughed. "To be stranded on a deserted island with my very own swashbuckling pirate!"

"You!" Aine grimaced in good humor at her friend, then turned her attention back to shopping. She singled out an exquisite porcelain doll dressed in an intricately embroidered white gown and bonnet from a shelf of dolls. "My niece would love this. Wherever do you find things with such fine workmanship?"

"The elves make them."

Aine's gaze shot to Santa. Joy bubbled in his voice and shone in his brilliant blue eyes. *The man plays his part well.*

She paid for the doll and two toys for her nephews, then gave her scarf an extra wrap about her neck before stepping back outside into the cold with her packages. It had stopped snowing, but a steady breeze nipped at her cheeks as she walked in step with Holly.

"They don't have taxis in this town? Or are you just trying to torture me?"

"Aw, come on, Aine. It's only six blocks to my apartment, and when we get there I'll make you a nice bowl of hot potato soup." With a spring in her step, Holly hurried down the sidewalk.

"I must have been crazy to leave Florida to stay with you here in the frozen North for two weeks—even if you are my best friend." Her movements stiff with cold, Aine followed. She hadn't gone two feet when a small boy, coat unzipped and bare-headed, thundered down the sidewalk straight for her. In lightning-fast motion, woman and child slipped on the ice and tumbled into a snow bank. Aine took the brunt of the fall, stretched out on her back like a kid making a snow angel.

Planting an elbow in the middle of her stomach, the boy pushed himself up. "Hey, watch it, lady." His jaw quivered.

Aine broke into an open, friendly smile. "Sorry, little guy." She reached out to tousle his thick, slightly long black hair.

He yanked away from her and ran into The Christmas Store.

Aine struggled to her feet and brushed the snow from her backside. "Merry Christmas..."

Holly hurried to her side. "Kids! Who needs them?"

"I do." Aine reached down to retrieve her packages from the snow. "He's a cute kid. Wouldn't mind having one just like him."

"That what you wished for? Kids?"

"That's between me and Santa Claus." She shouldered her shopping bag and pushed Holly along the sidewalk in front of her.

"Aine! Aine! You'll never guess what happened today." Holly rushed into the apartment and slammed the front door behind her.

"The temperature dropped another forty degrees?"

"No, silly." Holly waved a plane ticket in Aine's face. The design department is being sent to Bermuda for a month—and I'm going, too. I got my promotion!"

"Fantastic!" Aine hugged her friend and they jumped up and down squealing like they had when they'd shared a room at the University of Florida six years ago. "Now all you need is a swashbuckling pirate."

Holly giggled. "That's the funniest part. The job is a photo shoot with pirate models on a real ship."

"Well, if you don't come back, I'll know Johnny Depp kidnapped you."

"In my dreams—or wishes." Holly scrunched her face. "Hey, wait a minute. Do you think...?"

"What? That Santa granted your wish? No. I think you finally got the promotion you deserve."

Holly smacked herself in the forehead. "What am I thinking? I can't go to Bermuda now." Her shoulders drooped and a deep sigh escaped her lips.

"Why ever not?" Aine picked up the airline ticket and waved it in Holly's face. "All you have to do is pack. Come on, I'll help."

"You. I can't leave you here alone. You're my guest."

"I can throw a 'Peter is a creep' pity party by myself just fine. This is your dream, Holly. You think I'd make you babysit me and lose this chance?"

"You sure?"

"Positive."

"Well, you can stay here as long as you like. My home is your home."

Aine glanced out the window at the falling snow. "Yeah. How can I leave this lovely weather?" She turned to Holly and grinned.

Holly grabbed a toss pillow from the sofa and threw it at her, but it missed its mark and hit the cat instead.

Yeoowwl.

"Ohmygosh, how could I forget Sugar?" Holly gazed at the snow-white cat hunched in the corner. "I can't leave her here by herself."

"She won't be alone. I'll be with her." Aine knelt and rubbed her hand down the cat's back, brushing her long fur with the back of her fingers. "We're buddies."

Sugar hissed and ran to the kitchen.

"I see." Holly laughed. "Doesn't live up to her name, huh? She just appeared on my doorstep a few weeks ago, and I couldn't turn her away. Had a tag with the name Sugar on it hanging from her collar, but no phone number or address. She really is a sweetie once you get to know her." Holly crossed the room to her bedroom door. "Come, help me pack. You can make friends with Sugar later. *If* you're serious about staying."

Aine rubbed the long red scratch on her hand. "I can think of lots better names than Sugar for a bad-tempered, skinny, ungrateful cat like you." She snapped the lid closed on the dry cat food container and left the cat to her Meow Mix.

She fixed her own breakfast, showered, dressed, called her parents in Florida, then her sister. The phone calls had been a mistake. Both her parents and her sister wanted her to come home. She certainly hadn't needed their reminders of Peter. They'd sided with him over her. 'After all,' her mother had said, 'he comes from a good family.'

Well, she planned to erase him and his good family from her mind. She didn't want to think about him ever again. She glanced at the clock above the kitchen sink. 10:00 AM. *Good grief, I thought it was at least two.* Nearly bored to tears, she grabbed her coat and scarf, pulled on her boots, and headed for The Christmas Store.

Something about seeing Santa and Mrs. Claus again encouraged Aine, and she hurried her steps. The sun peeked around a dark cloud, glistening gold on the luminous white snow coating a row of Scotch pines along the sidewalk. A cold wind slashed and shoved against her face, but the crisp, pine-scented air added to her happy feeling. She drew in a deep, invigorating breath and quickened her pace toward The Christmas Store.

The welcoming bell tinkled as Aine hurried inside the shop. Spicy aromas of ginger, chocolate, and peppermint drifted to her nose. "Mmm. Heaven." Only her second time in the shop, and already it felt familiar.

The store bustled with morning activity. Customers milled about the refreshment table, chatted in small groups, or examined the shelves of merchandise. Santa sat on his special chair, a child perched on his lap. A line of anxious children waited to hang their Christmas wishes on the tree. Odd, there seemed to be only one wish hanging on the tree. Hers.

The small boy sitting on Santa's lap looked familiar, but that was impossible since she'd never been to Holiday, Indiana before. The little guy scribbled something on his Christmas wish paper, grabbed the peppermint stick Santa offered, and scooted down. He reached up to hang his paper wish on the Christmas tree, and his jacket hood fell back, exposing a mop of black hair.

That's who he is. The little varmint that ran me down in the snow yesterday. The boy looked to be about six or seven. *Too young to be out by himself, that's for sure.* She stared at the boy. He looked clean, but ragged. The sleeves of his threadbare jacket barely reached his wrists, his jeans barely touched his socks, and one knee had a hole the size of an egg. Compassion squeezed Aine's heart.

The boy's gaze flitted all over the store before resting on Aine. His face paled and he flashed her a stricken look. He scraped the floor with one foot and lowered his eyes. "I-I'm sorry I knocked you down yesterday."

Before she could speak, assure him it was okay, he dashed past her. Her gaze followed him to a toy airplane hanging by a string from the ceiling. Poor little guy. From the looks of him, he'd not have a merry Christmas. His parents probably couldn't afford that plane or any of these fine toys and gifts. Maybe she could help somehow? Buy him whatever he'd wished for. If powerless to fix her own shattered heart, maybe she could help someone else's. Tears she'd held back for months flooded her eyes.

"Good morning, Aine." Mrs. Claus' cheery voice pulled her attention away from the boy to the friendly woman who today wore a white lace blouse with her long red velvet skirt.

She swiped her tears with her gloved hands. "Good morning, Mrs...Claus."

"Cute little guy, isn't he?" The old woman's eyes clouded with hazy sadness. "An orphan. Joey's mother died two years ago and he lives with an elderly great

50

aunt. Now she's not well." The white bun atop Mrs. Claus' head bounced as she shook her head and frowned. "His parents weren't married. The aunt says his mom never told the dad she was expecting. The only thing she ever told Joey was his dad is a pilot." She pointed to the blue plane hanging from the ceiling. "That's one of his Christmas wishes. Says his mommy told him his daddy flies a plane the color of his own blue eyes. Just like that one."

Aine mused over what the old woman had told her. "I'd like to help. May I buy the blue plane for the little boy and have it sent to his home?"

"That's very thoughtful of you, but I'm afraid the plane has already been spoken for. However, there is something you could do for me, dear. We like to take a photograph of all the people who hang a wish on the tree. It completely slipped my mind yesterday when you and Holly were in the store. I thought since Joey seems fond of you, I could photograph you two together."

Aine hesitated. "I'm sure you'd get a cuter picture of Joey without me spoiling it."

"Oh, no, dear. The two of you together will be just the thing. Stand over by the tree if you don't mind, and I'll fetch Joey."

"Mrs. Claus?"

The old woman turned back to Aine. "Yes, dear?"

"What happened to all the Christmas wishes hanging on the tree yesterday?"

"Oh, the wishes disappear from the tree once they're granted, my dear." She bustled to where Joey stood gazing up at the blue plane.

Although Joey seemed embarrassed, Mrs. Claus posed him and Aine between Santa and the Christmas tree. The joke Santa told did its trick and both Aine and Joey flashed big smiles for the camera.

"Don't move anyone. I want to get a couple more." Mrs. Clause snapped one photo after another with her Polaroid camera, handed one each to Joey and Aine, then added one to the collage of photos on the bulletin board behind the cash register.

Aine dropped her copy in her purse. *Cute kid. Wish I had one just like him.*

The next three mornings, Aine visited The Christmas Store, hoping to see Joey again. Each day she found only her and Joey's wishes on the tree, even though each day a steady stream of customers hung their wishes on the tree. Finally she could stand it no longer and questioned Mrs. Claus again about the missing wishes.

"I told you, dear. When the wishes are granted, they disappear from the tree. You have to believe in your wish. Perhaps you and Joey don't really believe."

Aine laughed out loud. She felt her face flush with embarrassment. "I'm sorry. It's just you sound so serious."

"I am, my dear."

Half an hour later Aine, crouched on all fours, tried to coax Sugar from under the couch. "Come on, kitty." She waved a moist kitty treat in front of the cat. "The package says this is the best treat ever."

The doorbell buzzed. Aine dropped the morsel on the floor and wiggled upright.

When she opened the front door she found a uniformed delivery boy.

"Ms. Aine Ross?"

"Yes. I'm Aine Ross."

"Special delivery." He handed her the envelope.

"For me? Who'd be sending me a letter here?"

The teen shuffled his feet. "Don't know, ma'am. Why don't you open it?" He turned to go.

Aine laughed. "Wait." She grabbed her purse from the table by the door and dug out a five-dollar bill. "Here's something for you. Merry Christmas."

The boy's face lit up with a grin. "Thanks, lady. Merry Christmas to you, too!"

She turned the envelope over and over in her hands. *Something must be wrong with Mom or Dad. Why else would I get a special delivery letter?* She made her way back to the couch and sat on the edge of a cushion.

Sugar dashed out and pounced onto Aine's lap. She batted at the paper with one tiny paw. Aine nudged the cat away gently with one hand. "Now you want to play? You'll have to wait."

Sugar settled back onto Aine's lap, kneading one thigh. The cat's eyes closed and she emitted a rumbling purr.

Aine stroked Sugar's soft white fur. "At least you have your claws in this time. Now let's see what's in this darn letter."

She slipped a long, tapered fingernail under the seal and slowly removed the letter. She unfolded the expensive-looking paper. *Congratulations, Ms. Ross! You are the winner of a seven-day, all-expense-paid trip to Hawaii. You'll enjoy a trip to a secluded island with Hawaii Blue Tours--dancing, dining, sailing, a dream vacation. Enclosed please find your plane ticket for Hawaii Blue Air, flight 111, departing Holiday International Airport, December 19, 2006 at 6:00 PM.*

Tomorrow? Aine turned the paper over again. That was it. Short and sweet. She checked the envelope and sure enough, a plane ticket made out in her name was tucked inside. Was this some kind of joke? She turned to stare out the window. Fresh snow fell from the darkening sky.

Hawaii in December? She searched the letter again and spotted an eight hundred number at the bottom of the page. A shock of excitement ran through her as she dialed the number.

Five minutes later she danced around the room with Sugar in her arms. Aine held the cat up and looked into her face. "What will I do with you?"

Sugar mewed and jumped from Aine's arms, pouncing on the shopping bag in the corner of the room.

Something about the way Sugar pawed at the bag gave Aine an idea.

"The Christmas Store. I'll ask Santa and Mrs. Claus if they'll watch you for a week. I'm sure they wouldn't mind."

A short while later, Aine bundled Sugar in a blanket and slipped her inside The Christmas Store shopping bag. She kept the bag closed and snuggled it to her chest to shelter Sugar from the wind on their short walk to the store.

As soon as the bell tinkled, Sugar peeked from her protective cover. She sprang from Aine's arms and ran across the room to Santa's chair.

"Ho, ho, ho." Santa reached down and picked up the cat rubbing against his soft leggings. "Look who came home, Mama."

Mrs. Claus scurried over and hugged both Santa and Sugar. "Blessed be, Papa, our baby is home."

"Sugar is *your* cat?" Aine crossed her arms and shook her head. "Great. I was going to ask you to cat sit, but since she belongs to you already, there's no problem."

Aine deplaned at Honolulu International Airport and searched the crowd. The sweet, exotic perfume of plumeria, ginger, maile, and orchids welcomed her. Mobs of people fought to claim luggage, meet family, and connect with their rides. *Silent Night* played on a ukulele blared from the loudspeakers between announcements of departing and landing planes. A circle of palm trees festooned with white orchid garlands, silver tinsel, and green and red bows horseshoed a giant mechanical Santa – barefoot and displaying a 'hang loose' sign while waving an armful of colorful paper leis, along with Mrs. Claus making a fashion statement by wearing a red flowered muumuu, a kukui nut lei, and a bright red hibiscus in her hair.

"That's more like it." She giggled at herself for thinking the Santa ensconced in a bright red outrigger canoe being pulled by eight dolphins more *normal* to her Florida upbringing than the Santa and snow she'd just left in Indiana.

Aine walked past the display and stopped in her tracks. The tall, dark and handsome fairy tale knight she'd just been reading about on the plane headed straight toward her holding up a cardboard sign: Aine Ross. But he'd traded in his medieval suit of shining armor for khaki shorts, a Hawaiian shirt, and flip-flops. And instead of heavy metal headgear, a red velvet Santa hat perched at a rakish angle on his thick dark hair.

"Ms. Ross?"

Aine nodded, and the Hawaiian knight handed her a bottle of expensive champagne and tucked the sign under one arm. "*Mele Kalikimaka.*" The beginnings of a smile tempted the corners of his mouth and her stomach lurched. "That's how we say Merry Christmas in Hawaii."

He pulled a dozen leis made from the petals of white orchids off one muscular arm and placed the flowers around her neck, then hugged her and lightly kissed one cheek. "Aloha."

"Thank you, Mr..."

"Jerald Garrison." A long moment passed between them. A light twinkled in the depths of his obsidian eyes—eyes that nearly stopped her heartbeat. "Just call me Jerald. I'm your official guide from Hawaii Blue Tours." He broke into an open, friendly smile.

She brought a hand to her cheek. The moment his lips had brushed it, heat surged through her body and it had nothing to do with the ambient temperature. "Thanks. You may call me Aine."

"Aine it is. That's an unusual name."

"I was named after my grandmother. It's Celtic for Joy."

"Fits." He reached for her carry-on bag, shouldered it, and helped her claim the rest of her luggage before guiding her to his waiting blue convertible outside.

Thirty minutes and nearly the same amount of miles down the road, Aine felt completely at ease with her guide. Resting her head back against the leather seat, she watched as city turned to country. "I thought Hawaii would be practically the same as Florida, but this is overwhelmingly beautiful. And the air is so sweet and fresh."

"Wait until we get to the kanikapila. Hope you're hungry."

"Kani..."

He laughed. "Kah-nee-kah-PEE-lah means to make music. Mom runs the Inn, and your welcome party has already started. You'll have a little plate lunch—or a lot if I know my mom. My cousin will tune up his uke, make some music, and you'll meet new friends and have a good time."

Aine searched Jerald's face as he spoke and sensed genuine caring and friendship. The bleakness and despair she'd felt the last month left her. The brilliance of Jerald's dark eyes and the strength of his chin sent a surge of desire through her body. She shivered. What was she thinking? It would be foolhardy to get involved with a man right now. She'd be gone in seven days.

The blue sports car rolled smoothly down the shell drive and stopped at the front entrance to the Inn. "This is it." Jerald jumped out of the car and hurried around to open Aine's door. "Welcome to Mama Lu's Paradise Inn."

"Charming. Not at all what I expected," Aine gushed. She stared up at the two-story brick building.

"You thought you'd stay in a grass hut?" A broad smile lit his face.

"Not exactly." Aine returned his smile. "But I wasn't expecting *Tara* way out here."

A younger version of Jerald ran out the front door and down the steps to their car. "About time you got here, Bro. Party's started out back." He held out a hand to Aine. "I'm Joe. I'll take your bags to your room."

56

Jerald guided Aine down a path and around the house. A long table overflowing with food was set up on the patio. The back yard—a white sandy beach—stretched to the ocean not thirty feet away.

"Jerald Garrison, 'bout time you got here." A pleasantly-plump, dark-haired woman wearing a bright yellow aloha muumuu and matching flip-flops grabbed Aine and spun her around. "Pretty little thing, this one."

"This is Aine Ross, Mom. Your new tenant for the next week."

"Welcome to Hawaii and to our hale, Aine. Just call me Mama Lu, honey, everyone does." She slapped Aine hard on the back and aimed a wink toward Jerald. "Sure are lucky such a pretty little thing won that tour. Won't be hard escorting this gal around the islands, huh, Jerald?"

"Put away your cupid arrow, Mom." Jerald glanced at Aine and shrugged. "She fancies herself a great matchmaker. If your ring finger is empty, you're fair game."

"Better not scoff at Mama Lu's magic, Little Bro." Another replica of Jerald, this one older, danced past with a beautiful Hawaiian woman in his arms. "Look what it did for Kari and me." His smile widened and he pointed to a picnic table crowded with eight giggling children enjoying their dinner.

Aine gasped. "All those children are your nieces and nephews?"

"That brood just belongs to Leo and Kari." He waved his arms wide. "Look closer and you'll see about fifteen more around here who belong to my other brothers."

Aine turned to Mama Lu. "Twenty-three grandchildren? How many sons do you have?"

"Six strong, healthy boys." Mama Lu's voice swelled with pride. "All of them married with children of their own, except Sammy and Jerald."

"Sammy's eighteen, Mom."

"And your excuse?" Mama Lu smiled.

Aine found herself instantly comfortable among the noisy, happy family, even though with her blonde hair and blue eyes she looked as conspicuous as a fish out of water. She glanced at Mama Lu, who met her gaze with a mystifying smile. A warm glow flowed through Aine and filled her with a strange inner excitement.

Mama Lu excused herself and Jerald introduced Aine to more of his family. When Mama Lu returned, she carried an oversized picnic basket and shoved it into Jerald's hands.

"I'm sure Aine would enjoy the view from the garden."

A few minutes later, Jerald lowered his body onto a cool stone bench in the garden and motioned Aine to sit beside him. She settled near him, her leg brushing his. A spark of fire ignited in the pit of her stomach. *Easy girl, just because you're in paradise doesn't mean you have to go all gushy.* She edged away.

Jerald removed the dishtowel covering the basket. "I'll bet you're starved." He placed the contents from the basket on the bench between them.

She hesitated when he handed her a plate.

He scooped up a tender steamed roll. "*Manapua?*" When she didn't answer, he said it slowly. Mah-nah-poo-ah. Rolls filled with chicken. You'll love it." He plopped it on her plate along with a large helping of shellfish marinated in soy sauce with rice and a dollop of coconut pudding.

"*Mai hilahila*—don't be bashful!"

After eating, they explored the garden, a world of lush foliage and tropical flowers. A haven of beauty appeared at every turn. The sound of traditional Christmas songs sung in the melodic Hawaiian language, accompanied by guitars and ukuleles, filtered through the garden from the party beyond.

Jerald's arm slipped around her shoulders and he pulled her closer. Her pulse quickened.

His lips brushed hers. "I've wanted to do that all evening."

Aine tried to throttle the dizzying current racing through her. She'd just met this man. What was he doing? What was *she* doing? Something about him drew her like a magnet. The garden's magic? Perhaps it was nothing more than the plant leaves swaying gently in the warm breeze or the soothing sounds of the surf a few feet away caressing the beach, but a magical, mesmerizing feeling overcame her and she melted into him, wanting more. Her lips parted.

"Hey, there's no mistletoe out here." The little girl's voice broke the spell and Aine and Jerald parted.

"Emmi, what are you doing out here?" Jerald scolded his niece.

"Daddy said for you to come back to the party with our guest of honor." She ran back down the path toward the house.

Aine started to follow, but Jerald pulled her back. His hands slipped up her bare arms, bringing her closer. His touch sent a warm shiver through her. Reclaiming her lips, he crushed her to him.

Her breath caught and her knees turned to jelly, but she pushed him away. "Your family is waiting for us." She gathered up the picnic supplies.

"Mama Lu won't mind if we stay here." He reached for the basket.

She shoved his hand away. "Jerald Garrison, if you think I'm going to stay in the garden necking when your whole family is not ten feet away, you've got another think coming."

He cleared his throat. "So, if the family wasn't so close, you'd stay and neck?"

For the next few days Jerald flew Aine around the islands in his private plane. They toured beautiful beaches, rich rain forests, and soaring mountains. By day they took advantage of sparkling waters to snorkel, scuba dive, and water ski, then lay on powdery beaches under a clear blue sky and soaked up the glowing sunshine. At night, when the city came alive with entertainment, they explored elegant boutiques, art galleries, and nightclubs.

Amidst the surprises and delights, a warmth...a spirit filled Aine's soul and healed the void Peter had left in her heart.

Jerald's hopeful gaze fastened on hers. He swallowed. "I'm sorry, Aine. I don't mean to rush you. I'd hoped you felt as I do. As if we've known each other longer than a week. I know it seems odd after such a short time, but I want to marry you, Aine. Spend my life with you." He traced her lips with a forefinger and his touch sent currents of desire through her. "I love you."

Moonlight bathed the beach. Aine ran her fingers through the silken sand. She'd shoved Jerald away all week. Checked her feelings. Too soon? Yes. No! Peter was the past—Jerald the future. She *was* sure. She couldn't fight her feelings—her body—any longer. She wanted him. Wanted him to devour her mouth, her breasts, her...everything! But it wasn't just physical. She loved him. Wanted his children. Wanted to be a part of his family. She'd found her soulmate. The *one*. Suddenly she couldn't wait to tell him.

"Jerald?" Tears filled her eyes--a mix of relief, surprise, and joy. Tears tempered by the bitter knowledge of past mistakes. How could she be sure? "I...I need to think." She pressed her palms to her temples.

"Shhhh. Don't worry about it, Aine. Maybe you're right. Maybe we need more time." He stood and brushed the sand from his pants. "Come on, I'll walk you back."

What had she done? She let him pull her up, but her knees turned to jelly. In a quick forward motion, he cradled her with his arms. Her head fit perfectly in the hollow between his shoulder and neck. She relaxed into his cushioning embrace.

Jerald took a step backward. "I'm sorry."

Aine squared her shoulders and ran ahead to hide the tears streaming down her face. She heard him curse behind her.

Aine dabbed her eyes with another tissue. She'd cried nonstop since returning to the mainland. She turned the note from Jerald over in her hand again. He said he'd wait. Said he'd call. He'd signed it *Me ke aloha*—with love. Why hadn't she told him the truth? Told him she couldn't live without him?

Empty and silent, Holly's apartment seemed a better choice than seeing her family right now. She paused at the threshold of the guestroom, taking a deep breath. Had it only been two days since her return? God, even that crazy cat would be a welcome sight right now. Too bad she was at The Christmas Store.

"The Christmas Store." She pulled on warm clothes and her boots. The store beckoned her. *But it's Christmas Eve. Will it be open?* She grabbed her purse and hurried outside, her heart beating like a drum.

Flushed and breathless, Aine turned the doorknob. The familiar jingle was a welcome sound. Her gaze flew to the Christmas tree in the center of the room and her heart fell. A tremor seized her body, and she choked on a sob. "No."

She ran to Santa. "Why?" she asked hysterically. "Why only mine and Joey's wishes left on the tree?"

Mrs. Claus offered Aine a fresh sugar cookie. "I told you, dear. Only the granted wishes disappear. Have faith, it isn't Christmas yet."

Aine didn't answer. Her shoulders slumped and she turned to leave. Before she reached the door, it burst open and Joey ran inside, pulling a man behind him.

Joey grabbed Aine around the legs and hugged her. "Look, Aine! I found my daddy and he brought me a blue plane—and I'm going to live with him." He waved the plane in the air.

Aine squatted, returned Joey's hug, then stood to introduce herself to his father. She froze. "Ohmygod!"

61

Familiar arms encircled her. She locked her arms around his neck, kissing him frantically.

Jerald stroked her back, her hair. His body melted against hers and he murmured her name. They clung to each other.

Jerald gazed into her eyes. "I was going to stop by your friend's apartment. I wanted to ask you something. And explain about my son. But Joey wanted to come here first."

"You don't have to explain anything to me. I'm glad Joey found his daddy."

"I want to explain, Aine. A letter from Joey's aunt arrived the day you left Honolulu, telling me of a son I never knew I had. I dated his mother in college, but we broke up before I moved back to Hawaii. She didn't like the idea of me becoming a pilot. She never told me about our son. After her death, Joey lived with his great aunt, but she has cancer and doesn't have long to live. I took the first flight to Holiday and here we are."

She swallowed, searching his face.

"I love you, Aine. If you don't mind a ready-made family, I want you to be my wife."

"Hey, what about me?" Joey tugged at Jerald's overcoat.

Aine and Jerald laughed. Jerald ruffled Joey's hair— hair just like his own. "I haven't forgotten you, sport. This is your new mommy. That is, if she'll have us?"

Joey jumped up and down. "Will you, Aine? Will you have us?"

"Yes," she heard herself say and turned to tell Santa and Mrs. Claus the good news.

They were gone, and so were *all* the wishes from the Christmas tree.

Be sure to check out Ann Marie's website
http://www.annmariebradley.com

Love's Eternal Hope

by Amber Dawn Bell

December 2005
Austin, Texas

Damn him to hell. What did he see in that home-wrecking bitch that made him think it acceptable to hurt everyone around him? What spell had she cast to pull him away from everything he claimed to love and cherish?

Hope Lacey roamed the empty shell of a house, absorbing twenty-eight years of memories embedded within its walls. The gnarled hands of fate squeezed her heart as visions of happier times seeped into her tortured mind. She'd raised kids and grandkids in this house, and every inch held a special memory. Acidic fire burned the inside of her stomach while angry ulcers two-stepped their way across the organ.

She'd been told she had to leave. Court ordered. The decision taken out of her hands. Her fingers curled into angry fists until sharp nails bit into tender flesh. Unanswered questions slashed at her mangled psyche. How could one person inflict so much soul-crunching agony? The emptiness of her once beloved home mocked her barren spirit.

Her belongings lay—boxed and stacked—in a sterile apartment where she'd have to begin life anew. The

63

buyers demanded she vacate the house by December 24th, allowing her precious little time to pack and move.

She'd not planned to spend Christmas Eve saying good-bye to a life she yearned to have back, but this was her last chance. Her daughter, Alyssa, expected her for dinner in less than an hour.

Stopping in front of the sliding glass door, she peered out the window into the backyard that had seen many good times. Trees wept their leaves in farewell, scattering across the yellowed lawn.

The swing—each of the grandkids had used it at one time or another—jerked and swayed in the chill wind. The same wind whistled and howled down the chimney as it had so many times over the years, rattling the glass door coverings. She pulled her jacket tighter around her and shivered. Salty liquid slid down her cheeks, burning her tear-chapped face.

Nothing would ever be the same.

Stomach churning, she swallowed a sob. Life forever altered through no choice of her own. Anger and sadness welled inside her until she couldn't hold it any longer. She collapsed to the floor in wrenching sobs.

How had life become so complicated over the last year and a half? Divorced, filed for bankruptcy, and lost her house. At times, she wanted to curl up into a tight ball and fall asleep never to wake again.

Loneliness had taken root and spread through her body like an out of control weed. Her kids supported her, and she appreciated their willingness to help, but they had their own lives to live, and so did she.

She longed for companionship to help end the desolate days of her existence, but would never remarry. No. She'd not make that mistake again. Never would she allow herself to trust a man or believe in his promises. A lesson hard learned, yet she craved the comfort of strong arms wrapped around her at night. Her cold, empty bed held as much appeal as a shark-infested reef. Yes, a companion would be nice.

Her sobs subsided and she pushed herself onto her

knees. Wiping the tears, she caught a glimmer of something shiny in the tract of the sliding glass door. She leaned over and picked it up.

Her favorite Christmas ornament, a nunne'hi of Cherokee mythology believed to be immortal, possessing magical powers. She'd bought it years ago at the Cherokee Nation in Oklahoma as a reminder of the Cherokee blood that coursed through her veins.

How had the ornament ended up here? She smiled. Probably her grandson, Caleb. Redecorating Nanny's tree remained his favorite holiday activity. She'd had to pack away the tree so fast she hadn't even noticed it missing.

Turning the ornament over in her hand, she studied the intricate beadwork. Long, black hair reached to its ankles and tickled her fingers. The nunne'hi enchanted her as much now as it had when she first found it. It had spoken to her in some way and had remained special through the years. Rubbing the pad of her thumb across the soft, doeskin dress, she sighed, knowing she would spend her Christmas in a small box-filled apartment that didn't even have room for her tree. A single tear trickled down her face, landing on the beaded dress of the Indian figure.

She closed her eyes tight and rocked back and forth, trying to comfort herself. "Oh, how I wish I could disappear into another time, to the land of my ancestors and its many mysteries. Anywhere to get away from this pitiful existence. I wish I had the chance to live back in a time where life was simple. Maybe even find a worthy companion to spend what's left of my life with." She opened her eyes and continued to stare at the ornament.

Maybe she could still explore the land her forefathers once traveled to find her true lineage like *he* had promised they would do. She snorted. Who was she kidding? She couldn't even afford to make her car payment this month because of the deposit she had to put down on the apartment.

Glancing around her yard one last time, she stored

away each and every precious memory. They had to last her the rest of her life.

The nunne'hi figure warmed in her palm. She dropped her gaze and stared in fascination as it began to glow. The soft sound of drums filled the silent room, beating a soothing rhythm that hummed its way into her body. Tiny embers of ethereal light flowed from the golden halo of beauty and swirled around her, performing a sensual dance. Her skin prickled as the light caressed her body, leaving her peaceful and euphoric. The scent of fresh rain and earth permeated the air, and she inhaled the natural essence, allowing it to filter through her. The strange feeling continued. All her troubles faded away, and she sensed something wonderful was about to happen.

A burst of golden light encapsulated her, then comforting blackness.

Hope woke, gradually becoming aware that she lay in the strong embrace of a complete stranger. She felt strangely at ease, his scent familiar, his touch soothing. Her mind denied the recognition, but her body screamed in opposition.

To clear her vision, she blinked several times. When her eyes came into focus, she found herself staring into the chocolate eyes of a bronzed god. She sucked in a breath. His long, black hair glistened in the bright sunlight as it cascaded over his broad, naked shoulders and brushed against her cheek. Strong, hard abdominal muscles pressed into her side reminding her she remained in his arms.

"Who are you?" A strange language poured from her lips. "Why are you holding me?" She clamped her mouth shut, startled when the unusual language continued to roll off her tongue.

She tried to move her head in an effort to see where she was.

"Be still," the stranger said as he searched her head. "No lump."

"What happened?" How could she speak and understand a language she'd never heard before?

"You fell and hit your head."

She again attempted to wiggle herself free from his firm hold, but it only encouraged him to tighten his grasp.

"Be still. I will take you to the village."

"Village? What village?"

He motioned with a jerk of his head toward a cluster of roughly hewn cabins. "My village."

He stood, lifting her in his arms as if she weighed nothing. A gust of hot wind blew a fluttering object toward her face, tickling her nose. She brushed the object away, but it remained attached. A feather.

She glanced down and saw she wore a tan dress decorated with beads and feathers. Strange. It resembled a costume she'd once made for Halloween when she went as an Indian princess, except this dress was made from real animal skin, not the imitation kind she'd used to make her dress.

Smoothing her hands over the soft length of her dress, she gasped. Her hands. Young and smooth. No age marks, no dry sagging skin, no brittle nails. What the hell had happened? And thin, a good fifty pounds had disappeared.

On the verge of flipping-out, she thought back to the last thing she remembered before waking. A wish. Beautiful glowing lights. Drums. The fresh smell of rain and earth. What had she wished? Oh yeah, she'd wished she could go back in time to be with her ancestors. Could it be? Ridiculous. She didn't believe in such nonsense, or did she?

It must be a dream. Heck, she could handle a dream and enjoy it too. In the arms of a gorgeous man, young and thin, what's not to enjoy? She giggled. The man carrying her frowned. God, he was handsome, all tanned and chiseled. An invisible web of attraction spiraled through her. She sure knew how to pick her dream lovers. Yes, she'd most definitely relish this dream. If

Demi Moore could do it, so could she.

Once they reached the village, she struggled to get down.

"No. Be still."

No? Not in her dream. She'd had enough of controlling men. "Put me down."

"No." He commanded, his brows puckered into a not unattractive frown.

She started to give him a piece of her mind until she noticed the crowd encircling them.

Naked children danced about, laughing and pointing. Women, wearing similar clothing to hers, approached to check the new female out. Some even had the nerve to poke her and pull at her hair. Her long black hair. Interesting. Last time she'd checked, it had been short and graying.

Keeping a distance, the men stared with piercing black eyes that gleamed from tattooed faces. They wore their hair in the typical styles of Cherokee men. She'd seen many pictures. Some wore their hair in a Mohawk, while others plucked a two-inch ring around the center of their hair. Some plucked all hair, except a small tuft right in the middle of their head.

Hope quirked her brows. The man holding her did not fit the image of the Cherokee. His long hair fell loosely about his shoulders and he bore no tattoos on his perfect features. Maybe he wasn't Cherokee, yet he said he was taking her to *his* village. She'd either find out soon enough or wake from the crazy dream.

In the center of the village, they passed a big round log cabin elevated above the other log houses. By the looks of it, she figured it must be some kind of religious building.

"Where are you taking me?"

"To the Long Hair Clan."

"What's a Long Hair Clan?" She'd read that Cherokees divided into different clans, but still lived together—however, she didn't recall that particular clan.

"They will take you." Irritation laced his deep voice.

"Take me where?"

He scowled. "Adopt you."

"Adopt me? I'm too old to be adopted." What did he mean by adopt?

"Quiet, woman."

Communication with this bronzed god had thus far proven difficult, if not impossible. Stopping in front of one of the smaller log homes, he kicked the door open and stepped in, then dropped her on the ground.

"Ouch." She rubbed her backside and glared at the barbarian before her. "Didn't your mother teach you any manners?"

"Stay." He glared at her as if reinforcing his command. Did she look like a dog? Would he swat her with a rolled up newspaper if she didn't obey? Really, like she was going to go anywhere. She didn't even know where she was.

She rolled her eyes as he continued to bore his eyes into hers. "Fine. I'll stay."

He knelt, grabbed her by the shoulders, and gave her a firm shake. "You will stay."

Her eyes widened and she gulped. Warm breath fanned across her heated cheeks. The smell of earth mixed with traces of leather drifted into her senses. Shudders radiated through her body from the intensity in his chocolate eyes, and heat rippled under her skin from his touch. She licked her dry lips, and his eyes dropped to follow the motion of her tongue. She gulped again.

Releasing her arms, he cupped her chin in his strong hand and tilted her head back. Her heart jolted and her pulse pounded as he traced the contours of her face. Tremors of arousal arced through her. A low growl sounded deep in his throat, then he stood and stormed out the door.

Hope released the breath she unknowingly held. Had he been about to kiss her? His full sensuous lips had hovered so close to hers she could have stuck out her tongue and tasted what he had to offer.

69

Covering her face with her hands, she shook her head. She'd behaved like some horny teenager controlled by raging hormones. Oh well, in a dream, she should be allowed her fantasies.

Still atingle from his touch, she couldn't help but wonder what else would tingle if given half the chance. She justified her thoughts by the fact she hadn't had the intimate touch of a man in a long time. Her old motor could stand a good tune-up.

Muffled voices sounded outside the cabin, but she couldn't make out the words. Several minutes later, the door swung open. A woman entered, followed by two men and the object of her new found lust. The woman knelt in front of her and took her hands.

"What is your name, child?" Her kind eyes endeared her to Hope.

"Hope."

A masculine voice bellowed, "Hope is not a name."

She snapped her gaze to the man who stood closest to the door. He wore a robe of white feathers, and his hair hung in elaborate twisted braids. "We will call you Fallen Hope. When Wolf found you, he said you fell and hit your head."

The younger man next to him, wearing his hair in a similar fashion, chuckled. "Fallen Hope is what we will call you."

Her bronzed god, Wolf, stared at her. She shifted under his scrutiny and wondered why he affected her so. The heat from his gaze sizzled her skin, leaving her breathless.

"Fallen Hope." She repeated the name to appease the man who insisted on the new name. In a sense, it fit.

He puffed up his chest. "I am the Peace Chief, True Arrow." He motioned to the woman kneeling next to her. "This is my wife, Sparrow." He tilted his chin toward the younger man next to him. "This is my son, Thunder." True Arrow approached Hope. "You now belong to Long Hair Clan. You will live here." He raised his hands and circled them around, indicating the cabin would be her new home.

Apparently, the Long Hair Clan had adopted her.

The chief and his son left, but Wolf remained, arms crossed over his chest and feet apart. He resembled the Indian statues found in tobacco stores. Was he to stay and guard her?

Sparrow noticed Wolf and shooed him out with sweeping movements of her hands. He moved toward the door and looked over his shoulder, locking eyes with Hope. Her stomach swan-dived to the floor and her face flamed from his blatant attention. A thrumming surged through her.

When he left, Hope sighed in relief. Much too intense for her taste, he wreaked havoc on her senses like no man she'd ever known.

"Wolf likes you." Sparrow smiled.

"Who is he? And why does he look different from the rest of the men? He wears his hair down and very long."

"You like Wolf, too?" She smiled again and nodded her head as if Hope answered in the affirmative. "He is the new War Chief and belongs to the Wolf Clan. He wears his hair long because he is touched by the ancients. He has magic and is honored by the gods."

Magic? Her dream kept getting more interesting. "He doesn't speak much."

"No. Even as a boy, he spoke little. Come, I will show you what to do"

Hope stood and followed Sparrow out of the cabin, trusting she wouldn't be required to help tan hide by peeing on it or some other disgusting chore.

Over the next couple of days, Sparrow showed Hope the village and the chores they expected her to do. It proved exciting and interesting, yet very exhausting. She learned to garden, weave baskets, and make clothing and beads. She reveled in the satisfaction of making do with what nature provided. It amazed her how much modern technology had made life easier, almost too easy.

Although the daily work changed some, one thing remained consistent. Wolf's constant vigil. No matter what she did or where she went, she could count on him lurking near, following her with his consuming gaze. An undeniable magnetism built between them, puzzling and exciting her at the same time. She wasn't sure if she should fear him or jump him.

She sensed and knew when he hovered close by the strange feeling within her body, an invisible force pulling them together like opposite ends of a magnet.

A distant rumble warned of a brewing storm. Flashes of light lit the sky as ominous black clouds gathered and advanced, morphing into eerie shapes. She watched as a gust of wind swirled dirt through the air, paying little attention to the task at hand.

"Ah, watch what you do." Sparrow's voice roused Hope from her musings.

"What?" Hope looked up at Sparrow then back to the basket she wove. She had missed sections, ruining the pattern. She flinched and wrinkled her nose. "Sorry."

"If you stop thinking of Wolf, maybe you would not make such mistakes." The mischievous glint in her eyes told Hope that Sparrow teased her.

The familiar vibration pulsed through her body, and she searched for the mysterious Wolf. She sucked in her breath when she made eye contact with the source of the invisible attraction.

His gaze raked her body, spreading tiny shivers from her belly to the juncture of her thighs where they settled into throbbing pinpoints of desire, and her nipples crested into peaks. How could a glance have such an effect?

Sparrow snickered and nudged her shoulder. "He desires you."

"No, he just thinks he is responsible for my safety."

Sparrow smiled and rolled her eyes.

Out of the corner of Hope's eyes, she caught a blur of movement and swiveled to see the origin of the motion.

A beautiful, petite woman glared at her with barely contained anger. Hope drew her brows together. What had she done to deserve such a hostile reaction? The girl curled her lips in distaste as she scanned Hope's basket.

"You call that a basket? Your weaving skills are as poor as the rest of your skills." Scorn shot from every pore of the girl's being. Hope stiffened. The girl huffed and spun, leaving Hope to stare after the hateful girl.

"What is her problem?" Hope turned to Sparrow and lifted her hands in question.

"Little Fire thinks you take what is hers." Sparrow nodded in Wolf's direction.

Hope gasped. "Wolf? I haven't done anything with him, much less take him away from her."

"She sees you as a threat. Little Fire claimed Wolf as hers. You must watch your back."

"But, I haven't tried to take Wolf from her. She has nothing to worry about." The dream turned in a direction Hope preferred not to go. She'd had enough of the other woman thing in her real life. She didn't need it in her dreams.

"Wolf pays you attention he does not show her. She has much anger that burns her inside. That is why she is called Little Fire. She belongs to the Paint Clan and is feared for her curses. Be careful, Fallen Hope, for today you have made a great enemy." Sparrow sighed and walked back toward her cabin.

Hope stood and glanced at Wolf. As if sensing her perusal, he lifted his head and met her stare. Her heart fluttered in her chest, and her head swirled.

A large raindrop splashed on her face. Even in her dreams, she couldn't catch a break. The sky opened and rain poured, plastering the doeskin dress against her body.

While deciding what to do, a strong hand grabbed her, dragging her toward the council house. He pushed the door open, and pulled her inside.

"What the—" Hope's words died on her lips as Wolf jerked her roughly against his hardness. Heat seeped into her and she melted into his warmth. Wrapping his hands around the back of her hair, he tugged, forcing her head back. His chocolate eyes darkened into ebony pools of desire, and she trembled with anticipation. Drops of water dripped from his hair, flowed across his chiseled features, and collected at the corner of his sinful mouth.

He swooped down and captured her lips, pushing open her mouth with his greedy tongue. Devouring not only her mouth, but also her soul. Hope allowed the invasion, reveling in the passion of the encounter. Never had she felt so consumed, so possessed.

She crushed her breasts against his chest, wanting, needing to be closer. He drew her tighter as if understanding her urgency. Wet leather and masculinity saturated the cabin, further weakening her resolve. Desire raced through her veins, singeing the intricate maze of vessels. Her womb tightened in unexpected spasms, and a tickling sensation centered and throbbed within her most sensitive flesh.

He deepened the kiss, branding her for all eternity and ruining her for any man that existed in her real world, for none could match the prowess of her dream lover. Releasing his hold, he allowed a small reprieve before he sucked her lower lip back into the warm cavern of his wicked mouth. She jumped and squeaked in surprise. Nuzzling his rain slick face against the curve of her cheek, he chuckled.

He unwound his hands from her hair and cupped her face. "You do not have the sense to stay out of the rain, woman."

What? She expected terms of endearment, not chastisement. She'd had enough of that from her ex. She didn't need her dream lover to point out her shortcomings as well. She lifted her chin in a haughty gesture. "I happen to like the rain, thank you."

The corner of his mouth lifted in what appeared to be the start of a smile. "A woman with no sense, and a big mouth." Before she could make a snarky comment, he bent and pressed his lips to hers, then bolted out of the door into the pouring rain.

What just happened? She opened the door and watched Wolf run toward his own cabin. It had been a long time since a man had made her go all mushy inside. At her age it was downright embarrassing.

A strange feeling grew inside her, and the hair on the back of her neck prickled in awareness. She stuck her head out a little further and looked around to search for the cause of her sudden uneasiness.

Like a viper erupting from its pit, Little Fire appeared within her view. She stood in the downpour staring at Hope, seemingly unaware of the rain beating down upon her head. If she didn't know any better, she swore Little Fire's eyes glowed red. Creepy. Sparrow's words came back to haunt her. She had warned Hope to watch her back, but she hadn't taken it seriously until now.

Retreating into the room, she closed the door and leaned against the wall. She would wait for the rain to let up before she made her way back to her cabin.

Hope woke early, antsy to start her chores. The encounter with Wolf replayed through her mind, making her crazy. She both wanted to see him, and at the same time avoid him. The newly awakened feelings had her out of sorts.

Walking through the village, she found herself searching for him. The more she tried to ignore her thoughts, the more intense they became. A slow hum flowed through her body. She felt him near. She bit her lower lip and resisted the urge to look around.

A long, muscled arm snaked out and grabbed her wrist, pulling her out of sight and into a secluded patch of shadows. Warm lips smothered hers with demanding mastery, and she drank in the soul-melting kiss. His lips departed hers, leaving her mouth burning with fire. She opened her eyes, and he had disappeared. Air whooshed from her lungs. Her legs quivered and her senses reeled from his passionate onslaught. She waited until her quickened pulse quieted, took a cleansing breath, then stepped out into the open.

As she rounded the corner, Hope crashed straight into Little Fire.

"This is your last warning. Stay away from Wolf. He is mine." Little Fire seethed with hatred. She shoved Hope out of the way and stormed off. Tongue-tied, Hope stared at the retreating form.

Throughout the day, Wolf would catch her alone and steal kisses. He played an exciting game, stalking and capturing his prey. The intimacy of his touch warmed her, breaking away the hard shell she'd erected around her vulnerable heart.

The final straw thawing her frozen heart occurred with the simplest of gestures, yet the most powerful. On her way to the river, Wolf stepped in her path. He brushed a lock of hair away from her face and ran his finger along her jaw line with such tenderness Hope thought she'd faint. The depth of affection in his eyes pierced her heart. He brushed a kiss across her lips and continued on his way. She could love this man.

Gasping, she covered her mouth with her hands as realization slammed into her. She already loved Wolf.

She wandered toward the river in a trance, unable to believe what had happened to her. Once she reached the water, she squatted and filled her container. Catching her reflection, she wondered at her youthful appearance. She touched her image, rippling the cool water. The magical changes transforming her into this beautiful creature amazed her. No wonder Wolf desired her. With a face and body like this, she all but beckoned for plucking.

Leaves crunching underfoot announced a visitor. She turned just in time to see a rock descend upon her. Earth shattering pain exploded through her head, followed by blackness.

Hope blinked her eyes open and moved her head.

Pain spiked through her skull, and she jerked her hands to the source of the pain. A gooey substance stuck to her fingers, and she drew her hands back. The metallic smell of blood hung heavy in the air. Her vision blurred and her stomach lurched. She swallowed to keep the bile from rising.

Strong arms scooped her up, pressing her against the familiar scent of Wolf, her bronzed god, her champion. He seemed to show up when she needed him the most.

Floating through the forest, clumps of green whirled around her making her nauseous. Soothing murmurs vibrated against her cheek, and the steady thump of Wolf's heart comforted her, allowing the agony to recede. She nestled into his warmth, feeling safe and secure against his muscled chest, and wondered at the bond that knitted this man to her soul. How could someone she barely knew have such an effect on her? She felt as if she'd known him her whole life.

Little Fire's face flashed into Hope's memory, and she moaned in distress.

"Hush, you are safe," Wolf said in a gentle voice.

"She...she tried to kill me. Little Fire." Hope choked the words past her quivering lips.

"I know. She will be punished," Wolf promised.

She believed he'd make certain Little Fire got what was coming to her.

Children's laughter signaled they'd reached the village. They entered a cabin that smelled like Wolf— earthy and masculine. He placed her upon a fur-covered bed. She opened one eye, testing her vision. Realizing the scenery no longer moved and contorted, she opened the other eye. Wolf ran his fingers against the side of her face and pushed back her hair.

"I have done nothing. Why would Little Fire do this to me?" She raised her hand to touch her injured scalp, grimacing from the contact.

Wolf grabbed her hand and squeezed. "You did nothing. When I saw her taunt you, I told her to stay away. She thought I wanted her, but I told her you were my woman. She did not like what I said."

"Your woman? You want me?" His chocolate eyes softened and she knew the truth. He felt the bond as keenly as she did. He loved her too.

"Your time here is short," Wolf said, rubbing her arm in comfort.

"How do you know this? What are you saying?"

"I know many things. My ancestors speak to me. They say we are one." He hooked his first two fingers together and pulled. "Our souls must join. We will seek each other through time, long after the body dies. You will soon leave, but we will meet again." He took her hand and brought it to his chest, placing it over his heart.

A shudder ran through her at his words. Words she knew to be true. "Why do you say my time is short?" Panic raced through her veins like a greedy germ, infiltrating every cell. She had finally met the person destined to spend her life with, yet she wouldn't be staying? How could the Fates be so cruel?

"You must go back to your time where you belong. I cannot keep you here."

"But, I don't want to go."

"I do not want you to go either, but you must. I will find you. This I promise." He sealed his vow with the press of his full lips against hers.

"Wolf, I feel strange..." Her eyes grew wide and the noises around her absorbed into the surrounding air. The ache in her head disappeared, and her body numbed.

"It is time for you to leave." He brought her hands to his lips and pressed a kiss on the sensitive flesh of her palm. "I will find you." His words echoed in her head. "I love you." She grabbed his hand and fought to remain with the one man who made her feel whole again. Her grip weakened. *No!* Her hand slipped from his.

A golden halo of light cocooned her. Drums beat steadily in the background, creating a soothing rhythm.

Golden light swirled around her, increasing in speed until it exploded into a burst of brilliant light.

Hope opened her eyes and focused on the backyard she'd looked into for twenty-eight years. She held the still warm nunne'hi in her hand. She shook her head to clear the dream that had held her captive then glanced at her watch.

"Damn." She sighed and turned toward the front door, stopping when something fluttered to the floor. She bent and picked it up. Her eyes widened and her jaw dropped. A feather.

The Entertainer wailed its melody within the confines of her purse. She fumbled through her overstuffed bag and grabbed her cell phone.

"Hello."

"Where are you?" Alyssa asked.

"I'm at the house picking up a few things I'd left behind. Why?"

"I just wanted to make sure you're coming tonight." Her voice had an unusually high pitch.

"Yes, yes. I'll be there."

"Great. Well, I'll see you in an hour."

"I'll be there. Bye." She pressed the off button. Her daughter sounded a little strange. Clearly she had something planned, and the excitement in her voice gave her away. She returned the phone to her purse along with the nunne'hi ornament and the feather.

As she drove home, she couldn't help but think back on her dream. Or had it been a dream after all? The feather was real. Very real. Where had it come from? She didn't remember seeing it before.

At the apartment, she wove her way between stacks of unpacked boxes, and then jumped into the shower. She dressed and put on some make-up.

Making it right on time, she put on a happy face and waited for the door to open.

Her grandson, Jarrod, opened the door. "Hi, Nanny. Merry Christmas Eve."

She smiled and wrapped her arms around him, giving him a big bear hug. "Merry Christmas Eve to you, too."

"Nanny!" Ashley, her granddaughter, rushed to greet her, pulling her brother out of the way. "It's my turn. Nanny, tell him to move."

"There's enough of me to go around." She laughed. What would she do without her grandkids? She existed for them.

Alyssa shouted from the kitchen, "We're in here, Mom."

As she walked towards the kitchen, a strange feeling moved through her body. Like *deja vu*. The closer she got to the kitchen, the stronger it became.

"Mom, I want you to meet someone." Alyssa beckoned her mother closer, then turned her palm over and extended it towards a man Hope had never seen before. "This is Tom, a coworker of Dan's." The man held his hand out and clasped Hope's hand in a firm handshake.

Recognition jolted her. His eyebrows lifted and he cocked his head to the side. Pulses of energy ran through their joined hands. Her belly flip-flopped. The scent of fresh rain and earth assailed her senses as a drum beat in the background. A slow smile spread across his familiar features.

He had kept his promise. He had found her.

Joy so huge welled inside her, threatening to burst forth like a confetti explosion. She wanted to shout her happiness to the world, but she feared her family would think she'd lost her ever lovin' mind. Heck, she almost thought she had.

"I've been looking for a woman like you," Tom said, winking.

"I know." Hope winked back.

They shared a smile and Hope sent a silent prayer of thanks. Her Christmas wish had been granted.

This time, she was glad her life would be forever changed.

Coming Soon
hppt://www.amberdawnbell.com

Operation Family

by Billie Warren Chai

A light snow swirled lazily through the frigid air before being caught in the violent whirling blades of the Apache helicopter as it sliced through the sky and toward Fort Heritage, Wyoming. With Christmas three weeks away, already a foot of snow covered the ground far below. Major Sean Spencer, United States Army, slipped off his sunglasses as the sun dipped beneath the horizon. Being one of the single officers without family in the area, he volunteered to be on standby alert so other members of his squadron could spend the holidays with their families.

He deftly landed the bird and shut it down. On the log he noted the starboard winch needed maintenance. Sgt. Mac McKinney finished stowing the gear and noted the supplies to be replenished as the rest of the crewmembers headed home.

"Why don't you head on home, Mac?" No doubt Sylvia McKinney had dinner waiting for her husband, complete with biscuits and gravy. Sean could really use one of her feasts, but he wasn't about to ask for an invitation again.

In the hangar Sean grabbed the stack of reports waiting for him as he watched Mac head out to his car. He dreaded the tedious daily routine of reading, initialing and signing the Army required. Seemingly oblivious to the snow, he quickened toward his quarters. He lived a Spartan life and his quarters reflected his lifestyle.

The sudden vibration and loud ring of his cell phone jarred him, breaking his concentration. He looked up at the clock. Twenty-two thirty hours. Where had the past three hours gone?

"Major Spencer speaking."

"Major, this is Long. We have a situation."

Long always had a situation and it usually involved a woman. "Tell her you have reveille at oh six hundred hours and get your butt in bed. Alone."

"That won't work this time, Major. The Madison County Sheriff's deputy says we aren't under arrest, but he'll only release us to our commanding officer."

Sean heard hee-hawing in the background.

"Can you come over and spring us, sir?"

"Just happened, huh, Sergeant? And who might 'us' be?" As if he didn't know it was Long, Taylor and Bale.

"It wasn't our fault, sir. We were in a fight defending a lady's honor. Honest, sir," he pleaded. "They'll release us, but only to a commanding officer."

In this snow it would take at least an hour to drive to and from the Sheriff's Station in San Gabriel, Montana, but he had no choice.

As he drove the familiar road, memories flipped by like a PowerPoint presentation set on high. All of them centered on Sergeant Ava Jefferson of the Madison County Sheriff's Office.

Her rejection still stung him deep and hard. His dream of marrying her crashed and burned when Ava flatly refused to quit her job as a deputy.

He'd told her no wife of his was going to risk her life because of a stupid job, where she could be shot down like a dog at any time. Three of his cousins were left fatherless when a deranged man killed his uncle—who'd been a police officer. Besides, his mother hadn't worked and neither would his wife. If he couldn't support a wife and family, he wouldn't have asked her to marry him.

A part of him didn't want to see Ava, but the flame of desire still flickered and he wondered if she'd be on duty tonight. At the Sheriff's Station he scanned the parking lot for her car, but didn't see it. Both relief and disappointment tugged at his heart. He pulled the collar of his flight jacket around his neck and shoved his hands deeper into its pockets as he strode toward the building.

The lobby had a small entryway with a walk-up window and locked door. There was a desk on the other side of the window. He pushed the buzzer and a few moments later a young woman appeared.

After quickly relating the situation he handed her his identification and a roster of his crew. She looked at the document. "I'll get Corporal Wilson. It'll be a few minutes." The window slid shut and she disappeared.

If his crew had been within arm's reach, he'd have strangled them right then and there. To paraphrase Bogey, 'of all the sheriff's stations in all the towns in the world, they chose Ava's.' He avoided places where she might be, and they drag him right into her lair. Tomorrow would be soon enough for their punishment—extra duty in the cold Wyoming winter was no picnic.

He waited, his temper spiking, until Corporal Wilson appeared. Wilson followed the book, but he had common sense and wasn't a *to-the-letter* man. Sean knew any break his crew got would be because of Wilson.

"Howdy, Major." Wilson opened a side door and ushered him to the holding area. He remembered the inner sanctum from his time with Ava. "They got in a fight at Unzipped."

Sean should've guessed the infamous strip bar was involved.

"But they didn't start the brawl," Wilson continued. "They ended it, protecting the...ah...ladies."

Women would be involved, too.

"Thanks, I get the picture, Wilson."

"I cleared it with Lieutenant Hudson. He said to give them a stern talking to and release them to their commanding officer. So, guess that's you. Haven't seen you in a blue moon."

The memory of Ava standing in this very hallway with a gun on her hip, khaki pants hugging her svelte body, cupping her cute bottom, and her shirt pulled across her perfect breasts crowded his thoughts. He even imagined he heard her voice in the distance. *Got to get over this, and quick, and get out of here.*

"Sgt. Jefferson," Wilson said looking past him.

Her presence washed over him even though he couldn't see her. His muscles tensed as he turned around to face her. Reality kicked him in the gut. Ava stood before him, beautiful and–*very* pregnant.

"Sean?" The clipboard clattered to the floor and her knees began to buckle.

He reached her in two steps and caught her in his arms before she crumpled completely. "Do you have somewhere she can lie down?" Despite her pregnancy, he held her easily, her head resting against his chest as Wilson led the way.

In the lounge he lowered her to a sofa and knelt next to her. His hand brushed the hair from her forehead and out of her closed eyes. The pounding of his heart resonated through his body. How could one woman do this to him? A special ops pilot. A hardened combat veteran. Used to command, he ordered Wilson to call the paramedics and to get a cool, wet towel.

Ava's green eyes fluttered, then opened wide. Instinctively her hand reached for her bulging stomach.

She was pregnant! Damn! Who was the father? She couldn't have been pregnant when they broke up. Ava wasn't the kind of woman who would have hidden her pregnancy from him. Or would she? Now early December, they'd broken up in late March or early April. His unit unexpectedly deployed in April. Stumps and horny toads, he was going to be a father!

Ava swooned as too many sensations and emotions flooded her. Sean here? A drum corps played off-key in her head. Sweat coated her body and her skin tingled.

The baby signaled its presence with a kick to the ribs. She flinched and touched the spot with her hand. A much larger hand covered hers and laced their fingers.

Major Sean Spencer stared down at her. She saw in his expressive, deep blue eyes that he knew she carried his child beneath her heart.

She struggled to get up, but Sean gently held her down and wiped her forehead with a wet cloth. "Just lay still, Ava. The paramedics are on the way." He leaned over and lightly placed a kiss on her forehead.

The world spun out of control. The same panic that had filled her on the day she confirmed the pregnancy burst forth from smoldering embers. She'd gone to the base to tell him about the baby. Break up or not, he had the right to know he was going to be a father. Sean wasn't there and the Army refused to tell her anything of his whereabouts. She'd left him messages to call until his voice mail stopped taking any more messages. Her letters were returned. Her mind finally formed the conclusion her soulmate and the father of her child was gone forever, but now, here he was. This had to be a dream. But a dream that talked to her, held her arms, and kissed her?

"Ava, don't move, honey."

She reached out and touched his cheek. Sean was alive.

The paramedics arrived and entered the lounge with Wilson leading the way. "She fainted in the hallway. Major Spencer carried her in here."

The first paramedic examined her while a second questioned her. "How far along are you? Can you feel the baby move?"

"I'm seven and half months along, due in late January. He's still very active."

Sean hovered nearby. Ava didn't know what to think. He jumbled her feelings. Relief filled her that he was here and knew about their child, yet anxiety tore at her. How must he feel to find out she carried his child and he hadn't been told? Could she convince him she tried to reach him? Would he forgive her? Why hadn't he answered her letters? Or called when he returned from his mission? Would he still want her or just the baby? Or maybe he wouldn't want anything to do with either of them.

"We called your doctor, and he doesn't think you need to go to the hospital, but you should get someone to take you home and call him in the morning for an appointment or sooner, if you have more problems," the paramedic advised.

"I'll see she does both," Sean answered.

She winced. Once again Sean presumed to order her life and she had to admit he had some right. After all he was the baby's father. But, if she didn't act now and left it to Sean, they'd be in front of the minister by tomorrow night and her career would be over the day after.

"I can take care of myself," she protested, trying to sit up.

"Sure," Sean snorted kneeling down next to her. "That's why I had to catch you to keep you from hitting the floor. As soon as I get my crew released, I'm taking you home. We have to talk about our baby." He stood and turned on his heel. "Stay right there 'til I get back. I'll drive you home," he rattled off over his shoulder.

There he goes again. If he thought he could order her around, he was wrong. A patrol officer came into the lounge and she asked him to drive her home. Sean may be the father of the baby, but he didn't own her. She'd made that quite clear last spring when he refused to listen to her hopes and dreams.

Deputy Boyd drove her home and helped her up the steps before departing. Once inside, she slipped out of her shoes and pulled off the constricting uniform. No sooner had she slipped a flannel nightgown over her head, than the doorbell started ringing incessantly.

She waddled to the door and opened it. Sean wore his thundercloud face.

"Come on in. I don't want to be the neighborhood show."

The room shrank when he entered. He removed his jacket and hung it on a hook as though he did it every day of his life. "I thought I told you to stay put," he growled. For all his gruff, he'd never intentionally hurt her.

She padded to a recliner and eased herself down. The chair had belonged to her grandmother and she enjoyed the warm memories. This wasn't going to be easy and she needed to be strong like her grandmother. Grandma Leota had been pregnant with her second child when her husband died of pneumonia. The chair gave her strength to go on when she thought about being a single mother.

Sean sat on the sofa near her. How many times had he lain there, his arms wrapped around her, watching television, talking, kissing and making love? In fact, the baby may have been conceived on it. While it seemed like old times, this was far from old times. As much as she wanted to climb onto his lap and snuggle into his strong arms, she couldn't live with herself if she did. She couldn't surrender herself or her child to a life without choices.

"You don't frighten me, Sean. I can take care of myself. Besides you had other things to do."

They sat looking at each other without saying a word. "Are you all right?" He asked it in that concerned, yet serious commanding manner of his.

Tension welled up in her. *I'm a police officer. A Sergeant. A supervisor responsible for a half dozen men.* She hated when she felt like this, like she didn't know her own mind, which right now she didn't.

"Yes, thank you. I tried to reach you." She couldn't stop the pain inside her.

"If you really wanted to reach me," he flung the words at her, "you could've."

She bit down on her lips to control her anger. Yelling wouldn't solve anything.

"You weren't at the base and no one would tell me where you were." She sat up and leaned toward him. "You didn't answer your phone. I left messages on your voice mail, you never called. I left a message with your commanding officer, and again nothing. I sent you letters, but they were returned to me as addressee unknown." She reined in her emotions with a deep breath. "I thought you were dead, killed in action on some secret mission."

His face went white. "Oh God, Ava, you thought..."

Without warning, he leaned forward and pulled her onto his lap. His hand caught her behind the head before he captured her mouth. Her lips parted to allow him entry. His hand caressed her stomach, swollen with his child.

"I'm so sorry. I didn't know," he breathed against her cheek before kissing her again. She'd forgotten what a great kisser he was. Kissing him back, she melted against him.

His arousal pressed against her hip. What had she done? In less than fifteen minutes, he had her eating out of his hand. She needed her wits, but they'd abandoned her. Damn. Raging hormones left her horny all the time and the one man she wanted held her. Another kiss wouldn't hurt. Or another.

Finally, Sean broke the kiss. "We need to talk."

"Uh-huh." She kissed him again.

"Ava," he said between kisses, "I don't want to hurt you. We have to stop until we see your doctor tomorrow."

Warning sirens went off in her head as flares flashed through the air around them. "What did you say?"

"I want to talk to the doctor so I'll know it's safe. I need to ask him some questions." His arms wrapped around her tightly. "I told you there would be consequences, and there will be. Tomorrow we can get the license and get married. I can move in here. I don't think the sheriff expects you to give notice, given your condition."

Fury blasted through her. Nothing had changed. He was still the arrogant bastard he'd always been. Quickly she pulled away from him.

"*I* will answer your questions. I am not marrying you tomorrow and I need my job to support my child."

"I can support us." He used that commanding tone she hated. He treated her like one of his men. "You don't need to work and put your life at risk. Our child needs his mother."

"Our child needs his father, too," she countered, struggling to get off his lap. "Are you going to resign your commission? Are you going to quit Special Ops?" She didn't want him to nor would she ever ask it of him, but he had to see what he was asking of her.

"No, I'm the best there is and the Army needs me. And with you staying at home taking care of the baby, someone has to support us."

She glared at him, then drew in a deep breath to calm herself. The battle could rage all night and she was tired. "What are your questions?"

"I want to know why you fainted. How you and the baby are doing? Do you know if the baby is a boy or girl?"

"No, I didn't want to know." Ever since she found out she was pregnant she'd envisioned a little boy with Sean's face, hair and smile.

"Does the doctor anticipate any problems? I'm about six months behind you and I need to catch up."

She baited him. "Assuming a lot aren't you? Maybe I don't want you here; did you ever think of that? I can do this by myself. I've done it for the past seven months." As soon as the words left her mouth, she regretted saying them.

He scooted her to the side.

She grabbed his arm. "I'm sorry, but it upsets me that after all this time you show up and start taking charge."

"This is my child, too, and you're not in this alone anymore, Ava. I'll always be here."

"Like you were for the past seven months?"

"That's not fair. We'd broken up. I didn't know."

"You didn't want to know either. As soon as you could, you went off playing your little war, putting your life in danger, oblivious to what was happening here. And now you come in here and demand I quit my job. You don't have the right."

"I have every right to do what I can to protect my child."

"So do I, Sean."

He released a weary sigh and looked at his watch. "We'll be at this all night. You need to get sleep and I have to go to the base in the morning and take care of a few things, then we'll meet with the doctor."

He hadn't heard a word she'd said. But she was tired—tired of being alone, tired of worrying about being a single mother, tired of grieving over the death of their relationship. She let him help her to the bedroom.

After getting her settled in bed, Sean walked to the door and turned out the light.

"Aren't you coming to bed?"

"I don't think it's a good idea. I'll be out on the couch. Just call out if you need anything." He moved away from the door. "Anything at all."

Frustrated, she buried her face in her pillow.

Sean settled onto the sofa with the afghan he found draped over the back. Sleep didn't come easily. He wanted to lie next to Ava, feel her curled next to him and wrap his arms around her. It took all his willpower to step away and not make love to her, hear her gasps of pleasure, and feel her hands stroke his body.

Thoughts hit him like flak. He was going to be a father. Despite her earlier statement that he assumed a lot, he didn't doubt she wanted him. She didn't love easily and no way would she shelve their relationship. It had to be hormones, the pregnancy, the shock of seeing him. But she definitely carried his child. Ava, the woman he loved, the child he longed for, in her body.

90

Unable to sleep, he got up and checked on her. She slept on her side, her back to the doorway. It troubled him that on some level Ava didn't trust him. Within days of their breakup, his unit had deployed to Afghanistan on another secret mission. He'd spent four months dodging bullets and trying not to think about her. When he returned home, he'd spent another two months sorting out all the things he hadn't been able to handle long distance, except Ava.

His mind had accepted her job meant more to her than he did. With a severe stab of guilt he remembered deleting the phone messages without listening to them.

Moving to the kitchen, he poured a glass of milk and sat at the table. He rested his legs on a chair while he thought.

A review of their relationship did nothing to lighten his mood or guilt. He felt alive with Ava. He wanted to do things with her. They shared hopes and dreams. When did it all fall apart? He pinpointed it to February when he'd asked her to set their wedding date. They'd chosen April twenty-fourth, her birthday. Within weeks they'd called off the wedding and gone their separate ways. She wouldn't quit her job when he'd asked her to. No, when he'd demanded it.

Her badge lay on the sideboard. The gun would be in her bedroom on the night table. Ava continued to work despite her pregnancy. It hadn't hurt her; she seemed healthy except for the fainting spell last night. The men she worked with respected her. The job gave her great personal satisfaction. She'd never do anything to endanger her child.

Time to face facts. This situation was his fault. He had no right to ask her to give up her career. She hadn't demanded he give up his career as a combat pilot. Both had dangerous jobs, but they were highly trained professionals and neither took unreasonable or unnecessary risks.

Another wave of guilt washed over him. It not only kicked him in the nuts, but bit him in the butt before taking up residence. Awareness struck like a Hellfire missile hitting its target. She didn't trust him because he didn't trust her. His unreasonable and stubborn demand for her to quit the job she loved had doomed their future. Now he needed to leave it all behind. He needed to show her he trusted her instincts and he wanted a future with her. By the time the sun rose he knew his next special mission and how to execute it.

Operation Family commenced at dawn.

Ava woke the next morning tired from a restless night. The baby had kicked all night and when he wasn't kicking, she dreamt about Sean. She decided to be firm. He would be a part of the baby's life, but she wouldn't compromise her job. No way would she quit.

A knock on the bedroom door roused her from her thoughts. She sat up. "I'm awake. Give me a few minutes."

"Can I come in?"

He'd never asked to come in before. Sean always did what he wanted and assumed it would be okay with her. She pulled the sheet up before she said yes.

He leaned against the doorframe in his old jeans and one of his army t-shirts —just like the one he left before the breakup. She thought of him every time she wore it, which was frequently. What was she thinking? She wanted to smack herself.

"I made coffee and there's orange juice. Which would you prefer? I can make pancakes, eggs and toast, bacon, oatmeal or cream of wheat. Your choice."

He gave her a choice? She stared at him in disbelief.

"Let me know when you decide. I don't have to be on base today after all, so take your time." He pushed away from the door.

"Sean?"

"What is it, honey?"

"Orange juice and toast, if it's not too much trouble." It wasn't all she wanted to say, but for now it was okay. "I'll be out in a few minutes."

"Why don't you stay in bed and I'll bring it to you?" He disappeared around the corner.

He returned in a few minutes with the food and a towel flopped over his shoulder. He hadn't shaved yet and his scruffy look excited her. A powerful longing to throw him on the bed overtook her. She pulled him down for a kiss, but he kept his balance.

"Eat. You can call the doctor about eight to get an appointment. If you don't want me to take you, you should call someone else. I don't think you should drive yourself."

Last night Sean had insisted he'd go to the doctor with her and ask questions. Obviously, during the night aliens had abducted him and replaced him with this well-mannered clone. Her mouth hung open, and she quickly shut it.

"You don't want to go with me?"

"Only if you want me to." His massive frame towered over her. "I'll only do what you're comfortable with." He kissed her forehead.

"Aren't you eating?" She didn't want him to leave. "Please, come eat breakfast with me."

"Okay, be right back." He returned a few minutes later with coffee, toast and a plate full of eggs and sat in a chair near her bed.

"I want you to take me to the doctor. I don't really think I need to see him, but I will. They'll do a sonogram. You can see the baby and listen to his heartbeat." She took a bite of his eggs and sipped the orange juice.

"It's a boy? I thought you said..." His face broke into a huge silly grin.

"I don't know," she confessed. "It just feels like a boy to me."

Sean took a drink of coffee and the smell of the pungent brew overwhelmed her. Damn, the persistent nausea. She made it to the bathroom before she lost her breakfast. Sean held her hair back, wet a washcloth and wiped her face.

"I thought I missed the morning sickness," he deadpanned. "Is this normal? My sister-in-law said hers was over after the first three months."

"Usually it is." She sat on the toilet lid. "But mine has been constant. Certain smells trigger it, like cigars, chili, or coffee. The doctor said as long as I can keep some food down, we'll be okay." She patted the baby.

"Damn it, honey, you should have told me." He took a deep breath. "Wait here." He put the cold cloth on her forehead and disappeared.

She closed her eyes and took a deep breath.

"Let's get you back to bed." He slipped his arms around her and picked her up. She wrapped her arms around his shoulders, her head against him.

Back on the bed, she noticed the coffee had disappeared. The fresh toast helped settle her stomach. As they ate, she told him about her pregnancy. The baby gave a particularly hard kick and she flinched. She scooted over and patted the bed motioning him to sit next to her.

"Ava, I want you as much as ever, but I don't want to take any chances." Desire danced in his eyes. She saw his erection pressing against his jeans.

"Come here, I want you to feel the baby move."

He sat beside her. She took his protective hand in hers and placed it on her abdomen.

"I think that's his head." The baby moved away as if he didn't want to be touched.

Later at the doctor's office, when Sean seemed reluctant to accompany Ava to the examining room, she took his arm and led him in.

"I want you with me."

He looked uncomfortable and out of place as he sat entranced listening intently to the baby's heartbeat and mesmerized by the images on the screen. Watching him, she was powerless to stop her heart from melting. She still loved him. She'd never stopped.

The sun peeked from behind the otherwise gloomy winter sky to reassure the world it was still there. This was a special day, and Ava felt like a little girl again.

They went shopping for baby furniture, and then together they spent the rest of the day assembling the crib, sitting on the sofa laughing, touching and watching television into the evening.

"I better head back to the base. I have a full schedule tomorrow." He scooped her into his arms. "First, I need to get you in bed."

Once again she reveled in his protective strength and manliness. He carried her carefully to the bed and gently laid her down.

"You're going to spoil me." She kissed him.

"You deserve to be spoiled, honey. Can I feel him move again?" She nodded and he put his hand on the moving baby. "Does he move like this all the time?" Joy beamed from his rugged, tanned face as he moved his hand deliberately.

"No, there are times when he sleeps. Unfortunately, it's not usually when I'm asleep."

"Hey, little guy, this is your daddy. Give your mother a break and let her rest." He spoke in his commander's voice, then winked at her with his baby blues. "Do you need anything before I leave?"

No, he couldn't leave. Pain clawed at her heart and her breath caught in her throat. "Why don't you stay here tonight? Who knows what might happen? I promise not to jump your bones." Although she didn't know how she could keep that promise.

"As much as I want that, honey, neither one of us is ready for that." He sat on the bed and wrapped her in his arms. Only when he wiped away the tears did she realize she'd been crying. "Don't cry, honey. I'll stay if you want me to, just like I did last night."

"I don't know what I want except I don't want you to go. I don't know if I can do this." She grabbed a pillow and hugged it tightly. "What do I know about babies? I know which end to feed and which end to diaper, but very little else. I'm scared."

He leaned back against the headboard and she curled up next to him in his arms. Her fears eased as Sean reassured her.

She studied his profile as they lay there. She knew it was important for a child to have two parents, preferably living together as a family. Sean wasn't just a man. Well-educated, he'd graduated from West Point and commanded a squadron of special-op helicopter pilots. Brave and strong, yet compassionate and caring, he'd be a perfect husband and a great father for their child.

They'd never discussed why he didn't want her to work after they married. Her hackles had gone up when he told her to quit her job and she'd never asked him why. Now was as good a time as any.

"Why didn't you want me to work after we married?" Her fingers traced lazy circles on his chest.

He stiffened, and then relaxed so quickly she wondered if she'd imagined it.

"I've thought a lot about that request since I saw you again. I talked to my mom and she said my sister Libby is expecting." He turned so she could see his eyes. "Again. This will be her sixth."

Their child certainly wouldn't be short of cousins.

"Mom claims Libby has no problem taking care of five kids, her husband and her full-time job while pregnant. In fact she told Mom she wouldn't have it any other way."

"Oh." The thought of all those babies stunned her. She seemed to have enough problems with one, and he wasn't even born yet.

"Anyway, let me tell you a little about my childhood. My mom didn't work, but the opportunities for women were different back then and living in Arizona on a ranch limited hers even more." Sean gently placed his hand over their ever active baby. "I remember Mom selling Avon and Tupperware. She even raised chickens and sold the eggs. She was always thinking of her children and their future.

"It took me awhile, but I finally realized the sacrifices she made for us. We were her full-time job and she was always there for us with whatever we needed. I guess you can say I'm an old-fashioned guy who believes a woman's place should be at home taking care of her children, like my mom, but to be honest, when I found out you were pregnant with my baby, the only thing I could think of was not losing you. I'm still an old-fashioned guy, who believes in God, country and mom's apple pie, but I'm also a man who can be flexible and if you want to keep your job, it's okay with me." He turned on his side and pulled her closer to him.

His fingers moved to caress her ultra-sensitive nipple. She moaned, wanting more. She remembered what it meant to have him around. "Sean, I want to spend the rest of my life like this, having your babies and waking up next to you." If he asked her to marry him right this minute, she would quit her job until the babies started school.

"I was wrong," he whispered, leaning over to kiss her sensitive breast. "I hope you can forgive me. I was wrong to make demands on you. I love you, Ava."

"You're forgiven. I want to make love to you. I need to feel you inside me."

"Are you sure it's safe?"

"Didn't you ask the doctor when we were there this morning? He said it's perfectly safe."

"Yes, ma'am." He was more than ready to do his duty and relieve all her pent-up sexual frustration.

Sean quietly followed through on Operation Family over the next couple of weeks despite his workload over the holidays. Now with Ava and his baby, he felt happy and complete. Ava returned to work, but chose desk duty.

Christmas Eve was two days away. He couldn't think of a better present for Ava than a wedding and starting their family properly. It took a little traveling, three days and five jewelers before he found the perfect ring, an emerald cut blue diamond flanked by sapphires. The moment he saw the ring, he knew it had been made for Ava. The matching wedding band had alternating diamonds and sapphires.

On Christmas Eve, as planned, he drove Ava to the doctor, then took her to dinner at the Officer's Club. He called in a whole lot of favors to arrange the details at the Officer's Club. She thought they were merely having a special Christmas dinner.

When the maitre d' seated them at her favorite table with a view of the snow-covered mountains in the distance, her eyes sparkled with approval. His heart pounded so loud and so fast he could swear she heard it. He barely tasted his meal.

"Any dessert, Major?" the waiter asked.

"Yes, I think so, what do you have?"

The waiter named off a list of desserts. "The lady loves strawberries. Do you have anything on the menu with strawberries? Perhaps you can check with the chef?" That was the code. It was now or never.

"Yes, Major." He turned and left. They drank sparkling grape juice until the waiter returned.

Ava graced him with a smile when the waiter sat a huge strawberry shortcake before her with a side dish of strawberries dipped in chocolate. If only she knew the trouble he'd gone through to get those darn strawberries in Wyoming in the dead of winter.

He gazed at her big brown eyes and held her small hand in his. She squeezed his hand and smiled at him. Never before had he seen so much love and warmth radiate from her face. Shawn knew the moment had come. "Ava, I love you. Will you do me the honor of being my wife?"

"Yes, yes, yes," she answered with no hesitation. Her eyes filled with happiness and tears of joy ran down her cheeks. "I'd be honored to be your wife." She kissed him. "I hope you don't mind, but I want to stop working until the last baby goes to school," she sighed, kissing him again.

"You can do whatever you want, honey. Just be my wife and let me take care of you."

She stopped and looked into Shawn's deep blue eyes. "It's almost Christmas Day. I wish we could get married tonight."

"That's quite a Christmas wish, but let me see what I can do." He stood and waved his hand toward the kitchen like he had a magic wand.

Immediately, as arranged, an Army Chaplain appeared in full dress uniform, followed by Sean's wingman, Captain Aaron Bryant, and Ava's best friend from childhood, Linda Stewart.

Ava screamed with delight, realizing what was about to happen. Nothing else mattered as she stood and hugged him. In the distance church bells and the sound of Christmas carols filled the air as the world celebrated the arrival of Christmas. He couldn't have given her a better Christmas present.

Sean married the woman of his dreams.

When the *San Gabriel Journal* reported the birth of a healthy baby boy, named James Sean Spencer, to Major and Mrs. Sean Spencer on January 12, Operation Family was successfully concluded.

Be sure to check out Billie's website

http://www.billiewarrenchai.com

The Gift of You

by Kimberly Ivey

Galveston, Texas
December 1974

"You wanna quit? Get out before I throw you out on your ear, you little tramp."

Liliana Brooks' feet couldn't propel her fast enough to the front door of Harry's Hamburger Palace. She'd endured all the abuse she could take from her boss, Harry Weiser—all the insults, groping and sexual innuendo. She yanked off her black apron and hairnet and flung them on the counter as he watched, then lifted her sweater from the hook and shoved open the door.

"Don't let the door hit you on the ass, sweetheart," came Weiser's final insult.

She pulled on the cardigan and ducked her head to shield her face from the biting sting of icy December wind. Sliding her hand into her front jeans pocket, she pulled out a hand sewn denim coin purse and dug around inside. *Rats!* Enough for a soft drink but not cab fare. She stuffed the purse into her pocket and peered through the restaurant's fogged windows. Harry glared at her from behind the counter. She couldn't go back inside to call her father to pick her up early. He'd be angry she'd quit her job and she feared his wrath. She looked both ways down a nearly deserted Broadway. Perhaps a brisk walk the few short blocks to her house

101

might clear her mind.

She crossed Broadway at 20th Street, contemplating what to tell her parents. *"Oh, I quit my job because Harry Weiser groped me again."* She could almost hear her father's reply: *"Well, if you wouldn't wear those tight jeans he wouldn't touch you."*

She thought of her precious baby boy and tears flooded her eyes. She'd silently promised to do better for Nicky, to build a good life for them. How would she support them now?

At eighteen months, the toddler had most of his teeth—two top ones in front like a baby beaver's—and a head full of soft, dark curls. He looked more like his father, probably one reason her parents hadn't wanted her to keep him. She wouldn't give him up for adoption. She couldn't. Her parents could push all they wanted, but Nicky belonged with her. She'd hold on to the hope they'd make it somehow.

She'd just crossed Mechanic Street when the sound of footfalls behind her took her by surprise. She turned, thinking it was David, a coworker who'd followed her with hopes of convincing her not to quit her job for the hundredth time. She slowed her pace to look back over her shoulder when someone knocked her to the ground. Her forehead hit the curb. She screamed and kicked as her attacker tore at her jeans. His hands worked their way over her body. Her booted heel impacted someone or *something*. She heard a grunt, followed by a curse. She rolled onto her back. It wasn't anyone she recognized. A dark hooded figure rose menacingly from the ground and came at her again, this time with what appeared to be a piece of pipe or a broken bottle.

"Where's your purse?"

She didn't carry a purse. Liliana jerked the coin pouch from her pocket and flung it at him, then rolled to her feet and raced down the darkened empty street. The man's feet pounded on the pavement behind her. A rush of adrenalin coursed through her veins as he grew closer. Why was he chasing her? She'd given him all her money. He grabbed her from behind and tackled her to the ground again, the impact knocking the breath from her lungs. His body covered hers. A grimy hand clamped over her mouth. A scream rose up within her, but no sound came forth.

Jake Delatorre sat at the green and white chrome dinette table in his Strand Street loft's tiny kitchen and swirled the scotch in his glass. He watched the mesmerizing dance of the amber liquid with partially melted ice cubes, then downed his drink. He loved the feel of fire in his throat, the tingle that shot through his skin and to the bone. *The warmth that helped him forget Diane and the baby.* He reached for the bottle again. A few more shots and he wouldn't remember at all. If he did, he sure as hell wouldn't feel the pain.

A scream, followed by the sound of breaking glass on the street jolted him back into the moment. Damned punk kids were at it again. Probably rival gangs fighting or vandalizing one of the vacant buildings. He scooted the chair back, retrieved his .44 caliber Ruger from atop the refrigerator and shoved it into the waistband of his pants. He'd scare them off before they thought of busting out his restaurant's window again.

He charged down the stairs, unlatched the heavy, eight-foot door and flung it open. In the distance two dark figures scuffled on the ground. He raised his pistol into the air and fired, piercing the silence of the night. Dogs barked. A light came on in the second floor loft apartment across the street. One of the figures rose from the ground and darted into the shadows while the other lay motionless.

With her heart pounding out a deafening tempo in her ears, Liliana struggled to her feet. She pushed the hair from her face. Thank God someone heard her cries and responded. Warm liquid trickled into her left eye. She blinked back the sting to see a man's silhouette moving toward her. Fear knotted in her stomach. Her attacker again? No, he'd been wearing a dark hooded jacket. This man wore a light colored shirt and pants. He was taller, thinner. Still, she remained wary. She turned to walk away, her legs thick and heavy like bags of wet sand. She wiped at the dampness on her face, smearing it, then stared at her hand. *Blood. Oh, my God.* Had she been shot? Stabbed?

The man took her gently by the elbow. "Come with me." He escorted her to a dimly lit building. "Did he hurt you?"

Yes. No. She wasn't certain. Her knees buckled as her head swam. She'd been robbed—*almost raped.* The man caught her before she slumped on the steps, then swept her into his arms and carried her into the warm building and upstairs.

He paused on the landing to look at her. "You're cold as ice, girl. Don't you have warmer clothes?"

Liliana didn't answer. Actually, this was the thickest sweater she owned. Nicky had been ill with two ear infections recently and she couldn't afford a new coat.

"The shot I fired scared him off," he told her as he ascended the final steps. "The guy's long gone by now so I doubt the police will look for him. If anything, they'll give *me* a citation for discharging a firearm within city limits."

Her teeth chattering from the biting cold, Liliana clung to him like a lifeline. His body was warm and his shiny dark hair smelled fresh like herbal shampoo. Using his foot, he nudged open a door and carried her into a living room and set her on an orange and brown floral print sofa.

He stood back and looked at her. "How old are you, kid? Sixteen? Seventeen?"

"Twenty," she whispered, her throat dry and aching from screaming.

He lifted a brow as if he didn't believe her.

"Could I have"—she swallowed hard—"a drink?"

He left the room momentarily and returned with a bottle of cola and an opener. "Would you rather have something hot?" he asked.

"No, soda's fine." Liliana settled into the sofa and eyed him cautiously. He was a handsome man with dark, collar-length hair and a moustache. Early to mid thirties she guessed.

He uncapped the bottle and handed her the drink. She took a swig, letting the cool liquid slide down.

He left the room again and returned with a wet cloth, then took a seat beside her on the sofa.

"Tilt your head more to the light and let me see how bad you're injured."

Liliana stiffened, not because it hurt, but because it was a bit unsettling to have a strange man touch her so intimately. Especially one who smelled as good as he did. She studied his eyes—as blue as Galveston Bay in summer. He was actually pretty cute for a guy his age. She rather liked his cologne, too—woodsy and sensual— not cheap smelling or overpowering.

He blotted her forehead gently. "Looks like a small break in the skin at the hairline. You might need a stitch or two." He thrust the cloth into her palm, then closed her hand around it and pressed it against her forehead. "Hold it firm for a moment until the bleeding stops. I'll call the police so you can make a report."

Turning away he reached for the phone on the end table and dialed *o*.

"Jeans, a white shirt and a brown sweater," he told the police. He glanced at her feet. "Black boots. No, she's not a... Yeah, I'm sure. Twenty," he spoke into the phone. He turned back to her. "The officer wants to know if the guy was your boyfriend."

Liliana shook her head *no*.

"Not a boyfriend. No, I didn't ask and I'm not going to insult her by asking that." He gave a heavy sigh. "Look, are you going to send someone or not? Good. She'll be here."

He hung up and turned back to her, irritation clearly etched on his face. "Cops will be here in a while— whenever the hell that is." He lifted a white, crocheted

105

afghan from the sofa's arms and draped it around her shoulders. "Your um...blouse is torn."

Liliana looked down. Mortified, she jerked the blanket tight around her.

"A pretty young girl shouldn't be out alone at night," he scolded. "You're lucky this time. I've seen you walking after dark before. Coming home from work again?"

She nodded.

"Where do you work?"

"Nowhere now. I quit the Burger Palace tonight."

Awkward silence stretched between them as Liliana stared at the soda bottle on the table and read and re-read the logo, ingredients and company information. Why didn't he say anything? Was he going to lecture her, remind her how foolish she'd been to walk alone in this neighborhood?

He cleared his throat. "Do you want a job?"

She looked at him, certain she hadn't heard correctly. "What?"

"I'm hiring for my diner downstairs, The Greasy Spoon. I need waitresses, cooks, cashiers, dishwashers for the grand re-opening. Do you have any experience in one of those areas?"

Was he serious? Why would he offer her—*a stranger*—a job? "But you don't know me."

He studied her a moment. "I know all I need to know. You need a job and I have a slot to fill."

Liliana shook off a chill that wrapped around her. Why had he offered her work? *Maybe he's like Harry Weiser and thinks you're an easy target.* She dashed that thought away as soon as it came. This man was different. She saw it in his kind eyes, felt it in the gentle care he'd taken with her. If he was going to hurt her, he wouldn't have called the police. He also wouldn't have covered her with the blanket. "I need to think about it."

"I'd like an answer now."

She fiddled with the fringe on the edge of the afghan and contemplated his offer. *Pushy fellow, wasn't he?*

106

"You don't give a person much time to think, do you?"

He shrugged. "I figure 'a person' knows whether they want to work or not. So what will it be?"

"You sure are insistent, mister..."

"Sorry." He offered his hand. "Jacob Delatorre. Everyone calls me Jake."

She liked the name—rugged and masculine. It suited him. She accepted his warm hand.

"Jake," she repeated. "I'm Liliana Brooks."

After the police took her report and left, Jake found safety pins to secure the front of her blouse. He then drove her to the emergency room a few blocks away and stayed with her while she had one stitch put in her temple. Afterward, he drove her home.

They sat quietly in his car outside her house. Although the lights inside were off, she was certain her father was watching from the window.

"Thank you for everything, Jake. I don't know what would have happened if you hadn't come to my rescue."

He stared at her a long time, as if he wanted to say something, but couldn't find the right words. As she gazed toward the house, ice cold dread hit her in the pit of her stomach. If Nicky hadn't been inside, she might never have come home. She turned to look at Jake. Even in the dark car she could make out the features of his handsome face.

"You never answered my question about whether you wanted the job," he prompted.

His voice was smooth and sensual and the butterflies in her stomach prevented her from speaking. She never thought she'd find an older man attractive. Liliana nodded. "Yes, I want the job."

"Good. Report for work at seven on Monday morning."

Nervous, she opened the passenger door and got out. She looked at the house and her knees trembled. "Thanks for everything."

Jake watched her walk away, her hands shoved deep

into her sweater pockets, her head bowed like a beaten puppy.

She paused at the front door, waved goodbye and his heart squeezed in his chest. What was wrong with him? She was a kid—even at twenty—and he was way too old to start behaving like some moony eyed adolescent. Besides, a pretty young girl like her would never be interested in a thirty-two year old man. He waved back. Once she disappeared inside, Jake pulled away from the curb and drove the deserted streets of Galveston for the next half hour, unable to return to his lonely apartment.

"Out screwin' another one tonight?" her father shouted from the darkened living room. Liliana paused in front of the door in time to see the orange glow of his cigarette as he took another drag. "Who was that man in the car, Lili?"

So he *had* been watching. "A friend."

"Friend my ass." He switched on a lamp. "It's two-thirty in the morning. What's wrong girl? Ain't one bastard child enough?"

Her father's tall figure rose from the chair and moved toward her. Every muscle in her body tensed as she braced herself for a blow that didn't come.

"I know what you're doing. You're hopin' to make another baby so you can get welfare and not have to work at all."

"I was at the emergency room for the past two hours getting a stitch in my head. Call the hospital if you don't believe me." As she brushed past, his hand reached out and snagged her arm.

"Weiser called hours ago. He said he had to fire you for coming on to him."

Coming on to him? Liliana stared at her father in disbelief. "Harry didn't fire me. I quit."

"You can't afford to lose this job. In the mornin' you call and beg him to take you back. While you're at it, you promise not to crawl all over him like a she-cat again. You need that job, Lili. Your mama and I can't keep feedin' you and that squalling brat of yours."

Liliana bristled. *That 'squalling brat' is your grandchild* she almost reminded him. "It will be a cold day in hell before I set foot in Harry Weiser's restaurant again."

He smacked her across the cheek, propelling rockets of pain through her skull.

"You'll do as you're told and not argue! I ain't gonna have no lazy slut livin' under my roof!"

Nicky cried out from her bedroom. Thinking their argument awakened him Liliana hurried toward her room to comfort him.

"Yeah, you go and shut that kid up so I don't have to," he called after her.

Liliana spun about. *Had he threatened Nicky?*

Nicky continued to wail.

"I said shut him up, Lili, or I'll give him something to really cry about."

She could take no more. Her father might slap her around—even beat her on occasion, but he'd never lay a hand on her little boy! She hurried into her room, closed the door and checked on Nicky. He was fine, only upset. After giving him a hug and kiss, she dumped a coffee can full of coins and dollar bills into the diaper bag—tips she'd saved. Then she packed a few of baby Nick's clothes and diapers, lifted him from his crib and wrapped him in his warmest blanket. As she crept past the living room, her father surprised her from the shadows. He raised his hand to strike her again, stopping when he saw Nicky in her arms.

"Where you goin' now!" he hollered.

Nicky howled and buried his face into her neck.

"I'm taking my baby away from this house—to a safer place."

"Don't you mean to your lover's?"

Tears stung her eyes. *One foolish mistake and they never let her forget.* She opened the front door and broke into a run.

"If you leave, girl, don't bother coming back, you

hear?" her father called.

As if she had any intention of returning.

The pay phone at the convenience store was a block away. She had enough change for a cab, but to drive her where? The homeless shelter wasn't far, but had probably closed for the night as had the local churches. Panting, her breath white as smoke in the night air, she hurried toward the bright lights of the store.

Nicky shivered in her arms. "Everything will be all right," she reassured him as she opened the door to the phone booth and slipped inside.

Jake awakened to banging. *What the hell?* He jerked upright on the sofa and strained to focus on the wall clock. Three a.m. He must have fallen asleep after taking Liliana home. Who could be at his door this time of morning?

His breath caught when he reached the bottom of the stairs. Silhouetted in the blue moonlight beyond the door's window stood Liliana. Jake flung the door open and an icy draft swept through the foyer.

"Get in here, girl."

She entered with a bundle in her arms. Even in the dim light from the street lamp he saw the wet streaks on her face.

Gently, he caught her by the arm. "What's wrong?"

"I didn't know where to go. I was scared so I brought..." She lifted the blanket on the bundle to reveal a small, sleepy-eyed child. "I brought my son."

Jake blinked. *Her son? Why, she wasn't much more than a child herself.* He latched the door, then ushered her up the stairwell to his apartment, flipping on lights as he went. What a surprise. Liliana had a child.

In his apartment kitchen, he dug around for a cookie in the jar and poured a cup of milk for the boy. He took the child from her arms and set him on a stack of phone books in a chair.

So she had a kid. Funny she hadn't mentioned him before. He also hadn't noticed a wedding band on her finger earlier. He didn't see one now. Jake flinched when he saw the large, red handprint on her pale cheek. "What the...?" His gaze darted to the child.

As if she knew what he was thinking she said, "No, Nicky's all right."

Rage swept through him like wildfire. Wait 'til he got his hands on the sorry bastard who'd abused her. "Your old man hit you?"

She nodded. "My father, that is. I'm not married. Nicky and I live with my parents. He was angry I quit my job—that I came home late. I didn't know where to go. I called a cab to bring me here because I knew you'd know what to do." She wiped her tears on her sleeve. "I'm sorry, Jake. Maybe it was a mistake to come here. I just didn't know where to take Nicky. I thought you might know of a safe place for us to stay."

His heart broke at her words. He looked at the youngster who grinned at him, revealing his overly large front teeth. He smiled at the boy, then reached across the table and took Liliana's hand in his before realizing how forward he must seem. He'd only wanted to reassure her, but she didn't pull away as he'd expected she might, especially considering her earlier ordeal. He studied her oval face, her flawless porcelain skin and straight shiny red hair that fell to her waist. Her large, expressive brown eyes held him captive once again. Was it coincidence that brought her to his doorstep twice in one night? Or was this a sign?

"Dah," the child said, holding out his tiny outstretched hand.

Liliana's hand eased away from his and she straightened in her chair. The magical spell was broken. "No, Nicky. One cookie is plenty."

The toddler made a pouty face. "*Dah,*" he said more insistently.

Jake chuckled. "I think he's hungry." He rose from the table and tousled the child's soft dark curls on his way to the cookie jar. "Okay, tiger. You can have another."

Once he'd settled the toddler with another cookie, he turned to Liliana. "When he finishes his snack, take him upstairs and put him down. You two can sleep in one of the extra apartments tonight."

"I can't do that, Mr. Delatorre."

He sighed. "Didn't I tell you to call me Jake? Mr. Delatorre sounds old—like my father. Do I look seventy?"

A hint of a smile tugged at the corner of her lips, but faded as quickly as it had come.

"Jake, I can't stay here."

"Why not? I have four separate apartments over the restaurant—three of which are empty. It's only me and the rattling water pipes and an occasional ghost that wanders through."

Her eyes widened with interest like a child's whose curiosity had been piqued. "You have ghosts?"

"Just kidding. No ghosts that I'm aware of." He patted her hand again, noting how his seemed to swallow hers. "Stay, Liliana. You and your boy are safe here." He reached into his pocket, retrieved a key ring and slid one off. He placed it before her on the table. "Our apartments are keyed alike, but I promise not to disturb you."

She stared at the key. "I can't move in. I don't know you. And you don't know *me.*"

Oh, he knew her all right, knew they were a lot alike—both alone in the world and the unfortunate recipients of too many of life's hard knocks. Besides, there was the child to think about. He looked at the boy again whose face was smeared with cookie crumbs. *Cute little fellow.* Liliana raised the cup of milk to the baby's lips and the child's pudgy fingers closed around it.

"Me," he said, pulling it away from his mother.

Sadness washed over Jake like a wave, threatening to drown him in memories. He thought of Diane, how this should be his wife and their child sitting at this very table right now. Not wanting to remember, he shook the haunting image away.

Liliana loved her son—no doubt of that in his mind—and no matter the circumstances of his birth he believed her a good mother simply because she'd brought her child to the safest place she knew. He felt honored she'd thought of him in her time of crisis—which pulled him back to his previous question—was it destiny that brought her to him twice in one night, and two weeks before Christmas no less?

Once the child finished eating, Jake picked him up and motioned for Liliana to follow him to the apartment across the hall. He grabbed fresh linens and a warm blanket and helped get the baby settled to sleep. Liliana appeared restless.

"Would you like a cup of cocoa to help you relax?"

Liliana nodded.

She sat at the dinette table in his apartment's kitchen, fiddling with the gold butterfly pendant at her throat while he warmed the milk on the stove.

"Nicky's father abandoned me when he learned I was pregnant," she explained. "When his parents found out, they moved away. Doug expected to attend college on a football scholarship. He did, I assume. I don't know." She shrugged. "He didn't stay in touch. I quit school my senior year to go to work."

Jake spooned the cocoa into the hot milk, then whisked it around and poured it into mugs.

"I still live with my parents," she continued. "Not the best situation, as you can see but I'm hoping to get my own place soon. I don't have anyone I trust to take care of Nicky while I work except my parents, and as you can guess that isn't working out."

He set a steaming mug in front of her, then handed her a bag of marshmallows. "I'll help you find childcare while you work for me. Deal?"

She bit down on her lip and nodded.

He sat across from her, curious to learn more. "I know it's none of my business, Liliana, but how did a smart, beautiful girl like you end up in this situation?"

She straightened in her chair and pushed a giant

marshmallow around in her cup with her fingertip. "I wasn't very smart back then." She lowered her eyes. "I'd never had a boyfriend before. He was a football player at my high school and I was a nobody who thought he cared about me."

Jake's instincts had been right. Some jock had taken advantage of her naïveté. Even still, she must have fallen pretty damned hard to give her innocence away to the first guy with a classic line.

"So what's *your* story, Jake?" she asked, changing the subject. "You said you live here all alone."

Jake explained that his wife and newborn son had died five years before—complications of childbirth. He related how he'd thrown himself into his work to deal with his grief. "I opened The Greasy Spoon diner at another location two years ago, but with the restoration of the historic area of Galveston going on right now, I wanted to move my business to the Strand district. I hope to eventually purchase and restore a few more of the turn of the century buildings. I know this end of town looks derelict now, but one day it's going to be hopping with restaurants and stores and tourists."

"I love this area and always wished I could live here. When I was a little girl I'd sneak away and come here to play on the steps and in the alcoves of the empty buildings."

Jake noted how her sad eyes lit up when she spoke of her childhood. "Tell me more," he urged.

She smiled shyly. "You'll laugh at me."

"I won't."

"I pretended I lived in another time and wore long dresses with petticoats that swished when I walked, and I had rows and rows of golden curls tied in velvet ribbons. Mother gave me one of her old dresses that fell to my ankles and I always tripped over the hem. I pretended it was a ball gown." She took a sip of her cocoa. "Silly, huh?"

"Not at all." Jake tried to imagine the little girl she'd once been, playing along these streets. "So *you're* the one who started the Dickens on the Strand business?" he teased.

"Oh, you mean the event last year where local business owners dressed in Victorian era clothes for Christmas and sang carols by candlelight? I'd love to go to that."

"I'll take you. I'm a member of the foundation sponsoring the event."

She stared at him as if he were a god. "Oh, I couldn't. Do you mean it?"

"Of course I mean it. Besides," he shrugged, "I haven't celebrated Christmas since my wife died." *He'd had no reason to, until now.* She was silent and he wondered if he'd revealed too much.

"What would I wear? I don't have any old-fashioned dresses."

"Not to worry. I'll talk with a good friend of mine. I'm certain she'll have an extra costume."

"You're serious? You'd really take *me* to something like that?"

"I'll do better than that, Liliana. I'll take both you *and* Nicky."

At Jake's urging, Liliana agreed to move into the empty apartment across the hall from his. He solved the issue of childcare for Nicky by putting a playpen in the diner's office so she could work and keep an eye on her son at the same time. The other employees also pitched in to help.

Two weeks passed and Liliana settled into her waitress job. On mild afternoons Jake would take Nicky out on the stoop to feed the seagulls or to play games. Weather on the island was quirky—wintry one week, mild and sunny the next. He took advantage of every opportunity to play outside with the boy.

One afternoon, he and Nicky sat on the steps outside The Greasy Spoon, pretending to be pirates sailing their ship into Galveston Bay. Liliana had gone Christmas shopping for Nicky with Lucille Bikini, his cashier. A young man approached him and asked for Liliana. Jake immediately noted Nicky's resemblance to the guy and guessed he was the boy's father.

"Liliana isn't here." And as far as Jake was concerned, the prick could disappear back under the rock from which he'd come.

"You know where she is?"

"Nope."

"When will she be back?"

Jake bristled. *That was none of his business.* "I have no idea."

The guy sighed. "Fine. When you do see her, give her a message for me, okay?"

Jake shrugged. "Sure. Whatever." The guy pulled a crinkled slip of paper from his front jeans pocket and handed it to him. Jake glanced at it. *A phone number.*

"Tell her Doug McMasters is in town for a few days and needs to see her real bad."

Two days passed before Jake's conscience got the better of him. One evening after Nicky had been bathed and put to bed, he set a folding table on the roof for him and Liliana to dine by candlelight. He hoped she'd understand why he hadn't told her sooner of McMasters' visit.

"It's warm enough tonight to enjoy dinner outside," he remarked as he uncovered the casserole dishes containing leftover meatloaf and mashed potatoes from the diner. "Christmas Eve will be here day after tomorrow, and I'm hoping the cold front they're predicting arrives to cool things down for the Dickens on the Strand event."

Liliana popped open the caps on their soda bottles. "I can hardly wait. Your friend with the historical society was so nice. She let me have my pick of dresses. She even found Nicky an outfit. It's so cute with green velvet pants that come to the knee and—"

"Liliana," he broke in. "I need to talk to you about something. Don't be angry at me for what I'm about to

116

tell you."

She speared a slice of meatloaf and put it in her plate. "Why would I be angry? Hey, could you pass me the mashed potatoes? I'm starved."

Jake lifted the dish and handed it to her. His breath caught in his throat as he thought of what he was about to say. From this point forward, nothing would ever be the same again. He felt it in his gut. "A young man came into the diner a few days ago and asked for you." He watched as she cut a bite of the meatloaf.

"What did he want?"

He fished the note from his shirt pocket and placed it on the table before her. "It was Doug McMasters, Liliana. He wants you to call him."

She dropped her fork and it clattered onto her plate. With trembling fingers she took the slip of paper. "That's—"

"Nicky's father," he finished.

She stared at the note. "How did he find me?"

Jake leaned back in his chair and ran his fingers through his hair. "I didn't ask. I assume your parents told him you were living and working here."

Her eyes lifted to his. "Why would he come back *now*? He didn't want anything to do with Nicky—*or me*. I haven't heard from him in over two years."

Although he'd lost his appetite, Jake scooted forward and served his plate. He had a pretty good idea of why McMasters had come sniffing around. The no good shit probably wanted to patch things up with Liliana—thought he'd say those sweet seductive words he'd once used to get her into bed. What better time than Christmas to make amends—and take advantage of an innocent young woman a second time.

He stuffed a forkful of meatloaf into his mouth and chewed vigorously, not tasting it at all. The thought of Doug McMasters —*of any man*—touching Liliana made him want to punch something. McMasters didn't deserve her. He certainly didn't deserve little Nicky.

Liliana stared. "Wait. You said Doug gave you the

note days ago? Why didn't you tell me *then?*"

Angry, Jake swallowed his food, almost choking on it. Sputtering, he reached for his napkin and wiped his mouth. He *would* have said he forgot, but that was a lie and he damned well knew it. He hadn't wanted to tell her. She and Nicky were doing well now. Besides, what right did some punk have to waltz back into her life and disrupt it? In the few short weeks she'd lived in the spare apartment, he'd watch Liliana bloom. Gone was the shy young woman whose spirit had once been shattered. She laughed and told him of her dreams for the future—a future he secretly hoped one day might include him. At least he'd been counting on it when he picked out her ring.

He drew a deep breath and steeled himself. "Are you going to call him?"

"You never answered my question, Jake. Why didn't you tell me of Doug's visit days ago?"

"I think we both know why."

She rose from the table, but didn't look at him. "You had no right to keep this from me."

No, he didn't. But she had no right to make him fall in love with her—with Nicky.

"Liliana."

She turned her face away. He knew it then. *She was going to Doug McMasters!* He had to know the truth.

"Do you still love him?"

"Jake, please..."

She didn't deny it. He resisted the impulse to argue, to forbid her to see the punk. Liliana wasn't a child he could control. She wasn't even his woman for that matter. He'd fallen in love with her, but like a chivalrous fool he'd kept his distance, never even kissed her. Not that he hadn't wanted to. *Not that he hadn't fantasized of much more.* Still, he couldn't let her go without knowing how he felt.

He sprang from his chair and rounded the table. She cried out as he pulled her against him, her eyes growing wide as he bent to brush his lips over hers. He expected she might push him away. She had every right to be angry, but she didn't resist. Instead, her body melted against his and her arms slipped around his neck. He kissed her deeply, tasted her sweetness in a deep soulful kiss. She whimpered against his mouth as the kiss deepened and changed and she returned the kiss, meeting each thrust of his tongue. His palms cradled her delicate face, then smoothed downward over her long, slender neck and delicate shoulders. He broke the kiss and pulled back to look at her. Flushed cheeks and soft, passion misted eyes glittered in the glow of candlelight. *Desire mixed with innocence on the face of an angel.*

She trembled as he worked open the first few buttons on her blouse. He eased it from her shoulders, pleased to find she wore nothing beneath. She was beautiful, even more so in the glow of candles and he had to touch her to believe she was real. He'd not been with a woman since before Diane's death—hadn't wanted to until Liliana came along. He caressed her breasts, listened to her sharp intake of breath as his thumb pads brushed over tight, aroused nipples. She arched into him, her soft pleasured sighs threatening to drive him over the edge. She wasn't a virgin in the physical sense of the word, but he knew from her response she wasn't experienced either. No matter that he wanted her, the last thing he intended to do was seduce her like that no good scum, McMasters once had.

With everything in him he released her and reeled away, knowing if he looked into her eyes again he wouldn't be able to control his desires. He'd carry her downstairs to his apartment and make slow sweet love to her all night long. Something they'd both regret in the morning. After all she'd been through, she deserved more—a ring, a wedding, and the promise of love everlasting.

He listened to the rustle of her clothes as she adjusted them.

"Jake, please understand. I have to see Doug. What

if he wants to know Nicky?"

He clenched his teeth to keep from saying something regrettable. How the hell could she ask him to understand? And why did Liliana care what the jerk wanted? He'd abandoned the two of them for Christsakes! But more than that, what emotional hold did Doug McMasters' have over her? *A child*, came the voice.

"Fine. Talk to him," he growled as tears threatened. "Do what you feel is right."

As the sound of her footsteps faded, his heart seized in his chest. As much as he wanted her, he had no right to deny little Nicky from knowing his real father. Besides, what if she still loved McMasters and decided to reconcile? Did he have the right to deny Liliana the freedom to follow her heart?

The emptiness of the vast night sky threatened to swallow him. He reached into his pants pocket and pulled out the black velvet box and flipped it open. A diamond solitaire sparkled. He'd been waiting for the right moment to propose. Now, that moment would never come.

Cursing softly, he blinked back tears. He hadn't meant to love her and Nicky. He hadn't meant to give his heart so freely. He shoved the ring box back into his pocket and stared out over the rooftops of the darkened neighborhood. The only thing that love ever brought him was pain. He'd learned that cruel lesson once before. He sure as hell wouldn't make the same mistake again.

Jake had avoided her since they'd kissed—since he'd told her of Doug's visit. From his reaction it was clear he didn't want her to see Nicky's father. Still, she needed to know why Doug had contacted her after more than two years. While she had no romantic interest in him anymore, she wouldn't deny him the opportunity to have a relationship with Nicky if he'd had a change of heart. It was only right. Perhaps after their meeting she could put her unanswered questions to rest.

They met at the ice cream shop on Broadway. She'd barely slid into the booth when she realized Doug wasn't interested in Nicky. He ignored his son who babbled and shrieked, trying to gain his father's attention. Doug said he'd been accepted to State University on a football scholarship. He thrust a legal document in front of her, saying he needed her signature promising she wouldn't cause trouble with a paternity suit or child support should be make the pros in a few years. She left three minutes into their meeting—the paper unsigned—telling Doug McMasters to have a nice life playing ball, and to go straight to hell while he was at it.

Jake spent Christmas Eve day running errands, ordering new restaurant equipment, and doing paperwork in his upstairs apartment office—anything to keep from coming in contact with Liliana. He couldn't face her yet, couldn't bear to see the look in her eyes that would surely tell him she'd reunited with Nicky's father.

From his window he watched her and Nicky get into a cab. Going to McMasters he guessed. Earlier, she'd sent a note by his cook stating she couldn't attend the Dickens on the Strand event with him. She offered no explanation, but he knew why. She planned to spend the holiday with Doug McMasters.

Sick over the whole damned mess, he cancelled his dinner plans then drove to the seawall. He sat in his car and stared at the foaming waves as the evening sky turned a brilliant magenta and the surf a mesmerizing shade of electric turquoise. Another year over, another Christmas Eve, and he was alone again.

He tortured himself with thoughts of Liliana and baby Nicky, imagined McMasters bouncing the child on his knee at that very moment. He saw the image of a happy family, Nicky giggling with cookie crumbs smeared across his pink cheeks, a sparkling Christmas tree draped with colored lights and silver tinsel with piles of gaily wrapped packages beneath it. Liliana laughing—the light in her eyes for another man. Fighting back tears, he whispered, "I wish you were my family, Liliana—you and little Nicky."

He waited until dark, then drove through neighborhoods past brightly lit homes where families celebrated the gift of each other. How many Christmases had he prayed for his own family? How many more holidays would he spend alone? He couldn't return to the empty apartment—not tonight, not when the past collided with the present and threatened to consume him all over again.

Liliana enlisted the aid of a store clerk to help her load the Christmas tree and bags of decorations into the waiting cab, confident Jake would be at the holiday dinner by now. On the ride home she wondered if he was still angry that she'd met with Doug. Or was he avoiding her because he was embarrassed that he'd kissed her passionately the other night? She touched two fingertips to her lips, reliving the moment, recalling the flutter in her tummy when his lips touched hers and the caress she'd allowed. Her one sexual experience with Doug McMasters never came close to what she'd felt when Jake touched her. Had he also felt the spark between them? Had he wanted her as much as she'd wanted him?

Back at the apartment, she took Nicky upstairs and put him in his playpen, then returned to the curb to retrieve the tree and decorations. She mixed the ingredients for a coconut cream pie and set it to bake while she assembled the stand and artificial tree. While Nicky napped on a blanket beneath the tree, she strung bright lights and silver tinsel and hummed along to corny Christmas carols on the radio. Afterward, she placed a bright red sticky bow on top of Nicky's head, stuck one on hers then lay beside him and patted his back.

Only one more thing would make this Christmas Eve

complete—to have Jake here with them. "I wish Nicky and I could be your family," she whispered. "I wish we could all be together for Christmas."

It was time he faced the truth and stopped avoiding Liliana. At one in the morning Jake pulled up at The Greasy Spoon and parked at the curb. Glancing up at the second floor window he noted the light in her apartment was on. Good. She hadn't stayed the night with McMasters.

McMasters couldn't have Liliana, nor baby Nick. She was *his* woman and no matter the outcome of her meeting with Doug, he had no intention of giving them up without a fight. He dashed upstairs and unlocked his apartment door. First thing in the morning he'd step across the hall to her apartment and apologize for being a jerk. Then he'd cook Christmas breakfast for the three of them. He froze when he opened the door. Hadn't he turned the lights *off?* He pushed the door open wider and saw Liliana and Nicky asleep beneath a Christmas tree.

Where had *that* come from?

His eyes followed a string of twinkling multicolored lights strung across the pass-through bar where a jolly plastic light-up Santa stood sentry over a green pie. He blinked. *What kind of pie is green?*

Liliana stirred restlessly, then eased her arm from beneath Nicky's neck. "Jake." She yawned wide. "You're home."

Speechless, Jake stared at her for the longest time. She had decorated his apartment. Baked a pie. That could only mean one thing—Liliana had made her choice.

She pushed the hair from her face. "Do you like the decorations? Nicky and I did them all by ourselves. Well, Nicky slept mostly, but he helped pick out the garland on the tree and the twinkle lights. Oh, and the Santa Claus on the bar was his idea, too. Actually, he wouldn't let me leave the store without it." She rose from the blanket and stretched. "I hope you like coconut cream pie. I made one from scratch. It's green."

He eyed the pie again and his stomach did a flip-flop. "I've never had *green* coconut pie before."

"I tinted the filling to make it look *Christmassy*. I wanted to put a cherry on top, but the store was out."

He looked around the tiny apartment that had once been empty and devoid of love and his throat constricted. She'd done all this for him. Liliana loved him. She must. Still, he had to be certain.

"What happened with McMasters?"

She shrugged. "Who? I don't know anyone by that name. Oh, by the way, you do realize you're standing under the mistletoe?" She edged closer, an impish grin on her face. "You know what that means?"

He looked up at the ball of greenery overhead suspended from a string thumb-tacked to the ceiling, then back at her. Lifting on tiptoe she pressed against him and her arms slid around his neck. Her lips parted and her eyes closed. Jake dipped to kiss her, to taste the woman he loved with all his heart. Liliana had come into his life a few short weeks ago, a stranger whom he might have never met had it not been for fate. This was the dream he wished for, the gift of love from a woman, the gift of a child. He kissed her gently then pulled back to look at her—and the ridiculous red bow on top of her head.

It was now or never. Gathering his courage, he released her and pulled the black velvet box from his jacket pocket. He flipped it open to reveal the diamond solitaire. Her eyes widened.

"Liliana." He swallowed hard as his throat threatened to constrict once again. "We haven't known one another very long, but I've grown to love you and Nicky. I would be honored if you'd agree to be my wife. If you would allow me to be a father to Nicky—to adopt him and give him the Delatorre name. I promise to honor and love you both and care for you the rest of my life."

Teary eyed, Liliana nodded. "Yes, I'll marry you."

Nicky snorted loudly and stirred on the blanket. "Da-da!" came the toddler's cry.

Jake looked past her to the child, then back into her eyes. "Did he call me daddy?"

Liliana nibbled her lower lip. "Perhaps I should have asked first if it was all right?"

"You taught him to call me daddy?"

She nodded.

Nicky ran to Jake with his short, chubby arms outstretched. "Da-da."

Jake lifted the child and hugged him close, breathing in his sweet scent. "That's right, tiger." Tears filled his eyes. "I'm your daddy now, forever and ever." With Nicky in one arm, he gathered Liliana into the other and hugged her close. "Merry Christmas, Liliana."

"Merry Christmas, Jake."

Be sure to check out Kimberly's website
http://hometown.aol.com/kimberlyivey2/index.html

The Patient Gift

by Patty Howell

Lea grimaced as she pushed against the wind to close her front door. The quiet darkness of her home wrapped around her. She stood in the foyer shivering, once again safe in her solitude.

When she'd left her office at the bank, only a dusting of snow had covered the streets. Now, a little more than an hour later, double-digit accumulations enveloped the city, slowing traffic and bringing Philadelphia to a standstill. The winter wind's arctic howl and outer blanket of snow exacerbated the tomb-like effect inside her house.

Balanced on one foot, Lea reached down and tugged off a boot. It slipped and landed with a loud thud on the pine floor—the hollow reverberation, a reminder of the sheer loneliness of her life, pierced her heart. *Loneliness—a toothache in my soul.* Suddenly light-headed, she backed up, braced herself against the door and slowly slumped to the floor.

Hot tears flowed down her cold face.

A solitary sob stole the silence.

"I know it's futile to wish. But I wish...what? I don't know what I'd wish even if I did think it would come true." Lea scowled and shook her head. "Talking to myself. Not a good sign."

She closed her eyes only to open them again when she heard clicking crossing the foyer. Basil, her aged black lab, lumbered toward her, pushing his large head into her chest and rubbing back and forth.

"Hi, Basil, old boy. You need to go outside?" She stroked and nuzzled his head and neck. "You haven't given up on me. You should, you know." She took his big face between her hands and peered into his huge black eyes. The intensity in Basil's stare sometimes unnerved her, as if he had the power to look straight into her soul. His slobbery tongue lapped her face as though wiping away her tears. She swiped her cheek with her hand. "That's enough, Basil. I love you, too. Thanks for cheering me, buddy."

Yet no smile curled her lips. She once found such delight in everything: life, day-to-day living, Basil...and of course family.

Everyone told her it was time to move on. Simply put, the will and power to chisel away the calcified cocoon she'd let wrap around her heart eluded her—and it was her heart that had yet to recover.

Pulling herself together, she eased the other boot off and pushed herself upright. She opened the door and Basil slipped out. Setting her boots in the corner, she put her handbag on the foyer table and draped her coat over the final post. Although he didn't dilly-dally, pretty white snowflakes covered Basil's coat when he came back inside. A vigorous shaking scattered them onto the floor, vanishing instantly into little dots of water.

"Yeah, me too, boy. It is cold." Her arms wound across her chest and she rubbed her upper extremities with chilly hands. Another shiver—she needed to start a fire. While at work, she kept her thermostat at sixty-two to conserve energy—and prevent a high utility bill. She looked at the lever and nudged it to sixty-eight.

Basil went back to the kitchen, as she headed toward the fireplace. In her living room she looked at the brown boxes stacked in the corner that UPS had delivered. Still unopened, two were from her older brothers, two from close friends.

Four weeks until Christmas. It didn't seem possible

it had rolled around again. Her life had forever been altered at the beginning of the previous year—after the first three months to be exact. Since then she'd functioned like an automaton. Not one present had she bought, nor had she any intentions of doing so. She wouldn't get a tree...display any other decoration...or send cards. She dwelt in a state of suspended animation.

No. Pennsylvania.

Lea jerked around. No sooner had she balled up newspaper and shoved it under the logs stacked on the grate when she heard the whisper. And she could have sworn the susurration said "Pennsylvania."

Nothing behind her—no one else in the room. She shrugged. Maybe the wind? Immediately her eye caught movement by the doorway. She breathed a relaxed sigh when Basil came into the room, head down, tail wagging as he sauntered toward her, then nudged her hand with his nose.

She lit a match to the paper in the fireplace and watched the fat lighter take hold. Once the warmth spread, she stood and headed for the kitchen. She loved the comforting ticktack of Basil's toenails on the wood floor as he padded along behind.

"Hungry, boy? Let me put coffee on and I'll get you some food, okay?"

Halfway down the hall, a scuffing sound caused her to look back. Basil stopped, turned and looked straight at the front door. A shadow floated past the outer side of the windows. Her body tensed and her heart thumped, as she stared at the slim sidelights framing the entryway. Another movement, another scuff. Basil emitted a low growl.

"Easy, Basil. It's only the wind blowing the snow around."

A light tap on the door. She jumped, Basil barked. She stepped to the door and looked out. The porch light illuminated a tall figure with a hat and long overcoat.

With some apprehension she called through the door, "Who are you and what do you want?"

"Ma'am," a man's voice yelled above the harsh wind outside. "My car's stuck in the snow. Could I use your phone to call a tow truck? My cell phone won't pick up a signal."

Everything inside her said to tell the stranger to go away, in any case it wasn't her habit to turn away someone in need.

She opened the door. "Please, come in."

"Oh, no ma'am. I'd get your floor messy. I've been up to my knees in snow."

His voice a deep, melodious baritone carried a honeyed southern accent.

"It's okay. These wood floors have taken a beating over the years. A little snow isn't going to harm them." She moved aside giving him a wide berth and motioned him in. He wasn't only tall, but broad.

"Thank you." He entered and forced the door closed against the increased intensity of the wind.

"Here, let me take your coat. You look soaked through to the bone."

"It's all right. If I could just use your phone, please."

Lea nodded. "My phone's in the kitchen. I was on my way there to fix coffee. Would you care for some?"

"No, ma'am. I don't want to be any more of a bother than I've already been."

"It's no bother and it'll warm you."

"That's very kind of you."

Lea stared at the man as he removed his gloves and hat. He rubbed a thin stubble of beard between his thumb and forefinger and raked his thick hair back. Mesmerized, she followed the long, tapered fingers and clean, clipped nails. She hoped her mouth hadn't fallen open as she perused his gestures.

Neither spoke.

Finally, Lea swallowed and broke the silence. "My name's Lea—Leatrice Novak."

"It's nice to meet you, Lea. My name's Durham North."

Her eyes cut to his.

He shrugged. "I know. And, yes, I'm from North Carolina. Durham, in fact. Comedians for parents." He waggled his brows.

He bent and placed his hat and gloves on the floor, alongside Lea's boots, then shrugged out of his large coat. She took it and carried it to the kitchen. He followed behind Basil whose eyes darted between his mistress and the stranger.

Basil stood sentinel inside the kitchen door.

"There's the telephone and the Yellow Pages." She crooked her head to the old-fashioned phone attached to the wall, the directory on a small table beneath.

"I haven't seen one of these in years," he touched the receiver in its cradle, then turned his attention to the heavy book.

"My sister gave it to me Christmas before last." The words just slipped out and pain tugged at her heart.

Near the back door, she draped his wet coat over two hooks on a rack, tracing her hands across the soft cashmere. Who was this man who'd dropped out of nowhere? And why had he almost made her smile when he'd wiggled his brows like some old movie star? *Smile...maybe that's what I'd wish for. I haven't done that in...practically two years.*

Returning to the counter, she scooped freshly ground beans into a filter, poured in water and switched the pot on as he replaced the receiver.

"Please have a seat." She tilted her head toward the round table in the middle of the kitchen.

She stared at him, again, watching as he pulled out a chair and sat. His large size dwarfed the table. The dark brew finished dripping into the carafe—its tantalizing aroma filled the kitchen. She realized she was still staring.

"What do you take in your coffee?"

"That white powder stuff, if you have it."

"I do. You have a voice like a radio announcer. It's very nice...soothing." *Lord. Did I say that to a total stranger? What is wrong with me?* She quickly turned and poured the coffee, thankful her back was to him so he wouldn't notice the flush that had rushed into her face.

He took the mug of steaming liquid she handed him. "Thank you—for the coffee and the compliment. As a matter of fact, that's sorta what I do. Not the radio though. I record books onto CDs for the blind."

"That's wonderful." She sat opposite him and observed the man as he spoke. He *was* handsome. Light brown hair, long enough that it curled at the nape. His eyes were a deep ocean blue above a perfectly sculpted nose. He was quite elegant for such a large person. She estimated him to be in his mid-thirties—her own age. Then she realized he stared at her, as if awaiting a response.

"I'm sorry. What did you say?" Her face heated.

"I said the tow truck guy is out on another call. They didn't know when he'd get here."

She wondered what she'd do with him until then.

He must have sensed her discomfiture. "I suppose I should leave. Wait in my car—"

"N-no. Please don't. It's...well, I don't have many visitors. I apologize if I sent bad signals. It's just that—"

"You have nothing to apologize for. You've been very kind to a stranger in distress." His smile was enough to buckle her knees, if she'd been standing. Her eyes darted down to the cup cradled in her hands. Overcome by awkwardness, she pushed her chair back and stood. "I have to feed Basil."

"He's a very well-behaved animal." Durham's observation elicited a low snarl from Basil.

"Basil tends to disagree with your classification." Her eyes shifted to Basil and then back to Durham, while she prepared Basil's food.

"That's beautiful," Durham commented.

"What's that?"

"Your eyes, they're very beautiful. But when you smile, they're enchanting."

Flustered, her hand flew to her chest. "Me? Smile? I

doubt that." She shook her head. "I haven't smiled in—"

"Over a year?"

She was stunned. "How do you know that?" She couldn't hide the quiver in her voice.

"I'm sorry Lea. It was a joke. Well, not exactly a joke. It's a song I wrote many years ago. I cared for my parents for several years. Then Dad died and Mom followed almost a year to the date. I penned some lyrics about not having smiled. I apologize if the comment upset you."

She didn't know what to say.

"I didn't mean *you* actually smiled," he continued. "Your eyes did. They're very expressive, you know. I'm fascinated by eyes. You see, that's why I do the recordings. Both my parents were blind."

When she finished preparing Basil's food, she retook her seat. "Oh. I'm so sorry. That must have been very difficult. How—"

"That's always everyone's question. How did I cope? How did it happen? How long were they blind?" He finished the last dregs in his cup and she stood.

"More," she offered.

"Yes, thanks."

She refilled the cups.

"Please continue with your story." She was eager to learn about this man and his family. Then it dawned on her, this was the first time in...yes...in almost two years, she'd been excited about anything.

He laughed and it made her heart sing. How long had it been since she'd heard laughter in her home.

"I don't think I was telling a story." He shrugged his broad shoulders. "Be that as it may, I'll be happy to elaborate." He sipped from his cup after blowing a gentle breath across the steamy liquid.

Sensuous lips, she thought, full and dark. They appeared soft and kissable, and she wondered what they would feel like covering hers. Another warmth crept into her face at her runaway thoughts.

Durham didn't often talk of the things he was getting ready to tell her. For some reason, however, he did want to share with this woman he'd watched as she busied herself at the counter awhile ago. He wondered why such an attractive woman was home alone on a snowy evening. No, he revised—attractive didn't quite fit the bill. Lovely—yes—a more apt description. Gorgeous, expressive hazel eyes that projected intelligence, yet it was as if someone had turned a light out in them. Full, brown hair that fell to her shoulders in a smooth wave. A petite woman, she barely reached his shoulders. Black slacks and a trim, white blouse revealed curves in all the right places.

He closed his eyes and inhaled the steam wafting from his cup as though breathing in buried memories. He placed his cup on the table and stared into it for several moments before speaking.

"Mom and Dad had traveled to a remote area in Africa where they were doing humanitarian work in a small village. A terrorist faction of Al Qaeda raided the village. The terrorists held my parents for seventeen days and tortured them to get information they didn't have. The U.S. Embassy couldn't do anything about their release since we don't negotiate with terrorists. One of the men, my father said, went berserk. He burned my mother's face with a poker—right across her eyes—then did the same to Dad. The terrorists fled, leaving my parents to die. If not for a villager stumbling upon them, they would have. Doctors did everything they could, even transplants wouldn't work because the damage was so great."

He stopped and tilted his head toward the ceiling, then his gaze returned to the present and to her.

He swallowed deeply.

Horror stricken, Lea covered her mouth. "Oh, Lord! I am so sorry that happened to them."

She fought an urge to reach across the table and take his hand.

"This happened about fifteen years ago." He rubbed one of his arms as though warming himself.

"Fifteen years! I didn't know Al Qaeda existed then."

"It did. Al Qaeda's been around a lot longer than most people realize. The news media didn't make much of a deal about it."

"Again, I'm so sorry. So you said they died. Was it from their injuries?"

"Yes and no. Dad was sixty-five when they went to Africa, Mom sixty-two. At their age, I think it was too much trauma to overcome. They lived for ten more years. Well, Dad ten, Mom eleven."

"And you cared for them all that time?"

"Yes. We also had a nurse. She attended them during the day while I worked."

"It's somewhat ironic that you were recording CDs for the blind, wasn't it?"

"Oh, that's not what I did then. I didn't start doing that until after they became blind. I'd read to them every evening and it was actually Mom who suggested it." Durham smiled. "Thanks for jogging my memory. It's not that I forget—just don't try to dredge it up."

Lea wished her open-wound memory needed a catalyst. "So what did you do before?"

"I taught college English and drama."

"Well, that fits right in with what you're doing now. That's advantageous."

"You might say."

Lights reflected on the kitchen wall. The tow truck arrived sooner than expected. Listening to Durham, the time had passed too quickly. Retrieving his coat, she saw him to the front door.

Turning, he took her hand and brought it to his mouth, tenderly brushing it with his lips. The gesture, so ephemeral she didn't have the opportunity to protest. And once done, was glad she hadn't.

"Thank you for the enjoyable evening, Lea Novak. I hope I get to see you again."

"It was nice to meet you, also, Durham," she

managed to utter through constricted vocal cords.

Then he was gone. As quickly as he'd come. She closed the door and shuddered at the onset of emotions his lips on her hand had evoked.

Friday found her home alone as usual. Well, there was Basil. During the week, Durham North had frequented her thoughts. It was during the lonely evenings at home, Basil lying by her chair while she read, that she thought of him and tonight was no exception.

Each time he came to mind, little piercing stabs shot through her heart. *What are these pains? Are they warning signs not to open myself to vulnerability?* If they persisted, she worried she'd have to see a doctor. The mere idea made her want to retch.

You won't have to.

Where had that come from? It sounded audible, but there was no one with her. She stared at Basil. He sat attentive, watching the door.

The knock startled her. Basil didn't move— continued to look toward the door. She calmed, realizing it had to be someone she knew, otherwise Basil would have been in protector mode.

A glance through the sidelights and her heart leaped. Durham stood there in his big overcoat. She opened the door.

"Hi. This is a surprise."

"I hope a good one." He brought a hand that had been tucked behind into view. It clutched a huge bunch of flowers. "For you, my lady," he said with a bow.

Lea was speechless. "Th...thank you," she finally uttered, backing into the foyer. "Please, come in." She hung his coat in the closet, hugging the bouquet to her chest with one arm. "At least the weather's better than it was last weekend."

He chuckled. "You've got that right. How've you been?"

"Good. You really didn't need to bring flowers." She

stuck her nose into the flowers and sighed at the heavenly fragrance.

"Well, at least you didn't say I didn't need to come." He laughed, a deep, sonorous, beautiful sound.

"What I was hoping," he added, "is that they'd cheer you. I've never seen such a beautiful woman look so sad. And, also, I hope you haven't prepared dinner because I want to take you out."

"Oh, I don't want...I couldn't..."

Of course you can.

All right! *What the heck is going on here? Those aren't my thoughts.* She figured she hadn't gone that far south of sanity. And Durham hadn't said anything; she'd been looking straight at him. Her attention switched to Basil, who now stood by her side, his tail kicking up a breeze.

"Basil?" she queried.

"Sorry. Hello, Basil." Durham chucked the dog on the head, rubbing it gently. "I didn't mean to slight you."

"No, it wasn't that." Lea shook her head in confusion. "Yes. I'd be happy to have dinner with you."

Yet she wasn't happy about it at all. In fact, she dreaded it. Her home was her comfort zone—her safe haven. Her routine consisted of going to work, doing her job, then returning. As bank president, she dealt directly with the public only occasionally. She'd loved her job as teller—then, but that was before...

"I'll need to bank the fire first."

"I'll do that." He flashed her a heady smile.

She let Basil out to do his business, temporarily arranged the flowers in a vase, and retrieved hers and Durham's coats.

Dinner was at a local restaurant, nothing fancy. Durham said he'd chosen this particular place because of its homey atmosphere.

She asked him questions about when he'd established his recording company; names of some of the books he'd recorded. She noticed he seemed embarrassed to talk about himself. He didn't sell the audio books, but accepted donations from other benevolent souls such as himself. His parents had left a sizeable estate, so money wasn't an issue.

He asked her questions. And seemed to accept if she didn't respond, or skipped over some of his inquiries. She appreciated that he wasn't pushy and didn't pry, but let her reveal herself at her pace. It was as though he sensed she needed space to get used to him. His presence. Then every so often that annoying feeling around her heart. It puzzled more than worried her.

Half way through the meal, Durham took a sip of his wine. "Do you ever watch birds?"

"Sure. Usually flying away from the tree my car's parked under at the bank." She frowned. "They can really make a mess. If you mean actual bird watching, no I couldn't tell you a mockingbird from a... I shouldn't say that. I do know the differences in most of the common birds. Anyway, why do you ask?"

He chuckled at her commentary.

"My mother loved hummingbirds." He set his glass down, broke a roll and buttered it. "After she lost her sight, I maintained the feeder. It was off the breakfast nook, and she'd sit for hours while I'd be her eyes." He smiled in remembrance. "This one particular time in May, mating season for hummingbirds, the birds came to the feeder, a male and a female. They flew away from the feeder approximately six feet, then the male zoomed upward and immediately descended to dance with the female. Then they'd both rapidly fly away.

"It took me about a week staring through my binoculars before I finally located their nest. They make the tiniest nest, not more than a few inches long on a branch." He held his fingers a couple inches apart.

Lea had set her utensils down, captivated by his story.

"I watched the building process for hours. In another section of the tree a hairy, black spider had taken residence, and they'd plunder its space and grab

138

strands of web to reinforce their nest. It was really amazing. It was one of the things my mother said she truly missed about not having her sight any longer."

"It sounds like she truly loved that you maintained her feeder."

"She did."

Back at Lea's house they enjoyed coffee and afterward Durham bid her goodnight. Standing in the foyer, he leaned down and kissed her on the forehead.

As he drove away she closed the door, stood with her back pressed to it and raised her hand to the spot his lips had touched. Warmth she'd forgotten existed flowed completely through and engulfed her from her forehead to the soles of her feet.

Durham looked her phone number up the next day and called. She sounded more aloof on the telephone than when he was with her. Since the first snowy night, when she'd opened the door, he'd been drawn to her. Embarrassed by his fascination with her, he'd intentionally not called the first week. Let the days slip by, even though he'd wanted to. Oh, did he ever. He wondered what had made her so sad. He could have run a search on her name. But that wasn't his way. Now.

It had been at one time, with his parents. He'd worked closely with U.S. intelligence and military types after the debacle in Africa. Did a little reconnaissance on his own. Sometimes what the U.S. couldn't do legally, others could. And doing things outside the country wasn't all that difficult. A few connections, palms greased and he got answers. Then he took action. Those who'd harmed his parents would never harm anyone else. And although he was a sensitive, deeply caring man, he had no remorse.

However, that was the past.

It wasn't difficult to discern something traumatic had happened to Lea, nevertheless he'd learned to be a patient man. A few women had turned his head before, none who'd pulled at his heartstrings as she had. He wanted to know her—spiritually, emotionally, and yes, physically. He wanted to break through the pain that had enshrouded such a beautiful creature.

Recalling last night at the restaurant, telling her the story about the hummingbirds, he'd intentionally not told her about the female. As the birds had continued their nest building, the female took a precarious turn and one of her feathers stuck to a portion of the spider web. Webs are extremely viscous and if not for the temerity and persistence of her mate, she wouldn't have gotten loose.

Lea reminded Durham of that snared female. Something had happened to turn what he believed to be a normally vibrant person into the withdrawn hermit she'd become. He prayed she'd allow him to help lift her out of the abyss.

He called again the next day, and the next. No softening of her shell-like exterior was apparent. But he wasn't losing hope. He was patient.

One week before Christmas, Lea sat by her fire. She stared at the empty space that would in happier years have highlighted the Christmas tree. Then she glanced at the table beside her chair, the shelf at the bottom. Her Bible was there, which she hadn't read since the previous year. And her journal. Both undisturbed, except when she moved them to dust.

Basil reclined beside the table. He lifted his head toward her as she moved her eyes from the two books to the fire.

No, you're not going to burn your journal.

Yes, it had crossed her mind before to burn it. But she hadn't thought it just now. She looked at Basil again. He lowered his big, bulky head to his rug. She bent over and ran her hands down his back. He gave her such comfort.

That slight little pain in her chest caused her to sit back.

Basil's head lifted again, only this time toward the

foyer. "What is it, boy?" Maybe Durham was dropping in again. He hadn't mentioned it on the phone when she'd talked to him this afternoon. Although he'd been so kind to her, she didn't feel she could return his kindnesses. Didn't know if she'd ever be able to.

Yes, you will.

She vacated the chair, hands on her hips. "All right. This is getting more than freaky." She went to the kitchen and put hot water on for tea. Returning to her chair by the fire, she reached for her journal. Not really a typical written compilation of what people would write about their day-to-day lives, it was a book someone had given her years before. It had surfaced while cleaning out closets after...everything had happened last year. Sitting at her kitchen table she'd written in it a summary of what occurred. Just notes really.

A knock on the door. Durham always knocked, never rang the doorbell.

She jumped up and quickly moved to the door. She thought it was Durham, but she couldn't tell for sure. Something blocked the way. Opening the door, she stared straight into the face of—a huge Douglas fir.

"Greetings, fair lady," Durham called out. "Me thinks you are in need of this."

Almost...a little crook at the corner of her lips. His head had peeked from behind the tree just in time to see her 'almost' smile. "Come on," he encouraged. "I know it's in there. Come on."

And she smiled—a broad, completely open lipped smile. "Durham, the tree is gorgeous." Her eyes twinkled in delight.

He was about to comment about the smile, until her hand flew to her chest and the pained expression on her face stopped him in his tracks.

"What is it?" Durham took her elbow.

"I don't think it's anything," she said. "I'll tell you about it later. Let's get the tree inside."

141

The tree fit perfectly in the corner by the window, where she'd always put them.

"So, where might we find decorations for this glorious tree?"

"Come. You can help me get them."

The teapot blared from the kitchen. "Oh, let me get that. You want hot chocolate or tea?" Looking over her shoulder, she walked down the hall.

"Whatever you're having."

She fixed hot chocolate. Somehow it seemed more festive than tea.

They sat at the kitchen table sipping the frothy, satisfying liquid. "Durham," Lea looked him in the eyes. "I have something I want to show you. I'm not sure I can talk about it right now, but there's something I want you to read."

"Of course, Lea."

Lea returned to the kitchen and handed him her journal. He looked at her questioningly. She hesitated a second, trying to read what she saw in those wonderful, sky-blue eyes.

"Please read it. It's not long. Not at all, in fact. Then after you read it, don't ask me talk to me about it. Sometime we'll talk, but not now. Okay?"

"I understand. Regardless, there's nothing in here that could change how I feel about you. I want you to know that before I open it."

He pushed his empty cup away and she sat across from him. Then he opened the heavily-quilted front cover. The first page simply had written in lovely script:

Journal
Property of Leatrice Martin Novak

He turned the page and continued reading in what he assumed was Lea's handwriting.

January of my 34th year

Week 1 – Eric returned from the doctor's. He had some tests run last week.

Diagnosis – The doctor informed him he has lung cancer

Prognosis –

With chemotherapy and radiation – 6 months

Without – 2-3 months

After much consideration, Eric decided he preferred a better quality of life with the few months he had left.

Week 2 – Mother hospitalized. The diabetes finally attacked with a vengeance.

Diagnosis – Her legs needed to be amputated.

Prognosis –

Without surgery, gangrene would spread to blood.

Maybe 2-3 weeks without surgery.

Mother was 79 years old. Decided she'd lived a good life. Does not want the surgery.

February of my 34th year

Week 1 – Mother passed away

My older sister and brothers, many family and friends bereaved.

March of my 34th year

Week 1 – My older sister suffered massive coronary infarction. DOA at hospital.

This is too much to bear. She was my best friend.

Week 3 – Eric hospitalized.

Week 4 – Eric slipped into coma. My sweet, sweet husband passed away.

I'm closing this journal. I have no more to write in it.

As promised, Durham made no comment, but he couldn't deny the tears that sprang to his eyes. Across from him, Lea sat, tears streaming down her cheeks. He stood and gathered her into his arms. The wonderful citrus aroma of her hair teased his nostrils as he kissed the top of her head. He ran his hands down her shoulders and around her back, gently kneading his fingers into the sparseness of her.

Finally, her wracking sobs ceased and he pushed her a hairsbreadth away. He tilted her face up and with the backs of his fingers wiped the tears, stopping at her chin, which he held between his thumb and index finger. He leaned down and tenderly kissed the lips he'd dreamed about the last three weeks. Reserved at first, she slowly responded. He was a patient man and anything more would have been presumptuous.

"Now where are those decorations?" he said, keeping his voice light.

They spent the next two hours decorating the tree. She'd pull out an ornament that seemed to have special significance and delighted in telling him about it. Every now and then she'd stop, bite her lip and he'd detect a little choking sound. He let her react to each thing in turn.

Occasionally, he'd pop more wood onto the fire and stoke it. Just as he wanted to stoke a fire in her. He believed that beneath her surface there were smoldering embers waiting to be stirred. Like the embers inside him had been stirred three weeks ago, when he'd slipped off the road near her house. There were other houses he could have approached. Hers had drawn him. He looked at Basil, who stared at him.

"Oh," Lea laughed. This caught his attention right away. It was the first time he'd heard her laugh.

"What is it?" He turned to see the source of her amusement.

She held a small ornament in the likeness of a man. "Who is that?" Durham asked, walking over and observing it with her.

"Some years ago a company produced these as Christmas decorations depicting old actors and actresses. It's supposed to be Basil Rathbone. My mother bought it because she loved his portrayal of

Sherlock Holmes. It's where Basil got his name. When we first got him, he was one curious puppy. He smelled out every inch of this house before he decided it was to his liking. Mom started calling him Basil."

She hung the decoration on the tree and stood back. "Well, that about does it."

Durham put his arm around her waist and together they enjoyed the fruits of their labor.

"Thank you so much, Durham." Her gaze traveled to his face. "Thank you for bringing light back into my life. I fought it at first, but I see that's useless now." She stood on her toes and he leaned down. She placed her hands on his face and it was all he could do not to grab her. Her touch launched an emotionally charged jolt inside him. This time her kiss was seeking and he met her advances one on one.

Christmas Eve, sitting on the floor in front of the fire leaning against the couch, Durham's arm cuddling her close, Lea felt safe once again. The firewood occasionally crackled, the tree lights twinkled and every so often created glimmering sparks from the foil-wrapped presents nestled beneath. Basil lying at their feet completed her picture. Four weeks ago, she couldn't even have envisioned this scene.

The Saturday after they'd decorated the tree, Durham had picked her up and they'd spent the entire day shopping. She'd bought gifts for her brothers, their wives, her nephews and nieces, and for her brother-in-law. Lots of gifts. She'd walked around smiling so much she'd thought onlookers must have thought her daft. Gales of laughter surfaced over some of the silliest things: a delightful stuffed animal for a niece; trains that looked like puzzles and ran around magnetized tracks for a nephew; a talking, stuffed moose head with Christmas decorations for her brother, the hunter. Durham would take her hand or put his arm around her shoulders and laugh with her. Life again held meaning and she embraced it. That evening, before a blazing fire, they'd wrapped all the gifts. Laughing, touching, kissing. It was so right.

On Sunday, she'd gone to church with him. The first time she'd set foot in a church since early the previous year. The building didn't collapse and God wasn't mad at her.

She canted her head and her eyes found Durham's. "Christmas Eve...I can't believe all that's transpired in the last four weeks. My entire focus has made a 180-degree turn. And it's because of you."

He hugged her tightly and she shivered at the voluptuous sensations that skittered along her spine.

"Love, I don't think it's all because of me. You opened your heart. My mom and dad both talked to me before they died. They warned me about letting bitterness develop. 'If things fester and balloon inside, it can eat you alive,' Mom said. I knew they were right, and it takes diligence not to let it happen. Mom used to read the Bible every day and that duty fell to me. I'd read bits and pieces of it before, and listened to sermons at church, yet it never really had much effect until I started actually reading it to her. One scripture that stuck out, I don't remember where it is, anyway paraphrasing it goes something like this: 'That our fight's not against flesh and blood, but against evil powers of the air.' I took matters into my own hands once, before I saw the truth in that verse. I've done things in my life I can't tell you about now—maybe some day. It's not that I'm sorry I did them. What I'm trying to say is, if I'd known that truth before, I probably would've responded in a different manner. Does that make sense?"

"I think so."

"Well, anyway. I think there are powerful forces at work in the universe. I believe in God and this is such a powerful time of year...a time of miracles."

"I'm happy about our miracle, Durham."

Ask her now.

"Okay..." he said tentatively, unsure of what had

prompted him. Had the dog just spoken to him?

"Okay what, Durham?"

"Uh...I had planned on saving this for tomorrow." He got on all fours and crawled toward the tree.

He retrieved a small package from underneath and handed it to her. A puzzled expression crossed her features.

"Open it, please." Her eyes danced and sparkled from the light cast by the fire.

Lea took the package. Judging by its size he knew she could guess at what it contained. She unceremoniously ripped the paper off and opened the jewelry case. "Oh, Durham! It's exquisite."

"Honey, I wanted to wait until Christmas Day, but somebody,"—he cast a sideways glance at Basil— "thought I should do it now. Will you marry me, let me love and care for you the rest of your life?"

"I'm overwhelmed, Durham."

"You don't have to answer right away. I know it's sudden and probably too early for you, but will you think about it? I'm a patient man and can wait until you tell me yes or no."

She closed her eyes and his heart dipped. He looked at Basil. *You? You rascal dog. What were you thinking? It was too soon for her.*

Sitting with her eyes closed, at last Lea realized all those pains she'd been having were bits and pieces of hardness she'd finally allowed to fall away from her heart.

Her eyes popped open. "Yes, Durham, yes. I so want to be your wife." She threw her arms around him, nearly toppling him backward onto Basil.

I told you. I always know what I'm talking about!

"Lea?" He pushed her away and looked at her.

"Yes?"

"Have you ever had the feeling there's more to Basil than meets the eye?"

"Huh?...Basil? Well, I suppose he's a pretty smart

dog." Lea gazed at her furry friend. His piercing eyes stared back at her.

That's all you think of me...a smart, furry friend. As much as I've helped you...I guess a guy just doesn't garner a lot of appreciation around here. He lowered his brows and turned his head away from his mistress and soon to be master, as if in a snit.

Lea and Durham looked at each other and burst out laughing.

"So, you're the one who's been tossing thoughts my way." She rolled up on her knees and gave the big mutt a ferocious squeeze. "Mom was right. You are an awesome creature!"

I guess if I can use a jackass to communicate My purpose when someone doesn't pay attention, I can use a dog. Who says I don't have a sense of humor?

I love you and wish each of you a Merry Christmas!

Love,
God

Be sure to visit Patty's website
http://www.pattyghowell.com

In Time for Christmas

by Cheryl Alldredge

Summer 830 AD, Longstone Abbey off the coast of Northumberland

"Nay. Do not look at me like that."

Gunnar glowered at the image of the Christian God hanging above the altar, then looked down to the boy cowering at his feet. The child muttered desperate prayers to his God, in his native tongue. Gunnar had an ear for languages and had picked up many dialects in his years of summer raiding. He looked again at the accusing eyes in the rendering of the boy's God.

"I am not a despoiler of children," he said to the image.

Reaching down to the child, he clutched a handful of the flea-ridden rags on the boy's back and lifted his shaking form to eye level.

"Silence, whelp!"

The boy pressed his lips together in a tight line as his eyes went wide. He clutched a small iron box to his chest. Probably a relic from the altar. Some bit of flesh or blood stained rag—the Christians always collected such. Despite the child's current state of terror, Gunnar suspected the boy had courage. His eyes told him the boy remained behind to protect the relic when more than half the monks had fled the abbey the moment they'd spotted the dragon heads of his longships.

149

When Gunnar reached for the small box, the boy began to fight in earnest, proving Gunnar correct in his assessment. The whelp had courage, indeed. Gunnar wrenched the box away and the boy fell limp, defeated.

"What are you called?"

The boy lifted his head and looked at Gunnar from tear filled eyes. "Be warned, monster. You will regret the day you besieged God's house."

A tingle of something fearsome ran down Gunnar's spine. He'd been threatened many times, by far worthier adversaries. Why did this small child unsettle him so?

"Your name!" Gunnar shook the boy, determined to win this small concession.

"I am called Jon," he squeaked.

"If you wish to live, you will obey without hesitation and make no trouble." Gunnar would never intentionally harm a child, but sometimes they were easier to manage if they thought he would. He pushed the small box back into the boy's trembling hands. "And if you trouble me not, I will leave this in your care. It will be yours to safeguard always."

Jon wiped tears from his cheeks with the back of his hand, leaving dirty smudges in their place. He took a deep breath and nodded.

"Good." Gunnar sat the boy on his feet. "Stay close."

Christmas Eve 2006: Coastal New England

Beth stared at the colorful lights draped around her small Christmas tree. All the pretty lights in the world couldn't cheer her up after the evening, no...the year, she'd had. Would things ever get better? She'd begun to think she'd never have the family she dreamed of. Children to share Christmas morning with.

She loved children. Wanted them desperately. As a schoolteacher, she had a class full of children she loved, but none of them would be opening presents under her tree in the morning. None of them were *hers*.

Beth wrapped a blanket around her shoulders and

let her eyes drift to the ancient metal box sitting on her coffee table. The package had arrived earlier that day. The note that arrived with it had inspired her to attend the Christmas Eve service, to light a candle and make a wish for Christmas—what a disaster that had been. She'd seen Bert with his new wife. His now *pregnant*, new wife. A tear rolled down her cheek. He'd told her he didn't want kids. Told her that her nagging about wanting a family had pushed him away and contributed to the death of their marriage. Apparently, he only didn't want kids with *her*.

She lifted the note from the table and read it again, studying every strange word.

> *Dear Ms. Markam,*
>
> *The enclosed box might seem empty now, but it has been in my family for generations and I'm assured it once held something of great value—hope. The box has been passed down with each generation, always with the intent that it would be handed over to your family when the time was right.*
>
> *You see, our family histories, yours and mine, overlap if only you go back far enough to find the moment when this box was handed into the keeping of my many-times-great grandfather. I was given his name in his memory and am honored to give you the box he so wished for you to have.*
>
> *Along with the box, I'm to tell you this:*
>
> *"Though the hope that once dwelled here has flown, it will return. It only waits for a prayer to give it back its wings."*
>
> *Ever your humble servant,*
> *Jon Gunnarson*

Mr. Gunnarson was mistaken. There was no hope for her future and no amount of prayer would change that.

Winter Solstice 830 AD; the Trondelag, Norway

Gunnar stared, slack-jawed, at the slight form sprawled on the floor near the hearth.

"I tell you, my lord, she didn't come with the others. No one saw her until this morn." Jon's voice was crisp and eager. He never ran short of words, and this occasion was no exception. "It's the prayer. You made the prayer in the chapel yestereve, did you not?"

"Aye." He'd felt a fool, kneeling before the Christian altar, whispering his prayer over that ill-famed box, but done it he had. "But, I did not ask for a wench. Comely as she is, what use have I for a wench? She'll only cause trouble. Mayhap she kept to the shadows or spent the eve in someone's bed furs?" Gunnar reasoned the Christian God would have better things to do than send him a wench...even one with a creamy complexion and fine sable curls about her head.

Jon tugged at his tunic, unrelenting. "What *did* you pray for?"

"I prayed for good fortune...for the farmstead."

"Well, then. She must be tied to the farmstead's future. Mayhap she's a wealthy princess from a far land...or a healer."

Gunnar well understood why the boy would hope for a healer. All the way across the sea, Jon had warned him of the wrath of God, and they'd returned from the summer raids to find the farmstead beset by illness. Gunnar's parents and sister had already died and his older brother soon followed, leaving Gunnar to care for the land and its people. That had been only the start of the bad luck that had ended with him giving heed to the boy's admonitions to appease the Christian One God.

"More likely she is one of lady Asa's servants."

"She's far too fine to be a servant, my Lord."

Jon had a point. He'd never seen a woman with skin so flawless—and her hands, clutched at the top of the blanket, showed no sign of calluses.

Eric, Gunnar's right-hand man, came to stand beside him. "If you do not want her—"

"No! She's a gift from God for my Lord Gunnar."

Only a hand laid protectively on Jon's shoulder saved him from Eric's ill humor. Gunnar gave the boy his best disapproving look—modeled after the one his father had often used on him.

"I beg your forgiveness, Lord Eric." Wisely, the boy kept his eyes low.

The woman on the ground, roused by Jon's outburst, pushed into a sitting position and blinked sleep laden eyes. It was then Gunnar saw the tiny chain about her neck and the small silver cross that hung from it—an indisputable symbol of the Christian Savior.

"I'll be damned. She *is* a gift from God."

Beth awoke, lying on the hard ground. Had she fallen off the couch in the night? The radio she'd left on seemed to be playing a foreign talk show. The crackle of the fire worried her. She'd never left a fire blazing in the hearth before. The air smelled of smoke and...baking bread.

The shout of a young boy coming from a few feet away broke through the fog in her brain. Worried for the child, she pushed up and tried hard to focus on the room around her. She had to be dreaming. What she saw made no sense. Her cozy living room and brightly decorated Christmas tree had been replaced by something out of the Middle Ages. Rough-hewn timbers spanned above her head, difficult to see through the smoke that hung in a thick cloud near the ceiling.

Directly in front of her, men and women stood gawking at her as if she were a museum exhibit rather than they, themselves, being the oddity. The boy caught her attention first. Stick thin with yellow hair that capped his head like a bowl, he seemed perfectly fine despite his earlier shout. He smiled at her warmly—a direct contrast to the man standing beside him with a hand resting protectively on the boy's shoulder. The huge, monster of a man scowled down at her.

To be fair, he was more giant than monster. He wore plain woolen trousers with a shirt and overtunic of woad-blue. They looked like they came out of a costume shop, only they fit his powerful physique as if they'd been tailored for him. His icy blue eyes, just a shade paler than his tunic, softened as he squatted down to her level. The tip of one long, blond braid brushed against his knee, then slid along his leg to dangle between muscular thighs. Despite her best efforts, Beth's attention strayed beyond the braid, lingering on the bulge in the snug material of the man's trousers.

When she managed to pull her attention back to the giant's face, a Cheshire cat smile curved his lips and those clear blue eyes twinkled with good humor. Smiling, he was devastatingly handsome. Perhaps not in a conventional sense, but in a rugged-warrior way. As she struggled to gain some composure, pulling at the blanket around her shoulders, one blond eyebrow arched and his gaze swept her with a leisurely caress. She felt it to her toes...and all the more needy places in between. How long had it been since a man had looked at her like that? Of course, this was only a dream, a voice in the back of her mind pointed out. Only in her dreams would a man like him find her worth such a look.

Tempted to test the limits of the most vivid dream she'd ever had, she reached out and tentatively laid a hand on one of his knees. Solid. Very solid. The second eyebrow lifted and his grin widened.

"Well, you're too delicious not to touch," she said, fully expecting the dream to end at any moment.

Dream man threw his head back and laughed, then reached out and grabbed her by the arms, pulling her to her knees in front of him. "Aye, sweetling, and I will wager you will be honey to my tongue as well."

His touch, firm but gentle, sent a wave of warmth along her arms, but his words filled her mind with questions. Well, a few lusty thoughts *and* some pragmatic questions. "You speak English?" Albeit an oddly ancient sounding form of the language.

He nodded. "Aye, and Greek. I'm a man of wide travels and many talents, as you will soon learn. I've a mind to teach you a thing or two I learned in the far eastern lands."

Well, of course he spoke English and looked like a Norse God. It was her dream after all...though no one else seemed to be speaking English.

"Master Gunnar! Balthor is tearing wood from the chapel for the fire!" The shout came from a young woman who'd just barreled through a door at the far end of the hall. Maybe now they'd all start speaking English. In a dream anything could happen. But no, a man at her dream giant's side said something she couldn't understand at all.

"Curse that brainless ox," said the giant, before releasing her and straightening to his full, impressive height. Then he was gone. Dashing out the door, most of the crowd that had gathered inside followed.

Beth struggled to her feet. She had no intention of letting her giant escape the dream so quickly. Wrapping the blanket around her, she headed for the door. She reached the opening on the heels of a broad, rounded man with a bush of red-gray hair, and slipped out before he could close the door in her face.

Shocked by the icy blast of air that stung her eyes and the cold mush beneath her bare feet, she reminded herself it was only a dream. Besides, the scene unfolding captivated her beyond caring about a little discomfort. Her dream giant, Gunnar they'd called him, strode quickly through a snowy landscape toward a barrel-chested fellow with a long salt-and-pepper beard. Or maybe it was frost in his beard, she couldn't be sure. The whole world seemed to be covered in snow or frost. A gray pallor spread across the sky, shot through with the barest hint of light struggling up from the horizon.

Gunnar met the other man midway between a small

building with a wooden cross hung on the door and what looked like preparations for the world's largest bonfire.

The young boy who'd been at Gunnar's side came to stand beside her. "Balthor is none too happy about the chapel," he said. "He fears Odin will be offended."

Beth watched as Gunnar and Balthor argued... loudly. They looked as if they might come to blows at any moment.

"Why is there a chapel?" Beth wondered aloud. Could the letter about the prayer have triggered this dream?

The boy lifted his chin to look up at her. Tiny lines marred his brow.

"Lord Gunnar built it to beg God's forgiveness for raiding the Abbey last summer."

Beth couldn't see her giant begging anyone for anything, but she kept that to herself. The boy was obviously fond of him. "So, what is the fire for?"

"'Tis for the Jul celebration. Lord Gunnar says he can make the people tolerate the chapel, but he will not make them give up their holidays."

Beth's teeth had started chattering by the time the angry voices quieted, ending with Balthor returning the timber to the chapel. Gunnar turned toward the crowd of onlookers and bellowed loudly, sending them scurrying away. All except Beth. It was her dream and she planned to do as she pleased. When his gaze landed on her, a scowl darkened his face and for a brief moment she considered running like the others. Taking a deep breath, she held her ground.

As his long strides made short work of the distance between them, his eyes traveled her length, down and then up, creating a small tingle of warmth to combat the cold.

"Have you no more sense than a babe?"

Gunnar didn't wait for her answer. Before she even made sense of his question, he had her in his arms, carrying her back into the hall.

"Where are we going?" Feeling sleepy, an odd feeling to have in the middle of a dream, she found it hard to work up much real enthusiasm for her question.

"To the fire, you lack-brained woman. If you do not die of fever, you might well lose your toes to the cold."

Beth frowned. He sounded genuinely worried. Why would he care? After all, it was only a dream. She would wake up and then the cold wouldn't matter. She opened her mouth to tell him so, but the motion of being settled on a bench in front of the fire distracted her. She'd rather have sat in his lap. Yes, a nap in his arms, her cheek pressed against the warmth of his chest—that sounded nice.

She watched, unconcerned, as he sat across from her and lifted her feet into his lap. When he wrapped his large hands around her feet, warming them, a growing discomfort finally focused her sleepy, confused mind.

"Be still, woman."

"Beth."

"Beth? What manner of speech is that, little gift?"

"Beth is my name, you big oaf. And that hurts."

"I am called Gunnar, not Olaf and aye, it is bound to hurt mightily. 'Twas your own foolishness that caused this."

Beth continued to tug against his hold. She felt as if every blood vessel in her feet had turned to ice, then shattered. How could she feel this much pain if she were only dreaming?

Shaking, she watched the large, work-roughened hands dry her feet with a coarse cloth. He moved the cloth over her skin with brisk efficiency. A jagged white scar ran along his forearm, disappearing beneath the turned up sleeve of his tunic.

He was real. It was all real. The truth hit her like a punch to her chest. Her heart seemed to pause beneath her ribs, then pounded back to life at a rabbit's pace. Frantic, she looked around the room. A row of wooden tables and benches ran the length of the nearest wall. Behind the center table, a pair of wooden uprights had been carved and painted in vivid reds and blues. Along the opposite wall, a raised area was covered in tidy piles of woolen blankets. Every detail was as real as the man gently warming her toes. She'd gone to sleep in her living room and woken up in the Middle Ages. *Impossible!*

"I have to leave," she muttered. "I have to go home." Back to central heating and electric lighting. She twisted first one way then the other, searching the far corners of the room for a magic portal or a time machine. *Isn't that how time travel worked in the movies?*

"Best you stop your wiggling, or this will end with you warming your feet in my bed through the day."

Beth froze and her jaw dropped as she slowly straightened, refocusing her attention on Gunnar. The heels of her feet, tucked beneath his tunic and pressed against his bare chest, were very near his...*oh my.*

"Nay. Do not be giving me that look. Gift or no, I have much to do this day."

Outraged, she crossed her arms over her chest and gave him her best schoolteacher stare. He frowned, marring the smooth expanse of his forehead.

"Jon!" His shout scattered the small, curious crowd that had gathered nearby. It parted like the Red Sea, giving the young boy space to move forward. He stumbled, struggling to manage the heavy fur in his arms.

Gunnar's face lit up. The man seemed to change moods faster than a six-year-old.

"Clever as Loki, you are. And true as Thor." Gunnar gently moved her feet out from beneath his tunic and took the fur from the grinning boy. The troublesome man's praise clearly meant the world to the lad. As Gunnar stood and placed the fur over her legs, the boy dashed away into the crowd. "He will fetch boots for your feet. Stay here, little gift, and stay warm. I shall send Meg to attend you. She will find you a warmer gown."

The massive man cupped her jaw, stroking his

thumb across her lips. Her mouth went dry at the gentleness of his touch. "There are many preparations to be made before our feasting can begin again, but I will look forward to coming to know you better when the work is done."

Jon brought her a pair of soft leather boots, and the English woman, Meg, brought her a plain woolen gown and an overdress of hunter green. They proved warm and comfortable, if a bit scratchy. Beth stood in a small private room off the main hall and smoothed her hands down the fabric as Meg looked on approvingly.

"The color suits you." Meg smiled, showing dimples in her cheeks.

"Thank you, Meg. It's lovely. It's kind of you to loan this to me."

"Oh, 'tis not mine, my Lady. 'Twas meant for the Jarl's younger sister." Meg's smile dimmed. "She died last summer. So many died with the fever. She never wore it mind you. I'd only just finished it when she took ill. So do not fret about that."

Beth took Meg's hand to steady the girl. Illness would be a frightening thing to these people. No antibiotics, no medicines at all. Only superstition and fear.

"It's all right, Meg."

The woman nodded, then met her gaze. "You didn't come with Lady Asa, did you?"

What should she say? Superstition and fear. What would they make of her? Beth couldn't think of a thing to say, so she pressed her lips together and shook her head.

"Jon says you are an angel, come to change our fate."

Before she could respond, a tall woman with elegant features, a fair complexion and a disapproving glare appeared in the doorway. Her words were clipped and sharp and utterly incomprehensible to Beth. Meg squeezed her fingers and tugged her into motion.

"Come now, we must ready the hall for the night's festivities. Yestereve began the twelve nights of winter feasting that is the way of the Northmen."

The Northmen! Beth knew enough history to understand that she'd landed in a Viking farmstead. Or awoken there, more precisely. She couldn't fathom how such a thing was possible, but her senses told her it was so. As she stepped back into the central hall of the smoky longhouse, she saw women working busily and children playing at the far end of the hall. The older ones watching over their younger siblings.

The hall was more crowded than she'd have expected, especially knowing an epidemic had visited death upon them so recently. As Beth worked alongside Meg under the watchful glare of the woman she soon learned was Lady Asa, she felt the unease of the women around her. Several were openly afraid of Beth, though she sensed their unease had as much to do with Asa as with her sudden, unexplained appearance.

Talking with Meg as they worked, she learned that she and Jon and many of the others were thralls—slaves who'd been captured or bought at market. Despite their status, Meg claimed most were satisfied with their lives. Jarl Gunnar treated them well as his family had before him. They'd mourned the passing of those that had died, leaving Gunnar the last living member of his immediate family.

Several of the women working industriously along with the thralls were very much Norse in their look and speech, but Asa and a small group of women that seemed to move about the hall as if they were tied to her lifted not a finger.

"Meg, why are those women over there not helping?"

Meg adjusted the evergreen bow they'd been replacing. "They came with Lady Asa. She is a guest—an unexpected one. The weather makes visiting unwise this time of year. But come she did and seems to think she is already in charge of us, since none of the Jarl's womenfolk survived the fever."

A loud shriek had them both turning with a start. Asa shouted at an older Norse woman. They seemed to be arguing over the meal preparations. The two women faced off, hands on hips, inches apart. Beth had seen enough jockeying for position and politicking in the school system to realize she'd stumbled into a power struggle among the women.

Meg leaned close and whispered, "Lady Asa is a widow. They say her husband died in a storm at sea because he delayed coming home too far into the winter season. The man hated being in his own home, all due to that shrew. Mayhap she's the fate you're ta save us from."

"Oh Meg, I don't think..." Beth didn't know what to say. She wouldn't be there long enough to change their fate. She might well wake up in the morning back in her cozy, warm apartment. *That was what she wanted, wasn't it?*

If she wasn't going to stick around, it couldn't hurt to take a few risks. She stepped boldly forward and cleared her throat. The two arguing women turned on her, glaring. Beth focused on the older woman.

"Do you understand English?"

The woman tilted her head, paused, then nodded.

"Good." Beth looped her arm around the woman's shoulder. "If she doesn't like the way you're doing it, I say, let's let *her* do it. Where I come from today is Christmas. It's a time for peace. And I'd love to tell you about it."

Beth held her breath as the woman's face drifted from concentration to consideration. A slap of rapid Norse assaulted her as Asa pushed forward and grabbed Beth by the arm. Asa's face had flushed redder than the heat of the fire could account for.

Beth thought she'd end up with a black eye any moment, but the older woman spoke in Norse in a tone that rang through the hall. Immediately a hum of chatter spread through the hall and children began to appear from all corners. They gathered around Beth, clinging to her dress and pulling her toward the far end of the hall.

"Meg! Come on, you'll have to help me. I'm going to tell them a story."

"I will help you." Jon appeared out of nowhere, but Meg and many of the other women joined them, leaving Asa and her crew alone by the hot fire.

When one of Asa's servants hunted Gunnar down and bade him to attend her urgently, he couldn't imagine what life and death matter could have intruded on such a fine day. He found her, face pinched and brows drawn together like a golden caterpillar perched above her nose, standing near the fire. She pointed toward the end of the longhouse.

"You must stop her at once. She has all the women lazing about when there is work to be done."

Gunnar surveyed the preparations for the feast, then followed the line of her outstretched arm to a gathering of women and children. His little gift stood, barely head and shoulders above them, clearly in the midst of relaying some tale. Her face was animated and her gaze wandered from child to child, holding them spellbound.

"It seems to me the preparations are mostly done and what is left you have well in hand."

Asa sputtered, then collected herself. "She spouts Christian prattle. Surely you do not mean to let that...that...woman fill the children's heads with that One God nonsense."

Gunnar suspected Asa's worry had more to do with jealousy than worry over the children's religious teachings.

"Aye, Asa, I have no objection if she wishes to tell the children of the Christian God." He didn't go into the fact that he believed her a gift from that selfsame God. Many rumors were brewing about how she came to be with them for the feast, but he'd not yet bothered to make any bold statements. Let them get used to her first. "No doubt you have noticed the chapel that sits not far outside."

"Aye," she shook her golden head. "And I know you think it some manner of wergild you must pay for your raid of that Abbey this summer past. Ridiculous notion as that is."

His belly filled with rage that she knew so much of his business. *Those* were the sort of tales he needed to silence. Fighting down his temper, Gunnar sought to speak gently to this woman who deserved his respect.

"I would not build a chapel lest I intended to use it. There will be much Christian teaching here. Best you get used to the notion."

"You would force your people to abandon their gods?"

"Nay. As our feasting attests." Had she no eyes to see the truth of that? "I mean only that both the auld gods and the One God will be made welcome here." She looked ready to shout down the rafters, while Gunnar wanted only peace between them. "I will go and listen to her teachings and if there is anything I feel not suitable for the children to hear, I will put an end to it."

She looked somewhat mollified, so Gunnar bade her return to her womanly pursuits and headed to the far end of the hall. When he neared, Beth smiled and instructed the children to bid him welcome. Settling in amongst them, he urged her to continue. She did so, entertaining them with stories of a babe born in a manger and three eastern kings that trekked many miles to bear Him gifts.

Gunnar watched his little gift dancing around the bonfire. The flicker of the blaze revealed fiery streaks within the wealth of sable curls hanging loose around her shoulders. Her form was slender, but strong and nicely rounded in all the right places. She had a powerful ability to heat his blood. And he wasn't the only one. Half his men were drooling over her like hounds over a bone.

He'd checked on her throughout the day, knowing well that a man's peace was tied to the peace among the women of the household. He'd been well pleased to see her getting along with the other women—even if a few did still eye her suspiciously. Her peace making seemed a feat Asa had no hope of conquering.

Asa danced before the fire as well, but the tall golden beauty didn't raise his lust this night. Perhaps her display of bad humor at the feasting had dampened his interest. She had turned red with temper when he'd set Beth in a place of honor and bade her retell her stories for his men. With his help, of course, since many couldn't understand a word she said. When the men teased and heckled that no babe was worthy of such a grand tale, she only laughed and carried on. He found her to be a splendid storyteller, giving the tale life in the details.

He would have to deal with Asa and her father on the morrow. While he'd listened to Beth entertaining the children with stories of the birth of the Christian Savior he'd begun to understand why the Christian God had sent her. The certainty of his course of action had been growing within his belly throughout the day. During this feast of new beginnings, he would be making a new beginning of his own.

Getting to his feet, Gunnar waited for his little gift to dance her way nearer, then plucked her from the circle of dancing women. She squealed and laughed as he lifted her into his arms and spun her around, dancing his way inside and through the doorway that led to his private quarters. When he landed her on her feet, she looked confused.

"Is the feast over?"

"Nay, little one, the feasting will go on for days, but it is time we settled in to warm the furs."

Beth's gaze darted to his fur covered bed. "Did you say...we?"

Gunnar chuckled at the sudden squeakiness in her voice. "Aye. You and I. Together."

"Umm, I can sleep in the main...hall...longhouse ...whatever you call it." She waved her hand toward the doorway and attempted to pull away.

"Nay. It would not be safe for you to sleep there and you will need the warmth of another to sleep through the night with comfort." He watched her eyes take in his room, as if searching for a means of escape as she considered her possible arguments. Gunnar placed his fingertips across her lips before she spouted some nonsense that would make him crazy with jealousy. "Nay, little one. No one will warm you but me."

"And if I say no?" she mumbled behind his fingers.

Gunnar traced her lips, then caressed the tip of her chin before lifting her face for a kiss. "Then I will be forced to persuade you."

Beth's heart beat like a wild thing beneath her breast. Could she blame the mead she'd consumed for the fact it beat with excitement, not fear? Or should she blame her need of this man on the fact it had been a long while for her, or on the fact he was gorgeous? No. She realized the truth the moment his lips met hers. It was the tenderness in his touch each time he drew near—the warmth in his smile when he looked at her.

His lips caressed hers with unceasing patience, gently urging her to kiss him back. God help her, but she couldn't resist. She returned his kiss, meeting his pace as the kiss turned passionate. Urgent. His hands stoked the fire within her as they explored and caressed her through the coarse fabric.

"You deserve finer cloth," he muttered, pulling at the offending material. "Tomorrow I will have Meg begin a new gown for you from the cloth I bought last summer at Hedeby's market."

"I don't need anything special."

She didn't even know if she'd be there in the morning. Likely, she'd wake up at home where it was safe and familiar and...lonely. Beth didn't have long to dwell on that thought as Gunnar quickly gathered the cloth of her dress and pulled it off over her head.

She tried to protest, but her will failed her and her traitorous body offered little resistance. Being with this man felt right in some indefinable way. She'd felt drawn to him from the start and when he'd bragged of her storytelling abilities to his men and honored her at the feast, she'd felt as thrilled by his praise as Jon had been that morning. There was something magical about him. For tonight—this one magical night—she would be his woman and he would be her man.

Gunnar lifted her and carried her to the welcoming pile of furs. Naked atop the furs she should have been cold, but heat simmered through her, keeping her so warm she marveled that her bones didn't melt. She watched him strip away his garments with brisk efficiency, revealing work-honed muscles. The sight of him sent shivers through her. Her fingers itched to touch—to explore. When he slipped onto the thick pile of furs at her side she couldn't resist the urge. She stroked her hands across his chest, tracing the muscles until he stilled her hand, pressing it to his heart.

"Enough, little gift, or I will forget that I needs must persuade you." His lips tilted in a wicked grin.

Beth slapped his shoulder with her free hand. "Jerk."

"Nay," he said capturing the attacking hand in his much larger one. "You are always misnaming me. I am called Gunnar." There was only laughter in his words as he rolled over her, pinning her to the pallet. "Think mayhap you can remember it?"

Beth met his laughter with her own teasing. "Maybe if you used my name I'd use yours. I don't think you even know it."

Gunnar lowered his head, rubbing his cheek against hers, releasing a warm breath against her neck.

She squirmed, which only served to rub her breasts against the broad expanse of his chest.

Gunnar kissed a trail of tiny kisses along her jaw line, ending a hair's-breadth above her lips. "Beth," he breathed. "You are called Beth."

166

Beth woke to an outraged feminine screech. She pried open tired eyes to see Asa standing in the doorway firing off rapid Norse. She started to pull the furs across her breasts, only to find Gunnar already tucking them warmly around her.

"This is not your concern. I will handle it. Rest, my Beth."

With that he got out of bed and slipped into his clothes, conversing patiently with Asa all the while. Firmly, he led her from the room. Only then did Beth notice one of the English thralls standing near the doorway.

"What was that about?"

The woman hesitated. "I guess it must be finding her soon to be husband with a woman in his bed on her wedding day."

Beth couldn't breathe. The woman's words were like a deafening echo in her head. *Husband. Wedding day.* Then Gunnar's words added to the awful symphony. *Not your concern.*

Beth bolted from under the furs. She desperately wanted her own flannel gown, but all she found was the gown Meg had given her. She wanted to go home. Urgently. Now! In that moment she needed comfort and the only thing she could think of for comfort in the strange, unfamiliar time and place was her faith. She didn't know why God had landed her here. Perhaps it had been a punishment for her foolish declaration that prayer couldn't help her. That had to be it. The only course of action was to pray for deliverance. Forgiveness. Home.

Beth pulled on every warm layer of clothing she could find—even though Gunnar's were way too large—then made her way through the snow to the chapel she'd seen the day before. An air of quiet solitude reigned. It might possibly be the only quiet place on Gunnar's entire farmstead. Yesterday, there had been people everywhere. Not like at home. Her quiet...lonely home.

Beth stepped up to the altar prepared to pray to go back where she belonged. Surely she'd suffered enough. But it hadn't felt like suffering yesterday surrounded by children on Christmas day, or in Gunnar's arms on Christmas night. Not until today, when she'd learned he'd marry someone else.

Then she saw it. Sitting on the altar in a place of honor. A familiar iron box. The same box, looking perhaps a thousand years younger, that she'd received in a package from Jon Gunnarson. *Jon Gunnarson? Could it be?* Could little Jon be the ancestor of the Jon Gunnarson that had written to her of hope? And if she'd been meant to travel back in time only to return home more miserable than when she'd left, why send it to her at all? *Hope.* All it needed was a prayer, but what prayer? To return home?

She lifted the box in her hands. Something skittered along her nerve endings and she knew in that moment that if she prayed to return home, the prayer would be answered. God wouldn't have sent her without a way home. Did she really want to go home? Or should she stay and have faith that she'd been brought here for a reason? For a man who needed her? She could be a part of his home. Not just in his bed, but among his people. These proud, strong, joyous people.

"Beth! Please! Put the box down."

She turned to see Gunnar standing just inside the chapel.

"Please, Beth, that little box brought you to me—it could take you away, put it down, my heart. Do not leave me."

All trace of color had leached from his face and his voice shook. He might intend to wed that Asa woman, but he needed her. She heard it in his voice. She had to have faith. Carefully, she returned the box to the altar.

Gunnar strode the length of the small chapel and drew her into his arms. "My heart. Never leave me."

Beth pushed against his chest, making enough space to lift her head and meet his eyes. "I'm told you're getting married today."

"I feared you thought that. It is true I had planned to marry Asa. As Jarl, I need a wife to lead by my side and her father would make a good ally. We were meant to marry in the spring, but she forced my hand arriving here in the dead of winter. 'Twas then I realized she might not be the woman I once thought. Still I had made the bargain, so we were to wed today amidst the feasting."

Beth felt tears slip from her eyes.

"Nay, do not cry. I have told Asa I cannot marry her. I will pay the *mundr* to keep the peace as best I can, but I cannot marry her when the One God has given me you."

"Is that why you would break your betrothal, because you think God will punish you if you don't?"

"Nay. I would marry you and give you babes because you are the most precious gift I could ever hope for. The answer to a prayer I did not even know my heart was making."

"But you don't know me. I ...wait, did you say marry me?"

"Aye. And give you many babes."

Beth grinned. "I'd like that." She buried her face against Gunnar's chest to hide the tears of happiness that coated her cheeks. Men never understood happy tears.

"Beth?"

"Yes," she mumbled.

"I will take you to Birka and find one of the missionaries to marry us in a way that will please your God, but it will have to wait until spring."

"I understand. Meg said it isn't safe to travel in the winter."

"Aye. But...Beth?"

Feeling her tears subsiding, Beth tipped her head up to look at him. "Yes?"

"Do you think your God will mind if we begin making the babes now?" He asked the question with a wicked grin.

"I think," she said, feeling like her very most heartfelt and oft-made prayer had been answered, "that God will understand."

Be sure to check out Cheryl's website
http://www.cherylalldredge.com

Once Upon a Snowflake

by Shelli Stevens

Lilly Rawson flipped on her windshield wipers as the first snowflake hit her window. *Great, not only am I lost, but now it's starting to snow.*

"I gotta go potty, Mommy."

She winced. "Can you hold it, Ben? We'll be there soon. "

Her son yawned. "Okay, Mommy. Will you play *Frosty the Snowman* again?"

"Sure I will." She pressed the button on the CD player to start his favorite song.

We'll be there soon. Lilly bit her lip and tried to ignore the sudden lump in her throat. *There* was nothing more than a newspaper clipping with an address circled on it. Not much to base a future on.

"How 'bout now, Mommy? Are we there yet?"

"Almost, baby." *Liar.* But what could she say? They were making a big step and Ben needed to feel safe now more than ever. She could hardly tell him they were lost. "Try and sleep. I'll wake you when we get there."

If he brought up having to go potty again, she'd pull over and let him use nature's toilet.

Lilly struggled to see through the snow, which fell heavily now. She looked for a sign—any indication of where they were. The wind picked up, causing the snow to smash into her windshield and reduce visibility to almost nothing.

She glanced into the rearview mirror at Ben. His

eyes had closed. *Thank God.* He needed to sleep. Way too late for a four-year-old to be up.

I wish we could find someplace where we'll be safe and happy.

She lowered her gaze back to the road, just as a flash of light arced through the snow.

Lilly gasped and hit the brakes, sending her car into a fishtail. She tried to regain control of the car, her stomach lurching, but now the car was in a full spin.

Her headlights illuminated a tree, and a second later her car slammed into it. Pain sparked in her head, and then everything went dark.

"Wake up, sweetheart. Can you open your eyes?"

Could she open her eyes? Lilly struggled with the minor task, surprised at the effort it took. Her gaze locked on the deep blue eyes that stared down at her with a puzzling intensity. *Who was he?*

Snowflakes hit her face, cold and wet, increasing her ability to focus again.

He carried her! It finally sank in, as each step jostled their bodies together. But why? The accident!

"Ben!" She struggled to get out of his hold. "My son!"

"Easy, he's fine. My sister's already taken him inside."

"Oh, thank God." She went limp in his arms as the little energy she had drained away. Her head fell against his hard chest and she took comfort in the strong arms holding her. He smelled like soap, with the hint of a woodsy aftershave. She inhaled deep as her eyes drifted shut again.

"No, don't close your eyes, sweetheart." His grip tightened, fingers dug into her hip. "You could have a concussion."

A door swished open and warm air brushed over her face.

"Hi, Mommy! You finally woke up. Mindy gave me hot chocolate."

Lilly managed to lift her head away from the man's chest. Ben sat at a table a mug in hand. Were they in a restaurant? There were booths and tables throughout, and the faint smell of grease.

Her lips curled in a wan smile. "That's nice, baby."

"Mommy, you're bleeding. Did you get an owie?" His eyes widened, the mug stopping halfway to his lips.

The man carrying her set her down in one of the booths, and propped her against the wall with a small pillow behind her back.

"How's she doing, Logan?" A plump woman burst out from another door, waving a towel frantically in her hand.

"I think she's okay." The man named Logan grabbed the damp towel, then turned those intense blue eyes back on her.

"How are you feeling?" He dabbed the wet towel against her forehead, and she winced. "Stings a little does it? You're lucky—it doesn't look too deep. And the lump on your head should go down soon. I'm Logan. This here's my sister Mindy."

"Nice to meet you both. I'm Lilly. And you've met my son, Ben. Thank you for helping us." She hesitated, lowering her voice. "Where are we? I got lost..."

His thumb skimmed over her temple, as if checking for further injuries. Tingles of warmth followed in the wake of his touch, confusing her.

"Snow River, Oregon. Where were you headed?"

Good question. "I...Northern California. I start a new job there tomorrow."

"You're starting a job on Christmas Eve?" Mindy slid into the seat on the other side of the table. She looked a lot like her brother. The same blonde hair, same eyes brimming with a well of compassion and sincerity.

It sounded ludicrous, taking a job the day before Christmas. It was ludicrous! But she needed this job. The only option available right now.

"You got someone you want us to call, hon?" Mindy asked. "A relative? Husband?"

"No!" Her body tensed. There was only one person, but she'd never give them his number. She took a deep breath. "I mean, it's just Ben and me. How bad is my car? I should probably head out."

"You should probably keep your butt here," Logan replied, his frown deepening. "You can't be driving this late at night in a blizzard."

His concern touched her. To have this man, a virtual stranger, care for their well-being... *Stop it, Lilly. You're being ridiculous.*

"Mommy, I'm tired." Ben came over to their booth and yawned. "Are we sleeping here tonight?"

Lilly bit her lip. She didn't have the money to fork out for a hotel. She had just enough money for gas and food until they could get to California.

"I own the Bed & Breakfast across the street." Logan touched the side of her cheek. A gentle, non-threatening gesture, but it still sent those tingles through her again. "We have plenty of room, there's no one staying during the holidays. You can call your job tomorrow and explain about the accident."

If she did, they'd fire her. But then, chances were they'd fire her anyway. Especially, now, since she couldn't arrive by the set deadline.

Mrs. Benedict, the matriarch of the wealthy, prominent family she'd been hired to be a chef for, had been uncompromising about the start date on the phone. She suspected the job would be entirely too demanding, but the pay had made her agree to the outrageous terms. And they'd been willing to pay room and board for both her and Ben.

"I'm sorry, I can't." Her cheeks flushed with humiliation, as her chin lifted. "I'm sorry, but I don't...have any money right now."

Logan stared at her. Where had she come from? This pretty woman with the auburn hair and dark doe eyes. He considered himself a decent guy, but he couldn't help but notice the tempting curves while he'd carried her to the restaurant.

174

"Mindy, take Ben and get him set up in one of the rooms. I'll bring Lilly over in a couple of minutes."

Her eyes widened with panic. "No! I—"

"He'll be fine. Mindy has five kids back at her place. She's great with kids."

Mindy took Ben's hand and they left the restaurant together.

"Please, I just told you I don't have any money." She tried to stand, but he gave her a gentle push back onto the seat.

"We'll work something out."

Logan rubbed a hand over his jaw. He watched as her cheeks turned a flattering shade of pink again.

"Are you...are you coming on to me?"

Logan threw back his head and laughed. And she sure didn't beat around the bush. "Lilly, when I come on to you I promise it won't be subtle."

"When? You said when. Does that mean—"

"Sweetheart, you need to stop overanalyzing." He stood and walked behind the counter, grabbed a glass and filled it with water. Her gaze followed his every step.

She took the glass from him and downed the water in a few gulps.

He gave her a thoughtful look. "The cook here just quit two nights ago. It's been a little hellish trying to keep up. Do you know anything about cooking?"

In response, he received a glare. *Okay, apparently I just insulted her.*

"I'll take that as a yes." Logan laughed. "Look, your car's not drivable, and there's a blizzard outside. So tell you what. I'll let you have a room and work on your car, if you agree to work in the kitchen."

Her expression turned skeptical. "What are you, the town mechanic, too?"

"Pretty much." He shrugged. "It's a small town."

Her mouth opened a bit further and she glanced out the window. "I'm not sure that's a fair trade on your side."

"Let me worry about that." He extended a hand to

help her up, enjoying the delicate softness of her fingers as they curled around his. "For now, let's just get you and your son set up in a room. Sound good?"

She bit her lip, then nodded. "Sounds good. Thank you, Logan."

Relieved she wasn't going to try and leave in the storm, he smiled. His gaze landed on her upturned mouth. *Talk about temptation.* But now was hardly the time to try and kiss her.

"My pleasure, Lilly. My pleasure."

Lilly pulled the chicken salad from the fridge, humming along to the Christmas song that played on the radio. As she started to whip up some more for the looming dinner rush, she looked through the window on the kitchen door to the restaurant.

It seemed incredible, but the place was packed. In the middle of a snowstorm and on Christmas Eve, no less!

This morning, each time a new customer had come in, Mindy dragged her out of the kitchen for an introduction. Her head reeled from all the names and faces; such warm hearts and indiscriminating friendliness. One of those small town things. So refreshing.

Mindy used her hip to push open the swinging door to the kitchen. "Everybody's raving about your poppy seed chicken salad. I'm so glad you talked me into putting it on the menu. You're one talented lady, Lilly."

Lilly flushed with pleasure as she pulled another loaf of bread from the oven.

"It's not the salad, it's your homemade bread. Do you realize how rare that is in this business?" She breathed in the delicious scent. "I haven't had a chance to try the stuff yet, but probably gained five pounds from the heavenly smell alone."

"Well, aren't we just the perfect team then?" Mindy giggled. "I called Steve to check on the kids. He said they're doing great and everyone adores Ben."

Lilly smiled. What a relief. She'd been worried how Ben would react to the abrupt change of plans. "Your husband sounds amazing. I don't know how he can handle five children plus a stray."

"Lots of prayer, patience, and the occasional shot of Jack Daniels." Mindy winked and grabbed the plate of sesame-covered chicken strips. "Be back in a second for the pulled-pork nachos. You've got some creative recipes, Lilly. And the folks seem to love them!"

Lilly checked out the new order slips to see what was up next. The door swished open again.

"That was fast." She glanced up and the slip fell from her hand. "Logan."

"How are you today?" He stepped toward her.

Lilly swallowed hard. *Man, he looked good.* The blue flannel shirt brought out the color of his eyes, and the jeans hugged all his nice parts.

"I'm okay." Her breath caught as he reached a hand to the cut on her head. Every part of her body tingled with awareness, and she fought the urge to lean into him and close her eyes.

"It looks a lot better today. Scabbing over nicely."

Scabbing over? She scrunched her mouth, imagining the ugly scab on her forehead, and pulled back. *That killed the moment.* Which was probably a good thing.

"I checked out your car. It's in pretty bad shape." He grabbed a bowl and reached for her chicken salad, dishing up a hefty portion. "I'm going to need to order parts. It could take a few days. And with it being Christmas..."

"Oh." There went the job. She'd called her employer in California this morning, but had gotten the voicemail. Although she'd left her number, she doubted a call back would come.

"*Sweet Georgia.* This stuff is good. Did you make this?" Logan lifted another bite to his mouth. Her gaze honed in on his lips and teeth as he pulled the food off the fork. Now that was a mouth designed to please a woman.

Oh... She jerked her gaze away and picked up the order slip again. "Yes. I made it."

He set down the bowl and stepped behind her. His breath fell warm on the back of her neck, and a slow tremble worked its way from her toes to the top of her head.

"I like it," he murmured and settled his hands on each side of her body, boxing her in between his chest and the table. "You look real pretty today, Lilly."

"Are you..." Her heart skipped in her chest and she closed her eyes. "Are you coming on to me now?"

He laughed, tickling the hair braided at the back of her head. "I might be."

Why can't I resist him? She leaned back until her body came into contact with his. His woodsy aftershave teased her senses, his hard chest made her think about satin sheets and his hard body.

The door burst open and Lilly straightened, their bodies no longer touching. "How're the nachos coming?" Mindy pulled up short, her eyes going wide, before she shook her head and laughed. "Logan, are you harassing my cook?"

He stepped back, his laugh a bit guilty. "Just offering her a little help."

"Well, that kind of help is going to have to wait. Go help Steve with the kids or something."

"Actually, I need to get back to work on Lilly's car." He scooped more salad into his bowl. "Thanks for the lunch. I'll see you guys later."

Lilly, flushed and scatterbrained, reached for the nachos she'd started on a few minutes ago. "Hold on, I just need to add salsa and guacamole."

"Great." Mindy leaned against the counter, continuing to watch her with a curious smile on her face. "You like my brother?"

Oh how embarrassing. "I...he's very sweet."

"I think he's *sweet* on you."

Lilly plunked a scoop of fresh guacamole, then salsa

onto the nachos and handed it to Mindy. "How come a man like Logan isn't married? He seems the type women would claw each others' eyes out over."

Mindy took the nachos and shrugged. "There have been plenty of women who've tried to snag him. He's just never really been taken with any of them. Plus..."

Bingo! There was a plus! "Plus?"

Mindy hesitated. "I'd better get these out. Thanks, Lil."

What was the plus? Lilly watched her go, her curiosity piqued.

She left the restaurant a few hours later. Mindy closed early on Christmas Eve, giving Lilly the rest of the night off.

As she walked across the street through the snow, she wished she had boots. Anything more practical than her old sneakers, which just soaked up the moisture. The snow still fell, and she stuck out her tongue to catch a flake. It rarely snowed back in Renton.

Just before she reached the Bed and Breakfast, Ben charged across the yard, squealing in delight. A second later Logan appeared behind him, roaring as he swept the boy up onto his shoulders.

The breath caught in her throat and she raised a clenched fist to her mouth.

Ben giggled and screamed with excitement as Logan spun him around before gently lowering him into a pile of snow.

Lilly's heart twisted in a bittersweet knot, and she stopped before they spotted her. Wrapping her arms around her waist, she chewed her lip. Ben beamed with adoration for Logan, and Logan seemed quite taken with her son as well. Was this a good thing or a bad thing?

Logan glanced up and saw Lilly standing on the sidewalk. *She is beautiful.* Even in her disheveled state after just getting off work. Those jeans hugged the curve of her hips so nicely, and the oversized wool sweater did

179

little to disguise the swell of her breasts.

He leaned down to Ben. "Hey, Benny boy, will you run inside and check if dinner's almost ready?"

"Okay, Logan!" Ben tore off into the house.

Logan straightened and crossed the yard toward her. Lilly's eyes widened as he came closer, her tongue swept over her lips. His gaze honed in on the small movement. He had to kiss her. There could be no more delaying it.

He took her hand, pulling her close. The soft curves of her body molded into his.

She inhaled swiftly. "Where did Ben go? Is he okay? I was hoping to—"

Logan closed his mouth over hers, cutting off her panicked prattle. Her lips were soft, her sigh even softer. She'd seemed about to push him away, but the hands that had slammed against his chest began to slide upwards until they wrapped around his neck.

Logan groaned in approval and stroked his tongue along the seam of her lips. She followed his lead parting them and opening her mouth for him. When he slid inside, it was like coming home. Like her mouth had been designed for his kisses.

Her tongue darted out in tentative strokes to play with his. She tasted sweet, like she'd just eaten a piece of chocolate. And all of a sudden he wanted more, so much more.

"Mommy, Logan, dinner's ready!"

She jerked out of his embrace, stumbling backward so fast he had to grab her hand to keep her from falling on her butt. Raising a hand to her swollen mouth, Lilly stared at him—her eyes wild with panic—before she spun around and ran to Ben.

"Thank you, Ben. What are we eating, baby?"

Logan heard the slight tremble in her voice as she took Ben's hand and they walked away.

"Ham. Steve said it's for the Christmas Eve dinner. What were you doing with Logan, Mommy? Was he hurting you like daddy did?"

Like daddy did?

"Ben!" She looked back toward Logan, hoping he hadn't overheard. Then they were out of earshot.

Slow rage burned deep and his fists clenched at his sides. It would certainly explain her skittish nature. Why she ran from him? Maybe she was still married.

Questions flooded his brain a mile a minute, and Logan finally shook his head. He'd talk to her about it alone tonight. One thing for certain, if *daddy* showed up in Snow River he sure wouldn't get a warm welcome.

Lilly padded down the stairs of Logan's house, again pausing to admire the structure. It was a log cabin, only with two stories and modern day facilities. And it was beautiful.

She walked into the living room, which glowed with warmth from a blaze in the stone fireplace. Speakers softly played a country singer's rendition of *Have yourself a Merry little Christmas* as Logan tossed another piece of wood into the flames.

He glanced up, his slow smile igniting a burn deep in her center. Something she'd thought dead long ago.

"Did Ben go to sleep okay?"

"Of course." She sat on the floor next to him, curling her legs under her bottom. "I told him the sooner he sleeps, the sooner Santa comes."

His mouth twitched. "I think Santa might have already been here."

She looked at him quizzically before glancing at the Christmas tree. Where earlier there had only been a few presents underneath the decorated branches, there now lay piles of brightly wrapped gifts. Only a few of them were from her.

"Oh my. I guess so. For your nieces and nephews?"

"I think some may have Ben's name on them. Maybe even one or two for you."

Lilly's mouth gaped. The idea that he'd bought gifts for Ben and her almost brought tears to her eyes. "Logan..."

"Hey, blame Santa." He took her hand and brought

it to his lips, brushing a kiss across the back of her knuckles.

Tingles started in her hand and spread throughout her body. She lowered her lashes and tried not to sigh in pleasure. She felt so at peace, so relaxed being here with him.

"How about some cocoa?" He stood, pulling her with him.

"Cocoa sounds good." She followed him into the kitchen and leaned against the counter while he prepared their drinks.

"How did you learn to cook so well, Lilly?"

She hesitated. "I completed a culinary program at a community college. "

"Is the job in California a cooking job?" Holding two cups of steaming beverage in his hands, he led the way back to the living room.

"Yes. I'd be head chef for a wealthy family." She sat on the couch next to him, their thighs almost touching, and accepted the second mug.

He blew on his cocoa. "Do you think you'll be happy there?"

No, but I'll be safe. "Sometimes there are more important considerations." She lifted her cup to her lips.

"Are you running from someone, Lilly?"

Her hands clenched the mug. So he *had* heard Ben's comment earlier. "It's not what you're thinking."

"Isn't it? Any man that hits a woman isn't worth the spit on the ground. If you're in some kind of trouble—"

"I'm not!" She closed her eyes. "I...took the culinary classes as a way out. I knew if I could complete the program, and get a good job, then I could leave him. I could leave Ben's father."

"Were you married?" he asked gently.

She shook her head. "No, I was stupid, but not *that* stupid. I knew marrying him would have been disastrous. I waited for the perfect job to come along, so we could leave." She broke off, taking a slow breath in.

Logan put a hand on her knee and gave it a gentle

squeeze.

"Jared drank too much, slept around...and then one night he slapped me. Ben saw it happen." She covered Logan's hand with her own. "So I took the first job offered to me. It just happened to be in California."

"Does he know you've gone?"

She shrugged. "I left a note. He has to know."

"And do you think he'll come after you?"

"I doubt it. That would involve him getting off the couch and putting down his beer." She gave a weak smile, forcing the unpleasant image from her mind.

"I think you're a brave woman." He set his mug on the coffee table, then took hers and did the same.

When he traced a finger down her cheek, tears prickled behind her eyes. She didn't need his sympathy. She'd come this far on her own. The last thing she wanted was to be dependent on another man.

"Lilly," he whispered, just before lowering his mouth to hers.

I shouldn't do this. Her eyes drifted shut and she tilted her head up so he could deepen the kiss.

Logan's arms came around her, pulling her into his lap and cradling her body against his solid chest. His tongue slipped inside her mouth intimately.

She stroked her tongue against his, cautious at first, until the fire inside her grew and she returned his kisses with fervor.

He tore his mouth away from hers. "Don't take that job in California."

Maybe it had been a crazy thing to say, but the more Logan thought about it, the more it made sense. He didn't want her to leave. But she seemed a little shocked by his statement. Hell, it shocked him too. Her gaze, previously hazy with desire, became wary.

"Are you still going to California when your car's fixed?"

"I doubt they'll hire me now. The job started today."

"Stay in Snow River. You can work for Mindy." He kissed her forehead and tucked a strand of hair behind her ear. "I know it's not glamorous, or maybe as exciting. I'm sure it won't pay as well—"

"You want me to stay in Snow River?"

He brushed another kiss across her lips. "Yeah, Lilly, I guess I do."

"But why? You barely know me."

"Well, I like what I do know. And, if you stay, we can get to know each other better." He trailed his finger along the fast beating pulse in her neck. "Besides, if you don't have that job in California anymore, you'll need a new one."

Lilly dragged her bottom lip between her teeth and seemed to be thinking about it. She had the sweetest mouth he ever remembered seeing on a woman. He could kiss her for hours and not grow tired.

"I don't want to be a burden to you, Logan. Or anyone in Snow River."

"Mindy and Steve adore you, sweetheart." He slid down on the couch and brought her with him, until they lay facing each other, pressed close so they didn't fall off. "And Ben seems to like it here. What about you? Is it so bad in a hick town?"

"Not at all. I love Snow River." She sighed and rested her cheek on his chest. "Let's say I do stay—and I'm being hypothetical here—I would insist on paying rent."

"I don't need your money—"

"Fine, but *I'd* need to give it to you." Her nails traced over his chest, making the blood in his body rush south. "I need to prove that I can take care of myself and Ben."

He wanted to take care of them. The words sat on the tip of his tongue, even as he realized how crazy it seemed. But she was right, they barely knew each other. Yet here they were, snuggled up on a couch on Christmas Eve like an old married couple.

And more than anything he wanted to make love to her. But he sensed that rushing her would be a mistake. She needed to trust him. He wanted her to trust him before they took the next step.

She yawned and moved closer. "Thank you, Logan. For everything you've done for Ben and me."

"You're welcome." He stroked her hair again. She felt good against him—so small and curvy. His protective nature emerged full force. His arm under her shoulder tightened.

After a few minutes of silence he realized she'd fallen asleep. He heard it in the shift in her breathing, the way her body grew heavier against him.

Logan closed his eyes to rest. Just for a little bit.

Lilly awoke when a log popped on the fire. She lifted her head from Logan's chest, and looked at the clock on the wall. *Three in the morning!*

She slid from under his arm, hoping he wouldn't wake.

"Did we fall asleep?" Logan's eyes drifted open, trapping her with his piercing blue gaze.

Oh, to be able to just cuddle back up with him and spend the rest of the night here. "Yeah. I should get back up to my room in case Ben wakes up."

"Okay."

His sleepy smile and tussled hair made him all the more sexy. A man who one didn't say no to. She pulled herself off the couch and headed for the stairs.

"Promise you'll think about staying, Lilly."

She froze, her heart filled with warmth and hope. With the possibility. "I promise."

"Wake up, Mommy."

Lilly awoke to Ben's animated face beaming down at her.

"Santa came! There's lots of presents under the tree!"

"Baby, that's great!" She sat up and rubbed her eyes.

"And everyone's already here! Mindy said I should wake your lazy toosh up. What's a toosh, Mommy?"

"Never mind." She laughed and swung her legs out of bed. "Give me a few minutes to get dressed, Ben. Tell

185

everyone I'll be right down."

When she came downstairs fifteen minutes later, a wall of Christmas music, loud chatter, and the smell of burning bacon hit her.

"Lilly, thank God you're up!" Mindy looked over her shoulder from her post at the stove. "This is why they don't let me in the kitchen. I burn everything I touch!"

"Okay, okay, I'm up. Here I'll take over." Lilly washed her hands, then relieved Mindy. "Where are the kids?"

"They're drooling over the presents in the living room." Mindy poured her a cup of coffee and set it beside her. "I was going to make eggs and bacon, but I'm afraid I ruined the batch of eggs."

"I'll take care of it."

In under an hour she'd whipped up a coffee cake to serve alongside the burnt bacon. They ate breakfast at the large table in the dining room. Mindy's twin girls, about the same age as Ben, fought over who got to sit next to him. Their mommy finally explained they could both have their way by splitting up and letting Ben in the middle.

Logan sat next to her and leaned close. "Merry Christmas, Lilly. Did you sleep well?"

Better when I was in your arms. "Merry Christmas." She gave him a shy smile. "I slept okay."

"Just okay?" His eyes twinkled as he popped a piece of her coffee cake in his mouth. "Are you still thinking about it?"

She flushed. "Yes."

"Thinking about what?" Steve asked from across the table.

"I'm trying to convince Lilly to stay in Snow River."

"Really?" Mindy gasped. "Oh, Lil, you should! We adore you and Ben. Not to mention everyone in town loves your cooking."

Logan's hand came to rest on her knee, and she looked up to see the quiet intensity in his expression. *He really wanted her to stay.*

186

"Mommy! Your phone is ringing!" Ben slipped from his chair and ran, then charged back into the room, waving her cell phone.

Who would be calling on Christmas? Probably Ben's dad. She swallowed hard, her stomach dropping at the prospect. "Excuse me for a minute, everyone."

Logan watched as she disappeared into the other room. He hadn't missed the panic that had crossed her face.

"You've got it bad," Mindy said from across the table. "I haven't seen you this attached to a woman since...well, ever."

Logan smiled, but didn't respond. Instead he raised his cup of coffee to take another sip.

"She likes you, too, Logan. And she doesn't even know about—"

"I know," he interrupted.

Lilly returned, her expression a bit dazed. "That was the lady in California. She...she still wants me. I can start as soon as the car's fixed and we're able to make the rest of the trip."

His gut clenched. "What did you tell her?"

She raised her gaze and met his. "I told her yes."

Mindy's indrawn breath echoed through the room. Then she cleared her throat. "Come on, kids, who's ready to open presents?"

The children fled the room, screaming with excitement, as Mindy and her husband followed them.

"Lilly." He reached out to touch her, wanting to ease whatever emotion tore her apart. She pulled away, shaking her head.

"When the phone rang, I was convinced it was Jared." She looked up at him, her expression anguished. "I don't know if he'll come after me, Logan. But if he does it could get ugly. And I could *never* put you and your family at risk." She sniffled in an obvious effort to hold back the tears. "I should just go. It's better for everyone."

No way was he letting her go. Logan stepped

forward and she stepped back. They repeated the dance until she stood trapped by him and the counter.

"Lilly, you sweet thing." He cupped her face, stroking a thumb down the softness of her cheek and inhaling her powdery scent. "If he shows up, then I'll just arrest him."

Her eyes went wide. "Arrest him? How..."

"I'm the sheriff."

"But you're the mechanic."

"Yes." He kissed her forehead.

"And you own a bed and breakfast."

"Yes." He kissed her nose.

"Plus you're the town sheriff?"

"It's a small town, love." Then he kissed her mouth. Briefly, but sensually—a promise of things to come. "Let's go open the presents with everyone, sweetheart."

Her head spun as they entered the living room. Steve stoked the fire, while Mindy distributed presents as she sang along to *I'll be home for Christmas.* Could she do it? Stay here with Logan? He represented everything she'd always wanted. Everything she'd always wished for in the perfect man.

"Here's one for you, Lilly." Mindy handed her a small, rectangular box. "It's from Logan."

She took it and gave him a puzzled glance.

"Open it, Mommy!" Ben screamed. He'd already torn open a package and now clutched a shiny, black model race car.

She peeled off the paper and removed the lid. Her lips parted on a sigh as she stared down at the silver snowflake on a delicate chain.

Logan cleared his throat. "I wasn't sure what you'd like, but it seemed almost—"

"Magical." Tears flooded her eyes and her throat constricted. "I love it, Logan."

"A necklace?" Ben's nose wrinkled. "He shoulda got you a toy car too, Mommy."

She laughed as she gently extracted the necklace. "No, he shouldn't have. This is perfect."

Logan took the necklace from her fingers. "Let me put it on you."

Fingers brushed the back of her neck as he fastened the necklace. Goose bumps collected and skittered down her spine. She leaned back into him.

His breath tickled her ear. "Stay in Snow River, Lilly. I'm falling in love with you."

She closed her eyes, tears of happiness prickling behind her lids. "Funny you should say that." She turned to face him, giving a shaky smile. "Because I feel the same."

"Are they staying?" Mindy hollered from across the room.

He raised an eyebrow. "Are you?"

Biting her lip to keep from crying, she slowly nodded. "Yes. We're staying."

The room erupted with whoops and cries of excitement.

"Just answer me this, Logan." She hesitated. "How come you're still single? It's been driving me nuts."

"Oh, that." He dropped a kiss to her mouth. "Because I have a little money."

"A little money?"

"Actually, a lot of money from an inheritance. Mindy and I both do." He touched his nose against hers. "I've always wanted someone to want me for me—not my money."

She rubbed his nose in an Eskimo kiss. "Well, I don't care how rich you are, I'm still paying rent. And doing the cooking."

That elicited another round of whoops.

"Until we get married, of course."

Married? The idea took root and sent warmth throughout her whole body.

"Mommy?" Ben came across the room and tugged on her shirt. "The music keeps saying they'll be home for Christmas. Are we going home?"

"You know what, baby?" She wrapped an arm around Ben's shoulders and pulled him to her side. "We are home."

Be sure to check out Shelli's website
http://www.shellistevens.com

Joy's Christmas Wishes

by Gerri Bowen

"Lady Emily, do you like my father?" Joy hopped from one foot to the other as they walked outside. "You met him in London, did you not? He's coming here for Christmas. He promised."

Emily had no trouble calling to mind the handsome image of Lord Captain Geoffrey DeBohun—immediately replaced by the snarling face of a father who thought his children had been taken from him. Emily shuddered at the recollection of the unpleasant encounter, brief as it had been. Whatever might be said of Lord Geoffrey, the paternal instinct to protect and defend his children was fully developed. She smiled at the eleven-year-old girl beside her.

"Yes, I met him in London. He thought his brother, Wickerdun, had absconded with you and your brothers. He was most upset."

Joy giggled. "Now he knows we still live with my aunt, just in a different house since she and your brother married." Joy stopped and looked up at her. "I'm going to make Christmas wishes. My mother told us there are special times when wishes would be granted."

"Oh?" Emily cringed inside. From the moment she met Joy, well over a year ago, the child had fixated on the idea she should marry her father. Although pleased Joy considered her a potential stepmother, Emily believed any woman presented to Joy would have been a candidate. She hoped Joy wouldn't wish for what

191

couldn't be. "Be careful what you wish for, dear. You must not waste your wishes."

Joy shook her head. "I have thought about my wishes. I even asked Simon, Hunter and Henry, and they all agree with me."

Oh dear. She'd consulted with her brothers.

"I wish for my father to stay home, and never go out on a ship again unless he takes us with him. Oh, look!" Joy cried as she pointed to the sky. The stars were just beginning to come out. "Look, the stars are twinkling." Joy hopped up and down. "That means I get my wish!"

"What a lovely—"

"That was just my first wish." Joy looked into her eyes. "My second wish is for you to be my new mother. If you married my father, you would make him laugh and then he would not want to sail away on a ship. He would make you happy, I know, because Aunt Maddy says he made my mother very happy."

Emily smiled. "That's because they loved one another, dearest. Love does not—"

"Look! The stars are twinkling again! You're going to be my new mother!"

Emily nearly toppled over from the force of Joy's enthusiastic hug.

"There, see, the last of your bloody brood is accounted for," Ardmoor said to his brother-in-law as they rounded the terrace. "Told you Joy would be with Lady Emily. Maddy says they never need look beyond Emily to find Joy." Ardmoor paused to allow Geoffrey his usual admonishment about his language, then looked to see why Geoffrey remained silent. "Like a bloody leech," Ardmoor added, tapping his peg leg for emphasis, wondering if he'd get a response. But no, Geoffrey's gaze remained on his daughter and Lady Emily. Ardmoor was certain the pole-axed look on Geoffrey's face was due to Lady Emily's laughter and large smile as she hugged Joy. Not to be wondered at, the woman was attractive. *Interesting.*

The voices of Spode, his sister Maddy's husband, and Wickerdun, Geoffrey's older brother, broke the silence, and looked to pull Geoffrey from his reverie. Ardmoor looked back at the new arrivals, recalling Spode promoted a match between Wickerdun and his sister, Lady Emily. *Oh, very interesting. Brother against brother for the fair hand of Lady Emily?*

"Look who is here, Joy. Zounds, Em, but Joy is your veritable shadow!"

Emily looked up at the sound of her brother's voice, but her sight focused on Lord Geoffrey. His gaze was fast upon her. Emily couldn't tell what he meant by such an intent stare. Was he angry because she and Joy were sharing each other's company? She was grateful for Joy's squeal of delight upon seeing her father, for it broke the contact between her and Lord Geoffrey.

"Papa!" Joy cried as she hugged her father. "I told Lady Emily you were coming! You promised, so I knew you'd be here for Christmas." She drew back and looked at his face. "How long will you stay?"

"How long would you like, princess?" he asked as he knelt before his daughter.

Emily watched and listened, amazed that the surly, rude man of her recollection could transform himself into the smiling, soft-spoken father before her.

"Forever, Papa. We all want you to stay home. Even Simon and Hunter agree, and you know they always wanted to go sailing with you. Will you? Will you stop sailing your ship and stay home? Please?"

Emily inhaled sharply when Lord Geoffrey smiled. The man was heartbreakingly handsome when he smiled. She almost missed his next words.

"Yes, princess, I'm home to stay."

When the child turned and looked at her, Emily was positive her eyes must be as wide as Joy's. "You see, Lady Emily! I told you my wishes would come true!"

Lord Geoffrey looked from his daughter to her. Emily lifted her chin at his raised brows. He looked back at his daughter.

"Why aren't you in the schoolroom, Joy?"

"Papa!" Joy giggled. "It's Christmas! Miss Hanson went home to her family."

"The girl has attached herself to Lady Emily," Ardmoor drawled.

When Lord Geoffrey looked at her, Emily fought the urge to press her hand to her breast. Drat! She pulled her hand away from her chest.

"Has my daughter been incommodious, Lady Emily?"

"Not at all, Lord Geoffrey. Joy is a delightful girl. She's—"

"She's my daughter, Lady Emily," he said as he rose.

Emily's chin rose higher. "I'm perfectly aware—"

"Papa, Lady Emily said she would be pleased if I kept her company," Joy said as she pulled her father's hand. "I like her and she likes me, and I wish—"

"Joy!" Emily exclaimed. "You must take your father to the barn. Remember what you and your brothers wanted him to see?"

"Perhaps tomorrow," Spode said. "Time we head inside. I declare, it's cold enough the lake will surely freeze this night! Emily, allow Wickerdun to escort—"

"Oh please!" Joy interrupted as she danced from one foot to the next and turned her big, blue eyes to her relatively new uncle. "I want my father to walk with me and Lady Emily. Please?"

"Zounds!" Spode turned and smiled at everyone. "Can't resist so sweet a request now, can I? Of course your father and Emily will walk with you."

Emily placed her hand on the arm presented to her, while her other hand was gripped by a determined little girl.

The men didn't remain long in the dining room with their after dinner port, for which Geoffrey was grateful.

It appeared the Earl of Spode was unabashedly in love with his wife, and deliriously proud she'd presented him with an heir four months ago. He declared he preferred his countess' company to that of cigar-smoking, liquor-swilling men. Geoffrey understood that. He was glad Maddy, his sister-in-law, had wed a man who cared more for her than convention's dictates.

Geoffrey's gaze fastened on Lady Emily as soon as he and the other men entered the drawing room. She was seated next to Maddy, now the Countess of Spode. The two women spoke, but Geoffrey saw Lady Emily dart glances at him as he approached. He wondered if she might actually take flight if he addressed her. Ladies of her ilk seldom did more than gaze appreciatively at men of his kind—attractive yes, but a second son, captain of his own ship, a merchant, widowed, with four children. Since his brother had informed him an announcement of marriage might come from this visit, Geoffrey knew Lady Emily was forbidden to him. It mattered not. She'd avoided his gaze and conversation with him at dinner, which made Geoffrey perversely want to press her. Make her look him in the eye. Respond to him. She had no right to look so attractive. To cause his blood to heat when she looked him in the eye. Just like Laurel used to do.

"Well, Geoffrey," Maddy began, "I'm pleased by your decision to give up your sailing days and remain home with your children, where you belong. The boys have need of a father who will be present for them as they mature, not wandering about the world sailing the seven seas."

Geoffrey arched a brow. "I'd nearly forgotten how you're so effortlessly able to express your opinion, Maddy. I am duly chastised."

Maddy chuckled. "As if you ever listened to me."

"Oh, I listened," he replied, his eyes shifting to Lady Emily. She looked away. He looked back to his sister-in-law. "I just didn't always agree."

"Well, the children are ecstatic, especially Joy. Emily told me Joy made a Christmas wish for you to remain at home, and not long after, her wish came true!"

Geoffrey caught Emily's eyes. His pulse thrummed loud in his ears as he gazed into her eyes. What the devil was their color? He'd have sworn they were blue when he found her outside with Joy. Now they looked dark. "Is that so, Lady Emily?" He wasn't aware eyes could get so large.

"Yes," Emily replied, but had trouble holding his gaze. "She spoke her wish aloud and not long after, she said the stars twinkled at her. She was quite happy. I was afraid—"

"Afraid she'd be disappointed?"

The way she blushed to the roots of her hair was charming. Brown hair. He'd never been fond of brown hair on a woman, but Lady Emily's hair looked soft. Puffy, not pulled back tight the way so many women wore their hair. Inviting to the touch. He judged it was long, possibly down to her hips, and tried to picture what she'd look like with it loose and flowing. Her voice jerked him back to the present. Had he been gawking?

"Well, yes. Children do get their hopes up, and are often disappointed. I didn't want Joy to be disappointed. Yet..."

Geoffrey's gaze focused on her lips, seeing her bite on the lower lip and suck it in. His pulse thrummed harder. "Yet?"

"We can't always have what we wish for, can we?"

Geoffrey shook his head. He had no idea what she was referring to, and was grateful for his brother and Spode's approach. The urge to pull Lady Emily into his arms was almost overpowering. The same urge he'd had when he met Laurel.

Emily despised herself for not ignoring Lord Geoffrey's presence. Loathed how she watched his movements as he ranged around the room. Scorned herself for trying to hear his conversation. What was wrong with her?

She'd had two Seasons in London, both successful. Her first when she was eighteen. Four years later, when she put away her mourning clothes, she had her second Season. Countless men had vied for her attention, attempted to woo her; she'd felt nothing. At age twenty-three, she was no green girl dazzled by the first handsome man to look at her twice. Why then was her attention so focused on Lord Geoffrey? No, more than that.

An overpowering urge to gaze deep and long into his grey eyes. Touch his face. Hear him speak about his life, from childhood to manhood. To know everything about him. She wanted to be captured in his arms. Wanted him to kiss her. What was wrong with her? It was his brother, the Earl of Wickerdun, she was supposed to be considering as a husband.

Wickerdun was a large man, like her brother. Taller, broader than most men. Lord Geoffrey was only an inch or so shorter in stature, but still over six feet. And his chest was broad. She thought that might be due to setting sails or steering the wheel, or whatever it was that sea captains did. Fighting pirates? Had Lord Geoffrey ever fought pirates? Or the French or Americans? She'd love to hear those tales! Drat! Her attention should be focused on Wickerdun, not his brother.

It was so difficult. She'd known Wickerdun forever. Remembered him from when she'd been a young girl. She liked him, she really did. Oh, bother! How could she be expected to consider wedding Wickerdun when his brother was flaunting his broad chest, handsome looks and devastating smile in front of her?

"Lady Emily?"

Emily turned her head to see Wickerdun staring at her, his head tilted to the side. "Yes?"

"I asked if you would like me to turn the pages whilst you delight us by taking a turn at the pianoforte."

Had he spoken and she'd not heard? Judging from the faces of her brother and Maddy, she hadn't. How embarrassing! "Of course," she replied as she rose.

Geoffrey halted upon hearing the beginning notes. He'd planned a hasty retreat before subjecting himself to an abomination of what could be termed music. But this was no idle ivory banger. Lady Emily touched the pianoforte keys not only with talent in her hands, but passion in her heart. Just as Laurel used to.

He sat silently after she'd finished, wondering if the passion he'd heard in her music was present in other parts of her life. With a shake of his head, he rose. Likely she was typical of her class and upbringing. And destined for his brother.

Emily watched Lord Geoffrey exit the drawing room. He'd stayed while she played, but said nothing when she finished. Hadn't even applauded. Said nothing to anyone before he walked out. Why did that annoy her? He was nothing to her.

Ardmoor edged close to his sister. "Tell your husband it won't do, Maddy. Wickerdun hasn't a bloody chance in hell. It will be Lady Emily and Lord Geoffrey, mark my words. They couldn't keep their eyes off one another tonight."

"I know, I saw. Do you suppose Robert...?"

"You know Spode bloody well saw. He doesn't miss a thing."

Maddy sighed. "I don't want Emily to feel pushed into marriage with Wickerdun. Still, we may be reading more into this than we should. So they looked at one another, felt an attraction." She shrugged.

Ardmoor leaned close to his sister. "Have you known Geoffrey to look at another bloody woman since Laurel died? No, because he hasn't. It's Lady Emily's blood." When he saw her raised brows, he continued. "You said Spode told you we share the same blood. Well, Geoffrey appears to be drawn to women who have the wild blood.

Ergo, he will be overpowered by his attraction to Lady Emily's wild blood and pull a dash to the Scottish border just as he did with Laurel."

"Oh dear."

"Oh bloody dear is right! I needn't see your frown to know what your husband would think of his sister being tossed into the bleeding scandal that would ensue." Ardmoor shook his head. "Not the way to start a marriage. Not at his age."

"The day Joy met Emily, she told me that Lady Emily was going to be her new mother. Do you know the little dear made it one of her Christmas wishes?"

"Thought having her father home was her wish."

"Her first wish. Her second was having Emily as her new mother." Maddy looked at Ardmoor. "I think Laurel would approve of Emily."

"I bloody well think so, too." He grunted. "We just have to see they do this thing up the proper way. No dashing to Scotland this time."

"We can't interfere, Ardmoor! We must let them decide for themselves if they'll suit."

"I like Wickerdun," Maddy said.

Emily sipped her morning chocolate before she spoke. *Was Maddy under orders to find out if she'd made up her mind about Wickerdun?* "Yes, he's an agreeable sort. Always has been."

"Ah, you've known him for most of your life. Robert mentioned Wickerdun always came here with him on school holiday instead of going to his own home."

"Yes. I believe Wickerdun found our home and family preferable to his own."

Maddy smiled and nodded. "Did I tell you about the first time Robert introduced me to Wickerdun? My first impression was of a fool. A pleasant fool, but a fool none-the-less."

"I believe you did tell me that story."

"He's not a fool, Emily," Maddy said as she leaned close. "He pretended to be a buffoon to put me at ease. A fine quality in a man."

"Yes." Emily finished her chocolate and rose from the table. "You may tell my brother I'm well aware of Wickerdun's fine qualities, but I haven't made up my mind."

After learning Lord Geoffrey had gone riding, Emily judged it safe to visit the nursery, specifically Joy, without running into the girl's father. But that had to wait because Ardmoor insisted on speaking to her.

"They fell in love and before anyone knew what was what, the bl...young fools dashed to Gretna Green!" Ardmoor stomped his peg for emphasis.

Emily had heard this tale. "They were young and impetuous and in love. Your sister, Laurel, was what— all of eighteen? Lord Geoffrey not much older, surely." Emily shrugged. "It's in the past, and no good for the children to dredge it up."

"Ah, there you have it! No dashing off to Gretna Green again. Must think of the children. And your brother. Spode would bl...well have the man's ba...if you were the object of scandal."

What was Ardmoor implying? "I have no intention of dashing off to Gretna Green, I assure you."

"Good. All that bl...rot about Geoffrey being a womanizer, thief, and murderer is just that—balderdash put out by his father so he could get his hands on Geoffrey's children after Laurel died. Geoffrey's a good man."

Emily arched her brow. "As good as his brother?"

Ardmoor smiled. "That's for you to decide, my dear."

Due to the shrieking of the princess and the pirates, and the fact that he was the princess' personal riding dragon, Geoffrey wasn't aware of Lady Emily's presence until he realized his roar wasn't met with squeals of glee, but nervous giggles. He lifted his head and steadied the princess on his back as he sat back on his heels.

The woman's expression was priceless. Eyes opened wide in shock, her mouth agape, with her face turning redder by the moment. Likely she'd never seen the sight of a father playing with his children in the nursery.

"Lady Emily," Geoffrey said as he set Joy on her feet and rose.

"I'm sorry, I didn't think you'd—I'm sorry to intrude," she said as she stepped back.

"Just the person I wanted to see." He turned to his children. "We'll finish this later. Time to get ready for ice skating." He turned to Emily. "Would you care to join us?"

"Join you?" She looked like he was asking her to join him in plunging from the rooftop to the courtyard below.

"For ice skating. You do ice skate?"

"She's a wonderful ice skater, Papa," Joy said.

"She taught me how to spin fast!" Henry said.

"Bang up skater," Simon said.

"Top of the trees," Hunter added.

"Where do you hear such language?" Geoffrey asked. "Never mind." *Ardmoor. At least he remembers not to curse around them.* "So you'll join us, Lady Emily?" Her eyes darted from him to each of the children. "We really must talk."

"Talk?" She looked at Joy and then at him. "Er, I—"

"We'll meet you out front. Do hurry, the children are keen to skate whilst the ice is still thick enough to hold us all."

Her eyes were like mirrors, their color hazel, reflecting whatever color dominated her sight—shades of grey, blue, green and brown. Friendly eyes. He'd swear they laughed and spoke to him, yet he needed no sound to hear. Geoffrey wanted to spend the rest of his life gazing into this woman's eyes.

Once at the pond, with the children amusing themselves, Geoffrey skated alongside Emily, careful to keep close. "Lady Emily, I apologize for my behavior when first we met. It was unconscionable. I'll not offer excuses. I know I was too quick in jumping to conclusions. I'm deeply sorry for my thoughtless words, which I know now to be false. Please accept my humblest apology."

Emily turned to him and smiled. "Oh, apology accepted. I understood later why you were so enraged. Actually..." She paused and Geoffrey waited for her to continue, his heart still speeding from the sight of her sudden smile. "Although you were unaccountably rude, boorish and uncivilized, I admired the fact your concern for your children caused you to act like a madman."

"You admired that?" He wished she'd turn and smile at him again.

"I did." She gave him a quick glance. "Was that what you wanted to talk to me about?"

He smiled and shook his head. "Joy told me about her wish for you and me to marry." He caught her when she lost her balance, and steadied her. "She's convinced it will be so, because she said the stars twinkled at her." He peeked at Emily's face, hidden under a bonnet and scarf. "You needn't be embarrassed. It's not as if you put the idea into her head."

Emily looked at him in horror. "Oh, no, of course not!" she exclaimed, and promptly lost her balance. He caught her before she fell. "Thank you, Lord Geoffrey. The first day we met, Joy told me she wanted me to marry you so you would stay home."

"But I am staying home." He smiled when she blushed. "Her first wish, remember? Even so, she still wishes us to wed. My sons think it a splendid idea." He smiled at the quick look she darted his way. "What about you? Shall we?" This time when he caught her as she lost her balance, he pulled her down on top of him.

"Bloody ice!"

"Careful, Ardmoor. Maddy'll have my head if you come to harm! Had to promise I'd keep an eye on you."

"Treats me like I'm a bloody china doll! I won't break if I fall! Half my leg is gone already, and the peg can be replaced."

"Surely your sister worries about the part of you that can't be replaced," Wickerdun suggested.

"Just what we need, a bloody peacemaker." Ardmoor whipped his head around at the sound of Spode's low whistle. Looked in the direction Spode and Wickerdun stared. "Bloody hell!" The two men beside him remained silent while they watched Geoffrey assist Emily to her feet. The three men continued forward.

Geoffrey was positive she was as aroused as he. Well, perhaps not as aroused, but she was interested. There'd been no screaming for him to unhand her. No strident demands he release her. She'd stared at him with a look of wonder. His cheek still tingled where she'd touched and stroked. True, she'd been wearing mittens, but his cheek still tingled, which led him to wonder what it would feel like if her bare fingers touched and stroked. His mind conjured up a picture of her touching his bare body. Which in turn inflamed that part of him that had been idle for so long. That's when her eyes widened even more.

"I want to kiss you." It was a foolish thing to say. He realized that as soon as the words passed his lips. She struggled to rise, but collapsed and gazed into his eyes.

"Why?"

Geoffrey blinked. *Why?* "Why? Because...I've had the urge to pull you into my arms and kiss you from the first moment I saw you."

She drew back and arched a brow at him. "The first moment you saw me you accused me of conspiring to take your children from you. The words you used, however, were more colorful."

Geoffrey smiled and watched her eyes darken; his smile deepened. "True. But I was attracted to you, which might have angered me."

"Why should..."

Geoffrey looked up at the four pairs of eyes peering down at them. "We were discussing Joy's wish."

"Ooh, ooh! Has Lady Emily—"

Geoffrey broke in. "A lady's decision is never rushed, princess." He helped Emily rise, but growled softly upon spying the approach of his brother, Spode and Ardmoor.

Emily declined all offers to escort her back to the house. Knew her face didn't stop burning until she was in sight of her home. *Everyone* had seen her lying on top of Lord Geoffrey! What was she about? Why hadn't she immediately removed herself from his person? Emily covered her cheeks with her mittened hands. *She'd felt his desire for her!* She shook her head. It had been the most thrilling experience of her life. *Ooh, but she was wanton!*

The men gathered in Spode's library, Spode seated behind his desk, with Ardmoor and Wickerdun seated next to him. Geoffrey had the unsettling feeling of being back at school, waiting to be paddled for another *unfortunate incident.*

"Will you explain to me," Spode began, "what we saw on the lake?"

Geoffrey took a deep breath while casting about for a suitable reply that wouldn't offend. Impossible. "I asked Lady Emily to marry me. She lost her balance, and before she could fall onto the ice, I allowed her to fall on top of me." Geoffrey could swear he heard his brother's teeth grinding, but he kept his eyes on Spode. Spode's brows rose to nearly meet his hairline. "You asked my sister—"

"I bloody well saw this coming," Ardmoor declared. "Maddy and I discussed this only last evening." He nodded as three pairs of eyes swung to him. "Was obvious they couldn't keep their eyes off one another."

His brother looked at him. "Your offer for Lady Emily's hand in marriage comes rather suddenly. Why? Is it because you knew I wanted her as wife?"

"No," Geoffrey said. "No, it's nothing like that. She..." He shook his head, wondering if he could explain what he didn't fully understand. "I never intended to wed again. Then I met Lady Emily. I was drawn to her, but assumed her typical of her class. Too, I knew her destined for you, so I fought against the attraction. The more I saw of her, listened to her conversation, the more I realized she's different. This morning the children told me how Lady Emily has helped them since Spode and Maddy wed. How kind she is, how she tried to do the things Maddy used to do, but could no longer because of the baby. That's when I knew Lady Emily was very special. Then Joy told me about her Christmas wish for Lady Emily and me to wed, so I knew then I had to woo her and wed her."

"A Christmas wish?" Wickerdun exclaimed. "You would wed her because of a child's Christmas wish?"

"Umm," Spode said, his face creased with frowns.

"Don't make light of it, Wickerdun," Ardmoor said. "Not only is your brother drawn to Lady Emily because of her wild blood, but Joy's wish was uttered with the sincerity and purity of heart only a child can claim. Then, too, Joy has the wild blood, so that makes her wish more potent."

"And she said the star twinkled at her," Geoffrey added.

"Ah," Spode said, still frowning.

"Are you all mad?" Wickerdun asked as he looked at each man in turn.

"Not at all," Geoffrey said.

"No running to Gretna bloody Green this time," Ardmoor said.

"*What?*" Spode asked.

"Lord," Wickerdun said with a sigh, "I'd almost forgotten."

Geoffrey looked at Spode. "I wouldn't. I want a church wedding with my children present."

"You married in Gretna Green?" Spode looked from Geoffrey to Ardmoor.

"I was in the army at the time, but from what I was told, Geoffrey and my sister Laurel took one bloody look at each other and fell in love. Her first ball, and she and Geoffrey were caught on the bleeding balcony, so—"

Geoffrey cut in, "We decided not to wait, so we ran to Gretna Green. Never regretted it, the marriage that is, just the scandal it caused."

Geoffrey waited, knowing his future hung in the balance. Would the Earl of Spode allow his sister to wed him, or would he go through with plans for his sister to wed Wickerdun? Surely the man would choose Wickerdun.

And what of his brother? Geoffrey turned to look at Wickerdun. They were slowly beginning to know one another after so many years apart. Would this cause a breach that could never be mended?

"What did my sister say to your proposal?" Spode asked.

Geoffrey blinked. *Bloody hell!* "Ah. She never said as we were interrupted by my children." The way Spode tapped his fingers together didn't bode well, surely. "She didn't say no." Geoffrey thought back. "She seemed interested. She touched my cheek." *Why had he said that?* He didn't like how Spode sat back and stared at him.

"I withdraw my offer, Spode," Wickerdun said as he rose. "I've heard enough."

Geoffrey rose as well, but Ardmoor grabbed his arm and shook his head.

Emily paced in her bedchamber, awaiting Spode's request for her presence. It was only a matter of time. Her brother would demand an explanation, quite rightfully, too, after what he'd seen. What *everyone* had seen! Emily covered her face with her hands in mortification. She giggled. Oh, how it must have looked. Another giggle, and now a sob.

Had Lord Geoffrey proposed to her? She'd been told he was a great tease, a jokester. Before this morning she'd not believed Maddy and Ardmoor, seeing only a surly and solemn Lord Geoffrey. Had he been serious or making a joke? She groaned. What kind of sister was she, wondering if Lord Geoffrey had proposed to her when Wickerdun was awaiting her answer for his proposal of marriage? Surely Spode expected her to accept Wickerdun. He'd never allow her to wed Lord Geoffrey.

Drat! The image of Lord Geoffrey's grey eyes and his devastating smile kept getting in the way when she tried to picture Wickerdun. Also his...whatever it was, his male part. She'd never forget the hardness, or the sudden knowledge of what it was she was feeling. He'd known when she'd understood. That's when he said he wanted to kiss her. Emily's stomach flipped at the memory. She groaned. How could she possibly—with all due respect and honor—accept Wickerdun's proposal when it was his brother who had invaded her mind, and she feared, her heart?

"She may not accept me," Geoffrey said. "Spode might—"

His brother rested a hand on his shoulder. "I believe she will accept you, and I believe Spode will allow her to wed you."

As much as Geoffrey wanted to marry Lady Emily, he didn't want to lose his brother's friendship. "I never expected, or intended, to come between you and Lady Emily. If I could—"

His brother squeezed his shoulder. "Say no more on the subject. When I heard you say she touched your cheek, I knew it was over." Wickerdun gave him a slight smile. "So did Spode. Lady Emily is a fine woman. I shall be pleased to have her as sister-in-law. I shall rejoice at your wedding. Truly."

Emily smoothed the skirt of her gown until she could no longer avoid her brother's eyes. She looked up. "I don't want to disappoint you."

Spode exhaled. "That's not what I asked, Em. As for disappointing me, Wickerdun has withdrawn his proposal, so accepting him now is a moot point."

Her smile was immediate, but quickly faded. "Is he very angry? Oh, I don't want to come between you and Wickerdun!" Both hands pressed her chest. "Oh, no! Wickerdun and Lord Geoffrey!"

"Our friendship is strong enough to weather this. Rest assured the brothers have settled it between them. Now, judging by the smile I saw, you weren't going to accept Wickerdun's proposal. So, I ask again, shall I allow Lord Geoffrey to court you?"

Emily shifted. "Did he ask for permission?" She breathed a little easier when Spode smiled.

"No, he said he asked you to marry him. But I'd rather go through the formalities if you don't mind."

Emily smiled and nodded her head. "Yes, that would be best."

"I think we should go back inside, Em," Geoffrey whispered before nipping her ear lobe. He chuckled when she shivered and clung to him. "Really, we..." Well, he couldn't disappoint her if she wanted to kiss him, could he?

"Why can't we run to Gretna Green?" Emily asked after their kiss.

"Well," he said as he leaned his forehead against hers, "one, your brother would have my head, two, my brother would have another part of my anatomy, and three, Ardmoor says he'd teach my children every curse word he knows, including Spanish and Portuguese, if I dragged you north and caused another scandal. Fourth, Maddy would lecture me from now until my ears fell off, fifth, the children are looking forward to the wedding, and last but not least, our wedding is tomorrow." He smiled when she laughed.

"The six months have gone by quickly, haven't they?" She looked into his eyes. "Then there are times—"

"Like now when it seems like we'll never be allowed to be together alone—"

"For more than a few minutes—"

He held her closer while glaring at Ardmoor over her head. "Without someone coming to find out where we've taken ourselves to find some privacy."

Ardmoor winked at Geoffrey and silently backed away.

Geoffrey looked down at Emily. "I bless the day Joy met you." His chest swelled at her large smile.

"Don't forget her Christmas wishes."

"Never, my love."

"My dearest love," she replied, tugging on his head and meeting his lips with hers.

Be sure to visit Gerri's website
http://www.gerribowen.com

Miracles and Mistletoe

by Kimberly Grant

Marla passed the sewing needle through the last piece of popcorn. The fluffy kernel split into several bits and sifted to the floor. Spearmint green and candy-apple red lights shimmered and blurred beyond her lashes.

She scooped up the latest ruined bit of garland. If her fingers didn't still, she and Chance would never finish decorating the tree this Christmas Eve. But at least the popcorn pieces were more easily picked up than other fragments in her life.

Chance's warm hands gripped her shoulders, and he nuzzled her left ear. "You seem miles away."

Leaning back, she let the string of plump cranberries and white corn drape over her leg. "Just a little preoccupied."

"Don't worry." Gentle, ginger-scented kisses rained upon her cheek and chin. Chance sat down, pulled her body close and rocked her to the seasonal sounds of one-horse open sleighs playing on the radio. "If Doctor Hogan's office said they'd phone with the results, they will."

"Unless they've forgotten. Or there's bad news." Each word tasted worse, and their cumulative bitterness lingered on her tongue.

The mantel clock ticked off more seconds. In the fireplace, flames licked at the logs and spat sparks against the fire screen. One-thirty-six. Sandy, Doctor

211

Hogan's secretary, had mentioned the office closing at three on Christmas Eve.

An hour and twenty-four minutes remained until the long holiday weekend. The churning in her belly intensified as Marla glanced out the window. In light of the weather forecast, they'd likely already gone home for the holidays. Her fingers curled into a fist and then straightened. More tears burned her eyes, and she blinked them back. Chance's shoulder massage failed to dispel the myriad feelings refusing to settle and allow her soul some respite. The wind-driven snow beyond the picture window was anything but a blessing. Definitely, a curse. A frozen, unrelenting curse cast upon her.

The song ended. Another broadcast blared, warning of worsening weather conditions. A nasal-voiced man detailed the blizzard holding Baxter's Bluff and miles of Colorado mountain land in its icy grip. At Chance's urging, she stood and made her stiff-legged way toward the fireplace. Once there, he eased her onto the Navajo blanket and headed to the kitchen.

He returned bearing two steaming mugs of mulled wine. She gripped the handle of her cup and sniffed. Rich and full-bodied. Deep red, just like her blood when drawn by Hannah, Doctor Hogan's raven-haired lab technician.

On his knees, Chance tapped his steaming moose-patterned mug against hers. "Here's to many years of happiness."

The sip she took soured when it hit her throat. She forced the wine and saliva down and scrambled to her feet. "Have you forgotten my life has been marked?"

Chance nodded, a section of blond hair brushing against his right eyebrow. "You're not a target, Marla. You know as well as I those test results are going to be good news."

"If I knew, I wouldn't be breaking every other piece of popcorn and messing up what would otherwise be my second-to-most favorite day of the year." Her body met with the cold leather couch cushions, and she curled her legs underneath her.

"There's still another hour and twenty minutes until the office closes. They're probably just swamped with stuff at the last minute. I know the lumberyard was. Dan and I had a devil of a time while we answered calls and delivered those emergency loads the past day and a half."

Something burst inside her brain. Her scream filled the living room. "Those people were prepared. Prepared for bad weather. But I'm not prepared for an uncertain future."

After years of searching for a man with whom to share her life, she'd met Chance at a winter carnival two weeks ago. His blue eyes and heart-stopping smile nullified the wind chill and all else that magical Wednesday evening.

Those long legs, clad in faded denim and finished with cowboy boots of specially tooled brown leather, now carried him to her in shorter time than it took to swallow. He set down his mug, found a spot beside her and bundled her quaking body close.

"I know what's really bothering you." His words carried on the tang of Napa Valley grapes.

"Probably so, but that won't quell these thoughts. I need to know what's next in my therapy. If the tumor has shrunk, I can have the surgery. And we'll enjoy the weekend in Aspen as we'd planned. You made the reservations?" She reached up and combed the wayward shock of hair off his forehead.

Chance snatched her free hand. One by one, he kissed the fingertips and then positioned her palm over his heart. "Absolutely."

Laughter sneaked up from her belly and shot past her tongue before she could close her mouth. "Always a planner. So am I...well, I used to be."

He wrested the mug from her grasp and set it beside his on the glass partition resting atop a base of ornate iron branches. "Our plans will come to pass. And if it will get you under the mistletoe with me before sundown, go ahead and call the doctor's office."

Always the voice of reason, Chance Yardley ranked as one of the most eligible and attractive bachelors in this small Colorado town. He could split wood and ski better than most any man who ever stepped a foot onto wilderness territory. In the short time since their meeting, the seeds of friendship had sewn themselves quite deep and brought a desire and romance she'd never known before.

She wiggled from his embrace and sprinted toward the kitchen. Her navy blue socks met the linoleum, and she skidded to a halt in front of the wall phone. Silence came from the receiver when she placed it next to her ear. Thankfully, the electricity remained on, but for how long?

The scuff-scrape of Chance's boot heels came behind her. With his hand over hers, she replaced the receiver.

"Looks like we're in one of the areas with downed power lines." The sentence sputtered from her lips and died in the surrounding spice-and-pine-scented air. "How stupid of me, praying for a whiter Christmas than ever before."

"Not stupid, just sentimental." He twisted her loose ponytail into a coil and kissed the nape of her neck. "There's only one thing to do." Strong arms spun her around, tipped her back in a pulse-pounding dip and then hauled her upright. Another ginger-flavored kiss warmed her lips. "Have a whole bag of marshmallows and full mugs of mulled wine ready for roasting and toasting when I get back."

"Get back?" The words echoed in her mind and invisible yet icy fingers dragged to the base of her spine. "You can't go out in this weather. Weren't you listening to the announcer? Many of the secondary roads are closed."

Chance's wink shot straight to her heart. "A little snow and a worried woman never stopped me before, and they're not about to stop me now."

Each stretch of Marla's fingers combed the rabbit fur lining the leather gloves. Another sweep of Chance's arm, and the utility brush cleared a wider section of the windshield.

More bad news broadcast from the radio. She hummed along with the Highlander's engine. The back of her mitten cleared condensation from the passenger side window, and she glanced out.

Always the landmark visitors to this remote land parcel noticed first, the gleaming metal mailbox lay blanketed in snow. The ponderosa pines remained visible, and their stout wind-whipped branches swatted at the sideways snowfall. Chance tapped on the dry top section of the driver's side window, and she followed his pointing finger.

A slight twist adjusted the defroster control. No other man had ever made such a sacrifice for her. Two had claimed their undying love and devotion, but all bets and promises were off when they met someone else.

Chance Yardley was a different breed. Always wearing a wide grin. Hair the color of corn silk caught in sunlight. Eyes as blue as a Colorado sky when all the clouds stayed away.

Her tongue tingled from the mint candy, and a warm current threaded throughout her body. If this was true love, may God allow it to grow. Doctor Hogan seemed certain her ovarian tumor would respond favorably to the last dose of radiation. If so, and the blood test and MRI mirrored his faith, surgery would become possible and give her a new lease on life and love with Chance Yardley.

A click sounded, and the opposite door opened. A gust of wind slapped her cheek and whistled around her head before settling.

She drew in a cleansing breath and blew it out. "I'll pay for the gas."

Chance climbed behind the wheel and slammed the

door closed. "Not this time. It won't take long to reach the lumberyard." He grabbed a section of her hood and tugged. "Might as well take you there to make the call. Then you'll get your Christmas surprise a little early."

Though the tires devoured the drifts without problem, each dip or turn bumped Marla's body against the door or pitched her toward his side of the vehicle. Chance adjusted the heater to a higher setting. Anything was worth the risk to make Marla Anders, the woman he loved, happy this holiday season.

"You just bought this truck two months ago. It's not wise risking a wreck. Whether today or Tuesday, my hearing the news about the labs and MRI won't make any difference in the overall diagnosis."

He navigated a known sharp turn. "But it will make a difference in your holidays."

"What if the lines near Doctor Hogan's office are also down?" Marla glanced at him and then out her window. "Our braving this blizzard will be a wasted effort."

"We could play what-if until the spring thaw. It won't help matters. Today, on the eve of a Christian holiday, we're going to keep the faith."

Her body shrank against the seat, a dun-brown bundle, still as a lone shock of wheat in an after-harvest field.

He adjusted the flow of warm air her way. "You shouldn't be out in this weather if you're going to have surgery after the holidays."

Marla shifted in the seat, removed her mittens and fumbled with her lap belt. "If it weren't for this dreadful disease, I'd be healthy as anyone. And if I weren't a working-class woman and had a bit more money, a certain gift would be wrapped and waiting for you underneath the Christmas tree."

Chance shifted gears and navigated another hairpin turn in the mountain pass. "I already have the best gift of all this year."

Her tiny nose quivered much like a snowshoe rabbit's. "What if we get stuck?" She freed the buckling device of her restraint. Her glossy pink lips puckered. "My gym membership ended when they phased out my job at the lodge and I moved here almost a year ago. Sedentary secretaries aren't known for their muscles and skill at shoveling deep snow."

He focused his attention on the treacherous pathway beyond the windshield. "Muscles aren't important. Besides, you're the prettiest woman in this part of the wilds. Knew that the moment my skates hit the pond in Mariposa the Wednesday before last."

The red needle hovered over the white thirty. No sense risking a skid, but he just had to get her to a phone in time to reach Doctor Hogan's office. Her holidays hinged on news only they could convey.

"Really?" A rustling sounded as she unzipped the parka. The visor came down, and she fussed with her hair. "Lucky for you I put on some makeup while you were warming up the truck. Otherwise, you might get stranded with a woman who'd make you think twice about meeting her under the mistletoe."

Marla raised her arm. A shaft of sunlight struck the shocking-pink face of her sports watch. Only a half hour until Doctor Hogan and his office staff would sign out to the answering service and start their Christmas holidays. That meant three and a half days from the next sunset until they'd call with her results.

Chance rapped on her window. "I think we can make it. The drifts are pretty deep, but the snow's letting up some."

"I don't want you risking your life for me. Please, get back in here. Let's turn around."

No matter how many times she presented her case, Chance had a rebuttal and stance that defied defeat. They'd been safe from harm thus far, but there wasn't any promise their good luck would continue.

Her palm met with the dashboard. The stinging

traveled from her wrist midway up her forearm, and she flexed her fingers. Luck? Where was that when she needed some? If only those lines feeding her phone connection weren't downed by this dumb snowstorm.

Chance circled the Highlander a couple more times. No traffic approached in either direction. They were out here alone. But at least the near whiteout conditions had improved. Still, if something happened to Chance or his new truck, she wouldn't forgive herself.

Each time Chance looked heavenward, his breath formed an ice fog in front of his face. Who or what was he praying for? Today, Lucifer had her in his clutches and he wasn't letting go. Only a moron like her would let Chance pull down that winding drive and embark on this senseless trip.

Chance entered the truck, shifted gears and pointed the vehicle toward the lumberyard he co-owned with his father, Jake, and brother, Dan. "Give me a hint about what you got me for Christmas?" His tongue swiped along the narrow blond strip of whiskers above his upper lip.

"No way." She reached out, stroked his cheek and withdrew her touch. Messing with him while he was driving on dangerous roadways was a surefire way to cause an accident.

"I think you'll like what I got yooooouuuu..." His last syllable hissed out and faded.

A buck emerged from the berm on her side. Chance guided the vehicle to the left. The wheels did a wicked dance over the drifted snow, but he avoided the startled creature. Marla squeezed her eyes closed for a heartbeat and then glanced in the portion of the side-view mirror not coated with snow. Standing in the middle of the path they'd just driven, the buck with a trophy rack stared after them.

"Sure was close." Chance steered them back to the right. "God was with us back there."

Marla swallowed. Her pulse ticked faster than Missus Galloway's metronome during those horrible piano lessons so many years ago. No matter how hard she tried, she never became the virtuoso her mother desired.

Playing in those coffee bars and nightclubs isn't for any woman with morals. Ellie Anders' diatribe cycled in her mind. *Put your college education to proper use and stop being such a free spirit. Your spirit isn't free. It belongs to God, just like your soul.*

Marla chewed the stale wad of spearmint gum. The latest chomp caught her tongue in her teeth. She winced. God will have more than my soul if Satan doesn't stay away today.

Chance jostled her arm. "Everything okay over there? Seems keeping your Christmas present a surprise is bothering you."

Two blinks banished the approaching tears. "A surprise is bothering me, but it's one no one can see without an x-ray. Also one whose outcome they cannot accurately predict." Doctors were special, indeed, but her health rested in far more divine hands.

Since their departure, the wind changed direction and now hurled flakes in a northwesterly manner. Chance tapped the brake pedal. No doubt about it. The red-lettered sign of YARDLEY LUMBER was right ahead. Now Marla could make her phone call.

"Won't be long now. The cell phone I forgot to take with me is on the desk. Use that." He veered off the deserted roadway and shifted to a stop in front of the chained gate.

Marla toyed with the zipper on her pale blue parka. "You don't know how much this means. Not many would have ventured out because some nervous woman wanted to know her test results."

He leaned across the gearshift and kissed her full mouth. Her lips opened and deepened the kiss. A moan floated over her tongue and onto his. A lifetime of love with Marla would be the best reward of all.

Returning to his side, he turned off the ignition,

pulled out the keys and pocketed them. "Looks like the yard gate drifted shut. I'll have to shovel out. Stay warm in here, and I'll come get you in a couple minutes."

"But..." Her hand grazed his arm.

"Don't worry. We'll have plenty of time when we get back to enjoy Christmas Eve together."

Don't worry? Bits of peppermint lodged in Marla's back teeth. That was so easy for him to say. He wasn't the one harboring a time bomb inside his body.

But diffusing it would prove far more difficult than doing the same with her curiosity.

With each shovelful of snow Chance flung away from the gate, she shivered. His breath came out in fogged bursts. She opened the window a bit. He sang, "...was a jolly, happy soul." But Chance wasn't the type to sport a corncob pipe, and his nose was pleasant, not button-size at all.

She closed the window and closed her eyes. Their meeting at the Winter Carnival was the stuff of which storybooks are made. Chance had steadied her as they skated over the pond, telling her jokes and about his love of hiking and outdoor sports. He'd also mentioned a ski trip he'd planned for that weekend.

The ski trip he cancelled and instead spent a weekend getaway with her visiting an art gallery, touring a winery and enjoying two romantic Italian dinners among other things.

Her door opened. She blinked and pitched sideways. Chance caught her and eased her descent into a smaller snowdrift. His cheeks shone pink, but it wasn't any use telling him of his flush. Rugged men like Chance were born hunters and providers. His Alpha carried through to his core, but it was so heartening when his softer side surfaced.

Freeing herself from his grasp, she skirted the snow-crusted bumper. Her feet left the ground as Chance hauled her into arms that loaded lumber and more for his business customers six days a week.

"Can't have you falling down. I'll carry you until we're inside the gate." The wide grin parted his kissable lips. Lips still faintly scented from the mulling spices.

Marla looked at the sky. Snowflakes teased her cheeks and lips, bestowing icy pecks before melting into oblivion. "Are you forgetting I'm not the one who almost fell while removing ice skates?"

His warm, hearty laugh hit her face. "But only because someone bumped me from behind." He bounced her and, when she settled, played vampire with her neck. "Otherwise, nothing will ever knock me off my feet."

"Nothing?" Stop challenging him. Bachelors don't like having their commitment buttons pushed.

"Well..." He winked, sneaked through the open gate, and deposited her on the snow-covered driveway. "Almost nothing."

A miniature version of her living room tree held court in a corner of the showroom. Cast iron chimineas, gas-log inserts, and wood-burning stoves commanded most of the interior's square footage. Marla took a deep breath. Orange-oil polish, probably used on the front counter and cabinetry fashioned by Dan Yardley, filled her nostrils along with the rich natural wood musk.

"Fifty-five years is a long time for a family business to continue operations." She removed her mittens and stuffed them into the parka's pockets. A downward tug on the metal heart zipper opened her down-filled parka.

Chance ran his hands through his hair and brushed the remaining winter powder free. "My grandfather sank lots of time and sweat into this place. The three of us—my dad, my brother, and I—expanded into other sales to supplement those derived from the lumber."

Marla's waterproof snow boots squeaked with each step across the lacquered floorboards. Chance motioned her toward a hallway, and she followed him deeper into the building. To their left through the glass panel, the emerald-green shade of a banker's lamp caught the light of the active bulb beneath. He opened the office door and let her enter first.

Her gaze landed on the silver casing of Chance's cell phone. Only inches away lay the black and white console of the business phone. Chance picked up the receiver, listened for a moment and then replaced it on the base. On the wall behind the desk, a clock face lay in the wooden grizzly bear's belly.

Two-forty-one. The muscles in Marla's throat clenched, and her stomach somersaulted.

Chance's jaw relaxed. "Phone lines are down here, too." He pointed to the cellular phone. "But that should work fine."

The tiny white numbers blended together in her brain. Marla's tingling fingers punched each digit in the sequence. May I not dial somewhere other than the place I'm seeking. Five times the phone rang. Sandy always answered in a prompt and courteous manner, no matter how hectic the office schedule.

Marla sank into the leather captain's chair, swung right then left. Two more rings. No one answering. "They've likely gone home. But, if so, the answering service should have picked up."

"Hang up and try again. Maybe they're busy getting everything in order before closing down for Christmas." Chance poured water from the glass carafe into the coffeemaker.

Another sniff brought the scent of roasted coffee beans, and she disconnected the call. "Doctor Hogan wouldn't put his staff's lives at risk. He probably had them close once the first reports came through from the weather bureau." Her fingers fused around the phone's casing and refused to relinquish their hold.

Why not? Try one more time. She glanced at the wall clock. The slender black minute hand had swept into position over the ten. If no one answered now, they likely wouldn't until Tuesday.

Marla's scalp tingled. By Tuesday, she'd have every

auburn hair plucked out and lining the bathroom trashcan.

Once again, she dialed Doctor Hogan's office. If only she hadn't skipped church last Sunday instead of spending the time talking sexy to Chance...

On the third ring, Sandy answered.

A thousand pins might have pricked her body. Marla lunged from the chair, almost colliding with Chance and the coffee can over which he was placing a plastic lid.

"Sandy, it's Marla Anders. Has Doctor Hogan had a chance to review my lab results and MRI?"

The medical secretary excused herself from the call, and Marla sidestepped Chase on her trip around the office. Silent minutes passed, but at least she'd gotten through. Sandy wouldn't lock up the office and leave her hanging on the line.

Sandy returned with the news she'd placed the results on Marla's chart, but Doctor Hogan hadn't signed off on them. He'd tried reaching Marla earlier but couldn't. And after leaving the office about a half hour before Marla's call, the internist was on his way to meet his wife and two sons in Denver at The Madrington Inn for the Christmas weekend.

Another swallow took the gum down her throat. "But can't you at least tell me what they say? Or can Jessica go over them with me?"

As Sandy explained the situation further, a ball of fire caught in Marla's belly and shot toward her feet. Jessica had gone home just before the blizzard bore down upon the town, and Sandy couldn't reveal the results without a doctor's presence or signature. The popping and bubbling in her belly mimicked that of the coffeemaker.

Chance caught her by the waist and pulled her backwards. Their bodies collided just as her legs weakened to the point of wobbling against her one hundred and twenty-two pounds.

The secretary apologized several more times and admitted she would remain at the office until the storm subsided. And, before her husband arrived to pick her up, she'd also leave a message for the on-call physician about Marla's tests so he could access the results electronically. Still, a return call to Marla was at the discretion of the covering physician.

Marla gave the secretary Chance's cell phone number, thanked her and hung up. "Guess I'll likely find out on Tuesday. Doctor Hogan's on his way to Denver to meet his family. Maybe the on-call physician will contact me, maybe not. Doctor Hogan and Jessica tried reaching me, but couldn't."

"We could leave a message for Doctor Hogan at the Inn." Chance claimed two mugs from the plastic tray and poured them each some coffee. "He'll remember what those reports said."

"I'm not calling him after working hours. That's not..."

He held the pot midway between the coffeemaker and one of Yardley's promotional mugs. "Polite? Are you going to worry about manners or just plain worry and ruin your whole Christmas?"

"Give me a minute and we'll head back." Chance paused in front of the miniature tree. A minute was more than enough.

The lowest strand of white lights flicked off and on, compliments of a timing mechanism in the cord. He lifted the strand and straightened it over the branch sporting artificial pine needles.

A rush of water came from the kitchen nook. While Marla rinsed out the mugs and coffee pot, he'd take care of something far more important out here, and she wouldn't suspect a thing.

Only a slight tug freed the ornament from the tree. An angel with a frock of white satin and gauze smiled at him with her painted-on ruby lips. Filament secured beads on the hemline. Her tiny hand clutched a golden harp that matched the halo attached to her back by a fine-gauge wire.

Each year as long as he could remember Donna Yardley decorated this same tree, humming Christmas tunes and making sure the tree was positioned for praise from all who entered the business. Cancer had claimed the life of his hard-working mother. Now another person he loved suffered the same dreadful disease. Marla was special. No, special wasn't a strong enough word. In sixteen days, she'd brought him more happiness than a childhood puppy, ten fishing trips to his favorite creek, and everything else that didn't involve his family.

Soft footsteps came in the hallway. He tucked the angel in his inner jacket pocket and guided the zipper tab all the way to the top. Hopefully, his Christmas surprise would allow her to forget today's unsettling events.

"All ready," Marla murmured and came alongside him. "What are you doing staring at the tree?"

Think fast, or she might figure something out. He reached down and pulled the extension cord free. "Just turning off the lights." As he straightened, he noticed her stare.

Lower lip caught in her teeth, she heaved a long breath out her nose. "But the tree was on when we came in. Seems someone wanted it that way." Marla shrugged and met his gaze. "And wasn't there an angel on top?"

Chance fitted her hand in his and guided her toward the front entrance. "Granddaddy didn't like wasting electricity." And Chance Yardley didn't like wasting precious moments that could be spent with an even more precious woman.

The storm's wrath had waned, and the wind flicked flakes against the vehicle's hood and windshield. Marla buffed her mitten-covered hands over her legs. "You haven't said much since we left the lumberyard. I'm not even being serenaded with Christmas songs like you did a couple nights ago."

Chance's grip on the wheel relaxed. "You enjoy my

singing?"

She nodded. "Very much. Reminds me of summers spent in Texas with my maternal grandparents."

"One of my college buddies lives in Laredo."

His whistling wrapped around her better than her favorite woolen blanket. At passing Mister Floodgate's rancher and property, she began a silent countdown. The road conditions were pathetic, but they'd made pretty good time on the return trek. Her left arm shifted over the fringed suede shoulder bag, inside of which lay Chance's cell phone.

She huffed on the window glass, traced a heart in the dampness and wiped it away with her mitten. Doctor Hogan or the on-call physician would call. Holidays were a time of hope. Those white-coated guardians of health wouldn't let her down.

Marshmallows spilled from the bag and over the blanket. Marla speared two on the ends of the steel fork and leaned toward the flames. Both candied puffs caught at the same instant, and she pulled back. Blackened crusts formed, and one breath brought coils of gray-white smoke from the toasted treats. A few spots sizzled amber before extinguishing.

The thump of bootless feet came from behind. Chance had prepared their evening toasting beverage using the bars of dark chocolate she'd ordered from Missus Gardiner. A native of Baxter's Bluff, Harriet Gardiner was a pastry chef who'd won statewide and national competitions for her confectionary genius.

Chance settled onto the blanket beside her. She pulled off one of the melted marshmallows, and a slender ribbon of cream stretched between her hand and the fork tine before breaking. Taking aim on Chance's mouth, she delivered the sticky gift. A bit of candied white gloss covered his lips, but he'd consumed the rest.

"Something tells me you've had lots of practice doing that." His fingers closed over the remaining marshmallow and swept it from the fork.

"I—"

Over her gaping mouth, the gooey fire-kissed treat smeared. Some tucked inside and coated her tongue, and still more rested on the tip of her nose.

Chance doubled over, his heaving body bunching the blanket beneath. The whatnots in the curio cabinet rattled. Marla dropped the fork, licked her lips and set the laughter behind them free. They reached for each other and fell down, kissing, giggling and gasping for breath.

Pleasant notes of John Denver's signature song jingled from Chance's cell phone. Marla broke their bond and dashed toward the foyer. She picked up the phone, pressed the silver button and spoke in as clear a tone as possible under the circumstances.

Doctor Hogan's bass tone greeted her on the opposite end. He presented a synopsis of her lab and radiological findings. Then, he outlined the risks and complications of abdominal surgery and a colleague whom he recommended who practiced in Nevada.

Bottle rockets burst in her brain, and she swallowed hard. "Yes, Doctor Hogan. I appreciate your getting in touch with me." She grabbed the notepad and glided the pen over the pristine white page. "Tuesday morning at nine-thirty. I'll be there. God bless you, this Christmas and always...Yes, I'll take care. Merry Christmas to you and yours."

Her tingling fingers released their hold, and the phone glanced off her stocking-clad foot. She bent down, turned it off and deposited it beside the message she'd scribbled.

In the living room, Chance stood beside the tree, his arms outstretched. Her cold feet carried her to him, and she hugged him so close, the buttons of his evergreen corduroy shirt pressed into her cheek.

"Good news, honey?" His kisses swept over her scalp.

She wiggled from his grasp and looked into his

beguiling eyes. "The tumor has definitely shrunk. And my white count is great. Doctor Hogan wants to talk with me on Tuesday. At the same time, he'll get in touch with an oncologic surgeon colleague. My surgery will be scheduled soon."

Hints of spicy aftershave clung to his cheeks and lingered on her lips after another kiss.

Gold flecks shone in Chance's eyes. "With this weather, guess we won't get a chance to go tobogganing tonight?"

"Tobogganing? You never said anything about that before now."

Pinched in his fingers was a sprig of mistletoe. Chance held it over her head. "Part of my surprise. We'll postpone it for a couple days." He kissed her breathless, pulled away and, while her heart pounded faster, the man-who-made-her-holidays-happier stole another smooch.

She buried her face against his chest. "Having you here for Christmas Eve is the best present ever."

A slight step backward separated Chance from her embrace. "Well, I have something else I think you might like."

More kisses? Another round of toasted marsh-mallows in front of the fireplace? "I'll always like you best."

He lay down the mistletoe, reached behind the tree and produced a beautiful angel whose dainty body rested in his palm. Chance passed her the ornament. "Something for my angel here on earth."

White heat flashed from her neck to her knees. "Me? You think I'm an angel?"

"I don't think so, I know so." Chance lifted her so their lips touched for a second, and then he set her back on her feet.

Around the angel's waist, an organza sash finished in front. Below where the bow tied lay a tiny hasp. She opened the smiling ceramic-bodied cherub and smoothed the skirt. Golden heart links glimmered, and she plucked the piece of jewelry from its hiding place.

Chance teased the bracelet from her fumbling fingers and fastened it around her wrist. The symbols of love formed an eternal chain. He closed the angel and hung her from the topmost bough.

Without speaking, he hastened to the blanket, secured the roasting fork, and decorated one tine with a marshmallow. Only a slight extension of his arm into the fireplace caught the sugary morsel and delivered a charred coating.

He pulled the toasted confection from the fire, puffed out the flame and returned. Toe to toe they stood, the marshmallow less than an inch from their lips.

She shook her wrist, and the golden links whispered over her skin. "My bracelet is beautiful. I only hope the present I've gotten you makes you half as happy as I am. I'm surprised you haven't opened it yet."

Chance clutched her hand, his breath coming in warm huffs against her face. "I love you, Marla. And I hope this is the first day of many we share together. I want to be there for you, during the surgery and long afterward."

The cry corkscrewed up her throat, but she swallowed it whole. "And I want the same. A chance to explore all life has to offer with the man I love, trust and cherish."

Together, they leaned toward the marshmallow. Chance's teeth separated the treat's jet skin, and the molten center met her mouth. Laughing, they made short work of the campfire classic. Soon, only the empty tine remained.

He delivered a quick kiss. "We're sticking together already." The roasting fork struck the carpet.

She tugged him toward the fireplace. "Let's not take any chances. We have the rest of the evening together. There are plenty more marshmallows." Upon reaching the blanket, she let him go, turned and held his face in her trembling hands. "If one marshmallow gets us that close, more might make us inseparable?"

He tickled her sides and lowered her gently onto the woolen throw. "Marshmallows are only the beginning, Marla. Only the beginning for us and our love."

Be sure to visit Kimberly's website
http://www. grant-moore.com/kimberly/

The Christmas Wish

by Rebecca Andrews

"Look Daddy, it's Mommy!" Ryan Connor felt a moment of panic when his six-year old son, Kevin, dashed away from his side and headed to the back of the line.

"Kevin, stop," Ryan shouted. Tired, exasperated parents gave him a quick sympathetic look as he left his coveted spot near the front of the slow moving line and headed for his wayward son. He heard the excitement in Kevin's voice as he cried out 'mamma' and launched himself into a woman's arms.

Ryan's heart took a jolt and then filled with defeat. He'd hoped with therapy and time Kevin would come to understand the death of his mother nearly a year ago was permanent and not something nightly prayers, a birthday wish, or daily visits to Santa Claus could change.

Ryan approached, not knowing what to say to the woman who at the moment had her arms full of his son. The air froze in his chest and the world around him tilted when she raised her head and looked up. Then by sheer force of will he righted it.

Even as his heart galloped away in his chest, his gaze skimmed the delicate, pixie like features, wide, green eyes and a smile that made a man think of sugar and spice. And things not so nice.

Dressed in black pants and a red Christmas sweater that accented her narrow waist and lush curves, the woman was beautiful and a dead ringer for his dead wife.

"Valerie?" The shock of his own voice echoed in his head, even as he asked knowing it couldn't be true.

"No, it's Holly." She detangled herself from Kevin and with an instinct borne of mothers, carefully placed the little girl at her side behind her.

"Can I help you?"

Still in a state of shock, Ryan noted the face and body were amazingly identical, yet the voice was different. Warmed by a rich, lilting accent he couldn't quite place.

"Ask her, Dad," Kevin pleaded, in an over loud whisper.

"I'm sorry. This is all so embarrassing. I'm Ryan Connor and this is my son, Kevin." He settled his hand firmly on Kevin's small shoulder. "He...um...thinks you're—"

She took a step back. "I'm not who you think I am."

Although taken aback at her abrupt interruption, Ryan was stunned at the likeness.

"I know you're not—but, my son thinks...you're his mother."

Looking for something to disprove what he was seeing, he studied the woman's face one more time. Val's green eyes had held flecks of gold she'd covered with solid colored contacts. But this woman's appeared all natural—a true, pure green. The eyes staring back at him slightly angled up at the corners and her upper lip was without doubt a touch fuller, giving her more of an overall exotic look. A perfect look for a model. "And if I didn't know better...I'd think so, too." The woman appeared good and truly shocked at his confession.

She smiled then and Ryan felt as if he'd been zapped full force by a hundred mega-watts.

"Well, that's certainly not the kind of thing one expects to hear."

"Dad..."

"Kevin. Son..." Ryan wiped a shaky hand over his jaw. With the woman who could pass for his wife on so many levels standing right in front of them, it was going to be nearly impossible to convince Kevin that she simply wasn't his mother. "I know what you think, but this woman...Holly...isn't your mother."

"But Dad..." Kevin rolled his eyes in exasperation. "I wished it. I say my prayers every night *and* I asked Santa Claus." Kevin turned once again toward the woman, looked at her with such earnestness in his dark gaze, Ryan felt his heart constrict.

"I'm six now." Kevin announced proudly.

Holly didn't know what to think. The child, little boy handsome, full of charm, and a mirror image of the boldly striking father broke her heart at the faith he'd placed on a wish, a prayer and a childhood myth as he'd learn when he got older. And the father, even with the embarrassed flush staining his cheeks, and the exasperated pinch to his slightly crooked mouth, was gorgeous.

Since coming to the States almost a year earlier, she'd been mistaken nearly everywhere she went as the supermodel whose death had rocked the modeling world. As disconcerting as that had been, it was nothing compared to this little boy's declaration. Sorrow pressed heavily on her heart as she knelt in front of Kevin.

"I'm really sorry, Kevin. I can tell you miss your mum very much. I'm sure wherever she is she misses you, too. Though I may resemble her, I'm not her."

Kevin stepped closer and laid his small, trusting hand gently against her cheek. "It's okay if you don't remember. I'll help you."

Stunned by the innocence of his words and not knowing what else to say, Holly stood.

"I'm hungry and you promised I could ride the train," her young cousin, Abby, whined.

"But I thought you wanted to see Santa?"

"It looks like we're not going to see Santa anytime soon." Ryan directed Holly's attention to the sign that indicated Santa had gone to dinner and to one of Santa's Elves making her way down the line speaking to parents. Frustration and disappointment etched on the faces of parents and children alike.

"Right then..." Holly said, turning back to Abby. "What would you like to eat?"

"Dad, I'm hungry too. Can we go to the food court?"

The food court was a revolving door of humanity as people settled down for a quick break and a bite to eat before heading back out into the insanity for more shopping.

With Ryan and Kevin in one food line and she and Abby in another, Holly took a moment to study the handsome man.

Long legs covered in denim that fit snugly across his rear, and the polo-shirt he wore stretched nicely over an impressive chest and biceps. But his face drew her ultimate attention. Thick, sable, wavy hair, dark eyes to match and a strong jaw line made him wildly handsome. Yet his slightly crooked mouth lent an air of charm. This man could be trouble, because the simple sight of him made her heart dance.

"Dad! How come we're not sitting with Mom?"

Ryan swallowed hard to get his bite of food down. "Because, Kevin, other than her name is Holly, we don't know her. She's a nice lady who happens to look like your mom, but she's not. You need to understand that." His heart dipped at the heartbroken look that settled on his son's face, the same look he saw on his own face way too often. He'd give anything to erase it. "Eat up. You can play for a little while and then we'll go see Santa."

Holly gathered their trash and carried it to a nearby trash receptacle. She needed to collect Abby and head back to Santa's Workshop.

She watched Kevin leap off the slide in the enclosed play area and disappear under an array of multicolored plastic balls, and following him Abby jumped. Seconds later, they both emerged from under the balls laughing and headed back to the slide to do it all over again.

At the top, Kevin turned, looked directly at her, smiled and yelled, "Watch this, Mom." He jumped and her heart did an unsteady flip. She needed to speak to his father.

"Mr. Connor," Holly said sliding into a chair at his table. "You seem like a nice man. I'm simply having a hard time believing I resemble your wife that much."

"That makes two of us." Ryan shifted in his seat, removed his wallet and took out his favorite picture of Valerie. He remembered the day the photo had been taken like it was yesterday. It wasn't a professional photo, but one they'd taken with an impulsively purchased disposable camera on a sunny, spring afternoon in Central Park. Back then they'd been so carefree and happy. With one phone call the years of hard work Val had put into her career came full circle. And his life suddenly spun crazily out of control as the modeling agency she worked for planned to launch her internationally. They had her scheduled to fly to Milan to start shooting for the fall. Ryan smiled and let his gaze scan the face of the woman across from him again. Her hair was the same shade of copper, with subtle highlights that looked real and not bought and paid for in a pricy salon. The familiar delicacy of her face made his heart catch. The likeness was simply amazing. He handed the worn photo to Holly.

The supermodel whose face had appeared all over the fashion magazines stared back at her. Shock shot clear to Holly's toes. No wonder Kevin had mistaken her for his mother. Except for some very subtle differences, she could be the woman in the photo.

Holly's worried gaze met his and she laid a hand gently over his much larger one. "I'm sorry for your loss. This must be so difficult for you,"—she handed the photo back—"but you've got to find a way for Kevin to understand I'm not his mum."

Frustration laced his words. "Do you think I don't know this? I've had him in therapy, we take flowers to the cemetery once a week, still no matter how much it's explained to him, he still insists..."

He wiped a shaky hand across his jaw. She was right. Kevin needed to understand his mother was gone and not coming back. And it was essential Ryan convince him *Holly* was not his mother.

"I'm really sorry Kevin made you feel uncomfortable. It's been so hard on him since his mom died. Maybe if you spent some time with him, he'd realize you're not his mother."

Startled by his unexpected suggestion, Holly leaned back in her chair. "I hardly know you and I don't think it's appropriate. Besides what if it backfires and he believes more firmly that I am? You and I both know I'm not, but convincing that little boy's heart may be quite another matter."

In a flurry of excitement, Kevin and Abby rushed to the table. "Dad, Abby invited me to her party. Can I go? Can I?"

"When's the party?"

"Next Saturday," Holly supplied.

"I'm sorry, Kevin. We have other plans that night."

"But, Dad, she's going to have real reindeer from the North Pole and Santa's going to be there. Pulleeze."

"I'm sorry, son, maybe another time."

Ryan scrawled his cell number on a napkin and pushed it toward Holly, then stood. "I don't see any other way. I could really use your help. Please, just think about it."

Holly settled down with the romance novel she'd begun last week. Nothing like a little romance to stir an empty heart, she thought wistfully as her mind wandered back to the day's strange events and to the phone number Ryan had written on the napkin she'd tucked into her purse.

She couldn't concentrate on the book because Ryan and Kevin kept creeping into her thoughts. Father and son. She'd been caught off guard at the little boy's utterance, and then he'd launched himself into her arms, and for a split second she'd clung to that sweet smelling little boy and the long buried dream his words conjured burst to life. Straight away she'd squashed it down and released him. But, oh, how her heart mirrored the simplicity of his little boy's wish and prayer.

If only Santa could make wishes come true as easily as Kevin believed. And the tragedy was going to come when all of Kevin's wishes and prayers went unanswered and he discovered Santa Claus was a fraud. She knew what it felt like to lose a parent and time didn't lessen the impact. She could only imagine the heartbreak and sorrow of a child so young. Holly's loss had been twofold. The accident that claimed her parents' lives a few years ago had also narrowed her chances to nearly zero of one day having her own family.

With a heavy heart Holly sighed. She'd never been a mother and it was unlikely she ever would.

Yet that didn't stop her heart from aching with the sadness Kevin must be going through.

The question that kept repeating...did Ryan really need her help, or was his appeal just a lure to get her into their lives? Her heart beat with an excited little bump as she wondered if that prospect would be so bad.

"Mr. Connor, this is Holly. I've been doing a lot of thinking about what you said and maybe you're right. Maybe I can help convince Kevin I'm not his mum."

"Great. Just in case you decided to agree, I gave some thought to what we could do. The kids are out of school, and I'm officially on vacation, so I thought we might take the kids to see the new Disney movie, get some pizza, then check out the lights and tree in Rockefeller Center. And it wouldn't be Christmas if we didn't go ice skating."

Holly swallowed. Her decision this morning to spend time with Ryan and his son had seemed harmless. As she listened to the smooth, deep timbre of Ryan's voice, it caused little shivers to dance down her spine. She realized this decision was perhaps the craziest thing she'd ever done.

"Righto. I've got some things to take care of today and part of tomorrow. So, how about pizza and the cinema tomorrow eve?"

"Tomorrow's good. How can I reach you?"

"I'll call when I'm free and we can meet up."

"Great. I'll see you tomorrow. And Holly, thanks."

Dressed in tattered jeans that had seen better days and an old sweatshirt, Holly turned on the radio and let the station offering twenty-four hours of Christmas tunes filter through her work space with holiday cheer. With her hair pulled back, water bottle at her side, she sat down at her potter's wheel, dribbled water in the center, and anchored the piece of clay she'd chosen. She smoothed the edges to seal it and turned it on. She watched it go round and round as she took a moment to study it.

This particular piece was a bit larger than the last. She added water from the sponge, getting the piece good and moist. What she did was part intuition and part talent. Closing her eyes, she started at the top of the piece and let her fingers absorb the smooth slip and slide of the clay. She never knew what the blocks of clay would reveal. For her the magic of discovery was as exciting as the finished piece. Holly let the gentle pressure of her fingers shape and mold.

She worked for hours like that, letting the piece take shape. Getting a sense of exactly what colors, shades and textures would look best on the finished piece. Stopping the wheel for a much needed break, she stood, stretched, and looked at what was evolving. She smiled, visualizing the finished piece—the textures and colors of another truly unique piece. Her art agent was going to love this one.

Pride swelled; amazed at the success she'd achieved doing something she truly loved. Most of her pieces were on display in an upscale gallery in Manhattan. Though she'd never consider herself rich, she was well off. Considerably well off. She sighed. She'd been in the States almost a year, maybe she should consider looking for her own place. But what did one do with a house when there was no one to share it with? Images danced behind her closed eyes. Ryan Connor, big, strong, handsome. Kevin a miniature heartbreaker.

She blew out a deep breath and settled back down to work. No point in worrying about things she had no control over.

Ryan paced inside the pizzeria, waiting for Holly and Abby. He checked his watch again. Knowing because she hadn't called and canceled as he'd feared she might, they were just running late.

He heard her rich, lilting accent and the faint trace of humor in her voice as she opened the door and blew in with the rush of winter wind.

"Mom," Kevin yelled and ran toward her. Ryan felt like an outsider as she bent and caught his son once again in her arms and gave him a giant hug. As bad as he knew it would be on Kevin when he realized Holly wasn't his mother, the sight of them together warmed his heart.

Kevin stepped back as Holly removed her gloves and coat. "Dad kept checking his watch. He was worried you weren't going to come. I knew you would." Ryan could practically see the happiness that oozed from him.

"I wouldn't miss pizza and a movie." She helped Abby out of her coat.

Ryan hadn't considered the impact of seeing her again. And he sure hadn't counted on what felt like a hammer blow to the chest as he looked at her in jeans and a black sweater that outlined her sexy curves.

Within minutes, Kevin and Abby scampered off to play video games and Ryan and Holly sat alone—together.

"Would you like to play a game while we wait for the pizza?"

She smiled. "I thought we already were."

"Ah, yeah. No. I meant like...skeet ball?" Ryan turned and showed her the multiple lanes each with four different size rings you throw a ball into to get points.

"It's kind of like bowling, only better. Because when you're done you can turn in your tickets for some really cheap toy. Come on. It'll be fun. I'll teach you."

Ryan put tokens into the machine and the balls filled the holding area. He took the first ball and rolled it. It bounced with perfect precision into the smallest loop at the top, scoring the maximum points. His score flashed at the top of the machine. He tossed two more balls with the same result and then turned to Holly. "Ready to play?"

Stepping up to the game, Holly took a ball, gave it careful aim and sent it flying. It bounced, hit the safety net then bounced three more times before falling into the lowest ring. With a pout, she picked up another ball. Ryan winced when she tossed it harder. It bounced too high, went off the edge and slid down the side.

Frustration wrinkling her brow, she turned to Ryan. "I don't get it. I did the same thing you did."

Ryan smothered his grin as he picked up another ball and tossed it casually up and down. "You can't just throw it. And it can't be too soft or too hard. It has to be just right"

He tossed the ball at her and she caught it. "Let me show you," he said as he moved behind her. Pressed close, he inhaled, dragging her clean, sexy scent into his lungs.

He covered her hand with his and spoke softly into her ear. "Be ready to release the ball when I tell you."

She turned her head to look back at him.

"Ready?"

She nodded.

He pulled her arm back and swung it forward. "Release!"

They watched the ball sail up the middle, ricochet off the edge of one ring and sink right into the top circle. She scored the max points.

Holly squealed, spun and wrapped her arms around his neck. Her gaze locked with his and a powerful slam of something hot and steamy spiked in his gut. He sensed she felt it too when her gaze settled on his mouth.

"Well, that bloody well was fun," she said with a husky laugh and stepped out of Ryan's arms.

The intercom announced: "Queen of Hearts, pizza's ready."

"That's us." He showed her the oversized playing card bearing the Queen of Hearts, as they repeated the page over the intercom.

"I'll get the kids. You get the pizza," she said casually.

Holly crossed the game room, headed for the kids. Her heart was still knocking around in her chest. For one brief moment she'd shut her eyes and given herself over to the sensations of his hard body pressed against her. She took a deep breath and swallowed to help steady her heart.

She acknowledged the powerful attraction between them and wondered what his kiss would taste like.

When the evening wound down, Ryan helped her with her coat. "How can I reach you?"

Holly dug in her purse and pulled out a business card. She felt safe giving it to him, because it listed the gallery address and phone number, not her own. Quickly she scrawled her cell phone number on the back and handed it to him. And waited.

Ryan took the card, skimmed it quickly, then his gaze caught hers and a hint of a smile played at the corners of his mouth. Her name printed in bold read. Holly St. Nick.

He brushed a kiss to her cheek and whispered, "I'll call you later, Miss St. Nick."

"Hey, you." Holly felt the familiar tingle down her spine she'd come to associate with Ryan's deep, smooth voice. She turned and found him looking down at her smiling. Then she noticed he was alone.

"Where's Kevin?"

"Val's parents called and wanted to see him, so he's spending the next couple of days with them." His eyes scanned the area.

"Where's Abby?"

"She spent the night with a girlfriend from school. She'll be home later tonight."

Ryan's brows rose and his voice dipped seductively. "So it's only you and me, huh? Want to get out of here and have some real adult entertainment?"

"Why, Mr. Connor, are you reneging? I believe you promised to teach me to ice skate."

Ryan smiled. "Ice skating, it is then."

Although she'd seen snow and ice, she'd never skated before. She shivered in anticipation. After all, it was December in New York and she'd watched figure skating competitions on the telly before. But she'd never strapped a pair of thin blades to her feet and attempted to stand on them. She had to be honest with herself—it wasn't just the excitement of ice skating. Casting a sideways look at Ryan, her heart fluttered. For the first time, she and Ryan would be spending time alone.

Sitting on the bench next to him, she laced up her skates and glanced up to observe the skaters. Beginners were easily spotted, they hugged along the edge. More experienced skaters moved along at a nice pace enjoying themselves. And in the center, seasoned skaters spun, twirled and jumped with perfect balance and a grace she envied.

"Nervous?" Ryan asked

"Nah, looks simple enough, right? You center your body weight on these two thin blades here and try not to bust your bum."

Ryan threw back his head and laughed. "That would be about right." He stood and held out his hand. "I promise not to let you 'bust your bum'."

At the edge of the ice, Ryan pulled her close and lowered his mouth to her ear. "It's kind of like making love for the first time—a little awkward until you get lost in the sensations."

Holly felt like a fraud as she looked him in the eye and answered, "Right o' then."

Her hand in his, together they stepped out onto the ice. In a smooth move, Ryan spun, faced her and took both of her hands as he eased her onto the ice.

"Slide your right foot toward me, gently push off and let yourself glide. Now push with your left. Feel the smoothness of the ice."

Holly wobbled and Ryan kept a firm grip on her hands as they made the first pass around the rink staying close to the edge.

They continued skating at the rink's outer border with Ryan facing her as he skated backward. When he felt her confidence grow, he let go of one hand and moved to her side. They held hands and skated to the Christmas music. As they neared the corner, Ryan instructed her to cross her right foot over her left and ease into the curve. A few more passes around the rink and when she blossomed with confidence, he let go of her hand.

"Teach me to skate backward?"

He grabbed her and slipped her in front of him, pressing her back to his front.

His lips next to her ear, he spoke. "Lean against me, close your eyes and feel the rhythm of my feet." Then he spun them around. Holly squealed at the unexpected move. Ryan whispered once again in her ear. "This time use your left foot to guide you and ease into the corner."

Excited she was actually skating backwards, in an overzealous move Holly let go of Ryan and tried to turn back around on her own. The tip of one skate caught on the back of the other. She wobbled, lost her balance, arms pin-wheeled and she reached frantically for Ryan as she screeched his name.

Trying to stifle his laugh—and save her from busting her bottom at the same time, Ryan grabbed her around the waist. A high-pitched squeal and a grunt later, both lay sprawled on the ice in a tangle of arms and legs, laughing like loons. Holly turned her face toward him and in a moment of suspended time her laughter died as she reached up, cupped the back of his head with her gloved hand and eased his face toward hers. Her lips, slightly chilled, warmed instantly against his as she slid her tongue gently over the seam of his lips.

The role reversal surprised him and without hesitation he opened his mouth and let the heat of her tongue slide against his and warm him clear down to his toes and all the places in between.

From a distant place in his mind Ryan heard the shrill whistle and knew they needed to get off the ice. Breaking the kiss, he stood and hauled Holly to her feet and skated to the edge.

"Are you cold? Do you want to get something to drink?"

"No, I'm good."

"I want hot chocolate, though. Let's go get some."

Sitting on the bench letting the hot cocoa warm her hands, Holly felt embarrassed because she'd kissed him like a wanton woman.

"I'm sorry if I embarrassed you Ryan, I'm usually not so forward."

"Oh, you didn't embarrass me. Quite the opposite." Ryan tossed his empty cup into the trash bin. "Let's get out of here."

He wanted to take her someplace private to finish what her kiss had started, but he didn't want to seem presumptuous or scare her.

"Where are we going?"

"I haven't been to Rockefeller Center in years. I thought it would be nice to walk and look at the lights and window displays."

"Sounds like fun." Holly hooked her arm through his.

The sun was setting as they turned in their skates. They walked along the edge of the rink, shoulders brushing against the other now and again as the last of the skaters exited. They stopped in awe at the sheer size and beauty of the large, sparkling, horn-blowing angels. Holly had only seen pictures before of the most famous tree in the world that graced the middle of Rockefeller Center, and she marveled at how they found a perfect tree year after year. But standing before it was an experience she'd never had before. Never had she seen so many lights, or been so moved by something of its sheer size and beauty. There must have been millions of lights spread throughout the limbs of the tree.

In awe, Holly turned and caught Ryan watching her. When he moved toward her and caught her mouth with his, Holly knew without the buffer of the kids the attraction sizzling between them was mutual. And that only left one question. Would making love with Ryan be the beginning of something great or end in heart break?

People milled about in the crisp evening air, while the streets filled with noise, traffic and holiday cheer. They walked arm in arm, immersing themselves in the excitement of the hustle and bustle of shoppers as they filed from store to store hunting for bargains. Mixed in with the crowd of humanity, they laughed, and oohed and aahed over elaborately decorated window displays. Most stores had themed music playing to match the various scenes.

They stopped at the corner and Ryan laughed. "Kevin would go crazy if he could see this."

"What?"

"There's a Santa on every corner."

"I don't understand."

"I didn't either. But Kevin is convinced that if he asks Santa every day, then on Christmas morning a miracle is going to happen."

Her brows rose in confusion.

"He thinks Santa is going to bring his mother home for Christmas."

"He's going to be very disappointed on Christmas morning."

"Heartbroken, I'm afraid."

With coats, boots and gloves on, Ryan kicked the front door closed and pressed Holly against it. The feel of her warm mouth against his sent all hope of taking his time and doing things right, straight out the window.

Holly broke her mouth from his and stared up at him.

"I'm sorry." He brushed a finger tip over her lower lip.

"Bloody hell, Ryan," she said catching his hand. "Where's the bedroom?"

Minutes later, jackets, gloves and boots were scattered in the foyer. Their clothes strewn about on his bedroom floor.

Ryan gazed down at the naked woman on his bed. All softness, heat and unspoken promise. The magnificence of her nakedness left his throat dry and his heart sputtering around in his chest. Her smile mesmerized him every time she graced him with the honor of it. But her kisses zapped him with a jolt of sexual awareness that rocked the foundation of his world.

Holly's breath hitched at the sight of Ryan as he moved toward her. He radiated strength, determination and heat as he slowly and lazily lowered his hard body over hers without breaking eye contact. Holly felt as if she were on fire everywhere his body brushed as he pressed her to the bed and covered her mouth with his. She didn't pause to ask herself if she was ready for the desire she saw in his eyes. She simply squeezed her own shut and gave herself over to the feelings. Sensations bombarded her. She was drowning in the taste, scent and feel of him. With a gentle shift body to body, she arched as his mouth closed over her breast. Heat shot straight to her belly as her body rocked against his. A soft appreciative moan slid from her lips, and she wrapped her legs around his hips inviting him home. She clung to him, taking all he offered, hungrily meeting his thrusts.

His gut clenched tight, his willpower dwindling with each move and stroke of her hand and body against him. He could feel her climax building as she strained against him reaching for more. Slipping his hand between them, he stroked the swollen, sensitive bud that would take her over the edge. He whimpered as her body spasmed around him. His own heaved and shuddered with relief.

It had been a while since he'd been with a woman. Over a year to be exact. That had little to do with the way Holly made his world spin out of control.

Leaning on one elbow, he traced the shape of her face with his finger. More warm and content than he could ever remember.

"Wanna go for seconds?" Ryan asked as he nipped her shoulder.

"You can't be serious?" She laughed when he caught the tip of her breast with his mouth.

"Try me." He grinned as he rolled over and positioned her on top.

In the kitchen scavenging for something to eat, Holly found herself pressed against the kitchen counter instead, Ryan's lips grazing her neck.

"Ryan?" Holly laughed.

He looked confused for a moment until he felt the vibration again against his thigh and pulled back. With a silly smile he pulled the phone out of his pocket.

"Dad! Grams said she's not going to take me to see Santa. Said it's silly. That Santa's not going to bring Mom home."

Ryan sighed, exasperated.

"Daaad." Ryan heard the emotion building in his son's voice.

"All right, Kevin. I'll pick you up in an hour."

Ryan tucked the phone back in his pocket. "I've got to take Kevin to see Santa. I'll drop you at your car."

"Do you think that's a good idea?"

"Hell, no. I think you should spend the night. But I also don't want to break Kevin's heart and have it be my fault when his wish doesn't come true."

The next morning, Ryan headed down Broadway with a bag of fresh croissants. He passed a newsstand and the bold print headline, spread across the front, nearly stopped his heart. A national rag sheet sported the headline, *'Supermodel's death a hoax.'*

The picture on the front page showed a grainy color photo of Ryan and Holly holding hands as they skated around the ice rink in Central Park. The photo underneath it showed Ryan kissing her. Damn! Their first kiss and it had been caught on camera by some damned paparazzi.

He reached for his cell phone. He had to let her know what had happened.

"Holly, can you meet me at the Coffee House?"

"Is everything all right?"

"We need to talk."

Sitting across from Ryan, Holly's eyes misted over, further blurring the grainy photos.

The nice neat world she'd built for herself was beginning to crumble. All because she'd agreed to the crazy idea of helping this man and his son.

"I know the circumstances of our situation are...unusual. And it's suddenly gotten a lot more complicated,"—Ryan rubbed at the tension in his neck—"but none of that matters. I want to spend time with you. Get to know you better and see where this is going," Ryan said nervously.

"I don't think that would be a good idea."

"Why?" Ryan leaned back in his chair.

"Why, indeed. Because of this." Her eyes rested on the rag sheet. "And because I'm *not* her." She laughed bitterly. "I may look like her, but I'll never be her. I can't be a replacement for you, and it's not fair to Kevin." As the words tumbled from her lips they broke her heart, because in less than a week she'd fallen for Ryan and Kevin. Yet she'd known at some point her little part in the game would come to an end and it seemed the time was now.

She stood. "I'm sorry. I really am. I've had so much fun with you and Kevin. This week has been like a dream come true. Goodbye, Ryan." She kissed his cheek and walked away.

Ryan sat in stunned silence. He'd finally met a woman who would love not only him, but his son as well. He knew from the way Holly acted with Kevin that even if she didn't love him yet, he already held a special place in her heart. He couldn't believe he'd simply sat there while she told him goodbye and walked out of his life.

His gaze drifted back to the tabloid, to the photo of his and Holly's first kiss. Holly's words, 'I'll never be her. I can't be a replacement for you,' made his chest ache. Had that been what he'd done because she'd looked so much like Val? NO! Holly was warm, fun, loving, passionate and tender not only with him, but his son as well. Something Val had never been.

Holly might be the answer to his son's wishes and prayers—she was also the answer to his own Christmas wish. But the real problem now was how he would convince her that in less than a week he'd fallen in love with her—and that he loved her because of who she was and not a look-alike replacement for his dead wife. Only one thing mattered, getting Holly back into his life.

Ryan let the valet park his car. Kevin was mad and had pouted all the way to the Spencer's house because he'd wanted to attend Abby's party instead. Truth be told, it's what Ryan preferred also, but he'd been invited to this Christmas function months ago. Kevin's name was also on the handwritten invitation as the Spencer's daughter was also having a party.

"Good evening, sirs. May I take your coats?"

Kevin forgot to pout as he snickered at the Spencer's butler. Wiggling out of his coat, he was ushered around the adult party to the large room designed exclusively for children's parties.

Ryan made his way through the crowd, greeting the few acquaintances he knew. Though Holly had been in his life only a short time, not having her at his side laughing and smiling felt wrong.

"Ryan." Ashton Spencer, host and business associate, clapped him on the shoulder and handed him a glass of sparkling champagne. "Good to see you tonight. How is everything?"

"Good. Everything is good."

"Where's your son—Kevin, if I remember correctly?"

"Yes, that's correct. He was escorted to where the children are."

"That's terrific! Rest assured he's in good hands. My niece from Australia has come to stay and is overseeing the kids' party. She's been an absolute treasure since my wife's gone back to work. She takes care of Abby after school and our daughter adores her. Even took her down to Rockefeller Center to the mall to see Santa Claus last week."

The mention of Spencer's daughter's name, a woman from Australia, and the mall in the same breath sent disbelief spiraling through Ryan. His gaze swept the room until he found what he was looking for—a large family portrait on the wall: Ashton, a woman— evidently his wife—and the now familiar face of little Abby. Ashton's daughter. Not Holly's. So Holly was Ashton Spencer's niece.

Realization dawned. She was here in Ashton's house overseeing the Christmas party Kevin wanted to attend. Sweet, sexy, beautiful Holly.

"Is everything okay?" Ashton asked.

Ryan smiled. "Perfect. Everything's perfect. If you'll excuse me, I think I'll go check on Kevin." Could it be all Kevin's wishes and prayers had been heard? And answered?

Ryan stepped through the doorway and saw Kevin sitting on the floor next to a little blonde girl. The voice that flowed like warm honey across the quiet as she read *'twas the night before Christmas* from a large leather-bound book took his breath away.

Ryan moved quietly into the room and listened as she finished the story, the flavor of her accent washing over him.

Holly closed the book and raised her gaze, surprised when she saw Ryan. Somehow he'd discovered where she lived. Well, none of that mattered. She'd done her part to help Kevin realize she wasn't his mother.

"All right, let's put on our coats and go outside and feed the reindeer before they have to return to the North Pole to get ready for Christmas."

Twenty plus kids jumped up and ran for the patio doors. Ryan made his way across the room to Holly.

"How did you find me?"

"Must have been a little boy's wish."

Before she knew what was happening Ryan grabbed her and kissed her.

"Tell me you don't feel something and I'll walk away." Before she could answer, he kissed her again.

"This last week has been the best time of my life. I know you're not Val. I don't want a replacement mother for Kevin, or just someone to warm my bed."

She opened her mouth to speak and he kissed her again.

"I love *you*, Holly St. Nick. I want you in my life, snuggled up next to me at night. Please, say yes!"

This time, before he could kiss her again, she put her hand on his chest.

"I love you, too, Ryan."

Standing under the mistletoe, she poured all her heart and soul into her kiss.

Kevin watched his dad kiss Holly. He knew his real mom had left them and gone to heaven and wasn't coming back. Santa'd told him if he was a real good boy and wished real hard, he was sure to get what he asked for. Santa sure was smart for an old guy. At the top of his list was a new mom for him, and since his dad was lonely, too, he'd asked Santa to bring his dad someone nice.

Kevin smiled. He'd already started on his list for next year. He wanted a baby sister.

All I Want for Christmas is a HulaHoop... and a Mother

by DeborahAnne MacGillivray

"Allison, it's three days to Christmas Eve. Have you written your letter to Santa?" Shaking off pre-holiday blues, Keon Challenger glanced to the passenger seat where his elfin daughter sat, busy opening a box of *Chiclets*.

He spun the wheel of the black Lexus SUV, hearing the wheels sing against the pavement from the heavy rain. Today was the first day of winter. No White Christmas in the forecast—*yet*. Unseasonably warm for Kentucky, rain poured in sheets as if Noah were having a going-out-of-business sale. Despite, weathermen were keeping a close eye on a cold front bearing down from Canada. Timing was the key. If the Arctic air barreled in before all this heavy rain left, there'd be a White Christmas all right—they'd be up to their bloody hips in the stuff!

His daughter's head, with the riot of pale blonde curls, nodded as the vivid blue eyes looked up at him. "I did, Daddy, last night. I went online and sent it to Santa's email. That way I know he got it."

He smiled at this precious being. At five, his darling daughter sounded so mature in her speech patterns; her British accent only made her seem more precocious. Rather vexing at times, the teeny terror had a penchant for being bossy and took great pleasure in running his life. To say daddy was firmly wrapped around her little finger was putting it mildly.

The smile left his face. He should've remarried, given his daughter a mother. Plenty of women wanted *him*. At forty-three, he was fit and prided himself he looked a decade younger. Rich, cultured and Brit—a big turn-on for American women—*The Lexington Herald* listed him in the top ten bachelor catches for the city since his move from London two years ago. Regardless, he feared none of the ladies he'd dated would be a good mother for Allison. He needed someone who loved his daughter as much as she did him.

"That rare beastie does not exist, I fear," he muttered under his breath.

"What's a beastie, Daddy?" Allison's huge eyes stared at him as if he were the fount of all knowledge.

"A small creature."

She blinked. "What's a creature?"

"A small animal."

"What small animal doesn't exist, Daddy?"

He sighed at the pint-size Perry Mason. Allison's first word hadn't been Papa; it'd been *why*. He'd learned long ago she could *why* him to madness, so developed the habit of derailing her cross-examinations.

"Never mind, Munchkin. Tell me what you wrote Santa you wanted."

She popped a *Chiclet* into her mouth—a purple one—and chewed, then squinched up her nose. "Daddy, is that allowed? Isn't that like a birthday wish? You blow out the candles and you aren't to tell or it won't come true?"

He slowed the SUV to permit a silly woman, with a newspaper held over her head, to dash across the parking lot. The corner of his mouth twitched as he watched the compact derrière and full breasts jiggling. *Dear Santa, what I'd like to find under my tree...*

"Silly, Yank. Should carry a brellie instead of having a mess of wet ink dripping onto her hair and hands."

Allison popped her head up above the dash to see. "That's Miz Leslie, the new ballet teacher. I like her, Daddy. She's Scottish."

"New? What happened to Mrs. Henderson?"

She paused to insert a green *Chiclet* into her mouth. "Fell. Broke her hip. She's gone to Florida to get better and may not come back. Miz Leslie is her granddaughter. She's taken over teaching. She's pretty, Daddy."

*Uh oh....*time to change the topic. "So what did you tell St. Nick you wanted?" he asked, though his divided attention was still drawn to the sexy ballet teacher until she dashed through the front doors of the dance school.

"Lots of stuff, Daddy. Santa won't give me all, though I *have* been very good."

"Opening negotiations, eh?"

"Huh? Neg-oceans? What's neg-oceans, Daddy?"

"Why don't you tell me what's on your list, too, then maybe I can get some things Santa can't carry in his sleigh."

"I told him I want a pony. A kitty. A pair of skates. And a MP3 player...but,"—time to add another *Chiclet*—"I told Santa he didn't have to bring me those things if..."

Keon was going to toss that box of *Chiclets* out the window! "If...?"

"Geesh, Daddy, you're grumpy...like Scrooge on the cartoon."

He chided with humor, "I bear absolutely *no* resemblance to a duck."

"Quack—quack—quack." Allison giggled, then added another *Chiclet* to where her cheek pooched out like a chipmunk. "Mrs. Mesham told some lady friend on the phone you need to get laid."

Keon nearly choked that his housekeeper had said

such a thing, but had little time to recover as Allison plowed on with another *why* session.

"She said if you played hide the pickle you'd smile more often. What's get laid, Daddy? And what's hide the pickle? Is that like hide-n-go-seek?"

Forcing a smile, he made a mental note to interview for a new housekeeper after the first of the year. "Sort of an adult version...um...yes."

"When can I play hide the pickle, Daddy?"

Now he *did* choke. "Umm...maybe thirty or forty years from now after I unchain you from your closet."

"Silly Daddy."

"Go ahead and giggle, Munchkin. Daddy's quite serious."

He parked the car—sensibly reached for his umbrella—then came around to fetch Allison. Opening the passenger door, he waited while she stowed her precious chewing gum box in her coat pocket and gathered her pink, Retro-Barbie ballet case.

She finally looked up in seriousness. "I told Santa I really wanted a hula-hoop."

Keon grinned. "Like the old Chipmunk song?"

"Yep. A hula-hoop..."—her eyes fixed him—"and a mother."

Keon's laughter died. Well, bugger. Where did one pick up a mother? Did *K-Mart* have *Blue Light Specials—mothers aisle three, half-price for the next fifteen minutes...*? He could tell the past couple weeks Allison had been on a Mother Hunt. Mommy Mania occasionally reared its head, but now that dog had a bone between its teeth and wasn't letting go. The last two Christmases she'd done the same. This time the push was stronger. Something had set her off.

Keon sighed. He adored his small daughter, would walk through fire for her, nonetheless feared this *present* was beyond his ability. Hula-hoops had made a comeback. That much was within his power. Bloody hell, getting a pony would be easy if they had a place to keep one. Ponies, cats and dogs were just not part of life in a condo. Maybe he'd look for a place in the country, farther out, away from Lexington, a home where Allison could have her kitty and a pony. Possibly along the Palisades of the Kentucky River.

Allison suddenly dashed ahead of him on the walkway, running up the stairs and inside through the white, double-doors.

"What's with females, always dashing about without umbrellas?" He smiled, watching her, his heart full of pride in his role in creating this very special child.

Opening the door, he paused to shake the umbrella, then left it in the stand just inside. He'd been in the ballet school twice before, when he brought Allison to check it out and register, then back for her first class. Originally a one-story antebellum home, a ballet studio and small stage had been built on the rear back in the 1950s. Now the foyer and rooms of the original house served as the waiting room, offices and changing rooms for students.

One dressing room door was open and lights were on over the mirrored table. A woman bent over, switching from street shoes to ballet slippers.

"Morning, Miz Leslie," Allison called, sparkling happiness in her voice. Clearly, his daughter adored her new teacher.

"Good morn to you, Allison. You're early. Class isn't for another half-hour." She dumped the wet newspaper in the trash, then wiped her hands on a towel.

"That's okay, Daddy will keep me company 'til then."

Keon arched a brow. What happened to, *hurry, Daddy, I'm going to be late?*

"Daddy, this is Miz Leslie, my teacher. Isn't she pretty?"

The woman came out of the room and offered a warm smile. "Leslie Seaforth,"—she held out her hand to shake, then paused when her eyes locked with his—"and you're Keon Challenger, Allison's *daddy.*"

A light hazel, they reminded him of a cat. Never had he been so struck by the power, the force of a woman's gaze. Hard to draw air, it felt as though he'd absorbed a physical blow, strong enough to make him sway. Being typically male, he generally didn't begin his inspection of a woman so high up. Leslie Seaforth's eyes held him, mesmerized him, leaving him unable to think or move or breathe. All about him receded to dark grey.

He grew aware Allison had hold of his wrist and pulled him closer to the fae woman who had the magic to rock him. "Say hello to Miz Leslie, Daddy." The small child finally resorted to pushing against his knee. "You know, kiss her the way you do all the other women."

The twinkle of faery dust in the woman's luminous eyes winked out. "All?"

Reality returned and everything came into focus for Keon as he saw he dropped from the level of Prince Charming to lecherous Casanova in a sweep of the long, black lashes. He tried to laugh it off. "Out of the mouths of babes..."

Her faintly stubborn chin raised a notch as her expression hardened. "Actually, I find children rather accurate reporters of the truth. They haven't developed the proper lying skills."

Well, this is going downhill fast. He held out his hand to accept her shake, and for an instant feared she'd jerk back, loathe to touch him, but with a challenge flashing in those huge eyes she took it. Her hand wasn't small, but a strong one with beautiful fingers. A hand he could imagine running over his bare chest, or wrapped around his...Keon gave his errant imaginings a shake.

One shouldn't lust after his daughter's ballet teacher. *Bloody hell! How did he stop?*

She wore a lavender leotard; the pale, stretchy *Capezio* material did little to shield her from him noticing she had beautiful breasts. Large, firm and the size of grapefruits. He thought you had to be flat chested to be a ballerina. Gor, the situation was going from bad to worse, faster than Superman's speeding bullet.

He assured, "I fear Allison exaggerates—"

"Kiss her hello, Daddy." His daughter pushed on his

258

leg again, quite insistent.

Seeking to distract the teeny menace on wheels, he suggested, "Why don't you share a *Chiclet* with Ms. Seaforth?"

"Okay, Daddy."

Leslie Seaforth tilted her head as she watched Allison rush into the changing room. "Points for the deft derailing. Does she always insist you kiss women, or is that solely your initiative?"

"She only insists I kiss her auburn-haired ballet teacher." He couldn't resist the taunt, nor his predator's smile as she blushed.

Heat spread up Leslie Seaforth's body to her neck, then her face. She could barely think, so flustered by the potently sexual man before her. Males like him didn't walk through a ballet studio door every day of the week. Hell, they were rarer than hen's teeth, as Aunt Morag always said. Keon Challenger was hard on a female's system, a throwback to when men were men, and not kinder and gentler, politically correct, androgynous beings.

This man exuded enough pheromones she had a hard time thinking of anything but him. And when he spoke—the sexy British accent evoked a twinge of homesickness. The emotion was quickly overridden by flashes of him whispering dark words in the hush of deep night.

Rampant sexual attraction received a cold dose of reality by sweet Allison telling that her father kissed *all* the women. Yeah, Leslie believed that. This stud in Italian loafers and the John Phillips' suit didn't have to do one thing, just stand still and women would be all over him.

The kind of man any sane woman ran from, *heartbreaker* was stamped on his forehead. The type she wanted *nothing* to do with, having been down that road once before.

Allison returned with her box of gum and offered a green one. Then she took out another and put it in her father's hand. "Daddy likes purple ones."

He leaned over and kissed the blonde curls, then winked at Leslie as he popped the square of gum into his mouth. "Absolutely my fav." Her heart warmed as his rolling eyes said just the opposite. He mouthed the words, "Too sweet."

"Daddy said he'd help tomorrow," Allison announced with a beam on her face, while patting his thigh.

By Challenger's expression, Leslie saw this was the first he'd heard of *volunteering*. She almost laughed. This pint-size cherub had horns hidden in those pale curls and daddy firmly wrapped around her pinkie.

"Are you sure, Mr. Challenger? It'll be three to four hours for the dress rehearsal. That many ballerinas can be a bit fraying to male nerves." Leslie nearly shook, thinking of being around Keon Challenger for that length of time. Talk about hard on nerves—*hers*!

His hand touched his daughter's shoulder. "I always find time for Allison."

Leslie's heart thawed. Most fathers would ask what they were volunteering for, when it would be, how long, and then check their *Palm Pilot* to see if it could be penciled in. His putting Allison first said much about the man. His love for his beautiful little daughter was clear upon his face and in how he kept patting the child's shoulder or caressing her blonde curls.

Allison was a cutie. The precocious darling had stolen Leslie's heart the first time they'd met. The child obviously had the look of the mother, for she was angelic while her father was black-headed and had stormy grey eyes, which held a hint of green. Allison mentioned her mother was dead, but no details. It was hard to imagine the little girl with no mum to read her faerytales or kiss her booboos.

"It's kind of you to volunteer. May I offer refreshments, fortify you while you adjust to volunteering? Coffee, tea, soft drink?"

"Tea would be nice."

Struggling to keep her wits about her, Leslie found it nearly impossible to breathe when she stared into those stormy eyes. "You can relax in the salon. I shall fetch it."

"If you don't mind, Allison and I would enjoy keeping you company in the kitchen." He slid off his overcoat, handing it to Leslie.

She hung it in the closet. "Certainly. Come on through."

Allison knew the way and already had his index finger, pulling him along. She released her hold on her daddy when she spotted the pet carrier on the kitchen floor. "A kitty!" With a squeal, she was on her knees before it. "Here, kitty, kitty, kitty."

Leslie opened her mouth to caution Allison to keep her fingers back, but the minx had opened the carrier's grate door and the cat zoomed out. "Och, I was going to say don't let him out. He's a grump today. I had him at the vet's for shots."

"Poor kitty." Allison petted the fat orange tabby and he seemed happy to have an adoring audience. "What's kitty's name?"

"Alvin."

Allison giggled. "Like the chipmunk in the cartoons? I love the chipmunk song about the hula-hoop. It's Daddy's favorite song, too, isn't it, Daddy?"

"It is indeed." Putting his hands in his pockets, Challenger nodded. He lowered his voice, meant for Leslie's ears only, "You have Allison's heart with the puss. She's been begging for one for Christmas. Our condo won't permit pets. I'm considering moving to the country, getting a place where she can have a kitty, maybe a pony."

Assured cat and child were bonding, Leslie moved to the cupboard and took out the tin of *Brodie's Edinburgh Tea* and put the kettle on. "Children need space. Pets are good friends, teaches them responsibility and love. Plenty of room to burn up all that energy. I cannot wait to get away from Lexington each night and back to the river house. I fear I'm not a city girl."

261

"You live on the river?" Interested, Challenger took a seat on a stool by the counter. "I originally held back buying a place in the country, not sure I'd stay. Once I set up the offices for my investment firm, I'd considered going back to London. Only, I like it here. A nice safe place to raise a child. It was good Allison and I had a change of scenery—starting fresh. Now I'm thinking of staying permanently."

"The river area resembles Scotland. I don't feel homesick there. My gran wants to retire to Florida to be near her sister. I'm considering buying her home. It's a beautiful place." *Perfect for a family.*

"See, Daddy, kitties are fun!" She had Alvin's mouse-on-a-string toy and the silly, pudgy cat was jumping and showing off for her like a kitten.

"He doesn't usually take to children. He likes her. But then, how could anyone resist Allison?"

He smiled. "She's special, isn't she?"

"Very. You're lucky."

He grinned. "Being a proud papa, I'm prejudiced."

"You should be. Allison's remarkable." Getting the cups down, she glanced to the child laughing at the cat bouncing across the floor. "If you don't mind me asking, Allison mentioned her mother's dead..."

"Lemon, no sugar," he said for the tea. After a moment's hesitation he answered. "Meredith died in a car accident when Allison was barely two."

"Did you love her?" She blushed at her crass invasion of his privacy, but it'd popped out before she could stop the words.

His stormy grey eyes met hers with a levelness that said he gave her the truth, bald and unvarnished, in the simple reply. "Yes."

She was unable to break the stare, could lose herself in those shifting green-grey eyes. Her breath caught and held as they stripped her bare, not just her body—as men tend to do—*but her very soul.* She was oddly unsettled that he'd loved his wife. By contrast, Leslie knew her husband died loving another woman.

Sometimes she wished to know a man loved her with the conviction she heard in Challenger's words. Other moments, she feared she'd never open herself to the possibility of that pain again.

"I'm sorry. For your loss—and my vulgar intrusion."

Leslie lowered her eyes to the tea, mentally kicking herself for being insensitive. He was a stranger. What right did she have to pry into his life, his feelings?

It was Allison. The little girl needed a mother, but she wondered if this man would remarry or enjoyed playing the field. She gnawed on the inside of her lower lip. It was none of her business.

Only, she was attracted to him. Deeply. No man had slipped past her guards so easily since Kevin's death. She kept all males at arm's length. Problem was, the little girl had already stolen her heart.

Ah, the road to ruin. Keon Challenger was a heartbreaker of the first order. She'd be safer sticking her finger in a light socket than kiss him. *Oh, boy! Who put that silly thought into my mind?*

As she held the teacup out for him, it rattled in her hand. With a thanks, he lifted the cup and sipped. Mesmerized by the beautiful mouth closing on the Belleek China, a hot flush started at her toes, rolled up her body and came out in a blush. Overpowering arousal hit her lower belly like a fist.

And damn him—he noticed. Those eyes, the color of the North Sea in winter, moved down her body and then back up, not missing evidence of her reaction to him, hardly hidden by the lavender leotard. The black brows lifted in a taunt as the corner of his mouth tugged into an arrogant, sexy smile.

Perversely, she wanted to slap that expression off his smug face. Bloody bastard, she was sure small herds of women stampeded to make goo-goo faces before him. A woman would never feel safe, secure with Keon Challenger, always fearing aggressive females who'd stop at nothing to get in his bed, in his life.

"Do you need any help today?" he asked, glancing at

his watch. "I've meetings later this morning, but I could cancel."

"I can always use an extra set of hands. I'm setting up chairs and tables, checking to see if any light bulbs are burnt out in the footlights and such." She smiled, taking in his expensive suit. "You aren't dressed for that sort of thing. Thanks for the offer."

Allison dashed about with Alvin chasing the streamer of red ribbon from where Leslie had wrapped packages for a display for the recital. Silly—and cruel —her mind summoned a vision of Christmas morn, Allison opening presents and playing with Alvin, Leslie watching on with Challenger, sharing that special joy. A beautiful tableau that solidified in her heart, made her crave for it to be real. Swallowing her tea, she let the hot liquid scald the picture from her mind.

She didn't know this man, so it was stupid to spin fantasies. Too much to risk. She'd learned, only too well, hope led to heartache.

The light from the doorway to the classroom was blocked. Leslie glanced up from tying the strings on Allison's tennis shoes. She figured Challenger would pick up his daughter. Almost breathlessly, she found herself waiting for his return, found herself dreading it. She often saw the Black Lexus sitting in the lot waiting for Allison, though sometimes his assistant fetched the child when the father was tied up. His coming back wasn't a surprise.

Her reaction to him was. She couldn't draw enough air as she stared at the sexy man in worn blue jeans and black sweater. His black hair was windblown, not the polished businessman of just an hour ago. Vividly, she envisioned him standing along the cliffs of her home, watching the winding Kentucky River below. Her heart whispered this man could easily fit into her self-contained life.

If she dared take that risk.

"Talk about delusions," she muttered under her

breath.

Challenger looked down, feeling Alvin rubbing around his legs. "I'm dressed properly now. Put me to work, Teacher."

He and Alvin dodged as a dozen pint-size ballerinas shoved by him. The only one in the class who was five, Allison was so small compared to the girls who were two-to-three years older. Her face brightened when she looked up to see her father on the end of those long legs. She wrapped her arms about his thigh and hugged him.

"Love you, Daddy."

"Love you, too, Munchkin. Where are you and the herd of marauding midgets heading in such a rush?"

She grinned. "Cookies!"

"Only one. After we finish up here I'll take you to lunch."

"McDonalds!" she squealed.

"We'll see."

He turned, his eyes following the small girl until she disappeared into the kitchen. His love for Allison was apparent to Leslie. A few fathers picked up their daughters from classes. Some looked bored, others appeared rushed. She couldn't recall any watching their daughter with such pride, such true devotion.

"Thanks for the helping hands. The weathermen issued a warning the rain might turn to snow suddenly, so a couple other volunteers called and cancelled. I won't turn you down again."

It was foolish she knew, but her heart stuttered as he neared. Oh, being around Challenger wasn't wise. Then why was she so pleased he'd returned to help? He was here for Allison, not because of her. She needed a strong dose of reality. Taking a deep breath to steady herself was a waste. She drew in air laced with potent pheromones from this super attractive male.

"What's first?" He invaded her space, deliberately pushing her buttons. A flash in the stormy eyes said he was very aware of her reaction to him, liked that she was aware of him.

As sophisticated as a teen—an idiotic way to feel at age thirty-three—she blushed and quickly looked away, motioning to the chairs stacked in the corner. "Ah...we need to set them up in rows in two sections. Tables at the back for refreshments."

He leaned close and whispered with a grin, "Then I'm your man."

Mercy! *If only*...Leslie sighed.

She watched Challenger unfold the chairs and place them in double sections—twenty across with fifteen rows, which would easily hold the parents, grandparents, aunts and uncles. Balanced atop the tall stepladder, she struggled to change light bulbs in the overhead spotlights. And tried *not* to watch him. She suffered from mild vertigo, so she didn't need to keep switching focus points between the bulbs overhead and the sexy man working methodically on the floor below the stage.

He moved well. Confident. Muscular, though not in a bulky body-builder style. He was lean, hard. The man had beautiful thighs and one super arse!

Challenger made it damn hard to keep her eyes off him.

Which proved dangerous! Her vertigo kicked up as her eyes were constantly pulled toward him. Feeling a total dolt, she stared at Challenger, desire searing every fiber in her being. It was pathetic to want what you couldn't have, however she hadn't been attracted to a man like this in...well...*never.*

Oddly, it was true. She couldn't recall Kevin ever making her this breathless. Her whole life she'd instinctively shied away from men like Challenger, played in the shallows and fallen for a man who was safe. Or at least she'd thought he'd been safe. Boy had she been blindsided!

Allison was running up and down the aisles dragging a ribbon with Alvin trailing after her. Poor Alvin hadn't had that much exercise in years. For a cat disdainful of children, the feline certainly had taken to the angelic girl.

The ladder wobbled and she grabbed the sides to steady herself. Vertigo spiraled and everything seemed to bend in on itself. Leslie closed her eyes, willing it away, but the whirling wouldn't stop, making it impossible to focus on heights and see them in their real relation. Instead, everything undulated about her as if she were on a rollercoaster.

"People pay for this cheap high," she muttered, trying to make light of her weakness.

Leslie shuddered, truly terrified as the ladder rattled and everything about her turned to a whirl of colors, fearful she'd lost her balance. She had. For a breathless instant she fell backward, floating free in space and desperately arching like a cat—frantically clutching at anything to keep from falling to the stage.

Then her back slammed into something solid. "Shhhhh...I've got you."

It took a panicked breath to realize Keon's right arm was around her waist; his left had hold of the ladder, securing them. He remained that way, letting her regain her balance.

As the vertigo subsided, she became aware of other things, like the deceptive power of the man. He was strong, much stronger than the John Phillip's suit of the high-powered businessman had revealed. He obviously exercised regularly, for the arms felt like bands of steel, protecting her from falling. The strong pounding of his heart against her back. His radiant heat poured through her, calming her fear. It was so tempting to turn and bury her face against his neck, inhale the super-charged pheromones exuded by the sexy man. Let arousal drive the fear away.

"You all right?" he asked, his head against hers.

Leslie managed a faint nod. "Just a spot of dizziness."

"Spot, my arse." He growled. "I'm stepping down a rung and I want you to do the same. I won't let go. Just step when I say. We won't move until you have your footing."

Leslie did as Keon said and felt an utter fool for the whole episode. She was sweating by the time her feet touched the stage floor. Trembling, the worst of her fear ebbing, she allowed Keon to wrap his arms about her and just let her shaking fade. She welcomed that high body heat. Felt she could stay there for an hour. She liked standing in Challenger's embrace too much.

Keon finally stepped back, put his hands on his hips and fixed her with those stormy eyes. "You suffer vertigo?"

She nodded.

"Then why the bloody hell were you up on a ten-foot ladder? Of all the stupid, moronic, imbecilic..."

Allison came over with Alvin twining around her legs. She patted Challenger's thigh. "That's okay, Miz Leslie. Daddy's a Scrooge grouch with me, too. He just needs to play hide the pickle and get laid, then he'll smile more."

Leslie sniggered as she placed the cat carrier down and turned to lock the studio doors. "Hide the pickle, indeed."

Challenger explained his housekeeper had given that *medical diagnosis* to a friend over the phone and Allison overheard. Leslie had bit her lip to keep from asking all sorts of loaded questions that could've quickly spiraled out of control. Gherkin or Polish Dill, being one.

Bracing against the bitter wind, she shivered. She'd worn a light blazer to work, too light now the temperatures were dropping fast. Picking up Alvin's carrier, she hurried down the steps, only to have the Black SUV coast to a stop before her.

The tinted window of the passenger side rolled down and Allison's elfin face appeared. "Hi, Miz Leslie." She was on her knees to see out the window.

"Hello, Allison. I thought you already left."

"Daddy and I want you to come Christmas shopping

with us."

"If I have to suffer the Merry Ho Ho throngs, I thought you could come along and hold my hand. Men in such situations are apt to break out in a rash." He flashed that to-die-for-smile. "Please come."

Shopping with Challenger and his beautiful child. For a woman looking toward Christmas with only Alvin, it'd be a way to capture the missing, childlike magic of a holiday that promised to be lonely. Swallowing regret, she lifted the carrier higher. "Sorry, it's turned frigid. I have to get Alvin home."

Determination flashed in the grey eyes. "Then how about lunch?"

"Yea! McDonalds!" Allison bounced in the seat.

Challenger chuckled. "How about Burger King instead?"

"Scrooge McDaddy...quack—quack—quack." Allison wiggled her head back and forth as she quacked.

Seeing her hesitation, he added, "Alvin can come. I'm sure he'd love a burger."

"Yea! Alvin wants a Big Mac!"

Challenger shook his head. "If this child of mine could just get enthusiastic about things..."

Not giving Leslie a chance to say no, he hopped out of the car and came around. Opening the passenger door, he scooped out his daughter and spun with her in the air, then opened the backseat door and pretended to toss her in. She squealed delight and laughed, but scampered over to the far side, then buckled her seat belt.

He turned to Leslie. "Next, the moggie." When she still held back, he pressed, "Oh, come, come. How can you resist a Big Mac, the best fries around and my scintillating company?"

"I'm sizzalating, too!" Allison added, "Pleeeeeeeese."

Leslie *wanted* to go with them, however her protective mode kicked in. It'd be too easy to fall for both father and daughter, her heart already too close to weaving castles in the air. Only a fool would set herself up for that. Yet, as she met those eyes, the color of the North Sea, reason died a quick death and she threw caution to the wind. *Call me fool.*

With a resigned sigh, she handed him Alvin's tote, earning another of those sexy smiles, capable of melting her heart. He placed it on the seat next to Allison, who instantly complained.

"Daddy, can't see Allllllllvvvvvvvvvvvvvin! Daddy!"

"Ok-ay!!!" Imitating the cartoon chipmunk, he flipped the carrier's door to face his very insistent daughter. "There, you can see Allllllllvvvvvvvvvvvvvin."

Cat secured, he held the door for Leslie. As she slid onto the leather seat, she smiled up at him. He was good with Allison, not just there and seeing to her needs, but he interacted well with the child, their strong rapport clear in the banter.

She wondered if he'd been that openly loving with his wife. A slight twinge of jealousy shot through her, envying the woman. Did he have it in him to love again? As her eyes followed him striding around the car, she swallowed, forcing back the longing that had no right to live.

He climbed in and reversed the SUV. Pausing to wait for traffic before pulling out, he said, "I still think we should go to Burger King." He winked at Leslie to show he teased.

"McDonalds!" Allison piped on cue.

"She's a very good child, except she's a bit one-tracked when she wants something. Is McDonalds fine with you? I don't take her there often, so she's putting me on the spot in front of you." Challenger's eyes sought his daughter's reflection in the rear view mirror. "She's playing innocent like she cannot hear me, but she does."

"Quack—quack—quack," the voice from the backseat commented.

Leslie chuckled. "Sorry, Challenger, I think you're outmatched. Big Macs are fine."

"Daddy needs—"

"Munchkin, if you want a Happy Meal, you'd better

stop telling Miz Leslie what I need."

"Quack—quack—quack." Switching gears, Allison cried out, "Oh, look, Miz Leslie! Flakes!"

Leslie took her eyes off the handsome man to watch the huge, fluffy flurries. "Wow, perhaps we'll have a White Christmas after all."

"I want snow! Santa likes snow!" Allison kicked her legs in excitement. "Scrooge McDaddy likes snow! Miz Mesham said Daddy needs to do more with his pickle—"

"Allison Anne..." Challenger growled a warning.

"—than write his name in the snow. How do you write your name in the snow with a pickle, Daddy?"

Leslie tried to contain the laughter, only when Challenger's eyes met hers they both lost it. She enjoyed watching father and daughter fussing, the sort of chatter rising from their deep love. A pang of wanting a family twisted within her. She could see baking cookies, Allison playing nearby with Alvin, Challenger carrying in wood for the fireplace. Images of a quiet family life she hadn't let herself think about for the past five years. She pushed the yearning back into its shoebox.

"I haven't had a White Christmas in...well, I don't recall the last one." Leslie pondered wistfully. She watched the beautiful snow swirling thicker as it changed over from the rain. "Sadly, it won't stick. All the rain and the warm ground will keep it melting. Still, it's beautiful while it lasts."

Challenger coasted into the drive-in lane of Mickey-Ds. "Happy Meal for the quacking brat. A burger for Alvin. What will you have?"

"Big Mac meal, super-size me, please. I missed breakfast."

Challenger tilted his head, the grey eyes heatedly raking over her body. A cocky grin spread across his sensual mouth. "I love a lass with a good appetite."

Wanting to fan her face, the temperature soared in her skin as she caught he meant for more than food. Clearly he was flirting, nevertheless she feared Keon Challenger flirted as he breathed. What was done carelessly, second nature to him, could have a lass' heart going pitter-patter.

He gave the order to the voice on the speaker, then pulled around. As he waited in line, he turned on the radio, pushing buttons until he found one reporting weather.

"It's looking nasty out there, folks. The rain didn't move out and the Arctic air came in faster than predicted. It's overrun the warm front and prevents the rain from leaving. Temperatures are dropping fast, nearly twenty degrees in the last hour. Rain's shifting to snow all over the state. The National Weather Service has issued a winter storm advisory. Get where you're going. Make sure you're stocked up with everything you need...food, flashlight, batteries. Those of you far away from the cities might see you have plenty of wood in or crank up those kerosene heaters in case your power fails. Expect six inches of snow by nightfall and more on the way...could be one for the record books."

"Yea, Santa got my email!" Allison unbuckled the seatbelt and stood on the floorboard to see the thickening flurries. "Daddy, Santa sent us snow! Bet Santa will give me the other things I asked him for, too."

Leslie turned to watch Allison marvel at the snowstorm. "What else did you ask Santa for?"

The child grinned. "A hula-hoop and a mo—"

Accepting the sack of food, Challenger quickly shoved the box at his daughter even before he parked. "Here, Munchkin, Happy Meal."

"Hey, where's Alvin's? He wants a Happy Meal."

Challenger parked the SUV, but left the car on battery, the wipers running. At this rate, the snow was so heavy they'd be covered before they finished eating. He handed back a hamburger wrapped in paper. "Chow for the cat. Don't let him—"

Allison opened the carrier's door and Alvin hopped on top of it, ready for din din.

"—out." Challenger rolled his eyes. "He doesn't panic

in a car, does he?"

"It takes a lot to ruffle Alvin."

He watched her munch french fries. "I love their fries, too." Stuffing a couple in his mouth, he looked at the snow sticking to the side windows. "You seem wrong about the snow not sticking."

"I hope so. It'd be lovely to have a White Christmas."

Leslie concentrated on eating her meal. Being in the car with Challenger and his potent male pheromones swamped her senses. With the snow covering the side windows, they were cocooned. It was too close. She had to remind herself to eat her burge and not stare at the handsome man.

"That cute little Beetle convertible of yours is great for gas mileage, but you'll face problems getting to the river with this coming down."

Leslie saw the wipers moving the snow, falling faster than the blades could swipe the glass clean. "Alvin and I'll be fine," she said without much conviction.

"If it keeps coming down like this, there won't be a ballet recital."

"That will disappoint the students. They've worked so hard. We won't be able to reschedule it until after the first of the year."

"Alvin ate his burger. He wants more." Allison poked her head between the seats, then her small hand held out a slice of pickle from her burger and waggled it in the air. "Here, Daddy, you can play hide the pickle with Miz Leslie now."

Leslie nearly strangled on her coke.

"I think I'll leave Alvin out and stick *you* in the cat carrier." He snatched the pickle slice and ate it before Allison could carry on with her train of thought.

"Silly Daddy. You're supposed to hide the pickle, not eat it."

This time Leslie did strangle. "Here...feed Alvin part of my burger." She tried to keep a straight face, but the chuckle slipped out.

Challenger started to laugh, too. Wiping his mouth,

he shook a finger at her. "Not—one—word."

"I wouldn't touch it with a ten-foot pole."

Finishing the last slurp of his soda, he formed his face to seriousness and arched a brow. "The topic...or my *pickle*?"

By the time Keon neared the ballet studio, he'd reached a decision.

The snow fell heavier with each passing minute. So far the highway was just slushy with sporadic patches of ice, only he fretted about what Leslie would face the closer she got to the river house. The roads along the Palisades were steep and winding, often treacherous in spots. Under normal conditions, she said she had a forty-minute drive during rush hour. This was far from normal.

The day darkened due to the storm, with decreased visibility seeing traffic at a crawl. Everyone puttered along at 20 mph, forced to use headlights. It was still a couple hours until the evening rush. Even so, his anxiety increased. This being Friday, every mother's son would be leaving work early in hopes of avoiding the twilight snarl as conditions worsened. Instead of evading the mess, Lexington would have the weekend exodus sooner. Leslie would be right in the middle of that.

"People go nuts with the first snowfall. They forget how to drive, none have snow tires on their cars," Keon commented, setting the stage to asking Leslie to come home with them. "The police will be tied up with wrecks."

"The officers stop responding," she agreed. "You get to the point if it's a fender bender, just exchange insurance info and get out of the way." Leslie glanced over her shoulder to see Alvin rested quietly on Allison's lap.

"Garages will be swamped with emergency runs due to people skidding off the roads. Like that eegit there." He nodded toward a red Lumina off in a ditch.

Two more cars were off on the opposite side up

ahead. That did it! He wasn't about to let Leslie out in that mess alone. Only how do you ask your daughter's ballet teacher to come home for the weekend, yet convince her he wasn't trying to corner her to play hide the pickle?

Actually, he really would like to get cozy with Miz Leslie. The lady had a body that was hard to get off his mind. *But it was more.* A warmth about her drew him. He loved watching her eyes as she looked at Allison, saw the hunger there. Oh, Leslie was attracted to him. He spotted the pulse in her neck jump when his shoulder brushed hers. Her auburn hair was neatly coiled, ballerina perfect, at the back of her head. His groin throbbed as he contemplated uncoiling the long braid and letting it play over his fingers. Oh yes, Leslie Seaforth was quickly becoming an obsession, and not only with him, but Allison. This woman was already half in love with his daughter.

Suppressing a smug grin, he lowly sang, *"It's beginning to look a lot like Christmas..."*

Maybe Santa did read emails after all.

Clearing his throat, he tried to sound casual. "Leslie, perhaps you should come home with Allison and me. Everyone's leaving Lexington, heading toward Nicholasville and Danville to beat the evening rush. No one wants to get stuck in this mess. A killer drive in that Beetle of yours." Keon presented it as nothing more than simple logic.

He wanted her to come home with them and it had nothing to do with the bad weather. Allison did a "Yippie!" from the back seat, but then he didn't have concerns from how the *peanut gallery* would take the invite. He had a feeling Leslie Seaforth was the reason Allison was on her Mommy Hunt kick.

Leslie smiled sadly. "It's kind of you to offer, but I have to get home."

"I'll smuggle Alvin in under my jacket. The super won't know he's there," he teased.

"It's not Alvin. I can't leave Edward alone."

275

Edward? Who the bloody hell is Edward? Husband? Why did images of men battling with claymores arise to mind?

"Edward?" He patted himself on the back for the laid-back tone. Jealousy burned within him like a brand, the emotion knotting his stomach with an intensity he couldn't ever recall experiencing.

"The pony."

"Pony?"

Allison squealed and her head popped between the seats, her eyes alight. "A pony, Daddy! See Santa read my email—"

"Allison Anne, back in the seat belt." He pulled his *official daddy voice*—obey or you shall be sorry. He didn't think Leslie was ready to hear Allison's updated rendition of *Christmas Don't Be Late.*

Hell, *his* mind was forced to shift gears. A few hours ago, he'd gone to drop his daughter off for dance class. Now his whole world had turned upside-down. He had to deal with the suspicion Santa not only read emails, he read minds!

"I can't leave him alone. His water might freeze up. If it does, I'll have to carry it from the house. He'll need extra bedding and plenty of food so he has fuel to keep warm during the storm.

"Want to see Edward, Daddy!" Allison bounced up and down infected with pony-mania.

He cocked an eyebrow. "*Edward* the Pony? I thought ponies had pony names, like Trigger or Buttermilk."

She laughed softly. The musical sound, similar to wind chimes in a summer breeze, sent a shiver up his spine. It summoned images of that muffled laughter in a darkened bedroom. Such flashes fired his hunger to take, to claim, a warrior's need to possess her rising in his blood, despite his mind warning they were moving too fast. He was deeply attracted to Leslie, appreciated her fondness for Allison. There was a sense of belonging, a comfortable feeling of them...*fitting.*

The disc jockey broke into the cozy daydream with a dose of reality. *"Repeating, we have a Winter Storm Advisory. The roads are turning to mush. If you don't have to be out, stay home. If you're at work, leave early. The police ask you stay home once you get there. Salt and sand crews will be out; make their job easier by giving them less traffic. AAA is already reporting fender-benders. The temperature is dropping fast, people. Weathermen predict a foot of the white stuff by morning. Get home, prop your feet up by the fire and relax. Here's a song to lend seasonal cheer."*

Dean Martin crooned, *let it snow, let it snow.*

Keon smirked at the radio. "Sing it, Dean."

Leslie's neck whipped around as he passed the turn off for the studio. "Och, my car's back there."

"You won't need it. Since you won't come home with us because of Edward, then Allison and I shall go with you."

Keon pushed the buggy down the grocery aisle of Wal-mart, gathering food for three people—and a cat—like he played *Beat the Clock*. Not sure what ponies ate, he grabbed big bags of carrots and apples, just in case. Fortunately, the Superstore was on the way, off Nicholasville Pike. Even with the weather situation worsening, his SUV and its four-wheel traction would see they reached the river house easily. Once there, they'd have to stay put until road crews salted, sanded and plowed. Leslie said she was several miles off the main road, so it could be days until they cleared secondary lanes.

"Ah, sacrifices." A smile spread over his lips, saying he fancied spending the weekend getting to know Leslie Seaforth.

Christmas was always special because of Allison, only for the first time since Meredith's death he was in high spirits. Everything was magical again, filling his heart with a child's joy. The anticipation for the holiday had always been to see his daughter at her happiest. Her

277

merriment was his. This time, he relished the sudden rush of Christmas cheer zinging through him.

"Dear St. Nick, let it snow, let it snow, let it snow."

He'd left Allison and Leslie in the car. They'd keep it running and warm for Alvin, while he dashed in to pick up emergency supplies. If he knew his daughter, she immediately launched into her wish list for St. Nick. A Kodak moment. He would've loved to see Leslie's reaction. He just hoped it hadn't put her off. Somehow, he had an idea the lass took it in stride.

Always leaving shopping to his housekeeper, he'd never been in a Superstore before. Deftly wheeling his cart up and down aisles, dodging other frantic shoppers, he was getting into the groove of collecting stuff. "The male reverts to his caveman food-gatherer and provider. Me, Keon. You, Jane...*hmm*...Leslie." While visions of Leslie in one of those Maureen O' Sullivan outfits played through his horny brain, he paused by the meat case, eyeing the fresh turkeys. "Bet even Alvin likes white meat."

Selecting one, he added it to his growing stack of purchases. With the same relentless pace, he snatched up a couple pair of jeans for himself, two sweaters and underwear.

"Ah, the bare necessities!"

Thoroughly enjoying himself, he zoomed through the kids' department and snagged items for Allison. Happening upon the pet section, he found *recreational drugs* for the cat. So intent on evading other customers, who dashed about in the same frenzied manner, he almost missed the colorful hula-hoops sitting on the end of the aisle.

"Thanks, Santa." He blushed sheepishly when a passing lady glared at him as if he'd lost his marbles.

Taking the final turn to the registers, he stopped abruptly as he spotted the glass cases. He suddenly knew he had one more purchase to make.

Back at the car, he quietly slipped the hula-hoop in the back and then hid it with the groceries, not wanting

Allison to see it.

Leslie got out and came around to help him load. She rolled her eyes. "You sure you got enough?"

"Depends..." He bumped shoulders with her deliberately.

"Upon what?"

"Upon whether Alvin likes white meat or dark." Flashing her a wicked grin, he leaned close, invading her space to inhale her light, lemony scent. "Personally, being a breast-man myself, I like white meat."

Leslie chuckled. "Challenger, you should be outlawed."

Traffic exiting Lexington had been worse than Keon anticipated. Multiple vehicles were off the sides of the road; he'd stopped counting all the fender benders. It seemed flashing lights of cop cars and wreckers were around nearly every turn. Even after they passed through the small town of Nicholasville, about fifteen miles southwest of Lexington, they still had to fight the flow of people rushing home to Wilmore and beyond to Danville. Pleased that he'd insisted on bringing Leslie home, he was glad the Lexus had four-wheel drive. Without it, it would've been a nightmare.

As the car pulled down the winding drive, the pony heard it and came running from the barn. Allison zeroed in on the small black beast like a heat-seeking missile.

"Look, Daddy, Edward!" Even before they parked, she was unbuckling the seatbelt and opening the door.

"Don't let the..."—he frowned as she flung the door open and nearly leapt out—"...cat out." Alvin was right on her heels. "I hope he's good with being outside."

"Alvin loves to chase snowflakes." Leslie chuckled as the feline started doing just that. "Thank you."

He paused, caught up in those mesmerizing eyes. "For what?"

"Bringing me home. I appreciate it. You were right. I'd never have gotten through in the Beetle. I'm rattled as it is. Alvin and I would've ended up in the ditch somewhere."

His hand lifted and he dragged the outside of his index finger along her soft cheek. "You're most welcome, Leslie Seaforth. Hope your unexpected guests don't put a damper on your holiday plans."

Nervous, she started to glance away, but her amber gaze came back to him. "I'm happy to have Allison and you."

"And we're glad to be here." Catching himself before he kissed her, he opened the car door.

The landscape hit Keon with a deep yearning. This was the place his mind conjured when he dreamt of a property away from the city. Hunger and admiration filled him as he studied the sloping hillside and clever layout of the home and stable. The barn's rear was nestled against the bend in the steep hillside, while the house front sat on stilts and looked out over the river below. A view that would endlessly fascinate him, each passing season would render it another portrait of the Palisades' breathtaking splendor.

Right now, it was a winter wonderland. Nearly six inches of snow blanketed the landscape, lending a hush to the wooded terrain.

Keon loved the house, coveted it. He couldn't imagine one designed that could suit him better. A huge deck ran around three sides with an A-frame front, all glass, creek stone and redwood. The two-story structure was perfect. Nestled in the woods, the acreage was so isolated.

Ideal place for a child to have a pony and a kitty.

Leslie climbed out and came around the Lexus, watching him study the grounds. "Magnificent, eh? I love it. Plenty of privacy with the hills surrounding three sides, yet lots of open room for—"

"Edward! Look, Daddy, isn't he cool?" Allison came dashing up. She'd already turned the pony loose and had him in tow.

Keon laughed out loud. "*That* is Edward? That isn't a pony, that's a shaggy dog."

"Don't insult Edward," Leslie teased. The animal's head was barely above her waist as she patted the tiny horse's forehead. "He may be what they call a 'miniature pony', but he's a big horsie in his heart. My gran rescued him from a petting zoo outside of Lexington. She didn't like how he was treated so bought him for a ridiculously high price."

"He's just right!" Allison bounced, half climbing up his leg. "Daddy, I want to ride him. PLEASE!"

He looked to Leslie, who nodded. "I need to put him back in the barn. She can ride to there." He lifted Allison upon the fat pony's back, the child grabbing a handful of mane to hold on."

"I want him to run!"

"NO!" He made a grab for Allison, but the pony was already bouncing toward the stable. "I need to put a chain on this wild child of mine."

"Don't fret. Edward only has two speeds—slow and stop. He's very good with kids. Adores them."

She turned and smiled at him, her eyes shining with love for his daughter. As their stares locked, the smile slowly faded, awareness of him clearly spreading through her. Yes, she adored Allison, but her hunger for him had a raw edge. For the longest moment their connection held, neither able to break it. Barely breathing. Then he saw a flash of pain, of the child standing before the candy store with her nose pressed to the window. Wanting, but knowing she couldn't have.

His heart did a slow roll. He was in love with Leslie Seaforth. Had been since he first looked in her amber eyes.

Sorting out the mounds of sacks Challenger carried in, Leslie glanced over the kitchen counter and into the living room. Allison sat wrapped up in a cozy tartan, Alvin sleeping on her lap. The child rocked in the rocking chair, content as she watched the weather report.

"More snow, Leslie," she called. The little girl was

281

way too happy with the repeated pronouncements of additional snow and warnings everyone should stay home.

Obviously, Allison had decided she was no longer *Miz* Leslie.

Challenger came inside with another load of plastic sacks. Dropping them on the counter, he met her eyes and smiled sheepishly. He'd bought a lot of stuff, more than what three people would need for the weekend.

She raised her brows. "That turkey would feed a family of ten."

"Alvin and I have big appetites." The silly man grinned.

Inventorying the purchases, she had a feeling Challenger had an eye on Christmas, rather than just toughing it out until the plows came through. Her heart warmed at that notion.

She'd planned a quiet holiday with Alvin. Her sisters called and begged her to come home to England for the holiday. Oddly, she resisted. She didn't have the heart to watch other people planning a future of Christmases, when she was at loose ends...waiting.

No real reason to decorate when she was spending it alone, she hadn't even put up a tree.

With her husband's death behind her, she wasn't sure what she wanted to do with her life. Why she'd jumped at the chance to come to the States and take over the dance school after her gran's accident. A new start, a new direction. This season would be a quiet time of reflection, soul-searching hoping to find her way.

She glanced around the lovely home, at the wood panel walls, the massive creek stone fireplace and the high-beamed ceiling. The room cried out for a Christmas tree. A huge one, in the corner, loaded with decorations and knee-deep with presents underneath. The scent of baking gingerbread cookies filtered through her imaginings.

Returning to sort the groceries, she pushed the silly dream-building away. She'd learnt long ago that was the road to disappointment. If she permitted herself to construct a beautiful Christmas—the holiday in the heart—then the weather front would shift and Challenger, with his drop-dead sexy smile, and his darling little girl would be gone, off to the Christmas already planned.

Stomping his feet to shake off the snow, Challenger came inside, this time with a load of wood in his arms. "Another hour and you won't be able to see our tire tracks on the drive."

He stacked the wood in the built in bin, then went out for more. Two more trips saw them with plenty of wood for the night. As he squatted to his knees to build the fire, Leslie watched the man and child in the living room, pain twisting her heart. This was almost too cruel.

They fit so well...as if they belonged.

Fearful Leslie wouldn't eat proper meals, her grandmother had left her tubs of frozen soup stock. She started one to simmer while she chopped veggies to add to it. With a smile, she glanced at Challenger making a cocoa for Allison. Unlike most men, he seemed at home with such chores. Puttering in the kitchen with him again brought those longings for a family to her heart.

She couldn't help but ask, "Ovaltine? Don't most kids want Nestles?"

He glanced at Allison, now watching the *Cartoon Network*. Vintage Toons of *Auggie Doggie and Doggie Daddy* had her giggling. "Allison has a deep affinity for anything Retro. I think she must be reincarnated from someone who lived in the 1950s."

As a commercial came on, she wandered into the kitchen ready for her hot chocolate. "I want five marshmallows, Daddy." Grasping the countertop, she pulled up on tiptoes to watch.

"One." He shook his head.

She waved her fingers to say five.

"Don't be greedy, Munchkin. You had a pony ride, played with Alvin for hours and went to McDonalds."

He handed her the small cup with *one* marshmallow.

"'Kay," she grumbled and took it. Sipping, her eyes roved over the pile of sacks containing clothes, still to be put away. Something caught her interest. She picked up an aqua-colored box and held it upside-down. "What's this, Daddy?"

Challenger, pouring another cup, tipped the mug over. Quick reflexes, he caught it before the chocolate spilled more than a tablespoonful. He stopped, looked to the ceiling and then closed his eyes as if praying for the floor to open up beneath his feet.

"Daddy's got a headache," Allison said.

"Yeah, Daddy has a headache." He laughed and grabbed for the box where Allison was waving it in the air. After three misses, he caught her wrist and tugged it from her hand. "And its name is Allison Anne."

Snatching up the plastic sack, he shoved the box into it, only to have the bottom rip. His package of underwear, can of shave cream and the box of condoms tumbled to the floor at Leslie's feet.

Suppressing a smile, she bent to pick it up. Challenger blushed. She wondered when was the last time this dynamic man *blushed*. She tried to arrange her face to appear serious, but the smirk slipped out. "I believe you dropped this."

He shrugged, trying to be nonchalant. "You know, the bare necessities."

"*Bare* necessities?" Leslie nearly lost it.

Challenger snatched the box from her and shoved it under the packages of briefs and the pump bottle of *Kiss My Face* shavecream.

"*Kiss my Face* shavecream?" She steepled her fingers over her nose and mouth trying to keep in the laughter.

"They didn't have my regular brand."

Leslie's laughter was cleansing, chasing away the cobwebs of the past. Opening her fragile heart.

The chuckle died as she stared into those stormy grey eyes. *She was in love with Keon Challenger.*

Wanted him with a passion that left her breathless. Wanted him and his darling daughter in her life.

And that terrified her.

Allison yawned, nearly falling asleep in the dining room chair.

"You've had a busy day, Munchkin." Challenger suggested, "Why don't you go sit in the rocker until I'm done. Then I'll tuck you up in bed."

"'Kay." Allison slid from the chair and came to Leslie. Leaning against her arm, she looked up with big blue eyes. "Will you rock me?"

Leslie's heart squeezed. Touching her napkin to her mouth, she glanced at Challenger. He'd stopped eating and intently watched them, a banked question in his eyes. Scooting the chair back, she took Allison's hand and led her to the rocker. She helped the little girl into her lap and set the chair in motion.

"Can I ride Edward tomorrow?" Allison yawned.

"Depends upon the snow. Even if you can't ride him, you can help me brush him and feed him an apple."

"'Kay."

Leslie enjoyed cradling the small body, feeling her delicate muscles relax against her. It was both soothing and heartrending holding Allison. So easily, she could imagine doing this for more than just a few nights.

"I don't have a mommy to rock me." Allison's sad whisper spoke how important this moment was to her, too. "I asked Santa for a mother. Sometimes he doesn't give me what I ask for. Mrs. Mesham said I have to be very good to get what I want from Santa. I've been very good this year, Leslie. Long time ago, I asked Santa to bring my mommy back. He didn't. Last Christmas I just asked for a mother. He didn't listen then either. Maybe he'll listen this year."

Maybe. Leslie patted the child's back. She glanced up to see Challenger standing by the wall of windows, watching her hold his daughter. His expression was guarded, concerned. Fearful of what she saw there, she

285

quickly looked away to the fire.

Challenger was aware of Allison's needs. Would he ask a woman to be the little girl's mother when he didn't love her? She ached to hold Allison, rock her, play with her, watch her grow. And she wanted Keon. Only she didn't want to be just a candidate for Allison's mother in his eyes.

She wanted Keon to fall in love with her, just as she was in love with him.

Giggling, Allison held up her arms for Challenger to grasp. When he did, she did a complete 'Ferris wheel' turn. "Do me again, Daddy." Rolling his eyes, he helped the little girl summersault in the air. Of course, the laughing child instantly demanded, "Do me again, Daddy."

"No, you greedy child. Three spins is enough. Hop in bed." Challenger tried to sound gruff, but Allison ignored him and started to spin on her own. Instead of flipping her over, he just held her upside-down. "Oh, look, the naughty child is stuck."

Leslie smiled at their antics, clear the two often played like this. Challenger didn't just take his responsibilities of being a single parent seriously, he enjoyed being a father to Allison. Fearing she made a fool of herself by staring at him, she turned down the covers on the bottom bunk bed for the child.

When Keon finally set her down, Allison was laughing so hard she could barely breathe. Leslie feared the child would have trouble settling down to sleep, but she let out a giggly yawn and said, "Do me again. Do me again."

"No and that's final. You used up your spins for one night."

She pushed on his leg. "Then do Leslie. Do her, Daddy."

Challenger's flashing eyes met hers with a power that rocked Leslie to her toes. "Well, do you want me to *do you*, Leslie?"

Oh, man, what a loaded question!

"Mmm...well...uh..."

"I think the cat's got Leslie's tongue," Challenger goaded.

Allison crawled up on the bed and stuck her foot up for Leslie to pull off her sock. "Why does Alvin have your tongue?"

"Your daddy's teasing."

"Daddy's silly." She stretched and yawned again. "Do piggies."

The phone rang in the kitchen, causing Challenger to look at her. "Go ahead, answer it while I go on piggy patrol."

Leslie hated to leave the family moment, but knew it was likely her gran. She'd worry if Leslie didn't answer. With a last glance at father and daughter, she went to the phone in the kitchen.

Sure enough, it was Gran. "Leslie! I was beginning to worry. Are you all right? They say you're getting hit with a blizzard." Maggie Henderson's worry came through the wire.

Leslie carried the phone to the patio doors. Flipping out the overhead lights, she left the room illuminated by only the firelight. She stared out into the winter wonderland, the night landscape a world of magical blue-white. "Don't fash, Gran. Yes, it's coming down at the rate of a couple inches an hour. It's rather beautiful."

"I'm worried about you there. What if the electricity goes out? What if the phone goes?"

"I'm all tucked up. Plenty of food, heating oil and wood," she assured. "I have the cell phone."

"Yes, but you're alone, all the way out there. What if something happens?"

Leslie hated to admit Keon and his daughter were staying the weekend, fearful her grandmother would start planning a spring wedding. Since Kevin's death five years ago, the family fretted over her not 'getting on with her life', but none as worrisome as her

287

grandmother. Still, it'd ease her gran's heart to know.

"Actually, I'm not alone..."

"Alvin and Edward don't count, my dear. I'm talking about two legged animals, six-foot tall, muscles, preferably in a kilt."

"Not kilted, but I have one who fits that description under the roof now."

The bubbly laughter conveyed Maggie Henderson didn't believe her. "You were never a good liar, Leslie."

"And I'm not lying now."

"If you say. Anyone I know?"

"In fact, you've met him. Keon Challenger and his daughter, Allison."

"Och, you move fast, lass. You can't see me, but I'm bowing in your honor. How did you snag that big fish? Half the women in the state have been hot on his trail since he came from London a couple years ago."

"He invited me to lunch with his daughter and we were caught in the snowstorm. He wouldn't let me drive the Beetle back, but fetched me home in his four-wheel-drive vehicle. It was clear we're going to be stuck for the weekend, so he stopped for supplies. Please don't worry."

"Worry? I might be sixty-something,"— she cleared her throat—"but being snowbound with that man is every woman's fantasy. I won't keep you since you need to entertain your guests. And in case your phone goes down and I don't get to speak with you again, Merry Christmas, darling. Have fun unwrapping *things*."

"Merry Christmas, Gran." Leslie didn't bother to remind her grandmother cell phones didn't *go down*. The elderly woman just didn't get today's *newfangled things*, as she called them.

She paused, wanting to go back to Challenger and Allison, but in another mind feared the family intimacy she'd intrude upon. They belonged together. Bedtime was a special time. She had no right to impose just because Challenger had been kind enough to see her safely home.

A lie. She hesitated because, like rocking Allison, she hungered for these things, the quiet nighttime ritual, the gentle sharing of family life that was beyond her hope.

Treading silently down the hall, she intended to fetch extra blankets. Only the orange glow of the bedside lamp on low pulled her, just like that silly moth attracted to the dangerous flame.

Challenger sat holding the little hand of his daughter. "I'll leave the lamp on in case you wake up." He glanced at the cat stretched out by Allison's far side, clearly determined to stay. "And Alvin is here to keep you company."

"'Kay, Daddy." She patted Alvin. "See, kitties are nice. He'll protect me from monsters."

"He will most certainly." Challenger kissed her tiny finger.

Allison gave a big yawn. "Daddy, Leslie won't fit in Santa's sleigh. Neither will Edward."

He leaned over and kissed Allison's forehead. "Close your eyes. We'll worry about St. Nick tomorrow."

"'Kay, Daddy. Will Leslie kiss me goodnight?"

His back to the door, until he spoke Leslie hadn't realized he was aware of her presence, hovering at the door's edge.

"Come, Leslie, Allison Anne requests a goodnight kiss." His head turned and he offered a gentle smile.

A smile that turned her heart upside down. Leslie walked to the bed and leaned over to kiss the angelic child on the forehead. "Night, night, Allison. Pretty dreams."

"Night..."—another yawn came out—"I like it here, Leslie." She rolled over and her small arm loosely embraced Alvin.

With a last look at the precious girl, she followed Challenger to the living room. He added another log to the fire while she turned on the news to watch the weather update.

"*The Kentucky State Police ask everyone to stay off the roads. If you have a medical emergency, contact* your local police or the State Police Station nearest you." *The weatherman turned to the digital map to show what was happening. "This cold front is straight out of Canada with frigid air. It overran the rain, so now we have snow. Oh, boy do we have snow! Close to a foot. At this point we could have six-to-ten inches of additional snow before daybreak..."*

Leslie noticed Challenger smiled as he lowly sang, *"Let it snow, let it snow, let it snow..."*

"Are you a snow freak?"

He closed the chain mail spark guard and then came to sit beside her on the sofa. "I suddenly have a fondness for the stuff. Do you mind—being stuck with Allison and me through Christmas? I'm actually rather handy to have about. Moderately tidy, not averse to doing chores around the house, and I can tote water for Edward if need. This snow is giving me a wonderful opportunity to get to know you, a crash course on who Leslie Seaforth is."

"You might be bored to death." She suppressed the tight laugh wanting to pop out.

Challenger's presence was too intense, too unsettling. Even so, she forced herself not to look away from him, but watched his fascinating grey eyes. There was such warmth there. A complex man, a strong man, his love for Allison revealed how special he was.

"Not bore...never bore." Putting his elbow on the back of the couch, he inclined toward her. "I know we just met today, so things are moving a bit fast in some fashion. In others,"—he leaned forward and faintly brushed his lips against hers—"not fast enough. However, I'm a patient man. I can wait."

Leslie savored that kiss, the promise it held, yet she steeled herself not to read too much into it.

"Shall we get the baggage out of the way? Then we won't have to deal with it again. I said I loved my wife. I did. However, I didn't idolize her, saw her faults as well as her goodness. Had she lived, I'm not sure she would've been the mother Allison needs. A rising reporter for telly, she was very career oriented. She was, I fear, living for the chase of the next breaking news story. I'd hoped that would change. She was killed in a multi-car pile up on the M-1, rushing to yet another scoop, so we'll never know. I'd like to think she'd come to see Allison was the most important thing in our lives. Deep down, I have doubts. Deep down, I worry if our marriage would've survived that."

Leslie's hands fidgeted, not caring to talk about Kevin, for while there were possible problems ahead in the Challenger marriage, he'd loved his wife. "You loved her. She loved you. Anything is possible with love." How could any woman not walk through fire for this man?

"Sometimes." He picked up her hand and linked pinkies. "She loved me, but I think the career, the jazz of being a television reporter was a bit more important. In the final year of our marriage, this drive had strengthened, not lessened. I did more and more for Allison, to make up for Meredith not always being there. I wanted something more than the job—I wanted a family. My investment firm was doing well. I was in position to work less so I'd be able to give more to Allison."

She met the question in his eyes. "My turn?" When he nodded, she sighed. "I don't talk about my marriage ...the failure. Not sure what went wrong. Not meant to be, perhaps. Kevin was a sweet guy. Everyone liked him. He felt safe to me, someone I could trust with my future. I think what upset me the most—I never saw it coming. Everything was going along the same, rather happy—I thought. I go in one day to put away the wash and I find a small packet of letters at the back of his sock drawer. I admit it. I'm nosy. Your husband hiding letters in his sock drawer—what woman would put them back without reading?"

Leslie got up, nervous, and paced to the glass doors. She hated this—that the emotions could still provoke after all this time. "So dreadfully predictable...as you can guess, I found he was in love with another woman.

They'd meet when he was out of town for business. She pursued him; he was flattered. She was exciting, sexy, thrilling. I was dull, boring. Things fell into place, small things. How he suggested I cut my hair...lose a few pounds...start wearing sexy dresses. I'm a jeans sort of lass. What? Was I supposed to look like a Frederick's of Hollywood version of June Cleaver? I told him to get out. He said, thank you; I just made it easy. He'd wanted to leave for some time, but felt guilty. They were heading to a vacation in Spain when they were hit head-on by a drunk driver."

He followed her to the doors to watch the beautiful peace of the falling snow. "Early today, you asked me if I loved Meredith and I answered you."

"Instead of telling me to mind my own beeswax?" She chuckled, feeling the memories, the feelings of betrayal, of pain, fading.

Challenger asked softly, "Did you love him?"

Leslie stared into the grey eyes, knowing she owed him the truth. Nothing less. "No."

"But you were deeply hurt. He betrayed you, took a marriage you worked hard to make good and just tossed it and you aside."

"I thought I loved him. And I guess in a way I really did. But I wasn't *in love* with him. I didn't understand the difference." She turned away to look out to the snowy nightscape, unable to watch Keon's eyes any longer, afraid to see the pity in them for a woman who'd deluded herself into marrying a man who wasn't *the one*. She put her hand to the glass feeling the cool of the winter night. "I wanted a home, a family, that anchor they provide. I needed the security of belonging to another."

"You weren't wrong, Leslie. Those are good things to want. Meredith's and Kevin's deaths demonstrate how easily life can slip through our fingers. You need to reach out and find what you want, what can make you happy." Challenger moved so he could slowly place his larger hand over hers, matching the finger spread.

She tried to chuckle, but it came out self-derisive. "I'm not a competitive person. I chose a man I felt safe with. Instead, he taught me there's no safety. I fear if I sought love again I'd be this green-eyed monster. Every time a woman might look at him or he glanced her way, I'd twist inside with doubt. I'm not sure I could survive that pain again."

"Or maybe you'd get lucky and find the right man, the man who'd make you so secure, doubt would never come your way."

His head started to dip toward her as if he meant to kiss her, but a hard gust of wind hit the side of the house, rattling the glass. An intense chill seemed to come straight through the well-insulated walls.

Being a coward, she used the drop in temperature to end the emotional tell-all. "I better get some extra blankets. Little children don't have the body heat adults do."

Challenger's eyes said he saw she was running from him, but he let it pass, recognizing the intensity of what was rising still too new. He picked up his purchases and followed her. "If you'll show me where I am to..."

"Put your *bare* necessities?" She paused by the door to the huge walk in closet and flipped on the light. "Ordinarily, I'd put you up in one of the upstairs rooms, let you enjoy the view in the morn, but they get a bit chilly when the wind is up. "We'll be warmer down here and can hear Allison if she calls."

He arched a brow. "We?"

She crossed the hall and turned on a light in the largest bedroom downstairs. "Not the breathtaking view from upstairs, but it overlooks the river." She opened the curtains so he could see.

He moved to the bed, placing his purchases on top of the spread, then joined her by the window. The moody grey eyes assessed the huge deck and then cliffs of the river on the other side. A faint smile tugged at the corner of his sensual mouth.

"I find it hard to believe anyone can improve on

293

this." His gaze encompassed her. "Or what is before them."

With a magician's pass, he reached up and pulled the pins from her bun one by one. They clattered to the floor with a deliberateness that sent a frisson up her spine. What would it be like to make love to a man so focused, with so much recoiled power within him? Leslie wasn't sure she was strong enough to face the demand it'd require of her, knew she was helpless to resist.

He allowed the silken mass to slide through his fingers, a fire flaring within the grey depths. Slowly they traced over her face, assessing. "Your husband was a bloody fool."

Leslie fought the tears threatening to cloud her eyes, and swallowed the knot in her throat, almost swaying to the pull of his hypnotic power. The wind buffeting the house pulled her back from making a big mistake. A coward, she grabbed at the feeble excuse.

"I better get the blankets. I wouldn't want Allison to be chilled." She rushed from the room before her will— and commonsense—weakened.

The soothing scent of the cedar walls greeted Leslie as she entered the windowless room. Turning on the low-watt light, she allowed sensations to rush over her. As children, her sister, Dara, and she would come and sit in here on hot summer days, spinning tales of handsome knights who came to claim them.

The huge room was lined with racks of clothes on one side, floor to ceiling built-in drawers and cabinets on the opposite. In the far corner, boxes labeled *Christmas Decorations* caught her eye. Drawn to them, she pulled off one of the lids to reveal glittering silver and gold garland. She examined the ornaments her gran had collected over the years. Old fashioned, there was a beauty about them not found in the fancy ornaments of today.

Leslie picked up a tiny wooden rocking horse,

painted with red enamel and with white string for the mane and tail. She wondered if Allison would like it. Challenger said she loved stuff that was Retro.

"I was in love with the house before, but this cinched it." Challenger sauntered in, checking out the room-size closet. "Most houses don't have good storage space. Someone really designed this well. And wow...the scent's heady."

Leslie smiled, pleased he liked it. "My sister, Dara, and I used to sneak in here with our blankets and pillows and sleep. Once we hid in here when a tornado passed over. Since it's at the heart of the A-frame, steel beams are in the walls and ceilings for bearing weight. Excellent protection."

"What wonderful decorations. My Retro Baby would love them." He moved closer. "Beautiful treasures like these should be handled carefully, protected."

Leslie found it hard to breathe as Challenger stared at her, not the box containing all the makings of a beautiful Christmas. What she saw in those grey eyes felt like a physical blow to her heart. He watched her as if she was something rare, something precious, watched her with a banked hunger that both compelled him, yet scared him.

Unable to maintain the stare, she turned away, fearing it was a trick of the shadows within the cedar closet. Scared she was seeing what she wanted to see.

Going to the far shelf, she pulled out two tartan blankets and two thirteen-togs duvets, pretending absorption in removing them from their plastic cases.

"You're running from me, Leslie." He blocked her way.

"Don't think to use Allison against me," she whispered her fear.

It was clear Allison wanted a mother, needed a mother. He was aware of his daughter's Christmas wish. Oh, he was attracted to her. More so, he knew she was drawn to him and his child. She didn't want him to paint anything between them with the faery dust of love merely to lure her into being a mother for a lonely little girl. Oh, she wanted to be a mother to Allison, but her heart clamored for Keon to want her. *Just her.*

"Meaning?" A stillness about him unsettled her, similar to a wolf or a big cat watching prey. So focused, so intent.

She swallowed, summoning courage. "I've been hurt—"

"I'm aware. What happened before has nothing to do with us. I'm not the fool your husband was."

"I adore Allison. She's special to me. She wants a mother and I have a feeling you'll move heaven and earth to see her happy. I think you capable of using my physical attraction to you against me, using my growing love for Allison against me."

Keon moved so fast she barely had time to blink. She sucked in a hard breath as he knocked away the covers she held and then caught her in his arms. One hand on the small of her spine, the other at the back of her head, he kissed her. Oh, did he kiss her. Not a gentle first kiss, not one of seduction. This was a warrior home from battle, taking what he wanted, no holds barred, demanding all and would settle for nothing less.

He arched her body against his, let her feel the length of his arousal. Her blood vibrated until she felt dizzy. So close, the enthralling scent of male hit her brain full force, flooding her senses to the point it was painful. Her heart slammed against her ribcage and she tried not to take a breath, to inhale that heady, drugging scent of Keon Challenger. It wasn't the faint woodsy cologne or the clear whiff of soap with the hint of lemon. What clouded her brain was the scent of *him*. She wanted to bury her nose against the heat of his skin and just inhale that fragrance. Challenger smelled...*right.* Oddly, her mind registered she'd never sensed that off Kevin's skin. No female animalistic sense of finding *the one.*

Only Challenger.

Crippled by the fears and insecurities, she tried to

hold back. It was too much. *He* was too much. Challenger wouldn't let her, issuing the silent demand, *open to him.* Open her heart, her soul.

She almost cried out when he stepped back. The stormy eyes flashing in triumph, he watched her for a moment, then bent and picked up the quilts and blankets.

Leslie stood stunned, unable to move or think. Everything was too fast, too soon, yet she knew there was no turning back. Trembling, she put a hand to her heart to will it to slow.

Challenger paused at the door. "Don't *you* use me to get Allison either. Don't you think I see how you adore her, how you want to be a mother to her? Don't use me to reach that goal, Leslie. Yes, I want someone to look at my daughter the way you do, want her to have that comfort of being rocked and kissed good night. Just remember, I'm not the means to Allison. When you want me—and only me—come to me. When you come to my bed be damn sure it's only for *me.*" He tilted his head with a sexy half-smile that spelled checkmate. "Good night, luv. Pleasant dreams."

Shaken, Leslie watched Challenger stroll from the cedar closet with an arrogance that made her want to kick him in the arse. "Mercy. What am I to do?"

"Kiss me. I need something to warm me up—fast."

Leslie realized she was being kissed—by a pair of icy lips. She tasted tea and Krispy Kreme donuts—and Challenger. What a way to wake up. Sliding her arms around his neck, she enjoyed the gentle kiss.

What would it be like to wake up this way every morn?

"Daddy's kissing Leslie!"

Challenger chuckled and then pulled back. "Nothing gets past this child of mine."

Not hesitating, Allison crawled up on the bed. "Daddy got us a tree!"

Leslie yawned as Allison used the bed as a trampoline, nearly bouncing poor Alvin off. "So the city lad went out and hunted down a tree and dragged it back? I'm impressed, Challenger."

"I did indeed. A very beautiful one, too."

"How's the weather?"

"White. Very white. The weatherman said seventeen inches already. The whole state is snowbound. I'm sure the retailers are bitchin' and moanin'. Last three days before Christmas to shop and no one is going anywhere. The police are warning everyone stay put. Seems you're stuck with Allison and me—likely Christmas and beyond." She thought she heard him mutter, "W*ay beyond.*"

Reaching for her robe, Leslie paused. "It won't be a hardship."

"Good, get dressed while I change into some dry clothes. Then we can take the Munchkin to feed and water Edward."

"Edward! Yea!" Allison clapped.

"And then we can prepare for a very wonderful Christmas."

Leslie rocked the sleeping Allison. The little girl had worn herself out playing with Edward and Alvin. She glanced to the cat passed out in front of the fireplace. Poor kitty was exhausted, too. Partners-in-crime, Allison and he had been into every phase of decorating, 'helping'.

She smiled. "The tree is beautiful."

Kneeling in front of the fireplace, Challenger used the poker to make room for another log. "I don't think I've seen any to compare. Picture perfect. Told you the old-time ornaments would fascinate Retro Baby."

"It'd be a delight to see Allison ripping through the ribbons and paper. Shame we cannot load the tree with gifts for her."

He came and gently stroked Allison's head. "I have her hula-hoop. One of the four things on her *Dear Santa* list."

She looked up at him. "Four?"

"She requested a pony and a kitty, but I think she realized we didn't have the room. She was willing to settle on the two things most important to her—a hula-hoop and a mother." He squatted down so his eyes were on the same level with hers, his thumb gently stroking her hand that cradled Allison's shoulder. "We're a package, she and I. Not that big of a risk, Leslie. If you'd just open your eyes and your heart."

With such gentle care, Challenger lifted the sleeping child and then carried her to the bunk bed. A yawning and stretching Alvin followed.

Clearly the cat had done what she was too scared to do—claim the child and man as hers.

She stood watching the twinkling lights of the tree that reached eight-feet tall. So perfect. Only she wanted Allison to have something under it, more than just a hula-hoop.

Images of the cedar closet popped to mind. She rushed there and rummaged around, until she finally found the old toy chest at the back, hidden under a pile of boxes. So intent in uncovering it, she didn't hear Challenger's footsteps before he partially blocked the light.

"She's asking for you to kiss her goodnight." He glanced over her shoulder as she unwrapped the contents of the wooden box.

Unfolding the tissue paper, she revealed the vintage Bubblecut Barbie. "It's a collector's item since they only put out a small number with raven hair. She's still in her original black and white swimsuit, open-toe shoes and holding her sunglasses. I took such care of her. Gran said she put her away because some day I would have a little girl to share her with. And here are my sock monkey and a stuffed Snoopy. Do you think Allison would like these? I know they aren't new, but they were special to me."

Challenger picked up the silly monkey and smiled. "I had one of these when I was a boy."

Leslie felt unsure. Maybe Challenger felt she was insulting his daughter by offering her second-hand toys. "I'm sorry. I didn't think..." She snatched the monkey from his hand and pushed it back in the box, barely seeing what she was doing because tears flooded her eyes.

Challenger's hands took her arms and swung her around to face him. "Whoa, what's this about?"

"I know you can buy her anything she wants, I didn't mean..." She stopped talking, knowing if she opened her mouth a sob would escape.

"Leslie Seaforth, these treasures will mean more to Allison than a dump truck full of Harrods's best. My Retro Baby will be in toy heaven with these precious gifts from you. You could give my little girl a stick and I'm sure it would be the best stick in the whole world. She loves you, you know." He paused as if fearful of speaking the words. "And so do I."

Leslie's heart leapt, wanting to believe he meant them. Only a man once said that before and proved the vow to be made of nothing stronger than the tissue paper wrapped around the doll. She hated that scarred her, left her in such doubt—but loving Challenger and losing him would be so much worse. She knew she wasn't strong enough to survive that.

She was in love with this man with the stormy grey eyes. Nothing had ever felt so right. Nothing had ever been so terrifying.

"Come, lass, let's say nite nite to the Munchkin." He took the toys and set them carefully in the box. "Then we can talk while we wrap presents."

Too stunned for words, too fearful to even hope his love could be real, she allowed him to lead her from the closet and down the hall to Allison's room.

Allison was half-asleep, but she clearly waited for Leslie to come kiss her goodnight. Alvin was already curled up at her side, purring.

"Leslie, can I ride Edward outside tomorrow?" Allison asked, fighting a yawn.

She pressed her lips to Allison's forehead. "Probably not. The snow is too deep for him. You can take him some treats and brush him again though."

"'Kay." The little girl reached up, putting her arms around Leslie's neck and hugged her tightly. "Love you, Leslie."

Tears instantly filled her eyes as she squeezed back. "I love you, Allison."

Challenger's hand gently cupped the back of her neck, but then the fingers flexed harder, rubbing, the gesture conveying how deeply the scene affected him.

Allison whispered against her ear, "Shhh...it's a secret. I asked Santa if you could be my mommy and that Daddy and I can live here with you, Edward and Alvin. I'd like that very much. The bestest Christmas present ever."

Leslie was unsure how to answer the child. She'd love to assure her Christmas wishes did come true. Wanted them to come true. Still too scared to believe, she hesitated to give pledges she might not be able to keep. "Maybe if we both wish very hard."

Keon saw Leslie ran from him. After Allison had fallen asleep, Leslie used the excuse of visiting the bathroom and had hidden in there—likely crying—for the last half hour. Fine. Not that he wanted her to cry, but he figured she needed a little space and it provided him with the opportunity to set the stage.

He turned out all the lights in the kitchen and living room, leaving only the glow of the fireplace and the twinkling tree as illumination. As he rummaged through Leslie's CDs, he found they had similar tastes in music, so was delighted to locate precisely the song he was searching for—*Save Room* by John Legend. Finally, he moved the coffee table before the sofa out of the way.

Setting up the player, he picked up the remote and waited for her to come out. As moments passed, he figured enough with the water works, and went and rapped on the bathroom door.

"Come, Leslie. Stop hiding from me."

"I'm not hiding," came the muffled reply.

He rattled the knob. "Open up or the big bad wolf will huff and puff."

Just as he assumed she wasn't coming out, the lock rattled and she cracked open the door. She'd washed her face and brushed her teeth, the scent of cinnamon *Crest* lingering on her breath.

"What? You thought I'd give up and go to bed? Do you really think I'm so dull and predictable? Sorry, lass. My Retro Baby is sound asleep. The night is young. All sorts of magic and Christmas wishes lay ahead." When she just stood, blinking up at him with those huge brown eyes, he took her wrist and tugged her from her bolthole.

As they entered the living room, he hit the remote to start Legend crooning the seductive song. Leslie took in his preparations, that glint of hunger banked by fear flickered in her luminous eyes. "What's this?"

He handed her the on-the-rocks-glass with a scotch and water. "My baby girl is resting in Sugarplum land, riding Edward with Alvin in her arms. It's time for us. Just us."

He didn't give her a chance to protest, but pulled her into dancing, rocking to the provocative beat. The corner of his mouth lifted as they fell into an easy rhythm, her dancer's skill overriding her reluctance.

Spinning her out and then pulling her back, he sang along with Legend, *"Let down your guard, just a little...I'll keep you safe in these arms of mine..."*

He saw recognition flash on her countenance, with that kissable doe-in-the-headlights expression. And kiss her is just what he wanted to do, but if he did he wouldn't stop. He still had a few aces up his sleeve to win her heart.

"Hold on to me, pretty baby...You'll see I can be all you need." When he sang that portion of the lyrics, she stumbled, then stopped dancing completely. "Okay, I don't have the sexy voice Legend has, but it doesn't

mean the words are any less felt. I can be all you need, Leslie, if you give me the chance. I'd love to make love to you before the fireplace, but I figure you're too skittish for that right now, so I arranged something else."

"Challenger..." She moaned weakening resistance.

Ignoring her feeble protest, he led her down the hall to the cedar closet and pushed open the door, showing the candles he'd lit atop the toy chest. On the floor were the fluffy duvets and pillows. "I recalled how your sister, Dara, and you had slumber parties in here. Thought we might have a *slumber party*. We can talk and laugh all night, get to know each other to where you learn to trust me. You *can* trust me, Leslie. I'll never hurt you. Save room in your heart for me."

Leslie felt the light bulb go on in her head, and with it all fears vanished. This man's heart was so open, so full of love for Allison. He didn't just see she was properly cared for, he adored being a father to her. His banter and play with the child showed he put her first, held nothing back. He'd love a woman in the same way, in a way Kevin had never loved her. A man that full of giving had no dark shadows in his ego.

Now she felt a total idiot for letting the past hold so much sway, keeping her from reaching out for what she wanted so desperately.

Challenger lifted the back of his hand to the side of her face and stroked it in near reverence. In his eyes she saw all she needed.

"Seriously, I won't touch you or kiss you...we can—"

She grabbed the front of his shirt and yanked him to her. "Shut up and kiss me, or you'll make me think you don't want me."

His brows lifted, as the grey eyes telegraphed his mind quickly switched gears. A playful smile spread over those sensual lips. "And what if I'd rather talk than smooch you, you demandsome wench?"

Leslie slowly undid the buttons, grinning when she saw he didn't have on a t-shirt. All the better to have my wicked way with him. "You're telling me to take a chance. I'm convinced you're candidate for Father of the Year. Now convince me you're up to being Husband of the Year."

"*Up?*" His chuckle rumbled in his chest as she pushed his shirt aside, then kissed his neck. Wickedly, she thumbed his flat male nipple. When she tweaked it, he inhaled sharply and his body went taut. "I...I wanted to give you candlelight and romance."

"Scratch plan A." Leslie chained kisses up his neck, then nipped his jaw with her sharp teeth. His muscles jerked as if he were a marionette and someone just pulled his strings.

"Oooo-kay. With the remaining vestige of my sanity, my poor, bloodless male brain is trying to catch up to your wicked ways. Playing conquering warrior claiming the fair maid has possibilities, however I rather fancy being the abused sex slave, too." When she ran her hand up his pant zipper, he groaned. "Ever hear the term *playing with fire*, lass?"

"Walk in fire with me, Challenger. Kiss me."

"Burn, baby, burn," he whispered, then his mouth took hers in a kiss that held back nothing.

Using those mobile lips, teeth and tongue, he kissed her like she'd never been kissed before, yanking her body against his. She didn't feel like *boring old Leslie*. She felt like a woman in love, real love, the stuff poets wrote about, singers sang odes to, the thrill-you-down-to-your-toes sort of love that goes beyond the physical wanting something so pure and rare it could only be magic. *Yeah, burn, baby, burn.*

Her hands trembled as she tugged the shirt from his pants, then pushed it off his beautiful shoulders. Urgency clawing at her, she wanted to savor the sensations, the power, but the need was too compelling. She skimmed her arms up his, reveled in their strength, over the muscular shoulders and finally to weave her fingers in his thick black hair. Arching her body against him, she sighed at their perfect fit. A deep inner sense said that in his arms is where she belonged.

The passion, the need, the love he summoned within her was overwhelming. It was *agonizing*. It was too much…it was not nearly enough.

Keon wanted so many things, and like the greedy kid in the candy store, he wanted everything all at once. He wanted to worship her like a princess, to bind this wonderful lady to him so she'd say yes to being his wife. It was hard to imagine how little time they'd known each other; she seemed to be a part of him, to belong in his life. Short time aside, he didn't have a moment of doubt. This feeling of perfection, of the final pieces of the puzzle making the picture complete, had never been there with Meredith.

With Leslie everything was so right.

Only that awe took a backseat to his clamoring libido. He'd barely slept the night before, thinking of her just down the hall. Burning to go to her, yet wanting to give her time to adjust to the idea of Allison and him as part of her life. At war with his honorable side, the primeval male in him wanted to conquer her, claim her, bind her to him in the age-old fashion.

As he undid the pearl buttons on her sweater, his hands trembled. He wanted her so badly. "Lass, I'd like this to be special, but I'm fast losing my mind."

She tugged on his belt buckle to loosen it, then unsnapped his jeans. "Actually, fast has its appeal."

"You want fast?" He captured her other wrist and backed her to the wall, pinning her with his unyielding body. Holding her hands at the side of her head, he ground his pelvis against hers, as he kissed her with all the ravenous hunger clawing at him. She arched like a cat against him, seeking even more. "Wrap your legs around my waist."

When he released her wrists, she clung to him, her

fingers clawing into his biceps. Hands sliding over her body to that firm derrière, he skimmed her jeans down. She stepped out of them. His right hand fumbled with his own jeans; the left pushed aside her pale pink bra. He drew a sigh from her when he palmed her breast and squeezed, then brushed his thumb back and forth over the pebbled nipple. Leaning to her, he took the tip of her tight breast into his mouth, sucking hard. He'd mark her. Leslie's sharp claws flexed in response. She'd mark him.

Keon smiled, drawing in the scent of her arousal, the female fragrance clouding his brain. Unable to hold back, he jerked her up and impaled her on his hard length of flesh. Ecstasy rolling over his sense and slamming into his brain, he paused to savor the delicious marvel of being inside Leslie's tight body.

Of belonging to her.

"Sure you want fast?" He withdrew partially and then flexed his hips, going deeper in a slow, sure movement. "I can do slow, too." Repeating the action, he delighted in watching her passion play across her beautiful face. "Very...slow."

"Slow...ah...has...ahhhhhhhh...possibilities."

Keon wanted to prolong this madness, this beauty, but her body tightened as she climaxed with a force that surprised her. Surprised him, too, for she let out with the start of a loud moan. He promptly closed his mouth over hers, swallowing the keen. Holding the leash of control for a minute more, he slammed into her pushing her into a second climax even before the first ended. Her internal muscles clenched around him, dragging him with her into the swirling maelstrom. He could no more hold back than not draw his next breath. His body exploded, pounding in his blood to where he nearly lost consciousness.

"Challenger," she gasped as he let her slide to her

feet, "you sure do play hide the pickle well, but can we take this to the bed? I'm not sure I can stand after that."

He scooped her up and placed her on the quilts on the floor. "Oh, we'll get there…eventually."

"Leslie…" There was a small shake to Leslie's hand. "May I give Edward an apple?"

Allison.

She struggled to awaken, but it was damn hard. It hurt to move. There wasn't a spot in her whole body where she didn't ache. She moaned and tried to blink, but her eyes were crusted from sleep and tears. Glued-shut, they didn't want to open. Challenger and she had made love, talked, laughed and cried. *Best damn slumber party I've ever had.*

"I gave him a carrot and ten lumps of sugar. I wasn't sure if ponies ate apples, so I thought I'd ask if it was okay." Allison jabbered away.

Pony? Sugar? Carrots? Another sigh and she rubbed her eyes and yawned. "We can take Edward an apple when we go see him later."

"Oh, that's okay. He's hungry now. I can give it to him." A soft knicker followed Allison's words.

Leslie wanted to burrow down under the heavy duvet with that male body heat keeping the covers snug. Challenger was the best bed warmer. She smiled, thinking of many such morns to come, waking in his arms.

Now?

Her eyes flew open as she jerked to sit up. Only she recalled she had nothing on so tried to clutch the covers to her chest. Challenger's heavy arm had her and the blankets pinned. Her movements caused him to wake up. Giving a sleepy yawn, he raised up on his elbow to see his daughter.

"Allison Anne *why* is Edward in the bedroom? Ponies belong in the barn." Challenger rubbed his face, trying to wake up.

She grinned and then threw her arms around the

teeny pony's neck and hugged him. "Edward was cold and lonely, so I brought him in to be near the fire. Then he said he was hungry."

"Did he? Did he also tell you little girls who sneak outside when they know better and bring ponies into the house get a spanking?" Challenger leaned over and made a half-hearted swipe at her, but giggling Allison danced out of reach.

"Daddy's smiling! Did you play hide the pickle with him Leslie? Is she my mommy now? Did Santa give me Alvin, Edward…and Leslie?"

Leslie shivered when he leaned close and kissed her bare shoulder.

"This isn't how a woman might want to hear a proposal, but the kid asked a question. If you don't answer the pint-size Perry Mason she'll just keep gnawing on your ankle with why…why…why." When she hesitated, he said, "Maybe the question should be did St. Nick give Allison and me to you for Christmas. You going to keep us? We need you."

Leslie couldn't speak, her throat was so tight with emotion, so she just nodded. Allison gave a squeal of delight, which scared Alvin and set the pony to fussing.

Challenger laughed. "Allison, take Edward and give him his apple. I shall kiss Leslie good morning and then get dressed and we'll return Edward where he belongs, and you and I shall have a long discussion on little girls leaving the house without permission."

"Quack—quack—quack," was her departing shot as she led Edward from the room.

Leslie looked down at the sleeping child, tuckered out after opening all the presents on Christmas Day. She was curled up with Alvin, her sock monkey, the 1964 edition Bubblehead Barbie and the *Creative Logic* Mp3 player in the midst of all the discarded wrapping paper. She smiled at their little Christmas Angel.

"Told you Retro Baby would love Barbie and Sock Monkey." Challenger lifted the sleeping child to carry her to bed. "In case you haven't noticed, when she goes to sleep for the night, she's out. She wakes up at the crack of dawn, but never during the night, wanting a drink-a-water, or fearful there's a monster-in-the-closet."

Leslie stroked the pale curls, where Challenger held her draped against his shoulder. "She did love them."

"Thank you for making all her Christmas wishes come true. She got everything on her list—a kitty, a pony, your MP3 player—thank you, again." He leaned to her and kissed her softly. "A hula-hoop and a mother."

"What about you? I didn't have anything for you."

"My unspoken Christmas wish would've been for someone to bring the magic to my life, to fill my heart until Christmas morn was as special for me as it was for Allison. You're the answer to everything I'd want."

Leslie followed him to the bedroom to help tuck up Allison. The little girl was so exhausted from opening all the gifts, the turkey dinner and several trips to feed Edward peppermint candy canes, that she never woke and asked for a goodnight kiss. Leslie gave her new daughter one anyway, then patted Alvin, Allison's self-appointed protector.

Back in the living room, Challenger scooped up the hula-hoop and began using it. "You know, sexy lady, I have this feeling we could keep the hula-hoop going while we make love. Want to find out?"

Laughing, she allowed him to pull her inside the hoop's circle with him. They tried several times to set it into motion, but ended up laughing so hard her side hurt.

Challenger looked down, his love clear in his eyes. "Marry me, Leslie. As soon as the snow melts, we can get a license. Call your grandmother in the morn and tell her we want to buy the house. I'll pay whatever she wants, no haggling. I'd like to start New Year's with you being Leslie Challenger."

She smiled. "It has a certain ring to it."

"Ring to it...which reminds me." His right hand

reached into his jeans pocket. "I was saving this to last. Okay, not everyone gets an engagement ring from Wally World, but I was in a bit of a rush. It's not a diamond, just a citrine. Since the band is gold, she said it can be resized if it doesn't fit."

Leslie opened the box and stared at the yellow, oval stone, lovely against the black velvet of the box, barely able to speak. "It's beautiful. You're beautiful. But...why?"

"I saw it as I passed the case. I almost walked on by. But then a little voice warned me I'd need it. I never believed in love at first sight, but I fell hard for you the instant I looked into your amber eyes." When she continued to stare at it, he took it from her and slipped it onto her ring finger, the band going on easily. "I'll get you a more expensive ring once the snows melt."

"Touch my ring, Challenger, I'll break your fingers. This one is perfect."

He laughed, kissing her forehead and pulling her body against hers. "Hmm...up to a game of hide the pickle?"

"Ah, you sweet talker." Leslie hugged his chest tightly. "Always, Challenger. Always."

Be sure to check out DeborahAnne's website
http://deborahmacgillivray.com

Also Available from Highland Press

Highland Wishes
No Law Against Love
Blue Moon Magic
Blue Moon Enchantment
Rebel Heart
Holiday in the Heart

Coming:

In Sunshine or In Shadow
Almost Taken
Pretend I'm Yours
Recipe for Love
The Crystal Heart
No Law Against Love 2
Second Time Around
Dance en L'Aire
Enraptured
The Amethyst Crown
Eyes of Love

Cover by DeborahAnne MacGillivray
2006